P9-CRJ-910

"YOU LEFT A MESSAGE THAT YOUR TORTOISES WERE STOLEN?"

"What was said quite precisely was that they vanished," Holmes corrected me haughtily. "We have no evidence of a break-in."

I could tell I was going to hate this kid. "For your information, I just jimmied the entry gate open—and by the look of it, I could probably do the same with the front door. So unless Houdini's been here, I'd say your super juvees have been nabbed." I switched on a light and began to look around.

Holmes stood stiff as a board. "Would you mind not poking at anything before asking?"

He made me long for a cattle prod. "What time this morning did you realize that the tortoises were gone?"

He paused a moment. "I noticed they were missing two days ago."

"Two days?" I was stunned. "Were you waiting for them to magically reappear? Or did you think that they'd gone out for a Burger King fix? Why did you wait so long to report this?"

"I thought they might have been borrowed."

Maybe he'd been munching on magic mushrooms for the past two days. I'd have to report the kid to somebody—the job was crying out for a replacement.

9/04

Other Avon Books by
Jessica Speart

BIRD BRAINED
BORDER PREY
GATOR AIDE

Coming Soon

BLACK DELTA NIGHT

ATTENTION: ORGANIZATIONS AND CORPORATIONS
Most Avon Books paperbacks are available at special quantity
discounts for bulk purchases for sales promotions, premiums, or
fund-raising. For information, please call or write:

**Special Markets Department, HarperCollins Publishers Inc.
10 East 53rd Street, New York, New York 10022-5299.
Telephone: (212) 207-7528.   Fax: (212) 207-7222.**

TORTOISE SOUP

SOUP

A Rachel Porter Mystery

JESSICA SPEART

HORICON PUBLIC LIBRARY

AVON BOOKS
An Imprint of HarperCollinsPublishers

This is a work of fiction. Names, characters, places, and incidents are products of the author's imagination or are used fictitiously and are not to be construed as real. Any resemblance to actual events, locales, organizations, or persons, living or dead, is entirely coincidental.

AVON BOOKS
An Imprint of HarperCollins*Publishers*
10 East 53rd Street
New York, New York 10022-5299

Copyright © 1998 by Jessica Speart
Inside cover author photo by George Brenner
Library of Congress Catalog Card Number: 97-94764
ISBN: 0-380-79289-3
www.avonbooks.com

All rights reserved. No part of this book may be used or reproduced in any manner whatsoever without written permission, except in the case of brief quotations embodied in critical articles and reviews. For information address Avon Books, an imprint of HarperCollins Publishers.

First Avon Books printing: June 1998

Avon Trademark Reg. U.S. Pat. Off. and in Other Countries, Marca Registrada, Hecho en U.S.A.
HarperCollins® is a trademark of HarperCollins Publishers Inc.

Printed in the U.S.A.

10 9 8 7 6 5 4 3 2

If you purchased this book without a cover, you should be aware that this book is stolen property. It was reported as "unsold and destroyed" to the publisher, and neither the author nor the publisher has received any payment for this "stripped book."

*In memory of Mollie Beattie,
the first female director of
the U.S. Fish and Wildlife Service,
who kicked in her share of doors*

———

Thanks go to Ron Crayton for sharing his knowledge on Nevada and the Mojave Desert; George Stephen for helping bring the desert to life; Ken Goddard for technical and moral support; Jo Tyler for her continuing good suggestions; and my editor, Micki Nuding for pushing me further.

One

It was the glare that first caught my eye. Sun glinted off metal, creating a flare of light that spread out over the scorched desert like liquid fire. From a distance, the object looked like a large metal roach. It was only as I approached closer that the insect metamorphosed into a black pickup truck.

I'd been based in Nevada for three long, hot months now and had heard stories about vehicles breaking down, their occupants foolishly stranded without any water.

"First your brain begins to boil and then your skin shrivels and cracks open so that the fluid in your body oozes out. Great for mummies. Lousy for your complexion, Rach." Terri, my designated best friend from New Orleans, where I'd previously been based, had tried relentlessly to prevent me from moving out west.

"After that you become delirious, taking off your clothes and ripping out your hair while crawling toward an imaginary six-foot-tall piña colada," he had continued, handing me an icy cold drink complete with a blue paper parasol floating on top.

Images of piña coladas danced in my head as I veered towards the lone pickup. The brain-curdling heat was enough to make me give serious thought to shedding my clothes; modesty be damned. What prevented me was those ten mysterious pounds that refused to go away, along with the fact that I tend to resemble a boiled lobster when I'm out in the sun for too long. I'd taken to wearing my mop

1

of strawberry-blond curls twisted on top of my head rather than cut what I stubbornly considered to be my unofficial badge of youth. As for my complexion, Terri would have been apoplectic. His three cardinal rules were cleanse, exfoliate, and moisturize. My car got a better lube job than my face did, which was beginning to resemble the desert after a year-long drought.

I think the heat is best summed up by a local joke about a new arrival in Hell, who views its flames with trepidation. "But it's a dry heat," the devil responds.

A sandpaper-like wind blew through the open car window, rasping against my skin. Reaching into the cooler on the seat next to me, I pulled out a handkerchief as frigid as a winter day in New York and laid it against my neck, relishing the momentary rush of goose bumps. At one hundred ten degrees, it was another scorcher of a day in this blast furnace more commonly referred to as the Mojave, the Sahara of the West. The temperature hadn't dipped below one hundred degrees all week.

My prime objective had been to imagine myself encased in a giant ice cube—no easy task, considering that the pitiful air conditioner in my old Chevy Blazer was on the fritz. Even when it had been working full blast, the car was like a poor man's steam bath. So I couldn't imagine why anyone would be parked of their own free will in the middle of the Nevada desert.

I turned off the blacktop onto a dirt road, past leafy creosote bushes and an array of yucca cactus, their stems as long and sharp as a battlefield of upright bayonets in a land that takes no prisoners. I had heard that it wasn't uncommon to trip across bodies buried in the desert—so I came dangerously close to swerving off the dirt road as a figure rose up through hazy waves of heat like an unearthly specter. The form, resembling a demon levitating off the desert floor, slowly transformed itself into a tall, slim woman with a mane of jet-black hair. Looking just once in my direction, she sprinted over to the pickup and revved the engine. The tires spun giddily in place and the motor wailed to be set free. Finally finding the necessary traction, the pickup careened out, kicking up a line of dust devils in its wake.

I had no illusions about my popularity in these parts. To the local macho cowboys, who hate the government and anyone who works for it, a visit from a U.S. Fish and Wildlife special agent is about as eagerly anticipated as a case of the clap. But the fact that she had taken off without so much as the usual obscene gesture set my suspicions on edge.

I peeled out after the pickup.

My foot pressed down hard on the pedal as I edged closer to the vehicle's rear end. If nothing else, I'd at least get the license plate number. But my desert apparition apparently wasn't overly fond of the DMV either. There was nothing to see but two catchy bumper stickers, America's version of the haiku.

I flashed my lights and beeped the horn. In return, a tapered hand snaked its way out the driver-side window, the middle finger raised in a salute. She seemed intent on leaving me behind, eating her dirt. I hit a patch of soft ground and the back end of the Blazer fishtailed like a hula dancer out of control. The pickup raced ahead screaming in glee.

I've never been one to take competition lightly—be it in aerobics class, faced with a thonged twenty-something version of the Energizer Bunny, or in a showdown against taxis in the streets of New York. I had *no* intention of losing a game of desert tag. Straightening the Blazer, I took off once again, my blood pounding along with the whirring of wheels as I watched the speedometer climb.

The Mojave whipped by like a video on fast forward. A field of razor-sharp cactus sprang into view and I dodged the obstacle, feeling ready to take on the Autobahn, when the fugitive pickup suddenly spun out of control, twirling in a dizzying one-eighty. When it finally came to a halt, we sat hood to hood, clenched in a power truck showdown. But before I could react, the woman sent her vehicle speed-

ing backward across the desert floor, like a cartoon thrown
in reverse.

I jammed my foot down on the accelerator, feeling giddy
as I gained on my prey, only to watch the pickup whirl
around and perform yet another movie perfect one-eighty.
Zooming ahead, it left me behind in a shower of gravel and
dirt. I gritted my teeth in determination, flooring the Blazer
for all it was worth. The speedometer flew past seventy,
onto eighty, and was twitching toward ninety in a chase
that would have made the Dukes of Hazzard proud when
the pickup started to swerve like a drunk on a roll. I locked
on, moving in for the kill, only to feel the ground inexpli-
cably disappear beneath my wheels. The Blazer soared into
the air on invisible wings before plunging back to earth,
where it landed with a shattering WHOMP! I slammed on
the brakes, my head hitting the roof with a sharp jolt as the
Blazer skidded to a halt.

Damn! I growled in disgust and glanced in the rearview
mirror. A deep washout lay like a trench in the ground.
Though I'd been going fast enough to fly over the rut, the
crash landing had stopped me cold. Left with no choice but
to give up the chase and assess the damage, I tried to get
out, but the door wouldn't budge. I crawled out the window, cursing my miserable fate as I fell to the dusty desert
floor. Dragging myself up, I gave the door a hard, swift
kick before wrenching it open and climbing back inside.
Damn car—had to be male.

This was my new life in Nevada. I was no longer up
against those good ol' boys of the South who brazenly
stood with their rifles and plowed down a couple of hundred ducks in a field. Now I was dealing with a huge expanse of land and an endless number of culprits who were
good at hit and run, slithering away from the scene as cun-
ningly as snakes. It made me nostalgic for the bayous and
the rednecks of Louisiana.

Disgruntled, I drove back to where the pickup had been
parked, and walked over to a row of yuccas sporting black
ribbons tied to their stems. At the foot of each cactus was

a metal bucket buried in the sand, its rounded lip level with the ground. A piece of rough plywood had been placed across the top of each container, with just enough space left open so that small, curious critters could easily tumble inside.

Altogether, a row of twenty-five buckets sat planted as neatly as a flower garden. Most of them had already been emptied, but enough remained for me to guess what was going on. Some Wild West entrepreneur was illegally trapping reptiles to sell. A number of tarantulas, rattlesnakes, large, hairy scorpions, and an assortment of lizards sizzled in the sun as they clawed at the sides in a vain attempt to escape. Others lay at the bottom, already dead, or too exhausted to continue to try. If there's one thing there's an overabundance of in the Nevada desert it's reptiles and bugs. Weigh those against the savvy cockroaches of New York City, and it's a toss-up as to which makes me more squeamish.

But worst of all was that the remaining buckets also held baby desert tortoises—a threatened species throughout the Southwest. They were either dead or close to it, providing plenty of gourmet goodies for the trapped creepy crawlers to feed on.

I walked back to my Blazer, put on a pair of heavy leather gloves, and dug out a snap stick with a trigger attachment rigged onto its end. All my life I have begged relatives, friends, even perfect strangers to kill any spider in sight. I have an irrational fear of anything with more than four legs—and now I found myself trying to save the damn things. Taking a deep breath, I lowered the stick into a bucket and carefully grabbed onto one terrifying creature at a time, holding each one as far away as possible before releasing them under the blazing-hot sun.

Wildlife smugglers and traders don't share my delicate sense of what gives a critter its charm: reptiles are the species *du jour* when it comes to the illegal trade. A poached rattlesnake can fetch up to four hundred bucks, while scorpions bring in a quick seventy-five smackers. Even chuckwallas, the most common lizard in southern Nevada, will ring in at one hundred thirty greenbacks apiece. The mastermind who was operating this scam clearly had it down to a fine science, turning a fast buck by cleaning out the buckets every few days.

I straightened up and watched the phantom pickup disappear in a cloud of dust over the distant mountains, as the last scorpion to be released scuttled under a rock.

My stomach growled, reminding me I hadn't eaten breakfast yet. Getting back in the Blazer, I plunked myself down only to curse out loud as my rear end hit the blistering-hot seat and my fingers sizzled against the steering wheel. A tiny antelope squirrel seemed to chuckle in response as it scampered over a rock, trailed by a red-tailed hawk eyeing the critter for a quick breakfast McNugget.

I turned the key in the ignition and the Blazer groaned in protest. I had inherited the vehicle from the last agent assigned to these parts. He'd survived a full six months before calling it quits. Rumor had it that his breaking point came when he found himself stuck in the desert with no bathroom and a bad case of overindulgence in chili. All that's known for sure is that he turned up in the hospital that day with a dead rattlesnake in one hand, its fangs firmly attached to his butt, and a letter of resignation in the other hand. I was the latest replacement.

I'd requested a transfer from my first job as a rookie wildlife agent in Slidell, Louisiana. I felt the change of scenery might do me good. Actually a change of senior resident agent was more like it. I'd begun to chafe under the southern-fried wisdom of my boss, Charlie Hickok. When I'd asked for a transfer, Charlie had hit me square between the eyes with his I-taught-you-everything-you-know routine.

"Goddamit, Bronx. I just broke in your scrawny ass. Who knows what they'll send me next?"

The fact that he viewed my ass as scrawny almost made me decide to stay. But I also knew that the man would say whatever it took to avoid the trouble of breaking in another rookie.

I held firm against Charlie's tactics and applied for a place bigger than a duck blind and dryer than a bayou. I should have known there would be a catch. There was none of the shit-kicking, boot-stomping, wolf-yelping "How dare you ask for a new assignment?" that I expected from the upper echelon of the Service. Rather, the old boy network of Fish and Wildlife honored my request in their own inimitable way: I quickly found myself transferred to Las Vegas.

I could live with that. It has bright lights, like my hometown of New York, and almost as many porno theatres. Besides, the median age in Las Vegas hovers at around seventy-four. I like that. It tends to make me feel young. Las Vegas also comes alive at night, giving me an endless array of places to go when my routine insomnia kicks in. The only problem is that the wildlife in town is of the human variety.

Getting onto I-15, I headed south in the direction of Searchlight. The sky was the kind of blue that makes you feel the earth is topsy-turvy, like the sea is over your head instead of under your feet. The El Dorado range stood off to the side, the mountains protruding like the spine of a giant prehistoric beast slouching its way toward Mexico.

So far, the best thing about being out here was the speed limit. Seventy-five miles an hour in the slow lane and cruising. I had already developed a game where I'd see how far and how fast I could go before even catching sight of another car. More often than not, I'd glance down at the speedometer to find myself flying down the road at one hundred miles an hour, singing with Bonnie Raitt at the top of my lungs.

When Bonnie wasn't warbling the blues, the garnet and onyx rosary beads that were slung around my rearview mirror played their own tune, counting off time like a metronome. Each click of the beads reminded me of its original owner, Jake Santou—a homicide detective with the New

Orleans Police Department. If there's anything I've learned from my past it's that the more attracted I am to a man, the more trouble I get myself into. I was head over heels where Santou was concerned. I had needed to gain some distance and allow myself to come up for air. The problem was, I hadn't expected to miss him so much.

The rosary beads clacked together in a frenzy as I suddenly slammed on my brakes.

Searchlight is just a pimple on the map, like most towns in Nevada. If you're driving too fast, there's a good chance you'll miss it. Once again I almost had. Named after a popular brand of match, it was a booming gold-mining community in its heyday, with forty-four mines and a dozen saloons. Now it's a one-horse town consisting of a few streets dotted with the occasional shack and an array of broken-down motor homes. Ironically, the main drag is named Broadway. But unlike the Broadway of New York, with its neon lights and razzmatazz pace, the primary landmark in this town is a white mobile-home trailer, which houses both the courthouse and the justice of the peace. Holding that position is a lot like a game of musical chairs. Each new justice of the peace inevitably dips his hand into the communal till. And just as in the game Monopoly, he or she lands in jail. The turnover is amazing, even by New York standards. Yet oddly enough, it seems to be a necessary step in making one's way up Nevada's political ladder.

Harold Ames, the town historian, gave a stab at explaining it to me one day. "Some of our most prominent politicians have done time around here. It's sort of a badge of merit."

Considering the fact that the town is only an hour from Vegas, it somehow made sense.

Shifting into reverse, I backtracked and pulled into the Gold Bonanza, the only place in town to grab a bite to eat. A large neon sign flashed its $1.99 breakfast special, and there were enough cars and pickups to make you think they were giving food away. But in Nevada, there is no such thing as just a restaurant. The Bonanza was part casino, part coffee shop, and part karaoke bar. I'd also discovered the food was only partly edible, but I was rarely, if ever, given the opportunity to eat.

Opening the door, I was immediately enveloped in a cloud of smoke as I squeezed past the crowd at the slot machines, already busy at eight in the morning. The *ching, ching, ching* of slots swallowing coins accompanied the rumbling of my stomach as I pushed my way over to the hostess, Lureen. A relic who'd been working here as long as the Bonanza had been standing, Lureen had to be at least seventy years old. It seemed to be the required age to obtain employment in the place. Lureen's scrawny arms poked out of a sleeveless tiger-striped top. This morning her legs, the width of small chicken drumsticks, were encased in bright purple spandex pants. Rhinestone eyeglasses matched dangling earrings, while her hair, tinted cotton-candy pink, was swept up in a creation that defied definition.

I received my usual friendly greeting. "We're full up."

And as usual, I looked out at a sea of empty tables. "I see a table over there."

Lureen took a deep drag on her cigarette, blowing the smoke out through her nose in a slow, steady stream as she contemplated me through her force field of rhinestones. "It's reserved."

I tried my best imitation of Little Orphan Annie, only to remember why I had given up my career as an actress in the first place. "Come on, Lureen. I'm starving this morning. How about an exception, just this one time?"

Letting loose a deep, phlegmy cough, Lureen wiped her mouth with the back of her hand. "Listen, kiddo, why do you keep coming in for the abuse?"

"Heck, Lureen. It reminds me of home. Besides, you keep calling me kiddo. Who can resist that?"

Lureen crushed the butt of her cigarette into a coffee container while she reached into her breast pocket and removed a pack of Marlboros, the official cowboy cigarette. Taking her time, she flicked open a lighter encrusted with knockoff garnets and pearls. The fresh cigarette twitched between her lips in anticipation of that first lung-wrenching gulp of smoke.

"Don't matter what I call you, kiddo. We're still full up." Plucking at her hair, she pulled out what appeared to be a dead fly that had become enmeshed in her heavily lacquered helmet. "You keep coming back like a bad case of heartburn, girl. You're lousy advertising for our place. Do yourself a favor and eat somewhere else."

I knew it was a hopeless battle. As a Fish and Wildlife agent, I tend to be looked upon with all the affection given pond scum. Of course, there's a reason for that—one with four legs, a hard shell, and a neck with as many wrinkles as Lureen.

It all started when the desert tortoise landed on the endangered species list. Biologists claim the critters are dying because of stress from rampant development, grazing, and mining. Locals argue that God just decided it was time to do them all in. What it's led to are restrictions on federal lands where the tortoise exists—which is just about everywhere in southern Nevada.

Except nobody tells a cowboy what he can do. Certainly not the damn government. *Especially* not some greenhorn girl from back East. It's been war ever since, with me as the latest target.

I felt a body brush past me and watched as Clayton Hayes seated himself at one of the open tables. A local rancher, Clayton had recently sold his land to an environmental group, which turned around and converted it into a tortoise refuge. While the sale had made him the richest man in town, it hadn't changed his contempt for environmentalists one damn bit.

Clayton dressed as if he were still out riding the range. A plaid shirt and dust-bitten jeans were his daily uniform. Old, scuffed-up boots declared that he was still a cowboy at heart, even if some secretly whispered he'd gone soft and sold out. His face and hands, a rich, dark brown, were as tough and resilient as cowhide from years of working outside in sun, sand, and dry wind.

Walking over to Clayton, I pulled out a chair and sat down.

"How you doing, Clayton?" I asked, plunking my elbows down on the table.

Hayes gave me a sidelong glance before spitting a hunk of rancid tobacco into his water glass to create a brown sludge. "Go to hell, Porter."

"I'll buy you breakfast." I had learned the fine art of bribery in Louisiana. Besides, I figured $1.99 a pop wouldn't break the bank, meager as mine was.

But Clayton wasn't taking the bait. "You better save your pennies for that plane ticket of yours back home. Unless you want to hang around and join us for our barbecue, that is."

Invitations didn't come my way all that often. I decided to forego common sense and take the plunge. "What barbecue is that?"

"When we set the desert on fire and roast all these damn tortoises out of here." Clayton slapped his knee and broke into a cackle. He spat another slug of tobacco into his glass, and the liquid balanced precariously on the rim before sliding down onto the table to form a thin puddle of mud.

My stomach rumbled again, this time from the stench of chewing tobacco. "Better be careful, Clayton, or I'll have to cite you for polluting a public place."

Rolly Luntz, another local with a grudge, sauntered over to join in. Having retired after working forty years in construction, Rolly had become a resurrected cowboy. Today he was garbed in a denim shirt and jeans complete with a belt bearing a fist-size silver and turquoise buckle. High-heeled, pointy-toed boots that definitely weren't made for walking gave him more swish than swagger. Topping off the ensemble was a cross between a cowboy hat and Abe Lincoln's stove pipe chapeau. He was determined to look like a cowboy if it killed him. If he wasn't careful, it might.

"Hey, Rachel. Do you know how to get a tortoise off

the road when it's crossing?'' Rolly asked, a grin sneaking to first base across his face.

This just wasn't my day.

"If you catch 'em just right with your tire, they're like a hockey puck. You can shoot 'em straight across the road.'' Rolly chortled, his grin sliding to home.

This was the latest joke in a popular local game known as tortoise tiddlywinks.

"That's very clever, Rolly. Your jokes are getting better,'' I said in an attempt to improve cowboy–federal agent relations.

Rolly grinned in delight at the praise. "Heck, Rachel. I got another if you like.''

I held up my hand, cutting him off at the pass. "That's okay, Rolly. I'm trying to limit myself to one laugh a day.''

"Hey, Rolly. I've invited Porter to the barbecue we're having. Why don't you tell her what's on the menu?'' Clayton asked with a wicked gleam in his eye.

Rolly tucked his thumbs inside the waistband of his jeans and made an effort to puff out his chest. "Its gonna be real good this year, Rachel. What we're having us is a whole lineup of crispy critters, including some rigor mortis tortoise and shake 'n bake snake.''

"Don't forget about our chunk of skunk and swirl of squirrel,'' Clayton chimed in.

But Rolly wasn't to be outdone. "Yeah. And there's our smear of deer and poodles 'n noodles.''

The two men convulsed into a fit of the giggles.

"That's great, boys. I wouldn't miss it for the world. I especially want to be there so that I can serve you up something real special after I land your rear ends in jail. How about a helping of three-hundred-and-sixty days Hayes along with a serving of twelve-months Luntz? Sound good to you?'' I asked.

The two men stared at me a moment before breaking out into a roar of laughter. Rolly pounded on the table with his fist, causing Clayton's lethal concoction to spill over. The river of tobacco juice made a beeline directly for my lap.

Jumping up out of my seat, I decided to forsake a down-home western breakfast and opted instead for my regular: a cup of coffee, a bag of barbecue chips, and a Snickers bar to go. If possible, my eating habits have gotten worse: my idea of good nutrition now is Taco Bell Lite.

But before heading out, I went to the pay phone to check the answering machine at work. I entered my code, and a mechanical voice with all the warmth of Lureen informed me that I had one message. The call was from the Desert Tortoise Conservation Center just outside of Vegas.

It seemed three hundred and fifty desert tortoise hatchlings had just disappeared.

Two

The location of the Center is kept fairly secret because of the science-fiction-type research that's performed there. In a sort of Nietzschean superman twist, young hatchling and juvenile torts are fed what amounts to Michael Jordan's diet. The result has been a production line of "super juvees," tortoises three times as large as a normal reptile left to fend for itself. This would be my first visit.

I passed the 7-Eleven, the only civilization for miles around, and turned onto an unmarked dirt road. Dust balls of fine, powdery silt rolled off the sun-stunned desert floor, caking my Blazer in a replica of Miss Havisham's ancient wedding gown. Soon a cyclone fence came into view, racing alongside my car mesmerizingly, and leading to a locked gate. Beyond that lay the one-story Center, camouflaged the same drab beige as the land. I beeped my horn to announce my arrival and waited inside my portable sauna for someone to open the gate.

A funny thing happened in Clark County, Nevada, when the desert tortoise was placed on the endangered species list. Since the reptiles have their burrows just about everywhere, all construction was forced to a grinding halt. Housing developments came to a standstill. Schools couldn't be built. The new airport was put on hold, along with half-finished highways and casino hotels. What was at stake was money. Big money. Billions and billions of dollars.

Because Nevada's favorite colors are gold, silver, and greenbacks, money changed hands, and, in the blink of a

14

tortoise's eye, Las Vegas was back in business. The Fish and Wildlife Service was handed a large chunk of cash along with an offer they couldn't refuse: builders would construct a conservation center for tortoise research. In return, developers were once again free to obliterate the desert.

The conservation center quickly turned into a dumping ground, with captive tortoises breeding as prolifically as rabbits. In fact, the problem was now what to do with all the critters. It seemed someone had just created his own solution.

Five minutes had gone by, and I was still waiting to be let in. Having passed through the stages of steamed and baked, I was now well on my way to being deep-fried. Patience may be a virtue, but it's not mine. I was at the point where I'd kill for a Coke.

Getting out of the Blazer, I opened up my handy-dandy Leatherman—a multi-pliers pocket tool kit, complete with wire cutter, straight and serrated blades, screwdriver, bottle opener, metal file, scissors, tweezers, and nail file. In less than ten seconds flat, I managed to jimmy the lock and I drove on inside. So far, security at the Center was worse than my old ground-floor apartment back in New York, which had been referred to by the local Hoods 'R Us as an easy lay.

I walked through the front door and was greeted by an array of stuffed desert wildlife frozen in lifelike positions. Since no one running the Center was to be found among the lot, I made my way down the hall, passing one sterile enclosure after another, until I finally arrived at the darkened lab. A small, sparse room, its decor was wall-to-wall wire cages. Each pen was marked to identify the tortoise inside. All stood eerily empty. It wasn't the high-tech extravaganza I had expected for the millions of dollars that had been spent.

''What are you doing in here?''

I turned around and saw a young man in his early twenties, wearing a white coat as if dressed up to play doctor.

Remnants of teenage acne marred his face, and heavy tortoiseshell glasses gave him the air of a nerd. He stood ramrod-straight with his hands clenched deep inside his coat pockets and looked me over as if I were an annoying piece of sagebrush that had somehow blown in.

"I'm Agent Rachel Porter with Fish and Wildlife. You left a message that a number of tortoises were stolen?" I inquired, using my best official tone.

The young man made an effort to peer down his nose, even though I stood a good inch taller. He then began to sniff around the room, his nostrils dilating with each whiff, as if in search of a missing piece of cheese.

"I don't believe the term 'stolen' was used. What was said quite precisely was that they had disappeared," he corrected me.

I glanced at his name tag, which identified him as William Holmes. "Well, Bill, unless Houdini's been here, I'd say your superjuvees have been nabbed."

"My name is William, and we have no evidence of a break-in. As was stated before, they've simply vanished, Porter," he haughtily replied.

A smarmy wiseass who was probably getting along by living off grants.

"The name is Agent Porter. Would you like to tell me precisely what you mean by the term 'vanished'?" I responded.

The corners of William's mouth curled down as if he didn't have time for such nonsense. "What I mean is that they no longer appear to be here. However, no locks seem to have been tampered with and no windows have been broken. As to precisely what has taken place, I'm afraid I must unfortunately leave those details to *your* attention, Agent Columbo."

I already hated the kid. "For your information, Bill, I just unlocked the entry gate without a key. And by the look of it, I could probably do the same with the front door. With the kind of security system you've got here, who needs to break windows?"

I switched on an overhead light and began to look around.

William stood stiff as a board. "Would you mind not poking at anything before asking?"

If I'd had a cattle prod, I might have inquired as to what he meant. Instead, I made a slow survey of the room. None of the cages contained food or water and each pen door had been carefully closed.

"What time this morning did you realize that the tortoises were missing?" I inquired.

William paused for a moment before answering. "I first noticed they had disappeared two days ago."

"Two days ago?" I was stunned. "What were you doing all this time? Waiting for them to magically reappear?"

I'd have to report the kid to somebody. The job was crying out for a replacement. William refused to look me in the eye, which only annoyed me further.

"Well, what did you think? That they had gone out for a quick Burger King fix? Why did you wait so long before reporting this?" I asked.

William's lips barely moved as he spoke. "I thought they might have been borrowed."

I tried to give him the benefit of the doubt. Maybe he'd been munching on magic mushrooms for the past two days. But he just didn't seem the type.

"Borrowed? And what would they have been borrowed for?" I prodded.

William shot me a withering glance. "We do all sorts of experiments here."

Okay. So the place was a bordello for kinky sex. I still had to hunt down three hundred and fifty missing tortoises.

Turning to leave, I noticed a neon-green tortoise painted on the door to the lab.

I pointed to the painting. "Is this the work of some budding Picasso? Or is it so everyone will know where the tortoises are kept when they're not being borrowed?"

Holmes gave me a look to kill. "That appeared around the same time the tortoises vanished."

I stepped in for a closer view. The form appeared to have been hand-painted using a stencil. "So nobody here is taking the credit?"

"No. I guess that must mean you've got your first clue, Porter," Holmes said, folding his arms.

"And what would that be, Bill?"

A grin, reminiscent of a weasel in heat broke out across his face. "It obviously means that this is the work of some commando group of econuts, who slipped in during the night and liberated the tortoises."

The kid had to go. "Yep. You're right, Sherlock. I guess the case is closed."

I stepped past him and prowled around the rest of the building. The kid was right about one thing—there had been no break-in. It was beginning to look like an inside job.

I turned around and almost bumped into Holmes, who had been tailing my every move. "I take it that you've spoken with everyone who works here?"

Holmes pulled back an inch. "Of course I have. No one has the slightest idea what could have happened, but they are all very concerned."

If they were as concerned as Holmes, there was the possibility that the tortoises could already have been missing for weeks.

"I'd like a list of everyone who works here, along with their address and phone number," I informed him.

William eyed me suspiciously. "I already told you I've spoken with everyone. What do you want that for?"

Good thing the kid wasn't gunning to be a brain surgeon. "I have some follow-up questions. Is there a reason you should have a problem with that?"

Holmes didn't bother to respond.

"By the way, Bill, be sure to include a number where I can reach you as well," I added.

Hesitating for a second, he licked his lips. "Why do you need my number?"

"Backup for the raid on the commando group," I dead-panned.

Holmes jammed his fists into his pockets again and skulked off to make the list. When he finally returned, he held the piece of paper just out of my reach.

"Ask around all you want, Porter. But everyone who works here does so because they care about tortoises." There were tiny sweat marks on the paper beneath Holmes's fingertips.

"A lot of people in Nevada care about tortoises. Mostly for the wrong reasons." I pulled the list out of his hand and headed for the door.

"By the way, Porter. How did you know it was the super juvees that were missing?" he asked, his voice high and tight in his throat.

"Would you keep regular tortoises in a lab, each in individual pens?" I retorted.

Holmes stared at me without saying a word. I didn't bother to tell him it was the age and weight carefully listed on each cage that had given it away.

The best thing about driving through the desert is that you have plenty of time to think. There's nothing much else to do. I began totting up a list of suspects in my mind. So far, nearly everyone in southern Nevada was on it.

With the federal government owning ninety percent of the land in Clark County, there's little private land left to buy. Instead, miners and ranchers lease public land for pennies, but with restrictions attached in a big flashy bow of government red tape. When I'd arrived, I was informed that miners despise the tortoise because their presence inhibits mining. I learned that ranchers hate the critter since they're the cause of cattle grazing being curtailed. And developers routinely yell at me that they have no land to build on.

But my list of suspects didn't stop there. Wealthy collectors with exotic tastes hanker after the threatened creature as a "must have" pet. And in Vietnamese and Cambodian communities, they're lusted after at sumptuous banquets in the form of highly prized tortoise soup.

All of this left me with an endless number of places to begin my search. Frustration makes me hungry. I reached inside my bag of chips found it was empty, and decided it was time for lunch. There was one place where I could eat and possibly pick up some information as well.

The Mosey On Inn was a pit stop on the road to nowhere. A giant statue of Paul Bunyon took up most of the parking lot, and I had yet to figure out its meaning—there was nothing in sight to chop down. I parked next to Paul's boot and walked inside, where I spied Ruby at her usual spot behind the counter.

"Hi there, sugar. Mosey on in here."

Ruby and her husband had moved to Nevada three years ago. Her husband had declared it his retirement paradise; Ruby saw it as her hell. Having lived most her life in Nebraska, she'd been dragged out here against her will, kicking and screaming all the way. Ruby's worst nightmare came true when after only two months in Nevada, her husband blissfully dropped dead of a heart attack while experiencing a lap dance in Vegas. Ruby had found herself stuck in a trailer that had been bought with their life savings and working a dead-end job.

"What'll it be today, sweetie?" she asked, pleased at having a customer.

"A slice of lemon meringue pie and a jolt of black coffee would be perfect," I replied.

Ruby waddled back and forth filling my order, her ample rear end threatening to burst her uniform at the seams. The buttons on the front of her dress were equally strained, thanks to a bountiful bosom, which was further accentuated by a large, purple plastic orchid pinned to her chest. Ruby helped nature along by smearing a generous dose of rouge on the tops of her cheeks and then applying the same ruby-red paste to her lips. To top it off, tiny rolls of tight blond curls covered her head, resembling a serving platter full of miniature pork sausage. The effect was that of a kewpie doll on acid. Ruby had been out in the desert too long.

"So what brings you out here today, sugar? It can't be just our homemade pie." Ruby smiled at me.

She was right. My fork bounced off a slice that must have been coagulating for days.

"Some young tortoises are missing from the conservation center," I replied, slowly chewing on a mouthful of rubbery lemon curd. "I was wondering if you might have heard any news."

The Mosey On Inn is a hangout where information on illegal deals is regularly exchanged. It's out of the way, the food is bad, and word has it that Ruby gets a small cut on any business that goes down. My counterdefense was to ply her with makeup, perfume, and hair spray whenever she supplied me with any dirt. I pulled out a small bottle of White Diamonds cologne and slid it her way. Ruby eagerly snapped it up and squirted on her daily fix, permeating my coffee with its sweet, cloying scent.

"How about them wackos?"

The rasping voice came hurtling at me from the back of the room. Turning around, I saw a figure disengage itself from a dark corner and make its way to the front. The man was dressed in full camouflage, but it was his face that caught my attention. He looked as though he'd been caught in a napalm attack and just barely survived.

"The whole bunch of 'em are crazy as loons. Call themselves guerrillas. I call them flaming assholes," he croaked.

One eye was a mere slit. The other stared out from a puffy mound of scar tissue, where it burned with the intensity of a live ember. He held a cup of coffee in his hand, complete with a straw. Taking a sip, his mouth opened and closed like a fish stranded on land.

It took me a moment before I managed to gather my wits and reply. "Why do you call them wackos?"

The man fixed his good eye on me. "They're supposed to be a bunch of screwball scientists. Probably experimented with one too many chemicals, if ya know what I mean."

He took another sip from his straw. A dribble escaped

and worked its way down to lodge in the crook that had once been his chin.

"They're always bitching about miners and ranchers destroying the land. I hear they even laid down in front of some bulldozers at one mine. I say the damn 'dozers should have run them over." The man paused for added effect. "I hear they call that Center you're talking about a concentration camp. Hell, I hear they even lick toads." He gave me the eye.

I must have looked surprised.

"You know, getting high and having orgies and stuff," he said, continuing to stare at me.

"Do these scientists live around here?" I asked. It seemed far-fetched, but it was all I had to grab onto.

"Sure. Not far from me." He nodded in an indeterminate direction. "Just the other side of McCullough Pass."

I'd never been through the pass. There was no reason to go. Nobody would have thought of living there.

"I'm Rachel Porter," I said. "I didn't catch your name."

His good eye blinked. "That's because I damn well didn't give it."

He quickly looked around in all directions, hunching his shoulders up to what had at one time been his ears, before moving in closer. I saw that his fingernails were as hard and horned as tortoiseshell, and what few teeth he had were dark, like small lumps of coal.

"They call me Cammo Dude. You ain't one of those government stooges, are you?" he asked suspiciously.

I could tell I was about to step on a land mine. "I work for the U.S. Fish and Wildlife Service."

"So you're one of those no-good, jackbooted thugs who wants to take away our land and uses any eight-eyed, range-munching, rock-climbing, pseudo-endangered critter to do it?"

The Dude was close to foaming at what was left of his mouth.

I pointed down at my sneakers. "No jackboots here. I also don't know of any critter like the one you've described, but I'd sure like to see it. And finally, did you say that you live in the pass? I didn't think there were any private landholdings there.''

The Dude backed off immediately. ''What are you planning to do? Come in with some group of Rambos and kick me outta my home?''

Bingo. Cammo was living illegally on public land. I decided to throw him some rope.

''No. I don't believe in that. I think as long as you're not harming the land, it's nobody's business where you live. This is wide open space that belongs to the public,'' I told him.

Cammo hesitated, studying me intently with his one eye. Then he nodded in agreement. ''You're damn right it does.''

I gave the lasso a tug. ''But not everyone feels the same way. So I'll make you a deal. You tell me whatever you hear about those tortoises, and we'll keep where you live a secret.''

I was hoping to add Cammo to a small list of locals I could turn to for information. Hermits living in the desert have a knack for knowing about poaching and everything else that goes on.

Cammo thought for a moment. ''You got a deal if you get rid of those damn helicopters you government stooges have got flying around here all night. A man can't get his sleep.''

''I'll look into it.'' I figured the 'copters had to be part of a training mission at nearby Nellis Air Force Base that would probably end in a matter of days.

Having struck a deal, the Dude headed back to his corner table and I got up to leave. But before I was out the door, Ruby pulled me aside. The smell of her cologne almost knocked me over.

''Listen, sugar. You want to find out what's going on in these parts? You head over to see old Annie McCarthy,'' she said, shoving a paper bag into my hand.

I already knew what the package contained. Ruby had

studied my eating habits over the past three months. Horrified, she'd become determined to save me.

"The woman's been here forever and is into every darn thing you can think of," Ruby continued. "Word has it she's dealing in reptiles, too. If something's going on, you can bet your buns Annie's gotten wind of it."

I trusted Ruby on this. She was my Information Central. If the tortoises weren't part of a deal that Annie McCarthy was involved in, there was always the chance that she might decide to squeal on any upstart competition.

"If she's not at the ranch, she's probably out checking her claims," Ruby added.

I had a hard time imagining an old woman out prospecting. "She's a miner?" I asked, glancing inside the bag.

A ham and cheese sandwich was accompanied by a shiny red apple. I looked up at Ruby and smiled.

She pulled a lace hankie from her breast pocket and gave it a squirt of cologne. "Annie's a crazy old coot who stakes a claim on every piece of land she can. She must have at least eighty of them in the area. She's probably got a damn fortune in gold sitting out there while she waits to strike it rich. Annie's counting on some mining company to come in and cut her a deal one day," Ruby revealed. "In the meantime, she's dealing in reptiles and every other damn thing to get by."

I got directions to the ranch, along with a couple of Cokes to go, and headed out in search of what I hoped would become my own goldmine of information.

The quickest way to Annie McCarthy's was across a shaven mountaintop. Turning off the highway, I threw the Blazer into four-wheel drive, the gearshift shrieking in protest as I held my breath. It had given way on me twice before, and I prayed it didn't happen now. Mountain lions roam the area, and I imagined they might find my diet of candy and chips made for a tasty treat. The Blazer rumbled into gear as I headed up the mountain. Tall steel power line towers guided my way, silent sentinels standing guard over the desert. The wind had picked up, producing a low, mournful moan that trailed close at my heels, prodding me on as it nipped at the back of my Blazer, and the power lines began to hum in the wind. The sound surged its way through me, starting at the soles of my feet and coursing up into my torso, my heart, my head, and my hands until I vibrated in unison with the desert floor.

Thorny bushes of cat's claw dotted the landscape, intermingling with patches of buckhorn choya. I'd made the mistake of brushing up against a choya plant once, only to learn how lethal their needles can be. As I drove still higher, the choya was replaced by a thick carpet of teddy bear cholla. Soft and fuzzy on the surface, its spines have been known to pierce an unlucky foot straight through to the bone.

I reached the summit and looked down over the sheer drop that lay to my left as I rounded a curve. The El Dorado Canyon was spread out before me, surrounded by wedding-cake layers of mountains. The road spiraled down till it touched level ground, where it ran straight as an arrow, crossing the desert floor. A speck emerged in the distance, and soon Annie's ranch loomed ahead.

Old and run-down, the ranch consisted of an ancient stable with a galvanized tin roof, a fenced-in corral, and tall wooden posts erected as gallows from which slaughtered cows were hung. The main house stood off to the side, ghoulishly decorated with an array of animal skulls leering down from above the windows and door. A powder-blue Studebaker was parked next to a structure that I suspected was an outdoor shower, judging by the water tank perched on its roof. If Annie was home, she could hear me coming from a mile away.

I parked my Blazer next to Annie's car and took a look inside it. In perfect condition, the Studebaker put my clunker of a Blazer to shame. A light cream-colored blanket had been carefully laid across the front seat. Long, black dog hairs clung to its nap on the passenger side. I noticed that the clock still kept perfect time and the gas tank was half full.

I walked over to the house and tapped on the front door,
though I took it for granted that no one was home. Already
ajar, the door slid open at my touch. I called out Annie's
name, but received no answer. Hesitating for just a moment,
I walked in.

My footsteps echoed as I entered the hallway and peered
into the first room on my left. The kitchen was immaculate,
without a pot or pan in sight. I brazenly began to explore,
opening the cupboards, where dishes were neatly stacked
and glasses lined up as straight as toy solders. The pantry
revealed an abundance of canned goods along with large
bags of dog food. It was as if Annie was seriously planning
for a disaster, either natural or man-made. I swatted away
a group of flies that were congregated on top of an open
can of dog biscuits and then closed the lid. Walking over
to the table, I saw it was set for one, with each utensil in
its proper place. A paper napkin was neatly folded alongside a chipped dinner plate gaily decorated with faded blue
cornflowers daintily dancing along its edge. A water glass,
cleaner than any to be found in my own kitchen cabinet,
sat nearby. Balanced on its rim was another fly, patiently
waiting for food.

I walked back into the hall, where my next stop was
Annie's bedroom. An old walnut dresser stood inside, vir-
ginally draped in a swathe of hand-crocheted ivory lace.
Carefully arranged on top were tiny photographs lovingly
displayed in antique brass frames. Each photo portrayed a
beautiful young woman whom I assumed to be Annie. The
photos appeared to be from the 1940s, though none contained the desert as a backdrop. In some Annie beamed at
the camera, holding a small dog in her arms. Other photos,
yellowed with age, showed her gazing up at a handsome
young man adoringly. Still others portrayed her alone, an
air of melancholy lingering about her.

As I held a photo of Annie, a whiff of a scent intruded—
tinged with the distinct, sharp odor of ammonia. But something else was mixed in as well: the nauseatingly sweet
stench of decay. I took a deep breath, and the stench

reached down inside me, its fingers twisting teasingly at my stomach while numbing my brain. Tiny pinpricks of perspiration broke out on my face and over my body. I licked my lips, rough as an emery board against my tongue, to taste a salty residue of sweat.

For the first time, I became aware of how deathly still the house was. The only sounds were that of my own blood pounding through my body and the persistent buzz of flies, their maddening hum hanging like an off-key chorus filling the air.

My feet moved woodenly out of the bedroom as I continued my search. I passed a room Annie must have used as a study. A rocking chair sat in reproachful silence; on its needlepoint seat lay a copy of *Pride and Prejudice*, a bookmark napping between the last pages that had been read. A wooden case against wall held a treasure trove of books. On any other occasion I would have perused Annie's choice of reading material, curious as to how she filled her time, living all alone in the desert. But the air had grown more and more putrid, urging me on.

By the time I reached the end of the hall, the smell was so intense that I began to gag. But what I saw appalled me even more: an army of black flies buzzed angrily outside the last door, covering every inch of its frame. I glanced down and stepped back with a gasp as I saw where the insects were coming from. Hundreds of winged black bodies swarmed in the gap where the door met the floor, crawling over one another in a mad fight for space. Steeling myself, I pulled my shirttail out of my pants, held the fabric up over my nose and mouth, and gingerly pushed the door open with the tips of my fingers. Immediately, wave after wave of droning insects descended upon me like an angry tsunami crashing out of control. I shrieked and blindly swatted the air in a vain attempt to drive them away, covering my head and turning my back as the irate mob flew over and around me, filling the hallway beyond as they headed for the front door.

Only after the roar had died down to a low hum and I

could once again breathe did I dare turn and face the await-
ing tableau. The overwhelming heat in the room, mixed
with the origin of the stench, nearly flattened me as I stared
in horror. The remains of a badly decomposed dog lay rotting on the wooden floor of the bathroom. Covered with
flies, what little was left of the body was filled with a frenzy
of other bugs gorging themselves on the feast. But it took
a moment for my brain to register what lay beyond that.

A grinning skeleton sat in an empty bathtub. Its mass of
silvery hair, still attached to the skull, flowed down to cover
bony shoulders like a finely spun veil. It looked like a white
sheet had been thrown over Annie's remains, in either a
grisly attempt at modesty or a perverse joke. But then the
sheet began to move. I rubbed my eyes and took a deep
breath, my heart pounding like a fist against my chest.

Sure that my imagination was playing a trick, I slowly
inched forward, suddenly stopping dead in my tracks as the
sheet of white began to break apart. It was then that I realized the crudely made shroud was nothing but maggots.
Hundreds and hundreds of tiny twitching and twisting white
worms. They wriggled between Annie's bare bones as the
last witnesses to death, forming a living blanket of squirm-
ing, well-fed bodies.

My pulse galloped through my veins and my vision began to blur as my scream roared through the room. Reverberating against the walls, it shook the house, before
clutching at my clothes, my hands, and my hair. Death furiously tracked its way through the ranch, permeating every
nook, every cranny, the very air. I tore down the hall and
out the front door, where I leaned against the gallows,
throwing up my breakfast along with the sandwich and pie.
I was still shaking as I staggered to the Blazer and rinsed
out my mouth with a swig of warm Coke. Frantically digging through my glove compartment, I located my cell
phone. Grabbing hold of it as if it would save me, I
punched in the number for Metro Police. But when they
answered, I discovered that Annie wasn't the only one no
longer able to speak. Disconnecting the call, I sank to the
ground and cried.

Three

It took three attempts before I was able to call Metro Police and speak coherently. Two hours later, a squad car pulled up to the ranch. By that time I was thoroughly sunburned, unable to bring myself to venture back inside Annie's.

"Hey, there. You got something ripe for us?"

Ted Brady struggled out of the squad car. Though only twenty-eight years old, he already had the receding hairline of a middle-aged man, coupled with a paunch that pushed against the shiny brass buttons of his uniform. A light blond mustache stained his baby-fat face like a smudge that hadn't been wiped away.

I'd never met the man who swung out of the passenger side of the car. Tall, with a mop of white hair and a walrus mustache to match, he raised his arm above his eyes, squinting at me, before striding over to where I sat on the ground.

"Henry Lanahan. Forensics. Thought I'd join Ted for the ride," he said in way of introduction.

Lanahan shook my hand, then I felt myself being pulled to my feet. "Why don't we go in and see what we've got?" he added. His fingers rested lightly on the inside of my wrist, and I felt faintly suspicious that he was taking my pulse.

Brady stood with his thumbs tucked into his gun belt. "You up for that, Porter? You look like you could use a rest in my squad car. It's air-conditioned, you know."

The last thing I wanted to do was go back into Annie's

house, and I would have killed for a shot of air-conditioning. But the smirk on Brady's face brought me to my senses.

"I'm fine, Brady. I had plenty of time for my daily si-esta, waiting for you to get here," I smartly retorted. Will-ing my feet to move, I led the way inside.

By the time we'd reached the bathroom, Brady had a handkerchief pressed to his mouth. Lanahan was encased in a thick cloud of smoke, puffing on a cigar that smelled almost as foul as the room itself.

Brady took one look at the scene and the blood drained from his face. "Jesus Christ. What the hell?"

Turning on his heels, he ran back out the front door, and the sound of retching wafted toward us on dense waves of heat. It was almost enough to make me feel better.

"Well, this is something I've never seen before." Lan-ahan walked over to the tub and bent down close. "Ex-traordinary! Just look at this!"

I sneaked a peek as Henry studied the scene.

"You see, to a fly, the human corpse is the same as an animal. Free food and plenty of it." He prodded a cluster of the parasites with the tip of his nail. "They lay their eggs on the skin, and when the little buggers hatch, the maggots scoop in the grub with this tiny clawlike apparatus that's attached to their mouths. I like to call it a maggot's version of *The Last Supper*."

My empty stomach turned.

Pulling on a pair of latex gloves, Lanahan lifted Annie's skeleton up by the hair as maggots tumbled off. "I'd say they did a pretty good job, wouldn't you?" he chuckled.

Forensics humor—I'd never get used to it.

Henry clamped the cigar between his teeth and carefully stuck a finger through the bullet hole lodged smack in her skull. The tip of his finger wriggled in the air like a puppy dog's tail.

"Looks like a .38 slug to the front of the head," he attested.

Annie's skeleton grimaced in horrified silence as Henry

lowered it back down. Then he directed his attention to the wall directly behind her. Closing his eyes, he ran his fingers over the hole there like a pianist playing a riff, probing for unseen clues.

"Yep. I'd say the bullet lodged right in here," he stated.

"How long has she been dead?" I was curious to know how much time it took to descend to this state.

Henry shrugged. "Maybe a month. Hard to say right now. Give me a few days, and I'll know more."

I looked at Annie's corpse and felt exonerated for my junk food diet. If this was the way I could end up, I didn't see the sense in torturing myself with wholesome food and exercise.

Henry turned to face me. "Now let's check the pooch."

A halo of dried blood enshrined a skull picked nearly as clean as Annie's.

"Same thing here. A .38 right between the eyes. Nice shot!" Henry turned the head in my direction. "By the way, if you want to take a gander, you can get a good look at those maggots chomping away at what little flesh is left."

My stomach catapulted into a series of somersaults. Averting my eyes, I noticed the neon-green imprint of a tortoise on the wall near the sink. Stepping over bugs and past Lanahan, I moved in for a better view. It appeared to be identical to the one I had spotted at the Center.

I hated to admit it, but Holmes might have been onto something, after all. Maybe there *was* a group of eco-nuts practicing their own form of vigilante law. Still, I'd found no sign of reptiles being kept on Annie's premises. Adding it up, the shooting of an old woman who lived in a shack with nothing of value just didn't make sense.

"Looks like we've got the gun over here," Henry called to me over his shoulder.

I skirted the dog, joining Henry and his cigar on the floor, where we stared at the .38 Smith & Wesson revolver nestled beneath the claw-foot tub.

I shuddered as a bug skittered by. "How do you suppose the gun ended up all the way under there?"

Lanahan pulled on the nub of his cigar. "Good question. I suppose we could ask old Annie, but it don't look like she's gonna do much talking." Henry chortled and gave me a wink. He was turning into both a comedian and his own best audience.

At this point, Brady dragged his body back into the room. An unnatural pallor had replaced his normal ruddy complexion. I couldn't help the twinge of a smile as I caught him mopping the endless stream of sweat that had begun to pour off the top of his head.

Brady caught my eye and glared. "Don't start with me, Porter," he warned.

Propping himself against the doorjamb, Brady listened as Lanahan filled him in on what we had found so far.

"Sounds like a suicide to me," Brady proclaimed.

I stared at him in amazement as he wrung his handkerchief out onto the floor. "You're going to write it off as a suicide? You can't do that!" I exclaimed.

"What the hell would you call it?" he challenged.

I would have called it shoddy police work but kept that opinion to myself for now. "Murder is good for a start."

I quickly gave Lanahan and Brady a thumbnail sketch of the theft of the tortoises and then pointed out the hand-stenciled imprint that had also been found at the Center.

"It can't be a coincidence. There has to be some sort of a tie-in here," I insisted.

But Brady was looking to keep it simple and clean. "Maybe they're all tortoise fans who are into graffiti. Who the hell cares?"

His florid complexion was back, along with his cocky self-pride. "Look, Porter. This is the way it went down. What we're dealing with is a crazy old hermit who was looking to strike the mother lode. Suddenly, she wakes up one day and realizes it ain't never happened, ain't never gonna happen. Gets out her gun, plugs her dog, plugs herself. Zippo. The end. You want to claim the dog was mur-

dered? That's your area of expertise, Kemo Sabe." Brady's
lip curled up in a sneer. "Be my guest. But for chrissake,
who wouldn't be depressed living here? Jesus, just look at
this place. I'd kill myself, too."

Maybe it was the heat, but my fingers twitched to reach
for my own gun and pull the trigger. "Let me get this
straight, Brady. Your explanation of the events as they occurred is as follows. First set the table for dinner. Then
climb into a bathtub. Next decide to shoot your only companion between the eyes. Then shoot yourself in the forehead. And to top it off, throw the revolver under the tub
when you're done."

Brady picked his nose and wiped his finger on his pants.
"The dog must have kicked it there."

"That ought to look good in your report," I retorted.

I stepped back, then realized I was in a cluster of bugs
and shot forward, almost knocking Henry head first into the
tub. He managed to catch himself in time, but his cigar was
another matter. The stogie flew out of his mouth, landing
in the brown sludge of body fluid that had collected at the
bottom of the drain.

"Careful! I'm working here," Henry reprimanded me as
he scooped up maggots. He methodically placed the parasites inside a plastic container.

Brady took one look and blanched once again. "What
the hell are you doing, Lanahan?"

Henry chuckled as he ladled up another batch of the
grubs. "If it was suicide, Ms. McCarthy might have decided to ingest some barbiturates first. We'll find that out
by putting these little fellas into a blender, making ourselves a maggot milk shake, and testing the results."

This was way more than I wanted to know. I left Brady
and Lanahan to their own devices and wandered back outside.

The powder-blue Studebaker had taken on a lustrous
sheen under the sun, and I wondered what would happen
to it now. Walking over to the car, I found the driver's side
was unlocked. I opened the door and slid in. The blanket

thrown over the seat was warm, but it kept the seat from burning me. I peered underneath and was surprised to find that the leather had been maintained in flawless condition, without a gash or tear. I brought my foot to the pedal. The seat was adjusted just right for my height. I could still smell the scent of Annie's dog and I wondered what her life had been like, living all alone. Well, not altogether alone. She at least had a dog. I didn't even own a hamster.

Leaning over, I opened the glove compartment and poked around inside. Empty candy wrappers filled the compact space. Annie had obviously been my kind of woman. I closed it and turned my attention to the visor above me, pulling it down. Instead of finding a vanity mirror, as I had expected, a set of keys fell into my lap. The master key fit the ignition, but it seemed inappropriate to turn the car on. I sat still for a moment, the second key burning in the palm of my hand. Then, sliding off the seat, I walked around to the rear and unlatched the trunk, which opened without a sound.

Inside lay a tire iron, a wrench, and a navy duffel bag. For a moment, I wondered if I had discovered Annie's secret stash of reptiles, no doubt baked to a crisp by now. Bracing myself for the worst, I slowly unzipped the sack, ready to leap back at the first sound of a rattle or sight of a spider's hairy leg. But no mini-monsters were to be found. The bag was was filled with letters, all of which were addressed to Anna Bell McCarthy in Buda, Texas. The postmarks were dated from 1938 to 1942. Without thinking about why, I zipped the bag up and lifted it out of the trunk. Glancing furtively around, I stashed the remnants of Annie's life inside my Blazer.

"You still here, Porter?" Brady asked, slowly tottering outside.

Lanahan followed with a grin on his face as I closed the door to my car.

"If you like this place so much, I have a feeling you can get it dirt cheap," Brady suggested facetiously.

I'd caught a quick view of Brady's bachelor pad once.

It was a place that even New York roaches would have refused to call home. In comparison, Annie's house didn't look half bad.

He opened the cooler in the trunk of his squad car and threw me a beer. I popped the tab and took a sip.

"What happens now?" It would pay to know Brady's next move while I planned out my own.

"Now we clean up the mess." Brady wrapped an ice cube in his handkerchief and laid it against the back of his neck. "After that I file the report as a suicide. Case closed. Then tonight I get stinking drunk and try to forget what takes place when you kick the bucket."

He could have been describing my own plans for the evening. "You sure you don't want more time to rethink this case, Brady?" I asked, giving the man one last chance.

Brady swirled a swig of beer in his mouth and then spat it out, just missing Lanahan's shoe. "You wanna join the police force, feel free to come over anytime and fill out an application, and we'll see if we can't find you something to do. Otherwise, you stick to your work, Porter, and I'll stick to mine."

"There you go again Brady, assuming that what you do can be called police work."

Lanahan stepped between us like a referee at a boxing bout. "Why don't you give me a call in a few days, Rachel? Nobody will be signing off on anything until I've finished my testing. Then we'll take it from there. What do you say, old buddy?" Henry put his arm around Brady, holding the container of maggots close to his face.

Brady took a look at the maggots and pulled away, gagging at the sight. Lanahan winked at me, and I realized his sense of humor wasn't so bad after all.

Living in Las Vegas wasn't all it was cracked up to be. At least, it wasn't for me. There was no glamour in my life, no wild parties, no men banging down my door to show me a hot night on the town. Stopping by Taco Bell on my way home, I picked up a couple of burritos with a bag of chips as my vegetable.

Once again I was renting a place to live. I seem to have trouble when it comes to settling down. It's the thought of permanency that makes me nervous. Once that happens, you sink into the reality that this is your life. You buy furniture and dishes and hang bric-a-brac on your wall. Then you grow old, and before you're ready, you die. I figured the magic elixir of youth was staying mobile, and with the places I lived in, that had yet to pose a problem.

Along with my move to Vegas, I had decided to take the bold step of renting a house rather than the usual apartment. Well, not a house, exactly. A small bungalow, to be precise. A bungalow situated in a row of identical bungalows. Most people would have been appalled at units that sat practically on top of each other. It suited me just fine.

Just as in New Orleans, my new abode was decorated à la thrift shop specials. But the landlord had added a distinct touch of his own. The carpeting throughout was a shag that looked as if it had fallen into a humongous vat of Pepto-Bismol. The way I figured, it was a make-or-break factor. Either I'd like my life in Las Vegas enough to consider putting down roots, or the carpet alone would be enough to send me packing back home.

I threw my bag down on a table that the Salvation Army would have refused, and headed for the bedroom and my answering machine. The lack of flashing red lights confirmed that my personal life was comatose. I stripped off my clothes and turned on a Bonnie Raitt tape. Pouring a tequila in honor of my Mexican meal, I settled into a bubble bath with my burritos and part of Annie's stash of letters within reach.

I opened envelope after envelope, only to discover that what I had stumbled on were old love letters. They had been sent by a man who at one time had been her fiancé. Posted from Nevada, each letter told of a fortune in gold just around the bend, screaming out to be discovered. He would come home to her then. I wondered how long Annie had waited before giving up hope. And what had finally caused her to head for Nevada. I was beginning to discover that everyone has their own reason for deciding to live in the desert. It's a place where you can find yourself if you're looking or lose yourself if you choose. Then there are those who are running from something as fast as they can. Annie fell into one of those categories. So did I. I was still trying to figure out which was the perfect fit.

Visions of Annie in her tub flitted across my mind and I shivered, sliding further down into my blanket of bubbles as I poured another drink. Gut instinct told me that she had been murdered. I also knew I'd never convince Brady to keep the case open. My one hope was Lanahan and what he might find.

I concede that it's time to get out of the tub when my fingers reach the consistency of prunes. I opened my medicine cabinet and poked around for any remnants of lotion to slather on my skin, and was confronted by a bottle of Mylanta and memories of Santou. He practically lived on the stuff. In my twisted state of mind, I kept it in order to feel close to him. A pang of homesickness squeezed at my heart in a surprise attack.

To hell with pride. Picking up the phone, I dialed Santou's number. I had asked him for space and time. I guess I should also have asked for more frequent phone calls. I listened to the phone ring for a while and finally hung up. It was one in the morning, New Orleans time. I didn't even want to think about where he could be. I thought about him enough as it was. Every morning, noon, and night, not counting my dreams.

Terri had warned me that I would be lonely. His advice had been to get a bird. "You don't have to walk them, and they'll never break your heart."

He was wrong about that. I'd had a parakeet as a kid. It had escaped one day through an open window to perch on a tree. I had begged the bird to come back inside. Instead it had flown away. I should have taken that as a sign then and there that either birds weren't meant to be caged or I had about as much luck with them as I would in my future relationships with men.

That night, though I left the lights blazing bright, my demons hit in full force. A mass of maggots swam into my dreams. Emerging from a Pepto-pink milk shake, they crawled up into my bed to swarm on my body, covering me from head to toe. It wasn't until hours later, as my demons were finally leaving and deep sleep had begun to set in, that I wondered about Annie's closest neighbors.

HORICON PUBLIC LIBRARY

Four

Dawn was just creeping up as I started out the next morning. The sunrise, a crimson streak against the sky, stretched like an animal come to life. I barreled down the road serenaded by the demented yammer of coyotes ending their partying for the night. A kit fox loped over a rocky outcrop on his way home.

I stopped at the Mosey On Inn and stumbled inside for my morning transfusion of coffee along with directions as to where the group of wacko scientists were holed up. I also gave Ruby the news about Annie. Ruby took it in stride.

"These things happen," she casually informed me.

"Being shot in a bathtub?" I asked, surprised by her response.

Ruby adjusted her chest as she put on a new pot to brew. "Darlin', there are lots of bodies buried in holes out in the desert. The trick is to make sure you don't trip and fall in with them."

The words sounded like good advice through my tequila haze. I grabbed another cup of coffee and a bag of Doritos to go, but Ruby pulled the chips out of my hands, foisting a bran muffin on me in its place.

"You gotta eat healthy!" she called as I headed out the door.

The heat was already a sweltering ninety-eight degrees by seven in the morning and about as dry as a sponge held under a running faucet. I turned onto a dirt road and headed

39

toward the mountains, passing sun-bleached bones along the way. I only hoped they weren't human. The wind had begun to pick up, singing a mournful dirge through the needles of large barrel cactus as shadows of clouds tripped across the mountain face. I'd heard that with time you can learn to take the desert's pulse. This morning it was vibrating with life, even though none could be seen.

Shifting into four-wheel drive, I worked my way up and down switchbacks and over rocks, following Ruby's directions. After about twenty minutes of this, I began to think that she'd been wrong. It seemed inconceivable that anyone would want to live out here.

Then I heard the sound of gunshots. I turned off what Ruby had called a road and blindly followed the sound, but nothing came into view. Not wanting to risk losing my way, I was about to turn back when sunlight reflected off an object in the distance. I headed in its direction.

The closer I got, the less I trusted my eyes. There appeared to be a large wooden ark sitting in the middle of the desert. Unless I had just solved a biblical mystery, this was the home of the group of scientists I had been told about.

Then I caught sight of my welcoming committee. Ensconced in a beach chair was a bare-chested, middle-aged man with stringy blond hair. His sunburned beer belly hung like a worn-out tire over cutoff denim shorts. Cowboy boots covered his feet. He was bleary-eyed, with a fifth of Jack Daniel's stuck between his legs. He looked like he should have been on a beach, waiting for a wave to roll in, instead of working on his skin cancer in the middle of the Mojave Desert.

He waited for me to get out of the Blazer. "How ya doin'?"

"Hi. I'm Rachel Porter, with Fish and Wildlife," I said.

"So you're the new oinker, huh?" he commented, squinting up at me.

Somehow it didn't sound like scientific jargon to me. He

gave a wide grin as he brought the bottle of Jack Daniel's
to his lips and took a swig.

"Name's Noah Gorfine. Welcome to my ark." Noah
motioned behind him without bothering to get out of his
chair.

After Cammo Dude I thought I'd met all the loony tunes
around, but Noah was coming up number one on my hit
parade. If there was one thing I hadn't expected to find, it
was an ark sitting out in the middle of the desert. But then
again, I should have known better. In Nevada, nothing is
what you expect it to be.

"Why the ark?" I couldn't help but ask.

"In case it rains," Noah deadpanned.

"So where are all the animals?" I questioned.

Another gunshot rang out. Noah looked off in the distance and chuckled. "Don't worry. They're coming."

In the Bible, two of each kind were taken onboard the
ark. Heading our way was a twist on the story. A pack of
small, unkempt dogs began yapping their lungs out upon
catching sight of me. Breaking into a mad dash, the motley
brood lunged en masse, looking like out-of-control mops
as they nipped at my legs.

"Down!" A new voice issued the command.

The dogs immediately fell back in a ragtag semblance of
order. I'd been so busy swatting the little beasts away that
I hadn't noticed the woman who now stood before me. A
busty bleached blonde, she was dressed in a midriff shirt
cut to emphasize her abundant cleavage, a small roll of fat
squeezed out of the top of her hip-hugger jeans. She'd taken
the time to apply full makeup to her slightly bloated face,
and large gold hoop earrings finished off the ensemble.

Noah introduced us. "This is my number one mama,
Georgia Peach."

Georgia Peach looked like she had reached the summit
of ripeness long ago and was now careening down the other
side of the hill without her brakes on.

"So you're the new kid on the block, huh?" Deep and
gravelly, her voice sounded as if it had been run through a

meat grinder and then lightly sanded until it held a distinctive growl. "Guess they aren't going for perky tits and a tight ass these days."

I refused to take offense at a woman who resembled an over-the-hill biker chick. Still, I made sure to stand up straight, push out my chest, pull in my stomach, and clench my butt.

"It sounds as if you don't like the Fish and Wildlife Service very much."

"I sure as hell don't," Georgia growled.

"Any particular reason why?" I was curious to see if the desert tortoise came up on her list.

"Yeah, I used to work for them as a wildlife biologist. That's reason enough for me."

I couldn't have been more surprised if Noah had handed me an umbrella and correctly predicted an instantaneous flood. "What happened?"

"I wanted to be a *Playboy* centerfold. Can't you tell?" Georgia pulled a pint bottle of peppermint schnapps from her back pocket and carefully wiped off the top before bringing it to her lips.

"What are you doing now?"

Georgia pointed to the gang of oversized hair balls, which had begun to chase a panicky lizard. "I breed Lhasa apsos and sell them in Vegas."

With the way they looked, I found it hard to believe she could give the mutts away.

A movement caught my attention and I glanced at the ark, but the figure that had appeared quickly pulled back. Noah followed my gaze.

"That's my number two mama there. Suzie Q, get on out here. It don't look like this one's gonna bite."

The woman came out from behind the ark and stopped a few feet away from me. Standing six foot two with eyes of blue, Suzie Q lived up to her name. A mane of dark hair framed an elongated face. Her clothes hung loose on a stick-thin body as though they were dangling from a wire. Munching on a Twinkie, she stood and stared at me in silence. But my eyes were glued to what was sitting on her shoulder.

Noah glanced at me and chuckled. "That's Suzie Q's pet, Frank Sinatra. Want to say hello?"

What I wanted to do was get back in the Blazer and leave, but my feet were frozen in place. A large tarantula the size of a man's hand, Frank Sinatra could easily have replaced the star of *Arachnophobia*. Suzie Q kept munching away at her Twinkie, never taking her eyes off me.

Georgia's voiced jarred me back to reality. "So let's see what Fish and Wildlife has gone and hired themselves these days. Got a gun?"

My hand immediately went for the revolver stuck in the back of my jeans. "Why do you ask?"

Georgia licked her lips and smiled. "Just want to see if they hired someone who can shoot straight. How about we go a couple rounds?"

I followed Georgia, giving Suzie Q a wide berth as we headed toward the back of the ark. Strung out on a clothes-line between two tall Joshua trees hung photos of *Playboy* centerfolds from the last twelve months. Noah handed Georgia a .38 Smith & Wesson.

"Got a favorite bimbo you'd like to take out?" Georgia inquired.

I pulled out my newly issued 9mm SIG-Sauer. Besides being rusty on target practice, I was still getting used to the gun. But it held ten more rounds than my old .38, and the Service was a stickler for rules.

"I don't shoot at women." I tried to make that a rule, even if they did have better bodies than me. "How about some cans?"

Georgia looked at me a moment and then grinned. "Sure. I don't shoot at them either, unless they're screwing up my day. Noah just likes to hang them there so he can pretend it's his harem. Let's go over here."

We walked to where a black pickup sat. Plastered on its rear bumper were two ancient stickers declaring "Nevada Will Be Cattle-Free By '93" and "No Moo By '92."

Looking back at Suzie Q, I suddenly realized she was the woman I had chased in the desert.

Noah lined up three cans and Georgia took aim, easily knocking each one off its perch.

Twirling the gun around her finger, she moved away. "Your turn, Porter."

Noah sat the cans back up as I took careful aim, knowing I was being tested. I blew the first can off its roost and felt my confidence soar. I aimed at the second. Lining it up perfectly in my sight, I squeezed the trigger, but nothing happened. The SIG-Sauer had jammed.

Georgia broke out in a roar. "Don't you know that gun is for shit, Porter? That's how good the Service is. They've got you using a weapon that jams whenever it damn well feels like it. Hell, it's one way to cut back on retirement pay. Here—try this."

Georgia tossed me her .38, and I fired off two rounds in quick succession, knocking the cans to the ground and then hitting them again so that they danced across the desert floor. In some ways, shooting is a lot like playing darts, my all-time favorite sport. You just aim as if your life depended on it and pray for the best.

"Not bad for a government employee." Georgia pulled out her pint of peppermint schnapps and took a swig. Then she offered it to me. "Here. Have a swig. It beats the hell out of Lifesavers."

I took a drink and turned to Noah. "Aren't you going to shoot?"

Noah raised his hands in mock horror. "Hell, no. I'm a lover, not a gunslinger. I won't go near those things."

I decided now was as good a time as any to begin a bit of interrogation. "You may not be a gunslinger, but word has it you're a scientist. Any truth to that?"

Noah pulled a pair of mirrored sunglasses out of his pocket and put them on. "That was in my past life."

I tried to get a read on his expression, but it had now become impossible to see his eyes. "Did you work for the government?"

For a moment, as the silence of the desert closed in on us, I thought Noah wasn't going to answer.

"Yeah, I worked for the government and I got fired for my trouble," he finally responded.

It was obvious that I was treading on sensitive ground. "Why were you fired?"

Noah faced the sun. "They didn't like my personality. Can you imagine that?"

I pressed on. "What area of the government did you work for?"

"Bzzzzzz!" He sounded like the buzzer on a game show when the answer is wrong. "You just hit your limit for today, Porter. Time for my nap."

But I wasn't through with him yet. "Before you turn in for the day, did you know that a neighbor of yours was just found dead?"

Noah turned and gave me a cold stare. "Shit happens. Anyone I know?"

"Annie McCarthy."

Noah kicked the ground. "Son of a bitch. I knew it."

"Knew what?" I was back on the quiz show and going for the gold.

"Knew that ornery old witch would kick the bucket some day," he said without any remorse.

"You didn't like her?"

Noah took off his glasses and glared. "I didn't like the fact that she was staking every claim on the land out here and that she could sell all her rights to some big fucking mining company some day. There ain't nothing to like about that."

I wanted to keep him on a roll. "What's wrong with big mining companies?"

Georgia Peach walked away as Noah continued his tirade. "You tell me what's right about them! Look at those jerks on the other side of the mountain with their damn cyanide. They're poisoning the land and every creature in sight. You want to do some good? You should be hauling their asses in for killing birds who stop to drink from their poisoned ponds and for running over every tortoise that gets in their way.''

He'd piqued my interest. ''What mining company are you talking about?''

''The Golden Shaft. Their name says it all.'' Taking out a bandanna, Noah wiped his face, which had turned beet-red in anger. ''You can carry your little tin badge and your gun, but unless you put your ass on the line, Porter, you ain't doing shit.''

I bristled at his assumption. ''Listen, Noah, you're sitting out in the middle of nowhere griping about what's wrong. Have you ever put yourself on the line to make a change?''

Noah looked at me a moment. ''How the hell do you think I ended up here?''

Turning on his heels, he climbed up the ladder that led into the ark and disappeared from sight. I was left facing Suzie Q, who stared at me in silence. Two down and one to go. There was nothing to lose in questioning her as well.

''That was quite a chase you led me on the other morning in your pickup,'' I began.

Suzie Q leisurely tore the cellophane off another Twinkie as I watched Frank Sinatra—who, I imagined, was watching me as well.

She slowly took a bite and then licked her fingers. ''It must have been someone else. I rehearse in the mornings.''

I had to ask. ''What were you rehearsing?''

Suzie Q put a finger on Frank and stroked his back. ''My club act, of course.''

Of course. ''What club do you play at?''

Suzie Q's finger lingered in one spot as Frank arched his back. ''Any club that will have me.''

I imagined that knocked the number down considerably.

''I hear Annie McCarthy was involved in the reptile trade. Ever have any dealings with her?'' I asked, trying my best to ignore the fur ball with eight giant legs.

Suzie Q finished her Twinkie and held her hand up in

front of Frank to let him gather the crumbs. "I don't know what you're talking about."

I was beginning to wonder if Suzie Q and Annie might have been competitors in the trade. It could have been reason enough for Suzie Q to have knocked the old woman off.

"She collected lots of things to sell—like lizards and snakes, and that thing sitting on your shoulder," I said, pointing.

I could have sworn that Frank Sinatra reared up on his hind legs and hissed at me as Suzie Q left, too. I'd have to watch what I said from now on.

My boss Sam Morrell, senior resident agent and cowboy extraordinaire, sat poised at his easel, wire-rimmed glasses balanced low on his nose and a paint brush held high in the air. He was dressed in his usual outfit of neatly pressed jeans and down-home plaid shirt. His full head of white hair had been carefully combed, matching an impeccably trimmed mustache as soft and white as a lamb's tail. All in all, the man could have just stepped out of a Norman Rockwell painting. I stuck my head inside his office door. Without turning around, Sam knew I was there.

"What do you think?" His voice, soft and melodious, wafted across the room, settling on me as light as a blanket of down.

I walked in and glanced over his shoulder at yet another portrait of a cow. "Looks good."

All of his paintings looked exactly the same, but I knew better than to ever say so.

On a countdown to retirement, Sam lived for the day when he could move to his cattle ranch in southern Idaho. His wife was already living there along with his son, who ran the place. It was obvious that the ranch was never far from Sam's thoughts. His office walls were covered with his paintings, each one a meticulous portrait of a different cow from his herd. A small plaque nailed to the bottom of each frame identified its subject by name. It was the only way I could tell them apart.

"This one is Maizie. Ain't she a beaut?" Sam asked, beaming proudly at his newest creation.

We had a basic understanding where my job was concerned. Sam didn't much care what I did so long as I didn't make any waves that might jeopardize his retirement. I filled him in on Annie McCarthy's death, but it was already old news to him.

"Brady called me last night. Understand it was a suicide." Sam looked at me with an expression I had come to know. He arched his eyebrows and tilted his head as if he knew to expect trouble.

"That's how Brady chose to read the scene. I believe it was murder," I stated matter-of-factly.

Sam continued to paint without saying a word. I was used to my old boss Charlie Hickok's ways: he'd rake me over the coals whenever I said something he didn't agree with. I could live with that. I enjoyed duking it out and arguing to get my way. It was the silent treatment that killed me. And Sam was a master at it. I had become determined to outwit him at his own game, staying silent as long as he did. My cool lasted all of two seconds until I crumbled.

"Did you know that Annie was illegally dealing in reptiles?" I demanded in a rush.

Sam carefully shifted his weight back in his chair and slowly studied the painting in front of him before bothering to answer. "Sure did. Never could catch her, though."

It was a common problem. The reptile trade tends to be fast and furious, with both critters and people in and out quicker than you can snag poachers in the act. At one time, I had suggested that we set up a stakeout, anxious to make my mark and nab a few bad guys. But Sam had nixed the idea, claiming, "We don't have enough bodies to carry it out. Besides, nobody gives a damn anyway."

I offered another idea on Annie's demise. "Could it be that she got knocked off by a competitor in the trade?"

Sam chewed on that for all of a moment. "Nah. Don't sound right to me."

Sam clearly didn't want any uncalled-for investigations on my part. He considered himself a realist where wildlife crime was concerned and had more than once voiced the opinion, "I just try to do the right thing and forget about the fact that it's hopeless."

I still wasn't willing to buy in on hopeless as an option. Charlie Hickok had taught me to be a one-woman kamikaze hit team, to set my target straight for the jugular and not let go.

I tried another approach. "What about the fact that Annie had staked so many claims? Maybe she really did find a stash of gold and the wrong people found out about it."

Sam touched up a brush stroke on Maizie's muzzle. "Those claims ain't worth the fees she paid for them. Any fool knows that."

"Then what about those imprints of tortoises that I found both at the Center and at Annie's?"

Sam squinted at the painting and added a dash more blue to the sky. "Don't see no basis for a murder case there." He put down his brush and turned to look at me. "Forget about Annie McCarthy. That's Metro's business. What have you got on those missing torts?"

I let the subject of Annie drop for now and filled him in on my meeting with Cammo Dude.

Sam chuckled as he wiped spots of paint off his hands. "That crazy old codger runs around dressed in camouflage trying to make everyone think he was napalmed in 'Nam. Truth is, he used to run a meth lab up in an old shack back in those hills."

I must have looked puzzled.

"You know, the fifty-fifty drug?" Sam continued. "Take it and you got a fifty percent chance of living and a fifty percent chance of dying. Well, Cammo got a dose of both. He had a batch of meth cooking up there one day when the damn shack blew up on him. The fumes knocked him down to his knees and he hit a meth oil spill. Burned the skin right off his face." He lit up a Marlboro and studied his boots. "What wild goose chase did he send you on?"

I suddenly felt foolish. "He told me about a group of burned-out scientists up in the pass. He thought they might have something to do with the tortoises' disappearance."

Sam's head jerked up. "You been out there yet?"

His interest caught me off guard and I was suddenly cautious. "I was out there early this morning."

"Who'd you meet?" An ash from his cigarette fell onto the tip of his boot, but Sam barely noticed.

"A wildlife biologist who used to work with Fish and Wildlife by the name of Georgia Peach," I said, gauging his reaction.

Sam looked away, as if judging how much to reveal. "The boys back in Washington fired her a while ago."

Georgia had made it sound as if she'd left on her own. "Why was she fired?"

Sam picked at his plaid shirt, his finger twisting a piece of loose thread on one of the buttons. "She didn't agree with the Service's decision to put the desert tortoise on the endangered list. She made it enough of an issue that they asked her to leave."

Something didn't strike me as quite right about Sam's explanation, but I decided to let it slide.

"I also met a man by the name of Noah Gorfine."

Sam's eyes instantly locked onto mine. "Stay away from him, Rachel. The man's nothing but trouble."

I was surprised. "Why? What has he done?"

Sam's attention traveled down to his boots, where he brushed away bits of cigarette ash. "I just know he's considered a pariah by all the government hotshots. He used to work for the Department of Energy until he threw a monkey wrench into something big they were doing. Since then, anyone interested in a government career has been told to steer clear of him."

Sam walked out to the Mr. Coffee machine in the hall. Bringing back two cups, he handed me one. "If you want to keep your nose out of trouble, forget you ever met the man. If you want to get ahead in this job, keep with the program.''

Keeping with the program was like asking me not to eat, sleep, or breathe. I learned early on that part of my problem as a Fish and Wildlife special agent is that I don't fit into the mold. Higher-ups within the agency consider me one of those rare mutations that somehow manage to slip by without getting caught, bobbing and weaving, sliding in from the rear to kick down the door while no one's looking. At first I had taken it as a compliment, proud that I had proven myself to be so exceptionally wily. But all I'd accomplished by kicking the door in so hard was to land myself ass-smack in the middle of the Mojave Desert. Assignment-wise, it was the equivalent of being sent to Hard Rock, Alaska.

I had just begun to sip my coffee when my phone rang. Leaving Sam's office, I sprinted to my desk, knocking over a pile of unfinished paperwork as I reached for the receiver. I found myself faced with silence and then the sound of breathing. Along with no love life, I hadn't had many dirty phone calls of late. I somehow doubted that my luck had changed.

"Anybody there?" I asked.

I was just about to hang up when a woman's voice stopped me. "It would be worth your while to pay a visit to the Golden Shaft mine."

"Who is this, please?" I questioned.

"All you need to know is that birds and tortoises are dying there every day and nothing is being reported," the woman informed me.

It was my turn to be silent for a moment as I processed this information. "How are they dying?"

The voice on the other end snapped, "How the hell do you think? Birds drink from the cyanide pits. Haul pak drivers don't stop to pick up desert tortoises that wander into their way. They're being run over. Or even worse, they're buried alive.''

"If you tell me your name, I promise that it will be kept totally confidential," I offered.

The woman snorted. "Right. And good whisky is still a buck a shot. I need to keep my job, lady. You want to do something with the information I've given you? Be my guest. You want to sit on your ass like the State wildlife boys? Well, I can't do nothing about that. Let it be on your head."

Before I had a chance to respond, the phone clicked dead in my ear.

The Golden Shaft was the same mine Noah had complained about, and my mystery woman obviously worked at the mine.

Mines in Nevada ran on a self-reporting system that Sam likened to a fox declaring how many chickens he's nabbed in a henhouse. All wildlife deaths connected to mining activities were supposed to be reported directly to the Nevada Division of Wildlife. It seemed that few were. And when they were, nothing was done. It was only when endangered critters were involved that Fish and Wildlife stepped into the fray.

"In Nevada, mining gets what it wants. It's political suicide to go against the industry." Sam had pounded that into my head since my first day on the job.

It was well known that the mines greased State palms to turn State heads the other way. That was one of the reasons Fish and Wildlife was so disliked in Nevada: so far, the Service had managed to remain incorruptible.

I filled Sam in on the call and told him that I planned to drive over and take a look around. It would be the first mine that I had officially visited since being out here.

Sam wiped off his brush and scrutinized his latest painting. "That should be quite a treat, though I don't think you'll find the Center's missing tortoises there."

Standing up, he took hold of his canvas and hung it on the wall behind his desk right below a sign that read, "*The Golden Rule in Nevada is: He who hath the gold rules.*"

Five

I decided to play it politically correct and head over to the Nevada Division of Wildlife, the state agency that is locally referred to as NDOW. Not only was it time that I introduced myself to the head honcho of the division; I also hoped that a courtesy call would smooth any feathers that might be ruffled over my impending visit to the Golden Shaft mine. Sam warned me that I would be greeted with about as much enthusiasm as a hooker on a sex strike.

Monty Harris, head of the Las Vegas division, immediately ushered me into his office upon being informed of my arrival. A man as thin as a whippet, Harris sported a pair of muttonchops that looked like two dead coon tails slapped onto his face. A nervous twitch controlled the left side of his body, causing his hand and foot to jerk in unison as if he were about to breakdance. Brown polyester pants hung unevenly on his frame and his fingers picked at a tan rayon shirt that covered a concave chest. A utility belt was wound twice about a waist that I would have killed for, its zippered pockets secreting hidden treasures. Dark sunglasses masked Harris's eyes, and a mono-brow extended itself in one straight line above the bridge of his nose.

His breath whistled between his teeth as he aimed his body at the chair and nearly crash-landed. "What is it that I can do for you today, Miss Porter?" he asked.

The smell of stale sweat wafted toward me as I took a seat in the hard wooden chair facing his desk. Obviously Monty Harris was a nervous man. "I received a call about wildlife violations over at the Golden Shaft mine. I thought I'd go and check into it.''

The tip of a pink tongue flicked out from between Harris's lips and his eyes blinked behind their dark curtain as he looked me up and down before responding.

"And just who was it that gave you that kind of information?"

I had the distinct impression that Monty Harris would have liked me to be anywhere but in his office.

"It was an anonymous call," I replied.

The quick rat-a-tat-tat of a laugh escaped Harris's lips, ricocheting around the room like a bullet. "I'm afraid someone is playing a joke on you, Miss Porter. The Golden Shaft is an exemplary mine. In fact, the governor is about to bestow on it an award for environmental awareness and protection of the land. So you see, it appears that someone is pulling your leg."

The bony fingers of one hand lewdly played with a zippered pocket on his utility belt, then pulled the zipper open and rooted around inside. After a moment they latched onto their prey, a slim Tiparillo. Harris rolled the tiny cigar slowly between his lips and licked the filter, savoring the taste.

"I'm glad to hear Golden Shaft is setting such a good example, but I think I'll take a run out and check into it anyway," I responded.

Harris puffed on the Tiparillo as though it were a fine Cuban cigar. "If I were you, I wouldn't bother. You're just wasting your time. Of course, it might be that you feds have nothing better to do. But since you're new to this state, let me explain a few things."

I had become mesmerized by the tiny, coarse black hairs that poked their way out from beneath his shirt, and snapped my attention back up to his face. "Explain away. I'm always happy to learn something new."

"Everything pertaining to wildlife and the mines goes through this office. That means me." Harris hawked up a wad of phlegm, holding it in his mouth while he unzipped another pocket on his belt. Pulling out a wrinkled hand-kerchief, he spat into the fabric, wadded it up, and stuffed it back in its lair.

"What that means is that any bird or critter turning up dead is held for my agents." Harris leaned forward. "We're the only ones who do autopsies on dead wildlife for the mines. That's the rule. *Comprende?*"

I shifted in my chair, noticing the scorpion embedded in a glass paperweight that held down a pile of documents. "Do you happen to have a list of dead wildlife turned over by Golden Shaft to your agents in the past year?"

Harris's eyes narrowed and his nose flared, exposing tiny hairs that bristled like miniature porcupines on alert for attack. "There were none."

"So what this amounts to is nothing more than a crank call?" I persisted.

"That's right. That's just what it was," Harris replied. His sunglasses resembled two large, impenetrable black holes.

All my senses told me to stop right there. Which is exactly what made me barge ahead. "Would you happen to know how much NDOW has received in donations from Golden Shaft in the past two years?"

Monty's jaw hooked forward and the corners of his mouth curled tightly down. "You're treading on dangerous ground here. Let me tell you something, girlie girl. You ain't home. What you're up against is history. Mining is what built Nevada. It's what built the West."

I looked past the sunglasses into his eyes, and knew I should consider this a warning. I hate warnings. They're an unspoken challenge begging to be answered.

"In other words, don't bite the hand that feeds you?" I asked as innocently as possible.

Harris stared at me darkly. "Not unless you're prepared to be bit back."

I heard the mine before I actually saw it. The roar of trucks carrying one hundred ninety tons of ore apiece filled the air like thunder. I parked on top of a butte and pulled out a pair of binoculars to survey the scene below.

Long gone are the days of the small independent miner with pickax and shovel. Mines are now run by multi-million-dollar corporations complete with high-tech computers, earth moving equipment, and an arsenal of chemicals, all in search of microscopic flecks of gold.

For a while I watched the steady stream of trucks carried on tires that stand twelve feet in diameter, running twenty-four hours a day, seven days a week, three hundred and sixty-five days a year, their engines never dying. The shrill wail of a siren periodically pierced the low, steady rumble. Getting back in the Blazer, I wended my way down to the mine.

The closer I got, the more I realized that I was approaching a fortress that appeared to be more military installation than gold mine. Razor-sharp barbed wire surrounded the compound's perimeter, with guards carrying M-16 rifles posted at intervals. From the security alone, it appeared to be the mother of all mother lodes. The Fort Knox of the West. A posted sign appeared near the mine's entrance, warning "Use of Deadly Force Authorized." They needn't have worried. I had already taken it for granted that the armed guards were there for more than show. Still, it was nice to know they at least had the courtesy to inform me that I stood a good chance of being blown away if I made the wrong move.

I drove up to the front gate, where I was stopped by an unsmiling guard cradling an M-16 in his arms. I stated my business and waited expectantly for the guard to wave me inside.

"Are you one of the good guys or bad guys?" he asked.

I looked at him and cracked a grin, sure that he had to be joking. But he stared back at me with all the warmth of Godzilla.

"Fed or state?" he impatiently asked, his fingers twitching along the stock of his rifle.

"I'm with Fish and Wildlife," I replied, wondering whether that made me friend or foe.

He pointed to the office dead ahead. "Pull in there. Someone inside will help you."

I checked my rearview mirror as I drove away. My unfriendly guard was busy conversing into a walkie-talkie.

I walked into the main office, where a receptionist sat in wait.

"State your business, please," she said, barely bothering to look up.

I had the feeling she already knew, but I went along with the game.

"I'm with Fish and Wildlife. This is my first visit to the mine and I'd like to take a look around," I replied.

"You'd think we were running guided tours out here," she mumbled, picking up her phone and punching in some numbers. "Fish and Wildlife is here," she announced to the person on the other end. Hanging up, she glanced briefly in my direction. "You'll have to wait for the foreman."

I had no problem with that. At least it was cool inside the small room. I sat down on a gold vinyl couch and viewed the reading material on the table in front of me. *Mining Today* and *The Gold Review*. I passed up the magazines and studied the wall, where framed photos portrayed the wonders of gold mining technology at work.

Mines dot the landscape of Nevada, holding as much allure and promise as the main strip of Vegas does to a gambler on a roll. But few people realize what mining entails. One of the aerial photos showed a maze of roads and drilling activity on denuded land. The next photo zeroed in on a mountain that had been ground up into heaps of fine powder. Next to it was an explanation of the magic of cyanide, which is sprayed over these hills of dust. Cyanide percolates through the low-grade ore and then slowly trickles out, carrying with it specks of gold into fifty-acre collection ponds.

What was left out of the caption is cyanide's lurid history. Best known as the main ingredient in Jonestown's deadly Kool-Aid with a kick, cyanide was also the chemical of choice in the rash of Tylenol poisonings a few years back. More recently, it had been responsible for the deaths of thousands of migratory birds that stopped to drink from cyanide-laced pools as they passed by. Sam liked to refer to these chemical water holes as "hotter than a pistol—a bird flies in, it don't fly out."

With nothing else to look at I turned my attention to the receptionist, who was digging her hand into a can of peanut brittle.

"That'll kill your teeth," I advised.

"Yeah, like nothing else won't," she answered as she shoved a piece of brittle into her mouth.

Her nameplate said Dee Salvano. I had a feeling that was the only introduction I'd get.

"Have you worked here long?" I asked.

"Too long," she blurted. A small shower of peanut pieces flew out of her mouth, landing on her desk.

"Does that mean you'd rather be doing something else?" I inquired.

Dee fixed me with an evil eye. "In Nevada, if you don't work for mining, you're punching the register at a 7-Eleven, shimmying on a pole for a bunch of drunks with your boobs bobbing up and down, or kissing the government's ass as one of their toadies. Take your pick."

I decided it was best to end the conversation. I passed the long wait daydreaming about Santou's hands caressing my long-neglected body. A slow, sultry kiss was abruptly interrupted when the foreman of the mine planted his feet in front of me.

"Feds don't usually come here. What is it you want?" he demanded.

I glanced up at the man dressed in work boots, jeans, and a khaki shirt with a Playboy insignia sewn on the pocket. He didn't appear to be big on introductions, so I skipped over formalities.

"I'd like to take a look at your operation," I responded.

"What for?" he asked, his eyes narrowing in on me.

The name John was tattooed on a bicep that glistened with sweat. Since no hearts or roses surrounded it, I took it for granted that the name was his own.

"Because it's on my list of things to do while touring Nevada," I replied sweetly, wondering if I could fine him for annoying a federal agent.

John fixed his hands on his hips and pushed out his chest, as if to block my way in case I intended to make a run for it.

"If you're looking for wildlife violations, you gotta clear that with NDOW first," he insisted.

I was tired of sitting on a vinyl couch that had begun to meld to the underside of my thighs. The vinyl emitted a smooching sound as I stood up, as if in a farewell kiss to my rear end. All in all, not the sort of image I wanted to convey.

"As a matter of fact, I don't have to clear it with anybody, John. All I need is a complaint that trucks on this mine site have been routinely grinding desert tortoises underground without giving it a second thought. You remember those critters? They're on the endangered species list. And guess what? I recently received a complaint. So let's cut the games," I warned. "Just try stopping me from inspecting this mine, and I can guarantee you, the governor will find it highly embarrassing when he goes to present Golden Shaft with an award and discovers you've been slapped with a suit for noncompliance." If that didn't get me onto the grounds, I didn't know what would.

John folded his arms across his chest and stared at me a moment, as if calculating the best mode of attack. "How come you didn't call in advance? State officials always have the courtesy to call us first."

His Miss Manners was a hard act to swallow, but it was interesting to learn NDOW's tactics. It was smart of them to call ahead. That way there would never be violations around when they arrived at the mine.

Dee stopped chewing peanut brittle long enough to throw

in another interesting tidbit. "But I told you that Director Harris called to tell us she was coming."

John shot her a look to kill, causing Dee to choke on the current mouthful. I made a mental note of who else not to trust in this state.

John's hands crept into his pockets as he kicked at an imaginary spot on the floor with the toe of his boot. "Listen, I'm sorry I came down so hard on you. It's just that this is a busy mine and it's hard for us to take the time to show everyone around."

He leaned in close to me. "What say we give a donation to your office? I bet you could use a fax machine."

He was right. Our office was bare bones in terms of equipment. We were constantly being told to go catch the bad guys but were lucky if we even got so much as a pair of handcuffs with which to do it.

"Do I get that fax machine before or after I search for dead wildlife?" I asked, standing my ground.

John took a step back, his hands balling up into tight fists. "As far as I'm concerned, it's the state's job to protect Nevada's wildlife. Not some girl who's been given a gun and calls herself a federal agent."

I was getting nowhere fast. It was time to notch things up a step.

"Great. What say we get your boss's opinion on this, since he'll be the one that has to show up in court. I take it there's a manager you report to?" I asked pointedly.

John glared at me before rolling off down the hall. I turned to find Dee Salvano staring at me as well, a piece of peanut brittle frozen in midair.

"What's your mine manager's name?" I demanded.

Dee blinked as she put the piece of candy back in its box. "Brian Anderson."

"Call him," I ordered.

Dee obediently picked up the phone and dialed his number. "Mr. Anderson?" She paused as the voice on the other end barked out instructions. After a moment she hung up. "He knows that you're here, and—"

"Don't tell me. I'll have to wait."

Dee silently nodded as I took my seat back on the couch.

Another forty minutes came and went. I figured that by now there had been enough time to clear every critter off the place that might have been skulking around, dead or alive. But I was determined to stay put until I'd inspected the grounds.

I was just about to nod off when Brian Anderson rounded the corner and took hold of my hand.

"Agent Porter?"

I looked up into a pair of eyes as steely gray as a summer thunderstorm over the desert. A shaggy mane of silver hair framed the cheekbones I'd always wanted. A tight smile that was half grimace cut across his face, a perfect slash outlining picture-perfect teeth. If he didn't work out in a gym, I was a health nut. The guy could easily have landed a television series just by showing up for the audition.

"I'm sorry to have kept you waiting," he said in a harried voice. "I also want to apologize for John's behavior. I'm afraid we sometimes forget about manners, being under such a tight deadline."

His fingers were long and tapered, easily encasing mine, and his thumb rested gently at the pulse point along my wrist, which had begun to beat rapidly. I left my hand in his grip.

"What deadline is that?" I asked, trying to appear cool, calm, and collected.

Anderson's grimace softened and I realized that he was checking me out as much as I was him. I pulled my hand away.

"What I meant is that we're under constant pressure to produce. It tends to get to you after a while. Gets so bad around here that we even forget how to behave when there's a pretty lady around." He ran his fingers through his perfectly coiffed mane.

I wondered if that was John Wayne lingo for We've been busy stashing dead tortoises and birds away, but that's nothing for you to worry your pretty head about, little lady.

Brian held a can of Diet Coke out toward me. "I brought this as a peace offering. If you still have the time, it would be my pleasure to escort you around, Agent Porter."

Diet Coke. He knew how to get to a girl. I stood up next to Anderson's tall, lean frame and made a silent vow to lay off the Doritos and beat my body into submission until it resembled Cindy Crawford's.

We headed outside smack into heat as suffocating as plastic wrap. The light wind pummeled my face with minuscule grains of sand, causing me to squint as we walked around the grounds. I felt certain that Cindy Crawford would never subject her face to this.

Anderson took hold of my elbow as he steered me toward the main area of the mine. "Why don't you just tell me what it is that you're looking for, Agent Porter?"

"I was given some information that a number of birds have been found dead on the grounds and that your haul paks are running over desert tortoises," I said, overly aware of the feel of his hand on my skin.

He appeared to be genuinely surprised. "Really? I can't imagine that happening. At least, I haven't been informed of any incidents. We're receiving an award from the governor, you know."

I didn't say anything as we headed over to a tailings pond, where I examined the mesh netting that covered its surface, required by law in order to keep migratory birds away from the cyanide. It didn't take me long to find a number of tears in the mesh.

"I'm afraid you've got a problem here," I informed him.

Brian knelt down beside me. His arm brushed against my thigh, and my skin tingled at his touch. *It's just the heat,* I told myself, but I carefully shifted my weight so that there was some space between us as we examined the netting together.

"What can I say?" he asked, a tone of frustration creeping into his voice. "This is embarrassing, but as hard as we try, it happens."

He placed a hand on my arm and stood up, bringing me

along with him. "I understand if you feel it's necessary to fine the mine for this violation."

The guy seemed sincere. That alone rattled me. My philosophy about men is that if they look better than you, they shouldn't be trusted—and I was no easy touch. I moved back a step, hoping to break his force field of charisma.

"I'd like to check out the freezers," I said, determined to keep my mind on business.

"Of course."

We headed back toward the office, dodging giant haul paks along the way. If they weren't about to stop for us, there was no way in hell they'd come to an abrupt halt for a tortoise. The shriek of their engines made me wonder how anyone lived day in and day out with the noise. Loaded with two hundred tons of dirt apiece, the trucks shook the ground as we walked by.

Brian held the door open for me as we walked into the main reception area, past Dee Salvano's desk, and down a long hall to a room that contained a giant freezer.

"Let me do the honors," Brian offered, pulling open the large metal door.

The freezer was bare, without a trace of a bird or a tortoise to be found. Not that I had really expected anything to be there after my long wait in reception.

Brian waved at the freezer's empty shelves. "See? What did I tell you? Spic-and-span clean."

I could almost sense his relief. "How often does someone from NDOW stop by?"

Brian thought for a moment, a wrinkle marring his smooth brow. "Let's see. Not that often, really. What we do is call Director Harris whenever any wildlife is found dead on the grounds. But I can tell you, that doesn't happen very often. And it's never from cyanide poisoning."

I looked at his chiseled features and knew he was lying. "Never? They always manage to keel over dead from natural causes?"

"What can I say? I just hope it's not catching." Brian led me out of the room and into his office.

"How about some coffee?" He walked over to a small coffee machine situated in front of a window that looked out at the mine. "It's not very good, but I can guarantee you it doesn't contain any cyanide."

Just the thought of the long, dusty drive back to town was already making me groggy. "Great. I can use the caffeine."

Brian handed me a cup and settled back in his chair, crossing his feet on top of his desk. His office was spotless. Stacks of paper were neatly organized in front of him. An In/Out box held little correspondence, unlike my own, which was overflowing with letters I had yet to look at. I glanced around for the obligatory photos of a wife and multiple offspring, but none was to be found. In fact, nothing of a personal nature was in sight. No knickknacks, no diplomas, no funny coffee mugs. It was an office that anyone could have stepped into and claimed as their own.

Brian sat with his hands folded over a stomach that was as flat as a washboard. He seemed to be carefully watching me.

"Why Nevada?" he asked out of the blue.

"Just for a change of pace," I replied, trying to remain as noncommittal as his surroundings.

"This is a rough place for a woman alone." He shook his head. "You never know what you might come up against."

"And how is that different from any place else?"

Brian smiled enigmatically and shrugged. "I'm originally from Virginia and I find that people out here are different. They're not big on the federal government or those who try to uphold its laws. If I were a female in your position, I'd be scared."

I studied the man in front of me, but his face gave nothing away. "Are you trying to tell me something or just frighten me away?"

A flush crept over his face. "Sorry. I'm just one of those guys who gets protective when they're attracted to a woman. As one easterner to another, I don't know how you're finding it, but this is a pretty lonely place for a single guy."

Looking at him, I found that hard to believe. I suddenly felt self-conscious about the out-of-control curls on top of my head and the fact that what little makeup I had on had probably slid off in the heat. I wondered how Cindy would look after a morning of digging around in the dirt.

"Do you happen to know a prospector just down the way from here by the name of Annie McCarthy?"

Brian took a sip of his coffee and raised an arm behind his head. I noticed there were no sweat marks on his shirt, while I felt as if I'd been dunked in a barrel of water.

"Never heard of her. But small-time prospectors are a dime a dozen out here. In fact, they're the ones that are really hurting the land."

"Funny. I've heard the same exact thing about mines like the Golden Shaft." I raised the cup of coffee to my lips, making sure my arms remained tightly glued to my sides. "The thing about Annie McCarthy is that she was murdered. Is there any reason you can think of why someone would kill a down-and-out prospector in these parts?"

Brian focused his gaze on me, holding it for a moment. "Not unless her claims were of value. And if they were, believe me, I would have known about them."

He stood up and studied the landscape outside, giving me a good view of his butt. I wistfully wished my own looked that tight.

"I'm telling you, Nevada just isn't safe for a woman alone. At one point or another, you're bound to run into trouble," he warned.

I didn't bother to tell him that trouble is something I have a tendency to look for. Without thinking about it, my hand drifted to the SIG-Sauer tucked into the back of my pants. "Don't worry. I can take care of myself."

Brian turned back and softly smiled. The skin at the corners of his eyes crinkled, showing the first sign of an alluring physical imperfection. "I hope so. I'd like to see more of you."

He walked me out to my Blazer and opened the car door. "Come back anytime for a visit."

His hand touched mine, causing my pulse to race. I planned to take him up on his offer. But the next time, I'd know better than to inform anyone first.

I picked up Nevada's version of Chinese food on my way home—chow mein laced with jalapeño peppers—and ate my dinner straight out of its cardboard box. I'm a firm believer in the philosophy of takeout. If you live by yourself, why bother to cook? Taking it a step further, why dirty a dish if you don't have to? I shoved the uneaten portion inside my refrigerator, where it joined the ranks of unidentifiable food, some of which had already turned green with age.

As I shut the refrigerator door, the ground suddenly began to shake beneath me, making me swear that I'd never slam it again. Dishes in the open cabinet above my sink came to life, clattering precariously toward the edge. A pair of dirty glasses shattered to the floor. Then I remembered that Nevada is earthquake country.

"Great. I could have moved to California if I'd wanted to deal with this," I muttered, trying to remember just what one was supposed to do in a quake. It was either stand in a doorway or get under a bed, but I was too scared to remember which.

The trembling of the ground subsided before my own shaking did. I stood perfectly still, afraid that if I moved, my flimsy bungalow would come crashing down around me. But the quake had ended as quickly as it had begun— just one more experience to chalk up among my welcome wagon of greetings from Las Vegas.

I listened, sure that I would hear police sirens, the clanging of fire engines, or loudspeakers ordering an immediate evacuation of the area. But only silence filled the air.

I picked up the few shards of broken glass, then left the kitchen. I had put off checking my answering machine when I first arrived home, afraid that there would be no call from Santou. With the excitement of the earthquake over and nothing else to do, I wandered into my bedroom, where my heart leaped at the sight of two red dots blinking on the machine. I figured my chances were fifty-fifty.

Pressing the Playback button, I heard the upbeat voice of Duff Gaines, a reporter with the *Las Vegas Sun*.

"Hey, Porter. I hear a couple hundred tortoises were swiped from the conservation center. How about giving me a scoop on the story?"

I wondered who had blabbed the news to Gaines. I also cursed myself for ever having allowed my home number to be listed, so that people like Gaines could track me down.

Then Santou's voice wrapped itself around me, as sensual and smooth as a velvet glove, setting every nerve ending in my body on fire.

"Hi there, *chère*. Just checking in to see how that honky-tonk town is treating you. Things are hoppin' here. So don't bother to call back; I'm working late shifts these days. Take care of yourself, Rachel, and I'll speak to you soon."

The click ending the call was as unwelcome as a splash of ice water, bringing me back to reality. I was left feeling lonelier than usual. The overwhelming urge to call Santou back bubbled up, but I repressed it. It was a toss-up as to which was worse: wondering if I might catch him at home or knowing he was out and torturing myself with visions of who he was with. I chose to check in with the answering machine at work before consigning myself to another evening of TV.

One message had been left, delivered in a angry voice that bristled at me over the wire. "This is Harley Rehrer. If you want to know where your damn tortoises are, it's a no-brainer. The goddamn scumbucket environmentalists have been dumping them on my ranch for years. In my book, that makes the critters illegal trespassers and gives me the right to shoot the damn things on sight."

Rehrer had slammed down his receiver, abruptly ending

the message. It seemed as if everyone in the county was managing to find out about the tortoise theft, which left me wondering just what the hell Bill Holmes over at the conservation center was up to.

Six

Harley Rehrer is a legend in these parts. More than just a rancher, Harley is best known as the head of the local county supremacy movement, quaintly titled the Foundation for a Healthy Economy and Environment. The Foundation is made up of an angry group of miners, ranchers, and developers all hell-bent on one thing: wresting control of public land out of the federal government's hands—their motto being "Take your rules and shove it." The fact that federal grazing areas were now closed for three months every spring on account of the desert tortoise had brought the cauldron of resentment to a boil. I knew that dealing with Harley would be like stepping into an enormous, steaming cow patty in which, if I wasn't careful, I could sink.

I stopped by the office the following morning, hoping to enlist Sam for my visit to Harley's ranch. Unfortunately, I found him preparing for an escape to his digs in southern Idaho.

"I'm warning you right now to forget it, Rachel. We've already received a directive to stay the hell away from there and leave the man alone," Sam said, throwing some papers into his briefcase.

That was enough to make me decide that poking around had to be worthwhile. "Why? What do you think he'd do if I actually showed up to investigate his claims?"

Sam gave it some thought. "Well, what with your being a woman and all, I'm pretty sure Harley wouldn't blow you away. I guess you'd be alright as long as you didn't resist if he tried to arrest you.''

When I first arrived in Vegas, Sam had handed me a wallet-sized card. On it was the phone number for the U.S. Attorney in case any overly zealous cowpoke decided to place me under citizen's arrest. It was my introduction to the West and what I was in for.

Sam carefully wrapped up a canvas on which he'd begun a sketch of yet another cow head. "I hope you're not planning on doing something crazy and getting into trouble.'' He gave me a look as if he knew what I might be up to. "But if anything happens, give a holler. Though I'm not sure what the hell I'd be able to do.''

That was a consoling thought, but I somehow doubted Harley would allow me one last call before I was shot. I was so caught up in visions of being tarred and feathered and run out of Clark County that it took a moment for me to become aware of a thumping sound. This was followed by the scraping of claws against wood along with what I imagined to be the gnashing of teeth. I looked around.

"Have you buried anything in here that I should know about before you take off?'' I asked as Sam packed up his palette and paints.

He gave me a sour look and cocked his head. "It's a good thing you stopped by. Seems something was dropped off for you this morning. I found it tied to the front door.''

I followed the din as far as the bathroom. I couldn't think of anyone I'd met so far that would feel compelled to give me anything other than possibly a hard whack on the head. The racket behind the door grew louder as I put my hand on the knob, and I envisioned everything from a coyote to a large rat on hormones.

Sam grunted behind me. "Well, are you going to let the damn thing out or do I have to stay here and do it for you?''

I was tempted to shove Sam inside. Instead, I threw open the door, nearly knocking over my gift in the process. I came face to face with a dog, which resembled a Siberian husky but was much larger, that had effectively torn the bathroom apart. A bright-red bow was tied round its massive neck.

Sam sighed as he surveyed the mess. "I must be getting old. In my day, we just gave a woman a bottle of cologne. You got an admirer out there that you haven't told me about?"

I shook my head, equally puzzled. "Not that I know of."

I had never tied myself down with a pet, wanting to be free to come and go at will, no strings attached. Now one had literally been dumped on my doorstep. Commitment: just the word made me nervous. I looked at the animal with a wary eye.

"What makes you think this dog was meant for me?" I asked, hoping there might have been some mistake.

Sam lifted an eyebrow. "I've been here twenty years, and in all that time nobody's so much as offered me a free cup of coffee. You really think somebody's going to give me a dog?"

He scratched the side of his nose as he contemplated the critter in front of us. "You see that big red ribbon there? That's an announcement to expect a call for a dinner date. There ain't no women I know of lately who've been making eyes at me. And if they had, the missus would have hunted them down by now and run their fannies out of town. Nope—this critter is yours."

All three of us stared at one another.

"He already peed on the leg of my desk. Almost got me as well. And by the way, he left a present near your chair that you might want to clean up after you finish straightening out the bathroom," Sam added.

The dog sat down, contemplating me with the strangest eyes I had ever seen. Translucent gold, they seemed to look through me as if he could read my thoughts, making me feel that between us, he was the more intelligent of the two. Not to be outdone, I leveled him with what I considered to be an equally intense stare. But the mutt won the game unfairly, letting loose a loud bark that caused me to jump. Unnerved, I took a step back.

"Where did he come from?" I demanded.

"Damned if I know. But I think that note attached to his bow might give you a clue," said Sam, ever the detective.

I cautiously approached the beast, which had yet to take his eyes off me. I was aware that for an agent it didn't look good to appear frightened, even if the dog before me could have passed for Cujo. I slowly knelt down and carefully reached for the envelope stapled to his bow, nearly falling over as the dog licked my face with one swipe.

Sam muffled a laugh behind me. "Careful, Rachel. That mutt's a real terror."

The dog proceeded to sniff me up and down as I tore the envelope open and read its contents.

Since it seems likely that you'll continue to travel these roads alone, I've taken the liberty of providing you with a companion. He's trustworthy and loyal and will look out for you at all times. Besides, this gives me a good reason to call. Don't let the eyes spook you. That's the wolf in him. I know that you'll give him a good home and a proper name.

The note was signed "Brian Anderson."

"Hmph," Sam commented, peering over my shoulder. "So the mine is already trying to bribe you, huh?"

"It would seem that way," I considered what to do with the pooch, which was now sniffing my fingers. "When I got there, the foreman offered me a fax machine if I would just go away."

Sam gave me a sour look. "I would have taken the fax machine. God knows we could use it."

I was beginning to think Sam was right as the dog started to chew on the lace of my shoe.

"It seems Monty Harris tipped the mine off that I would be showing up. By the time I got there, you couldn't have found a feather," I informed Sam.

"Sounds like your first trip out was an educational one," Sam chuckled. "What you've got to realize is that these days NDOW operates pretty much on the donations that the mines give them.'' Sam scratched his head as the dog scratched behind an ear. "Of course, the string attached is, 'Keep the feds off our ass,' meaning you and me.''

Having sniffed to his heart's content, the dog now lay with his chin on my work boots. "What happens to people who buck the mining industry?'' I asked, wondering if anyone had ever dared take them on.

Sam chewed on that for a moment before answering. "You have to have a lead shield and stainless steel skin. Either that or you're history.'' His fingers idly combed a few stray mustache hairs back into place. "I guess it's something for you to think about while I'm gone.''

Picking up his unfinished canvas, Sam headed out to his Bronco. The office door slammed shut, and I suddenly felt terribly alone. My former boss had been endowed with a healthy case of KMA syndrome—or, as Hickok liked to phrase it, "Kiss my ass." Sam played it the opposite way, keeping his head low and steering for safe harbor. I knew what Charlie would have done where the mines were concerned. But this was Nevada, with an underlying violence ready to erupt—and I knew I was a moving target.

I looked over to where my newly acquired gift lay panting on the floor and went in search of a bowl for water. A thorough examination of the office turned up only Sam's mug and my own. I grabbed Sam's cup and filled it with water. Then, sitting on the floor, I placed it in front of the critter, who lapped up the liquid in record time.

I thought about traveling alone as a woman. Then I pictured Annie McCarthy with her dog. While I felt sure that her companion had also been loyal and true, in the end it hadn't much mattered.

I absentmindedly began to scratch behind the dog's ears as I thought about Brian Anderson. I found it hard to imagine someone that good-looking living alone, never mind being lonely. I could have put it down to my overwhelming distrust of the opposite sex; but something just didn't add up.

"Get a grip, Porter!"

I gave myself a hard mental slap. Here was a hot-looking guy hitting on me, and all I could do was wonder what his problem must be. No lack of self-confidence there. My thoughts drifted to Santou and the question of loyalty. Then I remembered that until last night I hadn't heard from the man in weeks. Obviously he wasn't sitting at home, spending his nights pining away for me. Maybe it was time I got out as well. Was it my fault if the first man to be interested in me just happened to look like Adonis?

I was startled when a large paw landed heavily on my shoulder. Looking into the dog's eyes, it was hard not to feel spooked. I knew that wolf dogs had a reputation for being ferocious. But then, that wasn't a bad quality to have in a woman's best friend. Besides, he'd be company. And given my lousy sense of direction, maybe he'd even be smart enough to point me the right way.

I christened my new companion Pilot.

I soon discovered that Pilot and I had something in common: we both like Bonnie Raitt. I blasted the radio, singing at the top of my lungs, and Pilot joined in, wailing the chorus. I felt good enough this morning to take a chance on stopping by the Gold Bonanza Cafe.

"What the hell is that massive mutt doing in here?" Lureen immediately complained.

This morning she was dressed to kill in lime-green spandex pedal pushers, the calves of her legs resembling desiccated twigs. A bright-red midriff top showcased a bare stomach with as many wrinkles as a retread tire. But my eyes were drawn to the glare coming off her gold sandals, which were decorated with an array of dime-store gems.

"Meet my new partner, Lureen."

Lureen scrutinized Pilot through her rhinestone glasses. "Well, if you think he's going to help get you a table, the aliens must have gone and sucked out your brain, girl."

Looking at Lureen, I seriously wondered if she'd ever had a close encounter of the third kind. I was about to head over for takeout when I froze in my tracks. Pilot had begun to lick the back of Lureen's withered hand, his body leaning firmly against her. I waited for the storm to erupt, only to be surprised yet again. Lureen looked straight ahead, never blinking an eye, as her fingers slowly crept up along Pilot's mane and began to stroke his fur. After a moment she cleared her throat.

"If you sit over there at the counter, I might have some scraps for your dog," she said gruffly.

I looked at the woman, too stunned to speak.

"Oh, alright," she grudgingly sighed. "I suppose we can dig something up for you, too."

Turning on her heels, Lureen headed into the kitchen.

I gazed at Pilot in amazement. He'd made more inroads in five minutes than I'd been able to make in three months.

I moved toward the bar with Pilot closely in tow, only to be pushed aside by a tour group of senior citizens sporting air-tight perms and polyester knits. Elbowing me with their canes, they took over the bar stools, ordering rounds of popcorn and beer to tide them over before reboarding the bus for Vegas. I grabbed the last seat as Lureen presented Pilot with an overflowing bowl of scraps that looked better than what I usually ate.

She placed a plate of scrambled eggs and toast in front of me as well, though her eyes remained focused on Pilot. "Come back tomorrow and I'll give him some good, meaty bones," she commanded.

I was dwelling on the joys of having a pet when I heard a voice behind me.

"Looks like you finally caught yourself a man, Porter."

I swiveled around to find Clayton Hayes poking his gums with a toothpick.

"Why, by golly, I was wrong. That's a dog you got there. But then, I guess that's better than nothing, ain't that right, Porter?" Clayton bantered.

I looked Hayes up and down. "In your case, Clayton, I'd stick with a dog any day." I glanced behind him, surprised to see Clayton alone. "Where's Sundance?" I asked, referring to his sidekick, Rolly Luntz.

"Why, he's out gathering tortoises for our barbecue. Still coming, ain't ya?" Clayton sucked on his toothpick, sliding it in and out between his lips.

I silently placed a bet on whether or not he'd swallow it and choke. I doubted if any of the the crowd at the bar would be able to move fast enough to apply the Heimlich maneuver—which would leave Clayton at my mercy. Maybe we'd negotiate about the fate of tortoises then.

"Or maybe you're too scared to come." Clayton grinned. "Maybe you heard who one of our speakers is gonna be."

"Who's that?" I inquired, digging into my food.

"None other than Shoot-'em-up Harley Rehrer," Clayton crowed.

Harley had recently gained added status by refusing to pay the government for grazing his cattle on public land. He now owed a whopping one hundred thousand dollars in fines and violations. While federal agents were itching to slap him behind bars, Justice officials were holding them back. Harley had recently issued a warning that any federal agents coming onto his property would be shot. Still smarting over the bad publicity from the shoot-outs at Waco and Ruby Ridge, the Justice Department wasn't sure they wanted to take on Harley as well. In the local cowboy's eyes, that made Harley Rehrer as powerful as God.

I finished my breakfast and turned back to Hayes. "Speaking of Harley, I plan on visiting him this morning."

Clayton stared at me as if he were looking at a ghost. "You're joking, right, Porter?"

I almost felt touched by Clayton's concern. "I don't see why there should be any problem. I'm just going out to pay a civil call. What's he going to do? Shoot me?" I began to laugh.

Tipping his hat, Clayton gave a slight bow in my direction. "Nice to have known you, Porter. Dead woman walk-

ing here,'' he loudly announced as he turned and walked
away.

If Clayton meant to throw me off balance, it worked. But
I wasn't about to let him know it.

The trip to Harley's ranch seemed endless, even with
Bonnie crooning the blues. A town consisting of a gas station and a diner flashed by all too quickly. Even cows on
the side of the road barely moved, hypnotized by the op-
pressive heat that pulsated up from the ground into their
hooves. A Mojave green rattler sunned itself in the middle
of the road, daring me to pass by. Four feet long and as
thick as a man's arm, the reptile barely bothered to lift its
head off the asphalt. Mesmerized by the warmth that penetrated its belly, it half-heartedly shook its rattles as if I
presented no more threat than a bug.

Cows were soon replaced by abandoned cars that littered
the desert floor like discarded tin cans. Lying flat on their
backs, their rusted axles reared up in surrender, their tires
long gone. Others had become targets for gun-happy cow-
pokes, with bullet holes pockmarking their vanquished
shells. It was clear that cowboys were little more than rednecks in chaps. Just recently one hotshot had used his
double-barreled shotgun to fill a thirty-foot Joshua full of
lead. In a twist of desert justice, the giant cactus had fallen
on top of him, creating the first cowboy voodoo doll in the
West.

The road rose sharply and then dipped out of sight, much
like a roller coaster that had reached its summit. I took the
plunge and found myself at the foot of the Virgin Mountains, where tumbleweed and cactus draped the desert floor.
Rocky plateaus rose off in the distance.

Following the directions I'd managed to scrounge, I
veered onto a dirt road, turning left at a creek, right at a
bush, and left again at a twig. I'd been told that I would
know Harley's dwelling when I saw it. My guess was that
it would be the only house around. I peered out of the dust
that covered my windshield like a ghost bumming a free
ride and caught sight of a decrepit drive. My eyes followed
its zigs and zags to a run-down ranch house perched on top

of a small hill. Word had it that Harley had a 7mm Magnum set up inside, mounted on a tripod facing the road. I figured I was already dead-center in its sight.

A wooden placard was mounted on a post at the entry to the drive. The sign held ten stick figures, each with a blood-red bull's-eye smack dab in the middle of its chest. A warning read, "Federal Agents: Enter At Your Own Peril." Not exactly your down-home western hello.

It seemed that the desert, along with its critters, was a brutal and unforgiving place. Everything out here threatened to either prick you, sting you, bite you—or maybe shoot you.

I had barely started up Harley's drive when he appeared on horseback to greet me. A plain-faced man, Harley had skin as coarse as a lizard's. He was dressed in a denim shirt and worn jeans, along with a red bandanna that peeked out from beneath a straw cowboy hat. When he drew closer, I saw the gun belt strapped round his waist, a .45 snugly bedded down in its holster.

I got out of the Blazer, leaving Pilot inside.

"Howdy there, miss." Harley brushed the tips of his fingers along the rim of his hat.

No "ma'am." I liked that. Who said he was such a bad guy?

"You lost? Or are you out here to try and do a story on me?" Harley cheerfully inquired.

Eyes as blue as a slow-burning flame took in every inch of me until I could have sworn he was flirting. I almost hated to burst his bubble.

"Good day, Mr. Rehrer. I'm Rachel Porter. I'm a special agent with . . ."

Harley's friendly demeanor instantly vanished, his voice turning as prickly as cactus. "Save it. I know who you are."

I noticed that his right hand wasn't far from his holster, his fingers jerking as if he had a bad itch.

"I got your message about tortoises being dumped on

your ranch and I was wondering if I could talk to you about it," I began.

"You want to talk?" he spat out, nailing me with his eyes. "Let's talk about my rights and how you've been trampling all over them. Let's talk about your wacko rules all because of some slow-moving critter with a hard top." Harley tore a dog-eared copy of the Constitution out of his shirt pocket and began waving it in my face. "Thanks to you, the American cowboy is a dying breed. We're the ones who are becoming extinct. Not some damn tortoise."

His eyes glared as if I were the Devil incarnate. It probably wasn't the right time to point out that Marlboro men always hung tough until the government threatened to yank their federal subsidies, then the howl could be heard from Nevada straight to the White House.

"You've taken away our birthright with all your gobble-dygook regulations and laws." Harley warmed to his topic like a preacher stumping at a local revival meeting. "When it gets to the point where I can't graze my cows because of a damned tortoise, that's where I draw the line. If it's between them or me, I say let's get rid of the damn things—and the people stoppin' me."

He grinned malevolently and looked beyond me.

A shiver tore down my spine, and I turned around, my skin clammy though the sun was set on deep-fry. Off in the distance, two ranchers were making their way toward us on horseback. If two is company and three is a crowd, four probably meant big trouble.

I turned back and looked at Harley, wondering what he had in mind.

"Gotta hand it to you. You got some timing there, Porter." Harley laughed grimly as the two men approached. "Those are my neighbors, Randall Jones and Deloyd Small. Besides being good, God-fearing men, they're vice president and treasurer of our Foundation. We were just about to have a meeting on what to do when it comes to dealing with federal agents. Maybe you'd like to sit in."

Visions of lychings danced in my head. It wasn't long

ago that a Forest Service ranger had been shot while sitting in his pickup, the bullet lodged right between his eyes. I didn't even want to think about the pipe bomb that had been set off at the federal Bureau of Land Management office in Reno. Or of the ranger who woke up to find the camper in his driveway ablaze like a charbroiled marshmallow.

Harley nodded to the men as they dismounted from their horses.

"Didn't know an outsider was joining us, Harley," stated one of the cowboys, as hard and lean as if he'd been sculpted from stone.

"Didn't know myself till just a few minutes ago, Randall."

Randall Jones looked me up and down. The brim of his black hat was pulled low to shade his eyes. Suspenders supported a pair of well-worn jeans that clung tightly to his hips.

"Beg pardon, ma'am, but is this a fed I'm smelling here?" Sniffing loudly, he slithered over to examine my vehicle.

Pilot let loose a low growl as Randall passed by. Randall growled back in return. A giggle drew my attention to Deloyd Small, who was anything but tiny. I'd rarely seen a hefty cowboy, but Deloyd was a mountain of flesh. His giggle escalated into a high-pitched titter that would have better suited a twelve-year-old girl.

Randall Jones and Deloyd Small were names that I had heard before. Like Harley, both men refused to pay the government for grazing their cattle on public land. Even more ominous, they'd taken potshots at the last Fish and Wildlife agent who'd dared to show up in these parts.

Deloyd's giggling scraped against my nerves like a tooth being hit with a drill. "The dog's a civilian. Otherwise, you've got it right, Randall. I'm with the U.S. Fish and Wildlife Service," I informed him.

Randall spat on the ground in response, leaving no doubt as to his opinion on my career choice.

I sidestepped the wad. "Harley here is claiming that tortoises are being dumped on this land. Is that what you and Deloyd think as well?"

Randall moved in close until we stood face to face, leaving me to wonder whether he was going to shoot me or ask me to dance.

"Damn right those things have been planted," Randall growled in an intimidating voice. "Deloyd has got 'em all over his place. Don't you, Deloyd?"

Deloyd glanced around as if watching the question go by, finally picking up on the prompt. "That's right," he agreed, his double chin shaking like Jell-O. "Damn environmentalists are so damn stupid, they put the wrong damn tortoises on my land. I'm telling you, those damn things ain't even the right damn color."

Having said his piece, he turned to Randall and grinned. I half-expected him to wag his tail. Instead, Deloyd's fingers picked at a group of angry red welts on his neck until one of the scabs came off. The thin trail of blood was a calling card for every gnat around, and small cluster immediately converged on Deloyd, who slapped at his neck with a large, meaty paw.

"Shit, that hurt. I need a drink," he announced.

For a God-fearing man, his language certainly could have been better. Waddling over to his horse, Deloyd pulled a canteen from his pack and proceeded to polish off the contents, the flesh under his neck bobbing like a turkey wattle.

Randall pushed even closer. One more inch and I'd be able to sue him for rape.

"Okay, Miss Hotshot Agent. Since you bothered to come all the way out here, why don't *you* tell us what's going on? How is it that we have nothing on our ranches one day and something endangered on them the next?" he demanded. "You can't tell me that's not a government plot."

I could have, but something told me it wouldn't much matter. Like Harley, both men were carrying .45s that hung like miniature saddlebags on their hips. I knew the situation called for the utmost diplomacy.

"You mean to tell me"—I snickered—"that you really believe the government is sneaking out here in the middle of the night?" I tried to hold back a chuckle. "And dumping hundreds of tortoises on your ranches—all in order to take back this land?" I couldn't help it—I howled with laughter.

All three men stared as if I'd gone mad.

Finally Randall spoke, angrily slicing the air with his forefinger. "That's right. And you want to know why that is?"

I tried to compose a serious face.

"It's because the government is planning to open this land to the Japanese. That's why," Harley boomed before I could answer. " 'We've bought so many damned TVs and cars from them that now we owe the Japs a ton of money. So the government has decided to sell them our land to blank out the debt."

As Lureen would have put it, either these boys were smoking some pretty strong weed or aliens had been sucking out their gray matter.

"Just think about it a minute," I began, repressing another suicidal impulse to laugh. "Your allotments of public land run on the order of thousands of acres, right?"

The men cautiously nodded their heads, waiting for the punch line.

"Do you realize just how many tortoises someone would have to dump here in order to have the critters running all over the place?" I asked.

"Not just anyone," Randall growled. "For all we know, it's you that's doing the dumping. After all, you're the damn critter agent. Let's see you laugh about that."

He didn't have to worry. The way they were all glaring at me, the urge had totally passed. Coming out here alone might have been a crazy idea.

I took a deep breath. "Look at it this way. If you figure that each tortoise is roughly one foot long by one foot wide, I'd need ten double-rigged tractor trailers filled to the brim just to haul the critters in. And," I added, certain this had to be the clincher, "just where would I get all those tortoises from?"

"Shit, Porter. That's an easy one." Randall flashed a wicked grin, as if I'd just willingly stuck my neck in the noose. "Ed Garrett says the Fascist and Weirdo Service is paying a group of eco-nuts living out in some ark to break into that tort hotel you got, steal the suckers, and then dump the little buggers on our land."

I groaned. One of six commissioners in Clark County, Garrett was an eager supporter of the county supremacy movement. He had recently introduced resolutions granting the commission power to veto the Endangered Species Act as to well as control all mining and development decisions throughout the county.

"And while we're at it, what about all those unmarked black helicopters the government is flying out here at night? Let's hear you explain those," Harley jumped in. He pushed his way in front of Randall as if to reassert his position as leader.

I was surprised to hear about 'copters again. Especially unmarked ones. As far as I knew, choppers coming from Nellis bore the name of the base.

"Can't answer that one, hotshot?" Randall sneered.

He was right. I didn't have a clue. Jones and Harley took a few threatening steps toward me, igniting a five-alarm fire in my brain.

"Maybe she don't want to," Deloyd giggled. Having walked back to his horse, he lifted a coil of rope off his saddle.

"I've heard about the 'copters and I'm not sure what's going on. All I can do is promise to look into it," I offered. But the trio weren't in a listening mood.

"If she doesn't want to answer, it's because she's afraid," Harley retorted, sticking his chest out like a bantam rooster ready for a fight. "It's because she knows that's how the government's bringing the tortoises in. The suckers are being airlifted."

"Now, you've got to know that's crazy. Do you really

believe that's something the air force would do?" I began.

"Or maybe government Rambo squads are performing secret maneuvers in the dead of night to raid us," Deloyd eagerly added. Caught up in the wave of excitement, he trotted over to join Harley and Jones.

The homegrown, ready-to-detonate militia slithered tighter around me like a large boa constrictor closing in on its prey.

"Those of us at the Foundation have decided that we're only going to deal with Ed Garrett and the county commission from now on," Harley informed me.

"That's right," Deloyd added. "And Garrett says you're one of the feds that's plotting against us." He ran his hands along the length of the rope.

It struck me as odd that an official I'd never met would bother to spend his time spreading rumors about me. "If I was plotting against you, do you really think I'd have the nerve to come out here alone?" I asked.

But Harley was beyond reason. "Garrett says that the tortoise is nothing but an excuse to kick us off our land."

Randall grinned, his eyes locking onto my own. "Since this is an official Foundation meeting concerning what to do with federal agents, I say we oughta hold this one captive."

"Wait a minute, guys. This is now going too far," I protested.

But Deloyd chimed in, thrilled at having a hand in deciding my fate. "Hey! How about we sentence her for something like treason? What do you think? That oughta make all those big government honcho types sit up and listen."

It certainly worked wonders on me. I slowly backed out of the circle on shaky legs toward my Blazer. I had almost reached the vehicle when the three musketeers moved in unison to stop me. Quickly jumping inside, I closed the door just as Deloyd reached for the handle. I immediately pushed the button down and locked myself in, then caught sight of Randall creeping up along the passenger side.

Picking up on my panic, Pilot bared his teeth and let loose a warning growl before hurtling himself against the car door. His massive head lunged through the open window, where he barked and snarled at the men lurking outside. For a moment, I wasn't sure it was actually any safer in my vehicle with my demon dog. Through all the frenzy, I spotted Randall raising a gun in Pilot's direction. I immediately pulled the SIG-Sauer from the back of my pants and took careful aim.

"Do it and you're a dead man," I warned.

Randall took his time, probably weighing the risks. I decided to help him along by slowly pulling back on the hammer. It took Harley to break up the standoff.

"Okay. That's enough," he said. "Nobody's gonna harm you, Porter. It was just a little game. You'd better be on your way."

I immediately turned on the engine and backed out of Harley's drive, never taking my eyes off the three men, who stared back at me in turn. I made my way down the dirt path, past the twig, the bush, and the creek that had led me in, constantly checking my rearview mirror for any sign that the game had continued. But not a cowboy was to be seen.

I hit the main road and floored the accelerator, relieved at having made it back to the blacktop alive. Glancing over toward Pilot, I suddenly felt grateful that I hadn't been alone. I grinned and finally relaxed.

Then, as often happens, fear was replaced by ravenous hunger. I tore through the blueberry muffin I'd picked up at the Gold Bonanza and was about to chomp down the tuna on rye when Pilot whimpered, sounding like a tiny, frail puppy. His giant paw landed on my arm, nearly knocking us off the road, and he licked my hand, his nose twitching toward the food.

"Okay, partner. Point made. Its fifty-fifty from now on."

Splitting the sandwich in half, I gave Pilot his due.

Seven

This seemed as good a time as any to meet the man of the hour, County Commissioner Ed Garrett. On top of everything else that I knew about him, I'd recently heard he was pushing a proposal to have federal law enforcement agents give up their weapons—the reason being that armed-to-the-teeth ranchers, like those I'd just met, were afraid of agents like little ole me walking around with a gun. While I was supposed to travel the road with nothing more lethal than a Coke can, it was deemed alright for overzealous westerners to be festooned with everything from handguns to bazookas that could be used to blow me away. Because of all this, Garrett had become as popular as Elvis and was now the star attraction at local rallies.

The Virgin Mountains disappeared behind me as I tore down the road, my sights set on Vegas. I hadn't been sure what to expect when I first landed in town. What I found was a sea of polyester and varicose veins. Tourism drives the city, which is dominated by the Strip, a three-and-a-half-mile runway of wall-to-wall casinos inundated with visitors in bright jogging suits and bulging fanny packs, where the only high heels are those to be found on hookers. Squadrons of senior citizens traveling via Nikes ply the Strip both night and day. Plastic cups filled with quarters in hand, they roam in bands from one glitzy hotel to the next with deadened eyes, praying for luck and a fortune as instant as a Cup O'Noodles.

Turning onto Las Vegas Boulevard, I got caught in the

usual time warp as I passed the Luxor's shimmering black pyramid and sphinx jealously standing guard. The Luxor had quickly become my home away from home whenever I needed a New York fix, with its deli offering of bagels and lox. Driving on, Egypt gave way to the Excalibur's medieval turreted castle, which led to the Mirage Hotel, spewing fire and water from its Polynesian lagoon. I glanced up at a marquee larger than my former New York apartment, where those two immortal vampires Siegfried and Roy looked down upon me as perfectly preserved as if they'd been dipped in formaldehyde, a white tiger sitting placidly by their side. Understatement is not in this town's vocabulary. The sky is the limit and in Vegas the sky appears to be limitless, making it the newest fast food version of the American dream.

Bearing left onto Bonneville, I slipped the grip of the Strip and headed for the Clark County administrative building. Like everything else in Vegas, the building is big, bold, and new—three prerequisites for success in this town. I parked the Blazer, left Pilot inside, and caught the elevator up to the county commissioner's floor. A receptionist too old to be a showgirl but too young for retirement took my name and buzzed Ed Garrett's office. She hung up and gave me a dazzling smile, announcing that he was indeed in and would be happy to meet with me. I followed her swaying hips down the hall and thought about trying to imitate her, but quickly shelved the idea. With my luck, I'd simply look like I'd been thrown from a horse.

Caught up in my thoughts, I nearly missed the swiveling of her feet as they pirouetted to the right and stopped in front of a large wooden door that stood open. I followed the wave of her hand, my attention drawn to the back of a massive black leather chair. Turned away from me, the chair faced a picture window that framed the sprawling Las Vegas Valley below. A ten-gallon Stetson hat was mounted on the head rising above the black leather. I stood quietly for a moment, finally clearing my throat. But the head didn't move. I was beginning to wonder if the county commissioner had chosen to expire rather than see me when the chair circled around to reveal a man with the build of a linebacker. Ed Garrett stood up and strode over, towering above me. Dressed in an elegant black suit, his Stetson hat, bolo string tie and lizard-skin boots marked him as a buckaroo cowboy with buckaroo bucks.

Garrett grasped my hand and squeezed hard. "Glad you stopped by."

I squeezed back as hard as I could, barely making a dent in the hydraulic press that passed for his hand.

"And why is that?" I asked.

"I wanted to see for myself what kind of woman chooses to do what you do." His dark, severe face encased a pair of eyes with all the warmth of two shards of black ice. Obviously he wasn't concerned about getting my vote come the next election.

"This kind of woman," I replied, vowing to bone up on my staring technique at home.

"From what I hear, you like to rile people up, Agent Porter. You place yourself dead center in the middle of a brushfire and then you fan the flames," Garrett informed me.

It's always interesting to learn how other people see you. Unfortunately it's never as flattering as I'd like it to be. I gave a firm tug until my hand popped out of his.

"You're pretty good at that yourself," I replied. "I paid Harley Rehrer and his friends a visit this morning. Your name came up about the time they were measuring my neck for a rope."

Garrett pointed an impeccably manicured finger at me. "Those folks you're talking about are my constituents. My job is to stand up for their rights."

I considered pointing back, but I knew that mangled cuticles wouldn't help drive my point home. "Don't be surprised if the next visit you pay your constituents takes place in jail."

Garrett returned to his desk and settled into the leather chair, which was molded to his contours. Opening a drawer, he pulled out a bottle of Chivas along with two small silver cups. Filling each to the brim, he slid one in my direction.

"What you've got to realize, Porter, is that it's not only ranchers who are being hurt but developers as well. And when you hurt developers, then you're hurting Las Vegas."

"As far as I can tell, the only thing hurting Vegas is overdevelopment," I said, pushing my untouched cup back across the desk.

Garrett sipped at his scotch, savoring the taste. "Nobody in this town ever said no to a developer before all this nonsense over turtles began. It's damn near high time common sense was brought back into the equation. After all, we're talking about the future of Las Vegas here." Garrett finished his drink, then reached for mine.

"Actually, what we're talking about is money," I retorted. "Like it or not, development is going to have to be reined in. In case you haven't noticed, building in the valley is impinging on the habitat of everything from endangered plants to bighorn sheep."

Garrett leaned back in his chair, his dark suit blending in with the black leather until all that stood out was his face. "You must have mistaken me for someone who gives a shit, Porter."

Without a doubt big development had mucho power in this county, and I was sitting across from its political hammer. They had to be paying him off big time.

"You might not give a shit, Commissioner, but I'm willing to bet a lot of voters in Nevada do." I sweetly smiled.

Garrett cracked his knuckles one at a time, giving it some thought. "Extinction is a natural process, Porter. That's just the way life is. Of course, you'll have to find a new job. Maybe something in the line of receptionist here? By the way, I require all my female help to wear skirts. Preferably short." Garrett grinned. "Now I have a meeting to attend."

I planted my elbows on his desk, making it clear that the interview wasn't yet over.

"One more thing, Ed. You've been spreading a rumor that Fish and Wildlife hired environmentalists to break into the conservation center and steal tortoises that were then dumped on ranchers' land.''

Garrett's eyes narrowed as he stood and approached my chair. "What am I supposed to think, Porter? After all, you've already met with those paranoids in the ark: an angry former Fish and Wildlife biologist, an illegal wildlife trapper, and a deranged nut who was fired for trying to sabotage the Department of Energy. Those three are the perfect blueprint for terrorist material. I, on the other hand, am involved with a group of defenseless ranchers working hard to feed their families.''

"Why, Ed, have you been following me?" The fact that he knew my whereabouts caught me off guard.

"I know about everything that takes place in this county." Garrett's eyes focused in hard on me. "Don't ever forget that.''

He placed his hand against the small of my back as I got up. Quickly turning around, I pushed it away.

"Good. Then you won't mind telling your troika to back off. I don't take well to threats," I snapped.

Garrett leaned up against the doorjamb so that I'd have to brush past him as I walked by. "People get mad, Porter. And when that happens, if I were you, I'd get out of their way.''

"In that case, Commissioner, I'd suggest you get out of mine.''

Garrett laughed and stepped aside. But as I started to leave, he suddenly placed a hand on either side of the door frame, blocking my exit. "We ought to go hunting together sometime, Porter. It could prove to be fun.''

I didn't bother to tell him that I'm not a hunter. I've never shot an animal. But I have killed a man. It's just one of the things that sets me apart from other federal wildlife agents. That and the fact that I'm a woman. Most consider the combination to be lethal.

I shook my head. "Commissioner, I have the feeling we'd be aiming at two entirely different things.''

Garrett quietly studied me a moment before removing

his hands. "Should I take that as a threat, Agent Porter?"

"Not at all, Ed," I assured him. "But maybe you should consider wearing something bright the next time you're out on a hunt. I'd hate for those constituents of yours to think they had some honest, hardworking official lined up in their sights and end up shooting you by mistake."

Since I was already in the building, I decided to pop down a few floors and pay a visit to my neighbor, Lizzie Burke, who worked as a computer programming whiz for the county. Lizzie had befriended me the day I moved in, introducing herself by bringing over a bag of tortilla chips, guacamole dip, and a bottle of tequila. I could always tell when Lizzie was home by the music blaring out her windows.

Determined to become a star, Lizzie's obsession was tap dancing. I had to give her credit. She practiced every spare moment she had, which was usually when I was asleep. It had reached the point where I now couldn't doze off unless the strains of *42nd Street* were bouncing off my walls along with the pitter-patter of Lizzie's tap shoes. In its own way, the din was as lulling as the sound of garbage trucks had been in New York. I had suggested she give her dream a shot by moving to New York or Los Angeles, where there was more work than in the Glitter Gulch strip clubs or the casinos. But Lizzie insisted she wasn't yet ready for the big time. I didn't have the heart to tell her that at twenty-eight years of age, her star was already on the wane for breaking into show business.

Lizzie jumped up from her desk upon seeing me, her mass of short dark curls bouncing with a beat all their own.

"Hey, Rachel! What are you doing here? Things slow today?"

All I was slamming into were dead-ends and angry ranchers, but I'd have my tongue cut out before I'd admit it.

"I was just here to meet with one of our county commissioners, Ed Garrett," I told her.

"That prick," Lizzie replied. "The slimeball is always trying to cop a feel anytime I pass by his direction."

Standing at five feet two, Lizzie must have seemed like easy pickings to a man of Garrett's size.

"Someday I'm gonna punch his lights out for him," she added.

Hailing from New Jersey, Lizzie probably could. Just the fact that she entertained the thought made me feel all warm inside.

"If you've got time, let's get some lunch. There's someone I want you to meet," I said.

Lizzie grabbed a shoulder bag almost as big as she was from under her desk. She never traveled anywhere without tap shoes, a leotard, and a recording of *42nd Street,* on the off-chance she heard of a job opening.

"I've got plenty of time, especially if you're talking about someone tall, dark, and handsome," she said eagerly.

I chuckled as she followed me to the elevator. "You just described him to a tee, Lizzie."

"Uh, it's not Lizzie these days, Rach. My new name is Tamara Twayne."

Lizzie's name changes happened on a monthly basis. Her life philosophy was based on a quote from Cher: "We all invent ourselves. Some people just have more imagination than others." Lizzie felt sure that if she just hit on the right name, everything in her life would fall into place. We'd already gone through Shana Shames and Lorna Loon since I'd known her. After those, Tamara didn't sound half bad.

We grabbed three sandwiches from a vendor's stand on the bottom floor and sauntered outside. I opened the door of the Blazer and Pilot jumped out.

"This is it? This is the big surprise? What the hell *is* this thing, besides huge?" Lizzie asked as Pilot jumped up, his paws reaching her shoulders.

"Meet Pilot, my new wolf dog." I grinned as Pilot gave her a slurp.

"Well, he is kinda cute." Pilot licked her again as Lizzie

struggled to hold her sandwich out of his reach. "What does he want? Me or my food?"

"I think it's your sandwich," I remarked. I unwrapped a ham and cheese hero for Pilot, who dashed over to me.

"Typical man," Lizzie grumbled. "Sees something he thinks is better and he's outta here." Lizzie took a bite of her avocado and alfalfa-sprout sandwich. "So what were you and Hot Hands Eddie talking about?"

"Development," I said. "Seems we have different views as to how much should be going on in the valley."

Lizzie almost choked on her lunch. "I would think so. You're talking to a man who's one of the bigwigs on the board of Alpha Development."

The name rang a huge bell: billboards for housing subdivisions slapped up by Alpha decorated the valley from one end to the other. It didn't take much to know that Alpha was the largest and most powerful development company in Clark County. No wonder Garrett was heading the drive to have all public land released to the county commission. The money to be made on such a deal would be mind-boggling.

"Along with that clown Harley Rehrer, he's scheduled to be one of the speakers at some barbecue the ranchers are having. They're hoping to get all the local yokels worked up," Lizzie revealed. "With any luck they'll storm the county building, and I'll be able to take a few days off and audition for some gigs."

Pilot had wolfed down his ham and cheese and was zeroing in on my turkey sandwich when a thought occurred to me. "Is there any chance you could access Garrett's personnel file? Maybe dig up some background on him for me?"

"You mean dig around for dirt?" Lizzie grinned.

"More or less. I'd like to know how long he's been on Alpha's board and who else might be on it," I said. "Also what other real estate interests he has."

Lizzie bit into a brownie that tempted me severely.

"If you can, there's something else I'd like you to check

out as well." I filled Lizzie in on the tortoise theft at the conservation center.

"So who are we targeting for the gig?" she asked, letting Pilot lick her fingers.

"No one yet. But I'd like to know more about the guy in charge of the place. His name is William Holmes," I told her.

Lizzie brushed back the hair from her eyes. "His check is paid by the county, right?" I nodded. "Piece of cake. Speaking of which . . ." Digging into her bag of tricks, she pulled out a pack of Ring Dings. All of one hundred pounds dripping wet, she could afford to eat all the sweets she wanted. Pilot and I both eyed her with envy, lusting after the chocolate cake that filled her mouth. At times like this, I didn't care if Lizzie was my best friend west of the Rockies. I hated the girl. Pilot let out a frail whine as the last Ring Ding disappeared. I couldn't have agreed with him more.

With time to kill and no clues to go on, I decided to pay Noah and the gang another visit. The rancher's accusations against them seemed absurd but had made me curious. Besides, I was hoping to talk my way inside the ark and do some snooping around. If I had to pick a suspect out of the three for any dirty deeds, my choice would be Suzie Q. I wanted a chance to quiz her more closely—preferably without Frank Sinatra perched on her shoulder, watching my every move. My fondest wish for Frank was a one-way ticket to the jungles of Venezuela.

The sky went from a brilliant aquamarine blue to Pittsburgh steel gray in the space of a half hour as I crossed the desert. The sky was in one hell of a pissed off mood. Clouds formed low and dark, like the back ends of the offensive line at a Giants game. The wind picked up, and soon it was rocking my car from side to side in an effort to dislodge it from the road, howling like a banshee demanding my soul. Dry lightning flashed in the distance, then suddenly everything became ghostly quiet.

I jumped as a bolt of lightning hurtled to earth nearby, its fingers splitting cacti like a galvanized pitchfork. My hair stood on end as a rush of electricity crackled through the air, roaring into my legs, torso, and arms, reaching my ears and causing their tips to tingle. Rain barreled down in torrents, and visibility plummeted to near zero. I slowed, passing cars that had the good sense to pull off the road. I was more into the sport of hydroplaning, my tires gliding giddily on a raging river of water—making good time while saving on gas, if I could just manage to stay on the road. The radio warned that a flash flood was in full force, and that I should cease, halt, and desist. I had never felt more invigorated in my life.

Shifting into four-wheel drive, I turned away from civilization and onto the dirt road that led to Noah's. The Blazer's engine groaned in misery and its tires spun. I navigated the mountain as best I could, going up and down switchbacks and floating over rocks, until the ark swam into view.

I pulled up, barely missing Noah, who stood outside screaming at the storm in a knock-down, drag-out with Mother Nature, clenched fists raised to the sky. Rain poured from his limp strands of hair, over his bare chest, down his tire of a stomach, and past a pair of flowery bikini bathing trunks, finally settling inside his cowboy boots.

"Come and get me, you motherfucking, son-of-a-bitch-of-a-bastard storm! What's the matter? Haven't you got the goddamn balls? I'm right here, you asshole!" he screamed at the sky.

I stood in the rain and stared, sure he had lost his mind. A brilliant downstrike of lightning hit close enough for me to hear its sizzle bore into the center of the earth. I stood frozen in fear until an ear-shattering clap of thunder jerked me out of my stupor, and Pilot and I made a mad dash up the steps of the ark to its door.

I pounded on it only once before Georgia Peach let us in. Pilot was immediately swarmed by the roving band of dust balls, yelping at the top of their lungs. Emitting a high pitched squeal, he dove over them to huddle at my feet.

"Glad to see you found some kind of friend out here, Porter, even if it is a damn wolf." Georgia snorted. She was dressed in a gold halter top that barely contained her chest. A black vinyl hip-hugger skirt revealed a pair of legs as sturdy as tree trunks. She padded away on bare feet, with each toenail painted a different bright, shiny color.

"You're just in time for my afternoon tea break." Georgia flicked on a blender, then poured out one of the best banana daiquiris I'd ever had. She may not have been up to snuff in the Lhasa breeding department, but she would have made one hell of a bartender.

I sipped my drink as I listened to Noah screech over the rain. "Should I ask what his problem is? Or settle for simple possession?" I asked.

Georgia grabbed a pack of Lucky Strikes from off a makeshift counter, pulled out a cigarette, and lit up. Inhaling deeply, she hacked out a cloud of smoke.

As I waited for her to reply, I checked out what the eco-gang called home. From the decor, it was obvious that Georgia was an equal opportunity drinker: all brands, shapes, and sizes of empty liquor bottles adorned a ledge that ran the length of the room. The kitchen sink was piled high with a jumble of plates, and bowls filled with day-old dog food sat hardening on the floor. It made my own kitchen look pretty good.

Thunder crashed as lightning flashed above the solar panels that had been built into the roof of the ark. On the floor, a collection of pots and pans plinked with the steady drips of water leaking from the ceiling. I glanced down at Pilot, who lay on one of the giant foam floor pillows, the mad frenzy of Lhasas now an adoring harem around him. A tie-dyed curtain closed off the other half of the ark, but a rustle betrayed the presence of somebody there.

Georgia flopped onto one of the pillows, sending a cloud of dust into the air. She crossed her legs, and her skirt slid up to her hips, as she pulled one of the dingy pedigree mops onto her lap. I sat down opposite her, focusing my attention anywhere but on her crotch. Pilot laid his chin on my knee.

"You might be just as wacky as Noah if you'd experienced what he's been through," Georgia finally answered.

I tamped down my impatience with a gulp of banana daiquiri.

"Noah moved out here with his wife and two kids a couple of years ago, after that run-in on his job."

"What run-in was that?" I asked.

Georgia ignored the question. "He parked a mobile home down on the other side of the mountain in a wash. It was a popular spot, close to a man-made lake where people docked their boats."

I couldn't get used to the idea of man-made lakes plunked down in the middle of the desert. It's all part of the illusion that one of the driest spots on earth is actually an oasis, complete with palm trees—which are trucked in. It's also one of the reasons why the county was now running clear out of water.

"One day, when Noah was in Vegas hunting for a job, a flash flood like this one blew in," she continued. "His family was home in their trailer when a solid wall of water came roaring down the wash. It was only five feet high, but that much rushing water is powerful stuff—every trailer in its path got knocked right down into the lake. It happened so fast, there was no escaping."

Georgia looked out at the storm. "Noah arrived to find his family standing on top of their mobile home, his wife clutching their fourteen-month-old son, while his four-year-old clung to her legs. They were screaming and waving for help, just like the others who'd been caught. But there was nothing that anyone could do. The water was still so wild, it would've been suicide to try to swim out. Noah had to stand there, watching his family drown as their trailer sank. Not long afterward, he came out here to the desert and built this ark."

The sweat on my skin had turned cold. I was surprised Noah was even as sane as he seemed.

"How did you meet him?" I asked, hoping to escape the nightmare vision.

One of Georgia's mops made a lunge for her drink, and she threw him off her lap. "Disillusioned government employees seem to have a way of finding each other. Isn't that right, Porter?"

I stared at her, not sure what she meant. "You've got me lumped in with the wrong crowd. I like my job," I replied after a long pause.

Georgia cracked a smile and slurped at her drink. "That's what we all said, Porter. But there's a breed of us who actually wanted to get something done. That's the rub. That's where big business steps in and digs its heel into your neck. Sometimes the government will go to bat for you, but most times it won't. If you've got any ethics at all, that's when you walk."

"And what makes you think that will happen to me?" I asked.

"First off, you're in Nevada, where money rules." Georgia's chest hit ground zero as she bent down to reach for her Lucky Strikes. She grabbed the pack and sat up, shoving a runaway breast back inside its golden holster with her free hand. "Second, I know your type. You're a do-gooder, Porter; determined to save the land and its critters. Face it: you're doomed."

Suzie Q's head popped out from behind the tie-dyed curtain and I caught sight of one of Frank Sinatra's hairy legs. "You're full of shit, Georgia. All you care about is what kind of drink to make next and selling those pain-in-the-ass mutts." Suzie Q giggled.

She strolled out, dressed in the same baggy tee shirt, loose jeans, and sandals she'd had on the other day. I wondered if the girl ever bathed. She stepped over us into what passed as their kitchen and dug through drawers and stray paper bags until she found what she had been looking for: a pack of coconut-covered pink marshmallow Sno Balls, a close relative to Twinkies.

"So exactly why did you quit working for Fish and

Wildlife? What happened that was so bad?'' I was curious to know what might await me in the near future.

Georgia squashed the butt of her cigarette on a small bare patch of floor before leaning back on her elbows, her chest straining to be set free from the skimpy confines of the halter top. "When you get to the point where you can't do your job because your own agency turns against you, it's time to get out.''

"You're still not telling me what happened.'' I wasn't letting Georgia wiggle out of this as easily as she had her halter top.

"Jesus, you're dense, Porter. If I wasn't such a humanitarian, I'd let you run smack dab into trouble without a second thought.'' She hacked on a lungful of smoke as she lit up another cigarette. "I went up against a mining company with what I considered to be a shitload of violations.'' Georgia took a deep puff, her information suspended in the air. "You do that in this state and you're history.''

I finished my drink, running my finger inside the glass to scoop out stray bits of banana. "What mine did you go up against?''

Georgia finished off her daiquiri, the foam settling on her lips. "The Golden Shaft, that perennial favorite of politicians and government alike.''

The woman had my attention. "But I've been told that Golden Shaft is an exemplary mine. They're even receiving an award for environmental awareness.''

Georgia grinned. "Doo dah, doo dah. Don't that beat shit. It's amazing what those boys back in Washington can do. Violations miraculously disappear with the whisk of a pen.'' Her grin quickly vanished. "I was rewarded with the choice of transferring to scenic Newark or quitting.''

I looked at Georgia Peach and wondered if she had lost her marbles in the process. "So you quit and settled here near the mine? Why?''

"Those assholes are bound to fuck up, and when they do, I'm gonna nail their balls to the wall.'' She got up and grabbed the blender, placing it on the floor. The horde of hair balls rose up as one unit and rushed over, stuffing their flat little snouts inside.

"All right, so I'm doomed. But I've still got a job to do. Where would *you* begin to look for three hundred and fifty missing tortoises?" I asked.

Suzie Q took a bite out of the Sno Ball and rubbed her tummy. "They're long gone by now," she replied with a satisfied air. "Kiss those little critters bye-bye. Right, Frankie?"

She raised a marshmallow encrusted finger and rubbed the tarantula's back, leaving bits of pink fluff in his fur.

"How can you be so sure that they're gone?" I felt Frank Sinatra's minuscule eyes zoom in on me.

"Because anyone with enough brains to steal the things knows that they're worth bucks. And when anything is worth bucks, you take it to Pahrump to sell. If you really know the business, your haul is stashed with Wes Turley, the best dealer in town," Suzie Q nonchalantly replied.

Pahrump was infamous for mercenaries, wildlife dealers, and other lowlife scum. Suzie Q plucked Frank Sinatra off her shoulder and held him a hairsbreadth from her face, giving me the creeps.

"They've disappeared into the pipeline by now," she cooed to Frank. "The only way she'll ever find them is floating in some Chinaman's soup. Isn't that right, sweetheart?" She brought her lips to what I hoped was Frankie's face and let loose a loud smack.

"She's right, Porter," Georgia chimed in. "It's all speed, scam, and scumballs out here."

Like she was telling me something new.

The door slammed open and a waterlogged Noah floated in out of the rain. He didn't bother to say hello but went straight for the Jack Daniel's. Screwing the top off, he wrapped his lips around the neck and hoisted it upside down, draining the bottle.

Then he stared at me and burped. "You asked me the other day why I got fired, Porter. If you're free tomorrow, come by in the morning and I'll show you. I promise it'll be time well spent. You'll get to learn one hell of a lot about this wonderful state we call home.''

Having said his piece, Noah fell back onto a cushion.

"Sounds good; I'll do that. But I want to ask you about something I've heard. Harley Rehrer and his friends claim that the three of you are responsible for the break-in at the conservation center. They believe you've been planting stolen tortoises on their land.''

Noah laughed, kicking his feet so hard that streams of water flew out of his boots. "You got to hand it to those boys. They're always good for a laugh.''

"I'm glad to amuse you, but that doesn't answer my question. Harley says you're doing it in order to have him run off the land.''

"That man don't know shit from shinola. Did he tell you they were the wrong color, too?'' Noah grinned.

"How did you know that?'' It was beginning to seem that everyone in Nevada was trailing me—I must have more charisma than I thought.

" 'Cause I've heard the same shit before!'' Noah boomed. "Harley's just kicking and screaming 'cause he and his honchos are afraid of losing their government subsidies. He wants to make sure all you good taxpayers continue to ante up the bucks. Hell, all of us want something: I want lots of young girls, and I'd let you pay for that, too.'' Noah grinned lasciviously.

I glanced over at Georgia Peach and Suzie Q, sprawled out on the cushions. As far as I could see, neither of them seemed to fit the bill.

"Not those two. Those are nasty, vicious females who bite and scratch,'' he growled and cocked his head at me. "If you're going to be swayed by Harley and his gang, you're in for a shitload of trouble—'cause we got us a whole lot of western lunatics out here. You're just beginning to scratch the surface, girl.''

I wondered if Noah included himself on that list.

*   *   *

By the time I headed back to Vegas, the rain had died down to a depressing drizzle, finally lifting to reveal a sunset of staggering beauty. Mauve and scarlet painted the sky as I drove toward the city, which shimmered under miles and miles of neon twinkling like thousands of pieces of gold. An army of Joshua trees appeared as if out of a mirage, their stout bodies and upturned branches resembling an army of inverted tarantulas. Growing to thirty feet in height, the cactus was named by Mormon pioneers who proclaimed the plant's big "arms" were pointing the way to the Promised Land.

Not yet having bought pet food, I picked up a bucket of Kentucky Fried chicken, extra crispy, along with soggy French fries and two sides of slaw, before going home.

After finishing dinner, I opened the button on my pants with a sigh of satisfaction, then decided to continue the process, stripping off the rest of my clothes. I climbed into the bath with a glass of tequila and tried my best to escape the day.

But images of Noah's wife and children kept creeping into the dark corners of my brain. Though I pressed the palms of my hands tightly against my ears, there was no blocking out the screams of a baby. I slammed the door hard on my imagination, but a little boy's fingers slipped inside and deftly pried open the door. He silently stared at me, his face a canvas of terror, as wave after wave of water touched his toes, moving up to his chest to lap at his chin. His mother's tears turned into rain that washed over the boy and then inched up, intent on taking her baby. And all the while, Noah stood on land, the roar of the flood drowning his screams as his family disappeared.

Determined to shake the image, I glanced down at my own submerged legs and was startled to see only a skeleton there. I watched in horror as the flesh began dropping off my hips and waist, then the disintegration crept up to my chest and throat. I tried to cry out, only to discover that skeletons are unable to scream. Water filled my lungs and I started to choke, a burning sensation cutting off my breath. Thrashing around, I woke up and realized that I had fallen asleep in the tub.

I toweled myself off and decided to call it a night. Crawling under the sheets, I drank one more shot of tequila. A whimper drew my attention down to the floor. It was Pilot, flashing the most pitiful expression I'd seen since my high school boyfriend had begged to have sex. Even worse, the ploy worked. I patted the covers and Pilot jumped up. Sprawling, he staked out his territory in typical male fashion. I lay down again as Pilot lodged his back against mine, making me long for Santou. At least I knew where Pilot was at all times.

Eight

Pilot woke me early the next morning. I put him out in my fenced-in backyard, then showered and dressed as I contemplated making the two of us breakfast. Visions of eggs and bacon danced in my head, broken by a rip-roaring commotion from out back. Pilot barked and snarled in a frenzy that had me worried I'd find him foaming at the mouth. Then I heard the rabid growl of Roy Jenkins, the neighbor on my right.

"Shut the hell up, damn dog! Porter, get out here!" he screamed.

I took a peek out the door and discovered Pilot had kept himself busy by digging a huge hole under the cyclone fence, heading straight into Jenkins's backyard. On the other side, Jenkins's three rottweilers hurled themselves against the chain link in a kamikaze attempt to get at Pilot. Pilot was the only one barking, though. The other three dogs merely uttered pitiful yelps, sounding like a chorus of high-pitched, squeaky springs, belying their vicious appearance. The dogs weren't suffering from sore throats: Jenkins had had the pooches surgically altered, removing their voice boxes after they woke him too early one post-boozing-and-brawling morning.

"Goddamit, Porter. What the hell have you gone and done, getting yourself a mangy critter like this?" Jenkins spat in fury.

Pilot growled at him in response.

"Jesus Christ, just when I was beginning to get a good morning's sleep!"

Jenkins was an angry little man. Though he had a body as solid as a brick outhouse, his head was too big for his torso. The bushy black beard and dark hair covering the tops of his ears added to his general appearance of a gnome gone wild on steroids. A perennially unemployed auto body mechanic, he had a backyard littered with car parts and broken-down bodies resting on cinder blocks.

Roy was always looking for an easy way to make a fast buck. His main problem was that there was too much empty space where his brain should have been. His last venture had led him to buy sixty AK-47 rifles as well as a hundred thousand rounds of ammunition right after the assault weapons ban went into effect. Roy had thought gun prices would go through the roof. Instead, they crashed straight to the floor. But it started him on yet another sideline. He now worked as a vendor at local gun shows, which were generally attended by the area militia. Roy called his business Born to Kill. His stand carried everything from video cassettes with instructions on how to be the ultimate sniper to cast saws that claimed to be able to cut the leg off a poodle in under twenty seconds. Roy's philosophy was summed up in a sign plastered on his front door: "Guns are like wives. If it ain't yours, don't touch." Fortunately his wife had the good sense to leave long ago.

"Why'd you have to go and get a dog, Porter?" Jenkins hissed. "Piss off too many people? Afraid you need protection these days?"

His breath was rancid as a dead raccoon, even from the other side of the fence.

"Hell, I'll come and stand guard over your body anytime, babe." Roy licked his lips.

I would rather have had a cast saw taken to my own leg. Jenkins thrust his hand through the chain link in a pretense of trying to pet Pilot, hoping to get on my good side. But Pilot could sniff out a rat. Baring his teeth, he growled.

Roy snatched his hand back, scraping his skin against the metal.

"Great! I probably got tetanus now," he complained. "Your dog went insane when I brought a bowl of dry chow outside. What are you feeding that mutt, anyway?"

"I was thinking of bacon and eggs." Roy probably ate dry chow himself.

"Good God, Porter. Get a grip—that's a dog you got there. You want someone to feed, you can feed me, sweet thing." An obscene glint lit his eyes.

"What, and take you away from all the hookers in town? Don't be silly, Roy," I responded.

Jenkins tugged at his beard while he eyeballed me. "I notice you never have any men coming around, sugar. What say I come over tonight and show you a good time? Maybe relieve some of that tension that gives you that unattractive bitchy edge."

I was glad I hadn't eaten breakfast yet. This way I'd just get dry heaves. "Sorry. I've got a hot date with Dr. Kevorkian."

I was afraid that Jenkins might be right about my tension and the lack of a man—but he sure as hell wasn't the answer. Just the thought of Roy *au naturel* was enough to keep me celibate forever.

Pilot and I piled into the Blazer and set off for our date with Noah under a clear blue sky. It was the kind of day that seized you by the throat and insisted you pay attention. The mountains in front of me looked like a series of vertebrae ready to erupt from beneath their skin, while barrel cactus festooned the side of the road, resembling bright-red balloons that had strayed from an all-night party only to settle in the middle of the desert.

I pulled up to the ark, where Georgia Peach and Suzie Q lay on two air mattresses, sunbathing in the nude, a pile of panting Lhasa apsos gathered around them. It wasn't a pretty sight. My stomach gurgled, and I regretted the fried-egg sandwich I'd bought when I stopped to get a bag of dog chow for Pilot.

Suzie Q stroked Frank Sinatra, who sat on the ground by her side. But what caught my eye was the fact that Frank appeared to be sucking on a shapeless mass of skin.

Georgia Peach noticed the look on my face and chuckled. "Frank is just finishing his meal," she explained.

I was afraid to ask, but there was no getting around it. "What was it?"

Suzie Q blinked through her wraparound shades. "It was a Mojave rattler."

Mmm. Yummy. I wondered how Frank Sinatra had managed to consume something that size.

Suzie Q must have read my thoughts. "First Frank crushes its skull with his jaws."

I was impressed that she could tell where his jaws were at all.

"Then he feeds on the soft parts, sucking on the snake till there's nothing left."

It was beginning to sound like a porn film.

Georgia Peach smirked at me. "It's a fascinating event, Porter. A twenty-four-hour eat-a-thon. You should come and watch sometime."

Yeah. It was on top of my list of things to do, right after spending the night with Roy Jenkins.

Noah climbed down out of the ark; thankfully, he was dressed in cutoffs and an explosive Hawaiian shirt.

"Okay, Perky. Let's go."

Oh, God. Not Perky. Anything but Perky. "I hate Perky," I told him.

Noah grinned. "I thought you might. Okay, in that case, let's haul ass, Red."

I hated Red, too, but decided to let it go.

He turned and headed toward a banged-up Suburban utility van. I followed, with Pilot bringing up the rear. It wasn't until Noah glanced around that he noticed there would be three of us traveling together.

"You don't intend on bringing that nasty critter with

you, I hope. I don't bite, you know." Noah smirked.

"Leave him here, Porter. He can play with Frank Sinatra and the dogs," Georgia called out.

After what I'd seen of Frank's handiwork, I had no intention of letting either Pilot or myself get anywhere within jaws range of the arachnid.

"Thanks, but Pilot likes to go for rides," I explained as I waved the dog inside.

A turquoise-blue disaster on the outside, with scratches and dents on almost every square inch of space, the interior of the Suburban held just as little charm.

Gold shag carpeting with a variety of stains covered the floor. The dashboard was crowned with an air freshener decorated with pictures of Jesus. A Star of David hung from the rearview mirror, along with a giant pair of fuzzy dice.

I looked at Noah and arched an eyebrow.

"I like to cover my bases," he replied as he slapped on a pair of Ray Bans.

Shoving a bottle of Jack Daniel's between his legs, he thrust the throttle into gear. We jerked off in a series of stomach-churning stops and starts, with a horde of Lhasas yapping behind and the Grateful Dead blasting off the interior walls.

Noah decided to take the scenic route. My back came close to being knocked out of whack as we jolted over rocks and plunged into small gullies. Then we turned a corner and headed down a mountain, and the Suburban almost slid off the road.

"Oh, shit!" I yelped, and grabbed onto the strap above the passenger door.

"That's exactly why I call those things shit handles, Red." Noah took a slug of Jack Daniel's. "It's a technical term I devised. I'm gonna suggest that Chevy use it as part of their next ad campaign." He grinned.

I looked at him and wondered what drug he'd dropped this morning, as strains of Jerry Garcia pounded in my head.

"So tell me what you know about a place called Los Alamos," Noah began.

I pried my fingers, one by one, off the strap. "Well, I know it's not Spanish for the Alamo." I leaned over and turned the Dead down a good ten notches. "Let's see. Isn't Los Alamos located in New Mexico?" I asked. Noah nodded as I dug through my memory. "And I'm pretty sure it was the birthplace of the atomic bomb."

"Very good. You get an A in history. More importantly, it's a facility that's run by DOE—or as you civilians call it, the Department of Energy."

"And that's where you worked?"

"Yep. Believe it or not, under this gorgeous exterior lurks a former physicist. I was in charge of working on a project to transform nuclear waste into harmless material."

"Is that possible?" I asked.

"Sure it is. The problem is that DOE doesn't want to spend the time or money to do it." Noah lifted his bottle and took another swig as we hit the main road at seventy-five miles an hour.

"And that's why you were fired?" Somehow this didn't seem like a good enough reason to me.

"Don't rush things, Porter. That's what I'm taking you to see," Noah responded.

About an hour later, we arrived at a spot that didn't look particularly different than any place else in southern Nevada. Drab green brush and scorched tufts of grass dotted the desert floor, with no other sign of life around. The only thing that stood out was a long ridge off in the distance. It rose up fifteen hundred feet, with a single dirt road leading to it.

A blanket of hot, heavy air wrapped itself around us as we got out of the van and surveyed the scene. I felt a nudge, and Noah handed me a pair of binoculars. I held them up, but saw little of any consequence.

"Take a good look, Red. This is America's dumping ground. In the past thirty years, nine hundred and twenty-five atomic bombs have been set off in this place,'' Noah informed me.

The number seemed unbelievable. ''But I'd expect the land to be a barren moonscape,'' I protested.

''That's the clever part. The majority of the bombs were set off underground, so that you can't see the damage— invisible contamination. But even those explosions were powerful enough to break windows in houses a hundred miles away. When they were set off above ground, you could see the fireballs all the way up in Reno.''

I lowered the binoculars. ''So what's this got to do with you?''

Noah unbuttoned his shirt, exposing a chest already the color of rare roast beef to the sun. ''You ever watch the evening news, Porter? Haven't you heard about the controversy over Yucca Mountain?''

I had vaguely heard about some sort of ruckus between Nevada and the federal government regarding a place called Yucca when I'd been in New Orleans. But Nevada had seemed like another world back then, and I had paid little attention.

Noah rummaged around in the glove compartment of his van and pulled out a bottle of sunscreen. Slapping the liquid on his chest, he heaved a sigh of contentment.

''Let me fill you in here, since you're obviously missing some important facts,'' Noah said. ''That big ridge you see over there, situated between Little Skull Mountain to the east and the Funeral Mountains to the west, is known as Yucca Mountain. This little gem has become the designated burial place for all the high-level nuclear waste in this country.''

I stared at the mountain, thinking maybe Nevada wasn't the place to live after all.

''There are more than a hundred civilian nuclear power plants, not to mention all the nuclear weapons plants, that need to dump their spent radioactive fuel someplace,'' Noah continued. ''The waste is in the form of nuclear rods, which are among the most highly radioactive objects on

Earth. Even the briefest human contact with this stuff can be fatal. And all this spent fuel is permeated with pluto-nium—which is used in making nuclear bombs. The tiniest flick of that stuff will leave you with a good case of lung cancer.''

Noah rubbed his hand over his stomach, as if calling on a magic genie, while he gave this some thought. "Right now, there are over thirty thousand tons of this shit looking for a place to call home. This hitting you yet, Red?''

"So, you said, the government wants to bury it inside Yucca Mountain?'' I asked, feeling somewhat like a dummy.

"That's the idea,'' Noah nodded. "It seems there was this little law passed back in 1982 called the Nuclear Policy Act. What it did was to make DOE responsible for solving this problem by 1998, and time is running out fast. Unless something is done by then, DOE is gonna have to start paying a shitload of damages to all these utility compa-nies—and hell knows, they don't want to do that.''

Noah bit off a hangnail, spitting it onto a nearby cactus. "So DOE, along with the nuclear industry and the U.S. Congress, looked around and said, 'Hot damn! We've al-ready made Nevada a hellhole. Why not just finish the job?' And that's how Yucca was chosen as the holy site. I call it the Screw Nevada Bill.''

I felt like I was back in Science 101, trying to understand what the problem was. "Okay. They bury the stuff. So then it's over and done with, right?''

Noah slapped his forehead in frustration. "The problem is that this stuff is going to remain radioactive for fifty thousand years, long after the canisters holding the rods have begun to erode and leak. I mean, we're talking hot, hot tamales. And it's not a matter of *if* it's going to happen, but *when* it's going to happen.'' Noah chuckled. "Even better is that these geniuses picked an area with three major fault lines running right through it, plus lots of other little ones branching off in all directions. This is basin and range country that's still stretching and fracturing.''

Noah pointed up toward the mountain. "See that area over there? That's the latest fault to be discovered, called the Ghost Dance. Hell, this state is one giant fucking piece of Swiss cheese—it has more earthquakes than any place besides California and Alaska."

Maybe dealing with Charlie Hickok hadn't been that bad after all. "Well, if there's such a problem, why not just move the damn thing somewhere else?"

Noah gave me a sour look before shaking his head. "Rachel, Rachel. DOE has already poured three billion dollars into this project. There ain't no way they're gonna pack up their show and take it on the road."

"But this is all just hypothesis, right, Noah? There isn't any proof that anything is really going to leak, is there?" I asked, trying my best to believe in the power of positive thinking.

Noah leaned over and planted a big wet kiss on my forehead. "My dear, that's why we're all going to go down the fucking drain—because of people like you. DOE maintains one hundred and twenty-seven nuclear facilities, and ninety percent of them leak. I don't know about you, but if I were placing bets in Vegas, I'd say it don't sound like good odds to me."

He was a man after my own cynical heart. "So how do you fit into this whole thing?"

Noah rubbed his hands together as if about to perform a magic trick. "Ah, that's the interesting part, Red. You see, when I was at Los Alamos, I conducted some experiments and discovered that if enough nuclear waste is packed inside Yucca, there's a pretty good chance that there'll be one mother of an explosion."

Noah pointed his finger toward the ridge like a cocked gun waiting to be fired. "Right now a labyrinth of bunkers is being carved inside that mountain to hold thousands of steel canisters containing up to seventy thousand metric tons of nuclear waste. This is stuff that's gonna be buried and left for eternity. Now, if any of that were to blow up for some reason, it could set off a chain reaction that would scatter radioactivity all over the place. We're talking major poisoning of both the air and underground water, Porter. Vegas would suddenly be the ultimate thrill ride.''

My Pepto-pink carpet was beginning to lose its charm. Maybe it wasn't too late to transfer out of this place. "Did you tell anyone about this?''

"Sure I did.'' Noah flicked his imaginary trigger. "I huffed and I puffed and I presented all my scientific facts and figures to the powers that be at Los Alamos and DOE. I got kicked out on my ass for my trouble. Since then, they've been busy as beavers trying to bury my opposition to the project.''

Noah picked up a piece of grass and twirled it between his teeth. "It's funny, Red. The dangerous thing about chasing after the truth is that you eventually find it. That's when shit really happens.''

I leaned down and plucked a piece of grass to place between my own teeth. But Noah knocked it out of my hand.

"Don't do that. It's probably contaminated,'' he said.

"Then why are you doing it?'' I challenged him.

" 'Cause I don't care,'' he answered in a huff. After a moment, he continued with his story. "I didn't go down without a fight, though. I released enough information to the press to bring the project to a temporary halt. I've become DOE's worst nightmare.''

So Noah Gorfine was a whistleblower. "Why in the hell would you live in Nevada, with everything you know?'' I asked, fully convinced there was a screw loose somewhere in the man.

Noah gave a devilish grin. "What else could I do that would gall DOE more than be a watchdog in their own backyard?''

"Do you expect to win?''

"Hell, no.'' Noah spat the piece of grass out from between his teeth. "DOE is the most powerful and dangerous agency in our government. They make the CIA look like a bunch of ninnies. DOE does what DOE wants. All I can do is annoy the hell out of them and make their lives miserable, like some damned gnat."

Noah spread his arms open wide. "Right now, this is federal land, half of which is managed by the Bureau of Land Management. Part of the holdup is that all this property has to be transferred directly to DOE first, before development on Yucca can be finished. Once that takes place, the Department of Energy will have complete and total control over what happens. All we can do is hope there's a fuckup somewhere along the line."

We climbed back into the van and headed for home in silence. But before we got to the ark, Noah made a detour toward the Golden Shaft mine. He parked the van on top of a ridge, and all three of us got out to gaze at the mine below. Noah pulled out his binoculars and scanned the area.

"This is interesting," he said, handing the binoculars to me.

Peering down, I saw that a giant boring machine was drilling holes in the side of the mountain. For the first time I also noticed that railroad tracks led into the main tunnel entrance.

"What do you make of all that?" I asked Noah, who had sunk to the ground in a half-lotus position.

"Beats the hell out of me," he answered, his face tilted up to the sun.

It amazed me that he could worry about radioactive contamination but not give UV rays a second thought. "Is there some reason you're turning yourself into a piece of charred beef?"

Noah let loose a low chuckle. "Cancer from the sun— that's a good one, Porter. I show you the most dangerous spot on Earth, and you're worried about a little sunburn. What a wimp."

Schmuck, I thought, deciding to let him burn to a crisp. I turned my attention back to the mine. "You know, I paid a visit down there the other day, looking for violations. I was kept waiting for hours while they probably cleaned up the place."

"You've got to learn to beat them at their own game, Red. They play dirty. You have to do the same," Noah advised.

I focused the binoculars on a tall, lean figure talking to the driver of a haul pak, and my skin began to tingle. It was Brian Anderson, looking good as ever. I must have spoken his name out loud, because Noah grabbed the glasses from me.

"Who did you say that was?" he asked.

"Brian Anderson, the manager of the mine." I realized that my heart was beating faster and wondered if it was the altitude. It couldn't have anything to do with the man below.

Noah grunted. "He looks familiar. But then, all those damn cowboy types look the same."

This cowboy looked better than any of the others *I'd* seen. And I had yet to thank Brian for giving me Pilot. I'd have to pay another visit to the mine and do just that.

We returned to the ark and I drove back to the office, where I found three red beeps blinking on the answering machine. Pressing Playback, I heard the voice of my mystery woman.

"I see you got conned, Porter. Too bad. I was hoping you were smarter than that. Maybe next time you'll wise up and won't tip NDOW about your upcoming visit."

The phone clicked dead in my ear, leaving me to ponder how she knew about my meeting with Monty Harris. That was one more person with access to my schedule. I glanced suspiciously around the room—I was going to have to check the office for bugs if this kept up.

The second call was from *Las Vegas Sun* reporter Duff Gaines, still trying to write an article on the missing torts.

I flipped Pilot a dog biscuit and thought about munching on one myself while I waited to hear the third message. The deep voice of Brian Anderson emanated from the machine, making him sound as good as he looked.

"Hey, Rachel. I'm hoping you liked my present. Please don't take offense; it's only that I hate to think of you traveling alone on the roads. In the meantime, I'm hoping you haven't gotten so attached to him that you can't break away to have dinner with me. How's tonight sound? Give me a call.''

My immediate reaction was a sense of exhilaration that I hadn't felt in months. My second reaction was a pang of guilt as Santou's image flashed across my mind.

''Get a grip, Rachel—the man's only asked you to dinner. It's not as if you're jumping into bed.'' I reached for the phone, my pulse racing a mile a minute.

My third reaction was panic as I wondered what to do with my hair. Five minutes later, I had agreed to meet Brian at the Golden Shaft at seven o'clock that evening. And my fourth reaction was, *I have nothing to wear.*

HORICON PUBLIC LIBRARY

Nine

"What do you think of this one, Rach?" Lizzie had pulled a skintight, strapless red leather dress out of her closet. "You'd look bitchin' in this."

What I'd look like was a tube of cheap lipstick. "Thanks, Lizzie. But I don't think it's me."

My own wardrobe was so bare-bones that Lizzie had decided to outfit me. I was trying to figure out how a girl as tiny as Lizzie could possibly have anything I could wear.

"What? You want something more conservative? Jeez, Rach. Don't you think it's time you busted loose?"

Busting loose was one thing; I just didn't want to bust out of the tube top that Lizzie next tried to foist on me. I'd have to break down and buy myself some new clothes one of these days. "Listen, Lizzie. I'm sure I've got something at home that will work just fine."

But Lizzie was not to be deterred. Other than being a star, her second dream was to have been a fashion designer.

"Alright! Alright! There's gotta be something in here you can wear." Lizzie sighed as her fingers flew through the closet bursting with clothes.

Sequined tops were passed over in favor of a black Lycra unitard that could have been worn by Michelle Pfeiffer as Catwoman. Lizzie held it against her body as she twirled around, modeling its finer points for me before thrusting it into my hands. I firmly handed it back, refusing to even try it on. Leopard-print stretch pants and a matching top met the same fate.

117

"So what kind of date is this? With the Pope or something?" Lizzie stood with one hand on her hip, her dark curls bouncing in all directions, her toe tapping a mile a minute. "You know what your problem is, Rach? You're not willing to try anything new. You've got to get some fashion sense—now, before it's too late."

I looked at the moppet in front of me and had a sudden desire to hug her and tell her to shut up at the same time. Living next to Lizzie was like never having left home. She had become family, with all the good and the bad that implied. I edged my way toward the door to make a quick escape, but Lizzie was too fast for me.

"Oh, no, you don't! We're not through yet. I've got at least a dozen more things for you to try on," she said, grabbing me. The growing pile of clothes on the floor at her feet was beginning to resemble the Luxor pyramid.

Unlike me, Lizzie had taken the time to decorate her bungalow. It was a mixture of *A Chorus Line* and *La Cage aux Folles*. Brightly colored leotards were casually thrown over chairs like slipcovers, while a variety of feather boas lay artfully draped across a coatrack. Worn-out tap shoes formed a jumbled pattern on her closet floor. But the highlight of Lizzie's bedroom was her collection of jeweled turbans sitting on hat forms, resembling a chorus line of decapitated heads.

I leaned against a wall that had been turned into a colorful mosaic of Broadway musical posters. All except for one, which was a picture of Marla Maples in workout gear. It struck me as odd and I asked Lizzie about it.

"She's my idol, Rach. The woman knew what she wanted and went for it."

"You mean her marriage to Donald Trump?" I queried.

"No! I mean getting a role on Broadway in *The Will Rogers Follies*. Okay, so she had to marry Donald at the time in order to do it. But the important thing is that she didn't let anything stand in her way. There's a lesson there. Personally, I think it's also that double initial thing," Lizzie explained.

I looked at her questioningly, not quite sure what she meant.

"You know, your name has to have the right ring to it if you're going to be a star," Lizzie elaborated. "Like Marilyn Monroe, Ricky Ricardo, and Loretta Lynn. The vibrations mix with electrical currents in the air, creating a sort of energy that people can't ignore."

"You mean like Betty Boop, Olive Oyl, and Lorenzo Lamas." Maybe she was onto something. "So how's Tamara Twayne working these days?"

Lizzie wrinkled her nose. "No action yet. It's probably not quite the right vibrational ring. That's why I'm trying Felicia Fargo next. I know you think I'm crazy, but what you don't realize is that Las Vegas is the hot spot for a lot of electrical activity. Things can happen in this place that don't happen anywhere else."

With enough neon in Vegas to light up a thousand miles of desert, there was no doubt in my mind that the electrical activity in this town was a light-bulb manufacturer's wet dream. And there was no question that plenty could happen here. I'd already experienced that first hand.

The idea of Las Vegas as a place where dreams can come true is a popular one. What few people talk about is the fact that Vegas can just as easily annihilate the dreamer. The town's dark, seamy underbelly makes it the perfect spot in which to self-destruct. After all, where else can you develop an overnight addiction, get instantly married or divorced, and commit financial suicide all in the same weekend? It's all here and it's all for sale. I liked the idea of Las Vegas as a sort of Sodom and Gomorrah. It was tantalizing to walk down the Strip and feel its magnetic pull. The trick was to not get sucked in.

I carefully stepped over Pilot, who was preoccupied with tearing a chew toy to shreds, as Lizzie reviewed yet another outfit.

"Don't take this personally, but this is from my fat period. Whaddaya think?" she asked, holding it up for approval.

I actually thought it looked pretty good. I tried on the sleeveless black dress and surveyed the result in her mirror. Lizzie's fat period fit my five-foot-eight frame to a tee. The ribbed cotton dress ended just above my knees, which meant it must have been down to Lizzie's ankles. Though form-fitting, it was still flattering. Enough so to make me nervous. My stomach was already in a mass of knots over having accepted a date.

"It's perfect, Rach. You look terrific," Lizzie announced. "Though the high neck does make you look a bit like a nun."

Considering the way the dress fit, I felt certain no one would accidentally mistake me for one.

"You're sure this isn't too much?" I asked, examining my image closely.

"This is Vegas, Rach. Too much is wearing a chinchilla coat in the middle of summer or dressing in a feathered G-string for church on Christmas Eve. Otherwise, I'd say you're pretty safe," Lizzie advised. "Loosen up: in a few more years, you won't be able to fit into a dress like this. So enjoy it while you can."

That was a cheerful thought. As it was, I wondered if I was pushing the line now.

Lizzie picked up the pile of discarded clothes and threw them into her closet. "By the way, I should have something for you tomorrow on that guy at the Center. I finally located his file. Jeez, what a pain in the ass—you'd think he was CIA or something, the way it was buried inside the system. But now I just have to access it."

I had a hard time reconciling the Lizzie before me, in her skintight, hot-pink pedal pushers, with the computer whiz she obviously was at work.

"Thanks for helping me pick out a dress, Lizzie," I said, glancing at my reflection.

I was still unsure if I was actually going to wear it. I knew I'd feel more relaxed in something a bit more demure. Say, jeans and a tee shirt. But I figured I'd solve that problem when I got home without hurting Lizzie's feelings.

"On the Holmes file, why don't I pop over tomorrow around noon and pick it up? I'll bring lunch," I offered.

"I'll need a lot of energy," Lizzie informed me.

"Okay. I'll throw in a couple of Ring Dings." Pilot and I headed out the door, but I wasn't about to shake Lizzie.

"Hey, wait for me. Who's going to supervise those all-important final touches?" Lizzie asked, closing the door to her bungalow behind us.

Back home, I fiddled with the TV until I found a show that Pilot liked, while Lizzie rummaged through my shoes and jewelry. My plan to change into something else had been foiled. I took one last look in the mirror. I had actually managed to make my hair behave so that it hung in long, loose curls reaching down past my shoulders. I prayed it would stay that way, not frizzing up until dinner was over. I grabbed my shoulder bag and automatically stashed my 9mm inside.

"Hey, Rach. You've got to learn to be a little bit more optimistic about things. I mean, just how bad do you expect this date to be?" Lizzie asked wryly.

I realized it didn't go with the outfit, but ever since finding Annie McCarthy's bones in a tub, I'd become more cautious about traveling unarmed.

"You'd be amazed how much better a guy behaves once they know you're packing," I told Lizzie. I walked out the door and headed for the mine.

The roar of haul paks permeated the air long before I reached the Golden Shaft. When it came into view, I was surprised to see that the entrance to the main tunnel was lit up, as well as an area that looked like an improvised landing strip.

This time the security guard with his M-16 didn't bother to ask if I was fed or state but nonchalantly let me through the gate. I'd assumed that office personnel would have gone home by now, so I was surprised to walk in and find the receptionist, Dee Salvano, still seated at her desk. The can of peanut brittle had been replaced by a glass jar of jelly beans, which Dee scooped into her mouth by the handful.

"Long time no see," she commented as I entered the room. "Is that your mine-touring outfit you're wearing tonight?"

She was the kind of gal I would have loved to elbow while pushing onto a subway. But since I was the proverbial stranger in a strange land, I held my breath and behaved.

"I'm here to see Brian Anderson," I replied, uncomfortably aware of what I was wearing.

"Lucky you." Digging through the jar, she located a purple jelly bean and popped it into her mouth. "He's in a meeting, so you'll have to wait."

That was nothing new. I carefully sat on the vinyl couch, fighting to keep Lizzie's dress from riding up my thighs. I noticed that the reading material hadn't changed, so I amused myself by trying to guess the number of jelly beans in the jar—a challenge, considering the rate at which Dee was eating them.

She suddenly pushed away from the desk and announced, "I'm going to the can. If anyone else pops in all dolled up, tell them to stay put and wait."

I sat alone in the deserted reception area, realizing that I had two options: either I could tip the jar over and cheat on the jelly bean count or I could follow Noah's advice and play by NDOW's and the mine's rules—down and dirty. If I timed it right, this would be the perfect opportunity to check the mine's freezer.

I looked down the empty hallway. Evidently any office personnel still around were tied up in the meeting. The only thing I had to worry about was Dee. There was no telling how soon she'd return.

Now or never, I thought.

I quietly made my way down the hall, gingerly approaching the bathroom, certain that Dee would come barging out and find me—but all was quiet on the bathroom front. It's hard to feel inconspicuous in a skintight black dress, but I did my best imitation of Nancy Drew, hugging the wall as I quickly tiptoed toward the freezer room. I tried the knob and let loose a sigh of relief. The door wasn't locked. Slipping inside, I shut it behind me.

The stainless steel freezer cast a morguelike pall on the room. A shiver rippled through me and goose bumps popped out on my arms—not an attractive asset to flaunt in a sleeveless dress, but, it couldn't be helped. Death gives me the jitters, be it human or animal.

I stood perfectly still and listened as hard as I could for any telltale signs, like the flushing of a toilet. But the building was ominously quiet. The sterile smell of rubbing alcohol pervaded the air, causing my eyes to water.

Great. There goes my makeup.

I walked across the floor and grasped the cool steel handle of the freezer, hesitating for a moment as I reflected on the repercussions of what I was about to do. It was certainly against every rule and regulation in the state of Nevada. I also knew that getting caught could very well blow my career to smithereens. On the other hand, if I didn't go through with it, I wouldn't be doing my job as far as I was concerned. Besides, this would even the score.

The freezer door squeaked open, sounding like an ear-shattering blast in my brain. Then I spotted the contents. An array of dead migratory birds littered the freezer, from sandpipers to ibis to sparrows. But what was hidden away on the top shelf took the prize. Five flattened tortoises lay stacked one on top of the other, looking like a short-order cook's version of hungry man flapjacks. I swiftly pulled all five of the torts out of the freezer and shoved their carcasses inside my bag.

I closed the freezer door, my goose bumps replaced by a sheen of cold sweat as I tried to figure out what to do next. I couldn't very well go to dinner with five tortoise patties thawing inside my shoulder bag. I wasn't even sure if I would make it down the hall unobserved, or if I'd be caught, tarred, and feathered on the spot. There were certainly enough dead birds stashed away with which to do it.

I looked down to see a reptilian leg sticking out of my bag and quickly shoved it back inside, then I opened the door a crack and peeked out. No one was in the hall. Scurrying through, I quickly made my way back to Reception, every nerve ending in my body on high alert. I expected to find Dee Salvano crouched in predatory expectation, her jar of jelly beans held high in her hand, waiting to konk me on the head. But the seat at her desk was still empty. I darted outside, hauling my booty with me.

A hot, breathless wind greeted me, working its way from my ankles to the top of my head in a binding rope of heat. I walked toward the car, fully aware that I'd have five defrosted tortoises on my hands by the time I returned from dinner. Grabbing a piece of canvas from the back of the Blazer, I quickly rolled the torts up inside. I only hoped no telltale scent of *eau de torte morte* would give my stash away.

Then I casually strolled back inside, where I was confronted by Dee Salvano, who stared as if aware of what I'd been up to.

"Taking an unauthorized stroll around the grounds?" she asked, smashing a black jelly bean between her thumb and index finger.

"I had a yen to hang out with the haul paks," I replied fliply. "I didn't think there'd be a problem with going outside to get some fresh air."

What I wanted to do more than anything was to jump in my Blazer and take off before anyone realized that the contents of the freezer had been snatched. "Listen, if this meeting is going to go on for a while, maybe it's best that I leave."

Dee cut me off. "Yeah. And the air around here is real fresh, and good whiskey is still a buck a shot."

The phrase ricocheted around my brain. Damn. Whaddaya know: I'd been right after all. I had figured Dee Salvano to be my mystery caller, with her pipeline into the inner workings of the mine and her smart-ass attitude.

I was just about to return a snappy retort when Brian Anderson rounded the corner, cutting off any chance I had to respond.

Fashionably dressed in a crisp white shirt with the sleeves ever so casually rolled, he was wearing jeans that looked as though they had been freshly washed and pressed. A full mane of silky silver hair framed his face. It was that off-handed aren't-I-attractive look I'd worked all my life to achieve, only to miserably fail. In my mind, the man was the image of what a modern cowboy should be: Tom Selleck and Sam Elliott rolled into one, with the perfect grin of Tom Cruise. Too bad he had a bunch of dead critters stuffed inside his freezer.

Brian took both my hands in his, squeezing them slightly as he greeted me. "Sorry the meeting went on for so long." He stood back and surveyed me up and down before twirling me around. "I'd have been tempted to skip it altogether if I'd caught a glimpse of you waiting out here looking like this."

Dee rolled her eyes and my face began to burn. As much as I like compliments, I never believe they're totally true. But this time, I found myself hoping Brian meant every word. His eyes gazed into mine and a wave of heat raced through me. I was becoming attracted to the man in a major way.

"What say we get out of here? I've got the perfect spot in mind," he said.

Without any warning, Brian leaned over and plucked something from my breast. Already nervous, I jumped back as if I were about to be attacked.

"A feather." Brian laughed, holding the wispy piece of evidence up to my face. "Your job must follow you wherever you go." If only he knew.

I wondered if Brian planned to clue me in this evening on the fact that his freezer was fully occupied. I seriously doubted it, though a girl could still dream. I turned back as we headed out the door, catching Dee's eye. But she gave nothing away.

Brian steered me toward his Jeep. "You can leave your vehicle here," he said, opening the car door on my side.

"That's fine with me." I just hoped none of his employees was as nosy as I was.

The sun was setting blood-red over the mountains as we headed down the road, the colors in the sky pulsating with the intensity of a beating heart. Just as quickly, the palette melted into shimmering twilight. This is when the desert comes alive. Purple mountains stain the landscape, as surreal as three-dimensional punchouts dropped by whimsy onto the desert floor. Gnarled and twisted Joshua trees are transformed into crusty old hermits, their bodies resuscitated by the crystalline night air. And the howls of coyotes turn your blood cold, though the temperature continues to hover at a sultry ninety degrees.

We careened down the deserted highway, passing two young girls on the opposite side of the road, their attire in startling contrast to the barrenness of the landscape around them. Flaunting iridescent blue eye shadow and ruby-red lips, they were decked out in hot pants and strapless tube tops, their hair teased into towering blond swirls. They couldn't have been more than fifteen years old. Leading a forlorn puppy on a rope, they were hitching their way to Vegas, part of the parade caught up in the hype of catching dreams.

"So how did you like my gift?" Brian asked, his eyes flickering over the girls. "Ever have a wolf dog before?"

I'd been so preoccupied with my thoughts that I'd completely forgotten to thank him. I hadn't had a pet, since the age of thirteen, when my mother got white carpeting and life as I knew it went out the window.

"He took a little getting used to in the beginning," I confessed. Then I thought of my confrontation with Harley and what might have happened if Pilot hadn't been there. "But I have to admit, I feel more comfortable with him around."

"Glad to hear it." Brian's teeth grazed lightly against his bottom lip, a movement I found somewhat unnerving. "Have you decided what to call him yet?"

"Pilot." I felt an unexpected pleasure in saying the name.

Brian gave me a questioning look.

"I have lousy sense of direction," I explained.

"You could always use a map," Brian suggested.

I laughed. "You've never experienced my map-reading skills. Somehow I always end up heading in the wrong direction. Having a dog could come in handy."

I was enjoying Brian's company more than I felt I should. I thought of the tortoises defrosting in the back of my Blazer, and a flash of guilt hit me.

"He's a wolf dog—there's a difference," he stated.

"Hmm. And what's that?" My body temperature soared as Brian's gaze traveled the length of my dress.

"Well, they're smart and they're loyal and they'll protect you to the death. Kind of what I look for in a woman." He nibbled at his lip again, and my nerve endings began to tingle.

"Had any luck yet?" I suddenly felt as if I were being sized for a collar.

"Nope. Not yet. But I'm hoping that will soon change." He caught my eye and held it, slipping the collar around my neck.

A mixture of attraction and wariness made for a heady brew. I tore my gaze away, deciding to break the spell.

"So have you found any dead wildlife since my last visit?" I asked, playing my own version of Truth or Dare. "Of natural causes, of course."

"Sorry to disappoint you." Brian glanced nonchalantly out the window. "But we still hold a perfect record. Besides, don't you think Monty Harris would fill you in if anything was found?"

"I don't know. Would he?" I asked, going for my own casual air.

Brian turned and stared at me, his eyes a stormy gray. "Evidently you don't think so. Is there something bothering you that I should know about, Rachel?"

I was tempted to confront him on the freezerful of critters

and get the matter over with. But thankfully, logic prevailed. Even though the tortoises looked like a clear hit and run, until I had hard-core proof as to what had caused their deaths, I knew there was no case. If I was going to get myself busted, it ought to be for a rock-solid reason. Besides, Lizzie would kill me if I sabotaged the date so early in the evening.

"Sorry. I've just had a hectic day," I replied. "Sometimes I forget there are other things in life besides business."

"I know exactly what you mean." Brian exhaled a deep breath, as if expelling the day. "What's say we shelve shop talk for tonight? I think we could both use a break."

His hand casually brushed along my thigh, causing my body to log in on the Richter scale.

"Where is it that we're going?" I asked, trying to ignore the tremors.

Brian's eyes danced, as if he could feel the vibration. "It's a surprise. Let's just say it's a piece of old Nevada that doesn't exist many places anymore."

Brian pulled off the highway and steered the Jeep onto a secondary road that skimmed the Arizona border. By now the surrounding landscape was black but for a slip of moon and some stars glittering as shiny as gold nuggets thrown up in the sky. Then the stars hurtled to earth, transformed into the lights of an elegant old hotel that twinkled as though on fire. We pulled into a parking lot filled with pickups and vans.

"You know, you're right," Brian said. "You do look tense. We need to do something about that before we sit down to dinner." His eyes gleamed in the dark, luminescent as twin moons.

"Just what did you have in mind?" I asked, my pulse liquid white lightning, leery of what the answer might be.

"Turn around and face the window," Brian said softly.

I didn't move a muscle, choosing instead to study the moonlight at play along the contours of his face.

"You're not afraid of me, are you?" He whispered the challenge.

Stars glimmered inside my body, raising the temperature of my blood to over a hundred degrees.

"Not one damn bit," I evenly replied.

I slowly turned away from him, my body issuing one set of commands even as my mind screamed another. His hands slid onto my shoulders and I nearly jumped out of my dress.

"Not too nervous, are you?" The warmth of his breath set my skin ablaze as his fingers massaged their way down my spine.

I told myself I should stop him—but my body had thoughts of its own. My muscles relaxed with his touch. Not only did the man look good but he gave a hell of a back rub. A slight moan escaped my lips, and embarrassment shot through me. But Brian didn't say a word as his hands continued to light tiny brushfires under my skin. Just as I felt sure I would melt into a puddle, he had the good sense to stop.

"There. That's the first part of the evening. Let's move onto the second."

What concerned me was what he had planned for the third.

Strains of country western music led the way through the front door into the Eureka Hotel. Once inside, it was as if we had been transported back in time. The hallway was covered from floor to ceiling in elegant red and black wallpaper, whispering intimations of a naughty Victorian brothel. Period furniture added just the right touch.

But it was the smoke-filled bar that recreated the wonders of the old West in glorious Technicolor. Raucous cowboys slugged down beers, laughing and cheering, as five-dollar bills flashed in the air. I stepped inside, curious to see what all the commotion was about. I pushed past startled cowboys too polite to put me in my place until I landed in front of the bar. A live rattlesnake lay coiled inside a large pickle jar. I watched as one cowpoke after another placed a hand on the outside of the container, while the other held a five-dollar bill high in the air.

"Keep your eyes open!" was the chant as the next man came up to bat. The challenge was for each contestant to keep his hand against the glass without flinching, as the snake lashed out in fury, striking against the jar. Cowboy after cowboy pulled back or blinked each time the snake struck, its fangs bared in frustration. A nearby jar filled with five dollar bills affirmed the fact that the snake was the winner.

"That's some sport they've got there," I commented to Brian. He had edged in behind me as yet another cowboy bit the dust. "Is this what's considered a good time around here?"

One half-soused cowboy turned to eyeball me. A snake-skin belt with a silver buckle the size of a baseball held up jeans that rested on his hips, leaving breathing room for a stomach that hung like a tired old hound dog. Glancing down, I saw that his boots were made of snakeskin as well.

Hitching his thumbs inside his belt, he moved in close, his beer-breath smack in my face. "You got a problem with this, little lady? What are you? Some kind of animal rights nut?"

After three months in Nevada, I was beginning to tire of the macho cowboy routine. Staring him straight in the eye, I matched him inch for inch, proving I wasn't so little. "What I am is a federal Fish and Wildlife agent. Have you got a problem with that?"

The cowboy spat on the floor, wiping his mouth with the back of his hand.

"Bullshit. You don't look like no federal agent to me. You look like some pussy city slicker come out to poke fun at us locals." He bristled. "You think you're so smart, you stick your damn hand out there. Put your money where your mouth is, girl."

Brian quickly put an arm around my shoulders in an attempt to steer me away. "She didn't mean anything by it. No harm done. We'll be on our way."

But my cowboy was itching for a fight. "What's the matter, little lady? You gone and got scared? Not so easy now, is it? Maybe you ought to apologize to all of us here. Or you need your boyfriend there to fight your battles for you?"

An older, broken-down cowpoke sneered, "You better do like he says. Otherwise he might end up sticking you in a jar for us to play with." He looked around the crowd and flashed a five-dollar bill in the air. "Who'd bet five bucks to see if this lady here would play like a snake and bite?"

A whoop of laughter broke out as Brian pulled on my shoulder, but I refused to budge. I'd had it with cowboy humor.

"What's the deal?" I asked the first cowpoke.

Leering at me, he flashed a lopsided grin in need of some serious dental work. "We've got a live one here, boys! Place your bets now."

"I asked, what do I get out of this contest, Roy Rogers?" I persisted.

He fixed me in his sights before edging up against me in a game of Mine's bigger than yours. "You get to walk out of here alive."

Brian immediately swooped in as my gallant knight on an errant mission. "Back off, buddy. If she's crazy enough to go through with this, let's just do it and get it over with."

I turned and shot Sir Galahad a look to kill. "Thanks for the support, but I can handle this on my own."

Brian threw up his hands in defeat as the crowd roared. They loudly began placing their bets, most of them running against me. I turned back to my Marlboro man and waited for an answer.

He shook his head and chuckled. "I just love easy money." A dribble of tobacco juice crept out of the corner of his mouth. "The deal is, you stare the snake in the eye, and if you don't move your hand or flinch when he strikes, you win the pot of gold. But take a good look there, gal. You see all those five-dollar bills? What does that tell you?'' He leaned over and whispered in my ear. "Let me clue you in. The snake wins all the time."

He reached into his pocket and slapped his own five-dollar bet on the bar. "And if you lose, you buy us all a round and admit you're a pussy city slicker."

"Is that what everyone does that loses?" I inquired.

"We're making a special exception in your case, little missy." He grinned at me again and winked, spurring on my urge to knock out his few remaining teeth.

"Then I have a rule of my own," I informed him. "If I win, you set the snake free."

Mr. Marlboro looked me over once more, more closely this time. "You're right. You are crazy enough to be a goddamn fed agent."

The crowd of cowboys erupted in laughter again. Then a rotund cowpoke with a body like a beach ball rolled his way to the front, his tummy jiggling as he held in a chuckle.

"What the hell, Sharkey. You afraid she's gonna win? Let her have the damn snake," he said magnanimously.

Sharkey pushed him roughly aside and turned back to me. "You got a deal. Now stop stalling and let's play."

I glanced at the snake, its coils already rattling, its tongue flicking toward me in eager anticipation. Evidently I looked like an easy mark to her, too. Somehow I knew the snake was a female, probably as tired of dealing with cowboys and their macho games as me. I edged over to the jar for a closer look, and realized the snake was much larger than I had originally thought. She stared back at me with unblinking, glassy eyes, conveying one pure and simple message: Sucker.

I heard the snickers building behind me and was aware that Brian was in the crowd, biding his time, while he waited for me to lose. A sea of faces gathered around the jar, intent on catching me blink.

I shut out the motley throng and concentrated. When worse comes to worse, I tend to fall back on my acting skills, meager as they might be.

It's a role, Rachel. Nothing more. If you pull this one off, you win the Oscar.

I focused on the jar, its sides slathered in spent venom. The snake was already agitated, its body squeezed inside a bottle that had long ago grown too tight. It dawned on me that she was kept there for more than just the amusement of a bunch of drunken cowboys. These rough and tough men were fighting hard to contain their fear of the unknown, of one more critter that couldn't be broken, no matter how hard they tried.

I gazed at the snake and a shudder ran through me. We were both scared. That's when I felt walls of my own close around me like a tomb.

It's a role. It's a role.

I repeated my mantra as I slowly reached toward the glass, locking eyes with the snake. I could pull this off. I had stared down worse threats in the subways of New York.

It's a role. Snakes are the one thing you're not afraid of.

Time stood still as the snake regally drew itself up to its full height. And then suddenly it was as if I had been sucked inside that same bottle, where I gazed out on the drunken crowd filled with blood lust and fear. The overwhelming silence of being in that vacuum had a calming effect on my nerves. The noise of the mob was muffled, the venom-splattered jar creating a stained-glass mosaic of jeering faces mouthing words I couldn't hear. The only sound was the hiss of the snake's tongue, flickering in and out in mesmerizing rhythm.

The flesh of my hand hovered closer and closer until it covered the side of the jar. I became perfectly still, caught in a web of morbid fascination. I watched as the snake pulled back, as though in a dream, and everything came to a stop. Except for the reptile, whose movements were crystal-clear. My chest rose and fell with the weight of my breath, and I felt the blood course through my veins. I froze as the snake's jaw unhinged, opening wide, its body sensuously swaying. Then, in a slow-motion dance of death, the reptile surged forward, its fangs bared, aching to plunge into warm, human flesh. I held my breath and waited, feeling the dull impact as the snake hit the glass and bounced off.

Freshly spent venom oozed inside the jar, mocking the reptile's infuriating impotence. A sour taste of bile rose up from my stomach, lodging in my throat. It was almost as if I had made the strike myself and missed. Sweat rolled down my face to my neck and settled between my breasts as I came back out of the bottle and took a deep breath. It was over. I was shaking, but I had won.

My victory was met by dead silence. Then the few cowboys crazy enough to have played the odds by betting on me whooped it up, demanding payment from the crowd. Brian's arm slipped around my shoulder.

"What else do you do for fun, and does it require protective gear?" he asked suggestively, leaning in toward me.

But my gaze was locked on my Marlboro man as he turned and motioned to the jar holding the snake.

"Here. Don't you want it now?" he asked belligerently.

I leaned casually against the bar, afraid that my legs might buckle beneath me. Somebody passed me a beer and I took a long drink, quenching my fear.

I looked Sharkey square in the eye. "The deal was that *you* set the snake free. After that, there's a round for everyone on me."

Sharkey gave me a look that his momma would have slapped him for.

"What's the matter, Sharkey? Afraid to pick up the jar?" a voice called out from the crowd.

"Hey, maybe he can pay the little lady to do it for him," someone else teased.

Sharkey growled at the bunch of raucous cowboys. Then, stepping forward, he placed one hand on the lid, carefully sliding the jar off the bar until the glass bottom nestled in his palm.

"Clear the way, goddammit!" he yelled. Pushing through the crowd, he headed for the door.

Once outside, he set the jar on the ground and stepped back. I noticed that his hands were shaking.

"That's great. But now you've got to open the top, Sharkey. Otherwise, the snake can't get out," I observed.

I saw Brian walk over to the Jeep and wondered if he had decided to leave me here. Instead, he came back with a pair of heavy work gloves.

"Give the guy a break, Rachel," he said, a chuckle escaping him.

Sharkey took the offered gloves, glaring at me the whole time. "What's your name?"

If Brian hadn't been watching, I would have been tempted to give him a fake one. I didn't need one more angry cowboy on my trail.

"Rachel Porter," I said.

"I'll remember that," he snapped.

Sharkey walked over to the jar and twisted off the top. Then, jumping back, he tipped it over with the toe of his boot. The snake lay perfectly still inside the glass, as if suspicious of yet another prank. Then, slowly slithering out onto the warm desert floor, she looked around at us. The coils on her tail rattled one final warning, and the snake disappeared into the black depths of the Nevada night.

I went back inside and claimed my own jar filled to the brim with five-dollar bills as a few happy cowboys congratulated me.

"Why do I feel you're more relaxed now?" The tips of Brian's fingers lightly touched my back as we crossed into the dining room and were led to a table. "Am I going to always have to get you so charged up just to calm you down?"

The sexual innuendo wasn't lost; I just chose not to reply. But he was right. I felt perfectly relaxed after winning the showdown. The adrenaline rush was addictive.

A small stage had been set up in the corner of the dining room, where a cowboy in a ten-gallon hat and fancy snakeskin boots plucked on a guitar, singing a forlorn tune. The melancholy melody pierced the air, the music spilling out of a jagged hole in his heart.

I had another beer while we waited for dinner and studied the man across from me. Everything about him came in a large, neat package. Too neat. It made me nervous. He was good-looking, intelligent, and employed, to boot. Why was he alone? It didn't add up.

"I'm beginning to think I didn't need to get you that dog after all," Brian lightly remarked. "I get the feeling you like taking care of yourself."

He was wrong about that. It was just that I was afraid of depending on anyone else—especially when it came to men. More than once, I had left myself wide open only to be let down. Even now, I was still confused about Santou.

"What about you?" I asked. "I don't see you settling down."

Brian took a sip of his scotch. "I want to; I just haven't had the chance. My job keeps me pretty occupied. Speaking of which, I hear you've been busy, too. Word has it you're riling up cowboys outside of bar rooms as well as in."

Word traveled fast. "What can I say? Harley and his friends have no sense of humor. Not to mention a complete lack of sanity," I replied.

Brian played with the ice in his glass. "You've got to understand where they're coming from. They've had rights to this land for generations. They don't like it when an outsider threatens to curtail what they do on property they think of as theirs."

"But it's not theirs, Brian," I corrected him. "That's just the point. They're renting federal land for close to nothing. That means there are rules they have to abide by."

Brian gave a slow smile. "I'm afraid not everyone agrees with you on that."

"So I've discovered—Ed Garrett, for one. Remind me not to vote for him in the next election."

"He's got a large constituency who back him, Rachel. I'd be careful there," Brian warned. "Ranchers, developers, and mining companies give him their whole-hearted support. And I agree that more federal land needs to be released for private use." His eyes lit up, warming to the topic. "There's still one hundred million ounces of gold buried beneath this state, just waiting to be dug up. All that's holding it up is government red tape."

"It's that red tape that protects every bit of land from being destroyed," I reminded him.

Brian was quiet for a moment. "You don't like mining companies much, do you Rachel?"

I liked them about as much as I liked wildlife dying from all the pollution mines create. Brian must have read my mind.

"You know, mines have cleaned up their act from just a few years ago. There was no law that netting had to cover tailings ponds when I first got into this business." Brian took a sip of his scotch. "In fact, my first week on the job, I learned that a doe was stuck in one of them. She'd gone down to get a drink of water and then couldn't get out. It wasn't the toxicity in the pond that was killing her but getting caught in the thick plastic liner. She'd been struggling for two days and nobody would help her out. By the time I found her, the doe was alive and alert, but both hind legs were destroyed. I had no choice but to shoot the critter.

"Afterward, I asked some of the workers why they hadn't stopped and gotten her out. Seems they were placing bets to see how long it would take before the coyotes reached her."

He looked back at me. "That was the attitude back then. That's changed now, Rachel. Rules and regulations are in place to stop that sort of thing. Sure, business goes on as usual. But we've learned to be much more careful."

I could have tossed a coin as to whether it was the melancholy music or Brian's tale that made my eyes mist over. If he had wanted to get to me, he'd hit the right spot. I found it hard to believe that this was same man who was hiding contraband in his freezer.

"Harley claims a handful of environmentalists are dumping desert tortoises on ranchers' land. Do you agree with him on that?'' I asked, secretly hoping he'd give the right answer.

Brian's eyes narrowed and the corners of his movie star mouth pulled down. ''You're talking about those kooks in the ark, aren't you? Take a word of advice: stay away from them, Rachel. Especially that nut, Noah Gorfine. The man is certifiable and capable of anything.''

''Why? Because he defied DOE on where and how to dump nuclear waste?''

Brian looked at me in surprise. ''You *have* been digging around. Don't dig too deep, Rachel, or you're bound to land in trouble, wolf dog or no wolf dog. You're sticking your nose in where it doesn't belong.''

I'd obviously struck a nerve. Brian downed his drink and ordered a second scotch. A double, this time. I decided to steer him back onto the subject of mining.

''If there's still so much gold out there, why isn't your company buying up claims from small miners in the area?'' I questioned.

Brian homed in on where I was headed. ''You're asking about Annie McCarthy, aren't you?'' I nodded my head. ''I don't believe her claims are of any value where gold is concerned. But I told you that before,'' he reminded me.

The waiter brought Brian's drink along with our meals.

''That's it. Enough business for tonight,'' Brian declared, his mouth softening into a smile. ''Let's talk about you, princess.'' He plucked a rose out of the Coke-bottle vase sitting on the table and gallantly offered it to me. ''Are you involved with anyone I should know about?''

It was the million-dollar question I'd dreaded, since I didn't seem to know the answer to that anymore.

I looked at the rose and 'fessed up. ''There's someone back in New Orleans I'd been seeing. But we haven't been in touch for a while.''

Damn. I wasn't sure why I didn't just say I was involved and have it done with. If only he hadn't told me the story about the doe—not to mention his obvious physical appeal.

Brian's fingertips grazed mine as he caught my eye.

"New Orleans is a long way away, Rachel. You ought to think about leaving yourself open for a relationship here."

I took the rose but had one more question to hit him with. "By the way, is there any problem with my doing spot inspections at the mine?"

Brian cut into his steak and took a bite. My question hung in the air until he finally answered. "I think you should leave that to NDOW. Otherwise you might get Monty Harris into a snit. And believe me, you don't want to do that."

"Why is that?" I asked, wondering what he knew that I didn't.

"He can make life difficult." Brian looked at me curiously. "Haven't you heard what happened to the agent before you?"

"You mean it was really Monty who bit him, and not the snake after all?" I replied.

Brian laughed and then shook his head. "You're close. Harris complained about him so much to the boys in D.C. that he was pulled from this post. Never heard where he was transferred to, but I have the feeling it makes Nevada look like paradise. I'd hate to see that happen to you."

I found it interesting that Sam had never bothered to fill me in on that tidbit.

When Brian dropped me back at my vehicle later that evening, I worried about the defrosted tortoises, but my Blazer wasn't giving away any clues.

"I had fun tonight. But now the pressure's on for me to find some critter for you to save on our next date. There will be a next date, won't there?" he asked softly.

I found myself nodding as Brian tilted my chin up and kissed me lightly, his fingers caressing my throat. My blood kept beat with my heart as his lips grazed my neck before working their way up once more to settle on my mouth. Then I felt the warmth of his breath against my ear, light as a feather.

"You like challenges, don't you, Rachel Porter? We'll

have to see what we can do about that,'' he whispered, the
words drifting softly inside me.

I rode home in a state of confusion, not able to figure
out who Brian really was. My body had a mind of its own
where he was concerned. And the fact that he had not only
given me a dog but tried to save a deer hit every weak spot
I had. That was the problem. My defenses were down and
I felt certain he knew it.

I was just beginning to catch a good whiff of dead tortoise by the time I arrived home. I unwrapped the reptiles
and carried them into the house, trying to fight off Pilot,
who was sniffing furiously away. There was no trouble fitting the smashed torts in my freezer. Nothing else was in
there besides the thin layer of ice that was just beginning
to form. It would be a good year before I'd have to worry
about cleaning the space out with a hammer and chisel.

I walked back into my living room, where I discovered
that the hand-me-down coffee table I'd recently purchased
suddenly had only three legs. Pilot lay on the floor contentedly chewing away at the fourth, which now resembled
a piece of abstract sculpture. Obviously it was my punish-
ment leaving him alone. Pilot raised his head with a sheep-
ish expression. What the hell, I thought. It was time for
new hand-me-downs anyway.

Tonight was one of those nights when I knew sleep was
hours away. I could tell from the music blaring next door
that Lizzie was still awake, too. But I wasn't in the mood
to talk about tonight's date. Not until I had sorted it out in
my own mind first.

Instead I dug out the rest of Annie McCarthy's love letters, hoping for some insight into what makes relationships
tick. But Annie'd had about as much luck with men as me.
Letter after letter revealed little other than that her fiancé
had succumbed to being one more stubborn old prospector
who had refused to give up.

Feeling as sorry for her as I did for myself, I was about
to put the rest of her correspondence away when a

spanking-new envelope caught my attention. Opening it up, I read it through once, and then again, not yet comprehending what it was I'd discovered.

Buried among Annie's old love letters was an application for a quit claim deed. My heart began to race madly, and I couldn't quite catch my breath. The application spelled out the sale of all Annie McCarthy's claims to Golden Shaft Mine. While the place for Annie's signature was blank, the deed had been signed by Brian Anderson representing the prospective buyer.

I poured a glass of tequila and downed it in one quick gulp as I looked at the deed again. This time I noticed the date as well. If Lanahan was right about Annie having been dead for a month when she was found, then the deed had been signed and dated just two weeks prior to that. I poured myself another shot of tequila, my hand shaking as I brought the glass to my lips.

Brian had lied to me. Not only about the wildlife deaths at his exemplary mine but about Annie McCarthy's claims as well. I could still feel his touch on my mouth, his body pressed against mine, as I saw Annie's skeleton grinning mockingly at me. I'd been played for a fool.

I washed my face and brushed my teeth, trying to exorcise Brian. Low, throaty laughter swelled up from behind me as my skin grew prickly cold. I knew it was Annie, laughing at one more woman who had been so easily conned. Nevada was quickly becoming a place where no one could be trusted.

Thoroughly exhausted and confused, I wanted nothing more than a deep, dreamless sleep. I walked into the bedroom, where a single message flashed on my answering machine. If it was Duff Gaines again, I would scream.

But the call was from Santou.

"Listen, *chère*. I'm flying out. We need to talk. I'll see you on Thursday."

That was in two days. No "Hi. How are you?" Just "We'll talk." It had to be something important. I knew

Santou hated flying even more than I hated being away
from the pulse of the city.

I went to sleep dreaming of Santou and Brian until they
merged into one.

Ten

Pilot woke me from a sleep so deep that I felt I would never make it up to the surface. Licking my face, he pulled at the covers with his heavy paw until I was forced to face the day. I felt downright domestic as I got Pilot his breakfast, going so far as to fix a bowl of Cocoa Puffs for myself. But the sour milk I poured on it brought me to my senses. Rummaging through my bag, I came up with the three essential ingredients to start off any day: chocolate, caramel, and nougat, all rolled into one sugar-packed Milky Way bar.

Then I fished through my freezer and dug out yesterday's catch. It was time to pay Henry Lanahan a visit.

Lanahan's office was set apart from the Metropolitan Police building. Far apart. Outside of town, to be precise. Rough cinder blocks as gray and cold as a corpse's skin comprised the facade of the Forensics lab. All the place needed was a hearse out front as its official car. I parked in the lot and let Pilot out of the Blazer to roam the lab grounds while I attended to business.

The atmosphere in the building was quiet as a newly dug grave, befitting what went on there. I stopped a woman with pale skin and sad eyes to ask the way to Lanahan's office. She wordlessly pointed a rail-thin finger down the hall and then crooked it to the left. I interpreted this to mean I should turn at the corner.

I found Lanahan in a room that was eerily cheerful. Large cut-out Halloween skeletons with movable arms and

legs hung from one wall, creating a mural of dancing
corpses. On his desk sat figurines of two skeletons dressed
as bride and groom. The room had a central theme, you
had to give it that.

Lanahan bounded up from behind his desk upon seeing
me. "Hey, Rachel! Glad you're here. You're just in time
to see something neat. Come and take a look at this."

I followed Lanahan's lanky figure down the hall, half-
running to keep up with him. He swung a door open, and
I found myself outside baking under the sun again as an
odor like week-old roadkill smacked me hard in the face.

"What have you got out here?" I asked, trying to inhale
as little as possible.

Lanahan took a deep whiff. "I call this Skunk Alley in
deference to its highly noticeable aroma. It's where I bring
things to rot."

I pulled out a tissue and held it to my face. "You don't
happen to have Brady out here by any chance, do you?"

Henry chuckled. "Are you asking or requesting?"

He led me to the testing area, where three dead cows
were laid out several yards apart, all in different stages of
deterioration. Lanahan pointed to the one furthest along,
which had dried flaps of skin gingerly hanging from its
bleached bones.

"This one is old Gracie. She's the closest to the way we
found Annie McCarthy. Gracie's been dead for six weeks
now, so I think we can pinpoint Annie's demise at around
the same time."

This put a new light on the quit claim deed to Annie's
land. It appeared that Annie must have died around the
same time that Brian had signed and dated the form.

"Have you come up with anything else on Annie's
death?" I inquired.

"If you mean, was it a suicide as Brady insists, yeah.
I've got some information for you on that. I measured the
angle at which the bullet entered her skull. It came from a
good six feet away with the bullet penetrating at a down-
ward angle." Lanahan helped me swat a cloud of flies

away. "All I can tell you is that she'd have to have been one hell of a contortionist to shoot herself like that."

"What about the gun? Any fingerprints on it?" I asked, hoping for a break.

Lanahan shook his head. "Not a one, sport." He grinned as he caught my morose expression. "What do you want? Things to be clean and simple? Whoever did it thought the thing out."

The flies regrouped and buzzed past us, heading for a ripe carcass. I didn't bother to wait for Henry's lead. I made a beeline back to his office, having had my fill of rotting meat. Lanahan poured me a cup of black coffee without bothering to ask.

"What about drugs? Did you find anything there?" I wanted to make sure there was no mistake that Annie's death had been a murder.

Lanahan poured a wallop of half-and-half into his coffee, which was immediately transformed into tiny curds. "There was no sign of barbiturates, but my concoction did make for an interesting milk shake." Lanahan took a sip, curds and all. "I offered some to Brady, but he turned me down. I'm thinking of marketing it as a protein shake. What do you think? You can bet some numbskull in Vegas will buy it."

I was busy thinking about Annie's quit claim deed and all that it signified. If her death wasn't a suicide, the case would have to remain open. That was the only way I'd ever hand over the papers I'd found. Even then, I knew it was dicey. If Annie had truly been killed in order to snatch her claims, then there was also a good chance that the deed would disappear once it left my hands. One lonely old prospector's death didn't add up to much against Nevada's political landscape.

"Then Brady will be changing his report?" I asked, just to make sure.

Lanahan grinned. "He'll have to, won't he?"

Henry poured more expired cream into his cup, making me wonder if his olfactory senses hadn't been affected by too much time spent in Skunk Alley. "Don't expect much to happen, though. With the crime rate soaring every day in this county, the death of a hermit tends to rank low on Metro's totem pole."

The thought startled me. "Does that mean that no investigation will be done?"

Lanahan arched an eyebrow. "Yeah, there'll be one. Maybe a quick look-see around the year 2002, if you can wait. Unless she had some relatives who care to put up a squawk."

That didn't seem very likely. As far as I knew, Annie didn't have a single friend. Except for her dog, Annie had been as alone in this world as she now was in death.

"Sorry. Anyway, her death will officially be listed as a murder on the autopsy report, if that's any consolation," Henry informed me.

It wasn't. I felt discouraged and was about to leave when I remembered why I'd come in the first place. Reaching into my bag, I placed the five frozen tortoises on Lanahan's desk.

"I take it you didn't grab these from some tourist scavenging a few souvenirs," Lanahan remarked, eyeing the torts.

"Can't say that I did," I responded, knowing better than to say any more. "I was hoping you'd do an autopsy on them for me."

Henry gave a sigh as he picked up one of the flattened reptiles, holding it like a frisbee. "Gee, I wonder what could have possibly done them in?" he drolly inquired. "Let me guess. You're not chalking this up to suicide, either. Just what is it that you're looking to find?"

"I'm hoping the lab can prove that the tread marks on the shells were made by haul paks," I informed him.

Henry glanced up at me. "Haul paks, huh? Doesn't that fall under NDOW's job description? From what I hear, wildlife autopsies of this sort aren't done without Monty Harris's personal authorization. What with the mines being involved and all."

"That's what I hear," I confirmed.

"So in other words I would have to believe that these tortoises were found someplace other than on a mine company's grounds," Henry continued.

"That would make sense," I agreed.

"Because, God knows, you're not the type of gal who would twist things around just to get what she wants," Lanahan attested.

"Certainly not," I concurred wholeheartedly.

"Right. Porter, you're a pain in the ass." Lanahan winked as he picked up the pancaked torts and walked out the door.

Back outside, I found Pilot digging a hole in the lab's front lawn. I could only assume the dog had been bred with a miner's gene.

Lizzie was next on my list, and I headed for the county building. I cut through a maze of industrial back roads, preferring to stay off the Strip at midday, when tourists are on the loose. Besides, passing Vegas' string of hotels in broad daylight is like seeing a showgirl without her makeup on. Illusion is everything. Cruising the Strip at night provided me with my necessary quotient of glamour and glitz.

I parked next to some palm trees and let Pilot out to lie in the shade, with a warning not to uproot what little landscaping there was. Then I headed inside. Lizzie was ready and waiting when I got there.

"Here's the information on your boy at the lab, William Holmes. Brace yourself. You ready?" Lizzie looked like the cat that just ate the canary.

"Should I expect some ground-shaking news?" I was low on blood sugar and in bad need of some food.

"Damn straight. I did a hell of a job digging this stuff up. You wouldn't believe what a bitch it was," Lizzie complained.

"Alright! Here are your Ring Dings. What have you got?" I asked.

Lizzie tore into the pack. Catching my eye, she tossed

me one. "Why don't you ever buy any of these for your-self?"

"Diet," I mumbled as I blissed out on the first bite.

"Okay, here's the deal. It turns out that Billy Holmes is none other than Ed Garrett's nephew. My guess is Garrett got him the job."

Lizzie was right: the news *was* a shocker. Apparently nepotism was alive and well in Clark County. And how convenient. It left me wondering whether Holmes's theory on the break-in had been initiated by his uncle, or the other way around. Since Garrett didn't much care about the fate of tortoises, it was interesting to note that he'd set his nephew up in charge of them. So much for my plans to knock Holmes out of his job.

"What about Garrett?" I asked. "Were you able to get any more information on him?"

Lizzie licked bits of Ring Ding off her fingers. "Sure did. Seems he's been on Alpha's board for the last four years. But that's not all. He's got company."

Lizzie paused and waited. Digging through my purse, I pulled out a packet of Yankee Doodles and threw them her way.

"Good going, Rach. Okay. Two of our other upstanding commissioners are also on Alpha's board. Jim Borden and Mike Sears. What is it they say? Scum travels in packs?"

Obviously what was good for Alpha Development was also good for half the members of the county commission. It certainly gave Alpha a foothold for any federal land that might be released.

"By the way, how did the date go last night? Did you score?" Lizzie asked, grinning provocatively.

"Yeah. I landed myself a snake." And I didn't just mean the rattler I'd won. "Take a look at this." I dredged through my bag and pulled out Annie's quit claim deed.

Lizzie took the paper and read it over. "Yeah, so what's the big deal? It's a transfer of mining claims."

"The deal is that Brian told me Golden Shaft had never approached Annie McCarthy. He made a point of telling me that her claims were worthless," I informed her.

"Well, obviously this deed never went through. You can see that she didn't sign," Lizzie pointed out.

"That's what I want to check out. Do you think you can tap into the Recorder's computer system for me?" I asked.

Lizzie wiggled her fingers. "Not to worry. These little gems can find whatever you need to know. But listen, don't jump to conclusions so fast. There's probably some good explanation. After all, you like the guy, right?"

"What excuse can there be? That it happened to slip his mind?"

"Maybe he felt it wasn't important since it didn't go through." Lizzie thought a moment. "Or maybe somebody else John Hancocked his name."

I shot her a skeptical glance. The problem was, I wanted to believe her.

"It could happen. Suppose someone outside the mine wanted to impress Golden Shaft by getting the old woman to sign away her claims? Brian's signature could have been forged on the deed to make it look official." Lizzie gave a smug smile. "Case solved."

"Anyway, complications have arisen," I said, wanting to move off the subject. "Santou called. He's flying in tomorrow."

"Ooh! This is so hot." Lizzie gave a quick shimmy. "A love triangle. Wear the black dress again."

That dress had already gotten me in enough trouble.

"By the way, I need one more favor." I pulled out the turkey sandwich I'd brought for her lunch.

"What? No soda?" she pouted.

I produced a can of Coke from the bottom of my bag. "I need to get someone's home address."

"So why don't you just call them and ask for it?" Lizzie opened the sandwich and sniffed at the meat. "Ooh, real turkey breast!"

"I'm afraid that if I call, she'll recognize my voice," I explained. "And she may not want to give it to me."

Lizzie nodded understandingly. "No problem. Just give me the name and number."

I did so, and she picked up the phone and dialed Golden Shaft. "Is this Dee Salvano? Hi, I'm with Publishers Clearing House. I'm just checking to make sure you're the Salvano we're looking for. Did you happen to send in an entry a while ago? Great. One more question. I need to verify that you are the correct person. Could you state your address for me, please."

Lizzie wrote it down and gave me a thumbs up. "Thanks, Dee. You're one of our three finalists. We'll be in touch if you're the lucky winner.

"Ta dah!" Hanging up the phone, Lizzie handed me the address with a flourish.

"I'm impressed." The girl deserved to be a star. "But wasn't that a bit risky? After all, how do you know that she even bothers to open junk mail, let alone answer it?"

Lizzie took a bite of her turkey sandwich. "Get real, Rach. This is gambling country. Who's gonna live here and not bet on winning a cool million?"

Lizzie had a point. My bungalow was chock-full of magazines I'd ordered from entering contests and then never bothered to read. I picked up my bag and headed for the door.

"Thanks for the help, Lizzie," I said, waving good-bye.

"Make it tuna next time," she called after me.

The conservation center seemed to be the next logical place to hit, after learning about Bill Holmes's high and mighty connections. But Holmes was nowhere to be found. If any of the staff knew where he was, they weren't talking. I cornered a portly guy in baggy jeans with ragged cuffs for a quick interrogation.

I hit him with a right. "Does Holmes usually take days off unannounced?"

"I don't know," the young biologist ducked.

I hit him with a left. "Did he call in sick?"

"Can't say," the scientist swerved.

I countered with a jab. "Is he at home now?"

"I'm with the Smithsonian. I don't know where he lives," my opponent blocked.

I moved in for the kill. "Then he *is* at home!"

"It didn't come from me!" The biologist quickly turned and walked away.

Uppercut and knockout.

I jumped in the Blazer and pulled Holmes's list of addresses out of the glove compartment. I also dragged out a map, hoping to decipher my way. Then I stepped on the gas and made a beeline for one of Vegas's newer subdivisions.

Holmes's street address was in the middle of a ritzy development. I double-checked his list to make sure I hadn't gotten it wrong; but there were no two ways about it. Holmes was living among the *crème de la crème*. Either he was quite a nifty saver or something else was supplementing his income.

I pulled into his driveway and let Pilot out as I headed for the front door. The doorbell chimed a few classical notes, but no one was home. That made it the perfect time to snoop around. I peered through the front windows and saw that Holmes was sorely lacking in the decor department. A purple bean-bag chair sat plopped in the middle of the living room, positioned in front of a thirty-five-inch-screen TV. Above it hung a black velvet portrait of Elvis decked out in enough sequins to have made Liberace drool. There was no other furniture in sight.

I moved around to the back of the house as Pilot occupied himself marking the only bush on the grounds. Rounding a corner, I nearly tripped over a makeshift cactus garden badly in need of water. Next to it stood a small plastic pool that was bare. I pulled an empty bucket up to the back window and turned it upside down to stand on top, catching a glimpse of Holmes's kitchen. This room appeared to be a little more lived in, with a yellow Formica table and four green plastic yard chairs. A clock with dice in place of the hours hung above his stove. On the floor was a plastic mat with a water bowl and a dish full of food that looked crusty and old. I leaned in closer, pressing my face against the glass to get a better view, when something jumped up, startling me badly. A tabby cat rubbed its body against the window and then turned to hiss at me, warning away an unwanted intruder.

I retraced my tracks to the front of the house in time to catch Pilot uprooting the lawn. Fortunately none of the neighbors had appeared to scream at us yet. I decided to press my luck. Heading for the double garage, I jimmied the door, pulled it open, and walked inside.

A flashy red Miata sports car sat ready to rock and roll. I supposed that if you were going to live in a neighborhood like this, you had to at least give the impression you belonged here.

I looked around his garage. It was obvious that Holmes was no handyman; there were no tools in sight—only a large garden hose that lay rolled up in the corner like a sleeping boa. For a moment, I seriously thought about giving his cactus a spritz. I walked over and tapped the hose with my foot, and saw a can of spray paint nestled among the coils. Leaning down, I picked it up, curious as to what Holmes could be decorating. The color of the paint was a bright neon-green.

Like the stenciled tortoise I'd seen at the Center and the one in Annie's bathroom. My mind began to race. It seemed possible that an arrogant little twit like Holmes would have the audacity to steal tortoises right out from under the county's nose—and it would help to explain his influx of extra cash. But I couldn't see him as a cold-blooded killer. Still, how many people kept cans of neon-green spray paint hanging around?

I put the can back and left the garage, closing the double door. Pilot sulked as I dragged him away from his work in progress, refusing to get back in the Blazer until I gave him a rawhide bone. At this point, a can of neon green spray paint would only prove that Holmes had bad taste. I needed something more solid to go on. I pondered the problem as

Pilot proceeded to decimate his toy, but nothing came to mind.

I pulled out my cellular phone and checked the machine at work in order to kill some time. To my surprise, Harley's voice came at me loud and clear.

"Listen, Porter. I'm calling about the other day. We better talk. You're a newcomer to the West and have to understand how things work out here. So I'm gonna give you a second chance. Head on out this way again and it'll be one-on-one this time. Just come alone and you'll be fine."

Interesting that both Monty Harris and Harley found it necessary to teach me how things work in their West. Though it was like learning ethics from Machiavelli, I'd be a fool to turn down his invitation. But, if Harley thought I planned to set foot out there without Pilot, he was sorely mistaken.

I was still thinking about Harley when my cell phone rang. As far as I knew, only Sam had my number, and I seriously doubted that he'd interrupt his downtime to jingle me for a chat. I fumbled with the phone, finally answering on the fifth ring.

"Hello?" I half expected the call to be a wrong number.

"Back off, Porter," a mechanically distorted voice hissed in my ear.

I glanced around, as if someone might be there. But not a soul was in sight.

"Who is this?" I demanded.

"You value your health? 'Cause you're about to lose it," the diabolical whisper threatened.

God, I hated anonymous threats. "Yeah, that's what my personal trainer keeps telling me. You wanna give me a clue here, buddy?" I asked belligerently.

"This is your only warning," the metallic voice continued. "Either stay out of the way, or we'll blow your fucking head off."

"It's thoughtful of you to call, but how can I stay out of your way if I don't know what you're talking about?"

My question was answered with a click as the line went

dead. I had no doubt that the voice meant every word it had said. The problem was that the message could have come from anyone and been about anything. And I'd be damned if I'd wind up the subject of some hackneyed obituary without knowing why.

I thought about my anonymous phone call on the way out to Harley's. I wondered if Holmes had spotted me at his house and was trying to scare me off. It could also have been either Randall or Deloyd, frustrated that I had walked away the other day. Let alone anyone connected with the tortoises, Annie, or the mine. But none of that explained how someone had managed to get hold of my cell phone number.

As before, Harley knew I had arrived by the time I reached the top of his drive. Dressed in the same plain shirt and worn-out jeans, he sat motionless on his horse, appearing to view me with much the same interest he would an itinerant piece of tumbleweed. I got out of the Blazer as he silently eyed Pilot. Then he slowly raised his focus to me.

"I see you brought your dog again," Harley commented in a flat drawl.

A large chaw of tobacco was pushed into one side of his cheek, making me think of a squirrel storing food for the winter. Harley turned his head and spat out a dark stream of tobacco juice, staining the dry desert floor.

"He goes where I go," was all I said.

Harley pulled at the brim of his hat. "You know, I'd have shot you by now if it wasn't for the fact you're a woman."

He was clearly a dyed-in-the-wool sexist, but whatever kept me from being gun bait was okay by me.

"Hell, you might as well come on up to the house. No sense in us facing off here in the middle of the road."

I got back in the Blazer and followed him over the rocky dirt path that I assumed was his driveway. By the time we reached his ranch house, a large covey of miniature Harleys had gathered to greet us.

"These are my kids," he said with a dismissive wave of his hand.

He tied up his horse as Pilot and I got out of the car. I counted fourteen children in all, ranging from about two years of age to eighteen. Each had a mop of unruly blond hair and distrustful blue eyes, with a mouth that turned down as though they'd been regularly force-fed spoonfuls of cod liver oil. His wife was nowhere in sight. I figured she was probably too tired to venture outside.

I was wrong. I heard a crash inside the house and a scraggly cat the color of orange marmalade came flying out through the front door spread-eagled, and landed at my feet. The feline pulled itself up, took one startled look at Pilot, and the hair on its head flew up as straight as a porcupine's quills. Pilot let out a roar and started to lunge. I grabbed onto his collar and dug my feet into the ground, but the cat wasn't sticking around. Emitting a bloodcurdling shriek, it took off around the back of the house. A similar screech arose from inside the ranch.

"Stay the hell out of this goddamn house, you miserable critter, before I cook your skinny ass and serve it for dinner!" a woman's voice threatened.

Another crash added emphasis to her statement. Except for the part about the skinny ass, I hoped she wasn't talking about me. I ducked as a pie tin flew over my head, scattering the children in all directions. Then Harley's wife came into view.

"This here is LuAnn." Harley nodded toward her, keeping his eyes carefully aimed at the ground. LuAnn's frame filled the doorway. After bearing fourteen children, she had apparently lost all interest in her appearance. Or maybe it was in order to keep Harley away. Part of her hair was pinned on top of her head; the rest hung in ragtag strings down to her shoulders. A faded cotton housedress, held together in front by a series of safety pins, was splattered with the remnants of eggs and oatmeal from that morning's breakfast. While the kids had inherited Harley's eyes, there was no mistaking the fact that each had her mouth. Deep creases at both corners of her lips split the bottom half of her face lengthwise. Her eyes, small though they were, appeared even tinier, lost in a sea of flesh, while her nose had the width of an animal's snout, all adding up to a slightly piggish appearance. She clenched a sharp paring knife in a hand as pink and round as a ham while she sized me up as though taking my measurements for that evening's dinner.

"What the hell is she doing here?" LuAnn spat, never taking her eyes off me.

"We're gonna talk," Harley sheepishly explained.

"Not in my house you're not." LuAnn squatted down, throwing the paring knife into the wooden step in front of her. Pulling it out, she threw it again, her eyes darting back and forth between Harley and me.

I made an attempt to be friendly. "I'm just here to understand your position, Mrs. Rehrer."

But LuAnn wasn't buying. "My position is that the federal government is nothing but an invading army, and as one of its soldiers, you deserve to be shot, hung, and quartered."

Okay. Her position was pretty clear.

"The trouble is that unless things can be worked out, the fines you owe will go even higher—and no one wants you to lose your house," I explained.

A grin slowly spread across LuAnn's face that made my skin crawl. "Ain't no way we're losing this ranch, girlie. Before that happens, I guarantee you'll be dead."

"Are you threatening me?" I asked, knowing full well it went way beyond that. The woman was far more frightening than her notorious husband.

"Whatever it comes down to. Whatever it takes," she answered in return, staring me square in the eye.

LuAnn continued to gaze at me long and hard as she grabbed her paring knife and stood up. Then she walked back inside, slamming the door behind her.

"Maybe we better go for a ride," Harley suggested after a moment.

That sounded fine to me. I headed for the Blazer, but Harley's voice stopped me.

"Not in that. We'll go on horseback."

Call me a city slicker. Call me a coward. But I'd never ridden a horse. It just wasn't on my list of things I was burning to do.

I watched in silence as Harley brought one of his horses out from the barn. He saddled him up and handed me the reins. I began to panic as I looked at the animal that towered above me. I knew that if I refused to ride, I'd be knocked down about ten notches in Harley's eyes. I was left with little choice.

"What's his name?" I asked, stalling for time.

"Terminator," Harley replied without the hint of a smile.

Just perfect. I hooked my foot in the stirrup and grabbed onto the horn of the saddle, trying to throw myself up onto the horse's back.

"Done much riding before?" Harley drolly asked, as he watched me make a fool of myself.

"A little," I grunted, before attempting the impossible once again.

Harley finally got tired of waiting. "I'll give you a boost."

He pushed me up onto the saddle, where I viewed the world from a whole new perspective. One that was high and unsteady.

"I'm gonna take you for a ride on my range," Harley said.

He slapped Terminator on the rump and we took off.

"You mean the federal range, don't you, Harley?" I managed to sputter as I felt myself slip from side to side in the saddle.

Harley pulled up beside me and leaned over until he loomed in front of my face. "I'm the public, which makes me the owner of this land. You think you're gonna come out here and tell me what to do?"

I held onto the horn with both hands as I leaned forward to meet him. "Say what you will, but this is federal land, Harley. That means it's owned by the entire public, not just you. Which means you have to obey the rules."

Harley sat back and appraised me. "You're either stubborn or stupid, Porter. Either way, you're asking for trouble. I got my rights and I don't like something being crammed down my throat." He focused his baby-blue lasers on me. "You know, I could shoot you right now and no one would ever find you."

"Yeah. But then you'd have to deal with my dog." I bluffed.

Pilot was paying little attention to either of us, having already run ahead, delirious at the sight of a jackrabbit.

Harley pulled a pack of chewing tobacco out from his shirt pocket as he continued to ride. Extracting a wad, he shoved it into his mouth with fingers as rough and callused as a horned toad, adding onto the stash that was already there.

"You're killing our way of life out here in the West," he said in between chews of tobacco. "You're slowly destroying our heritage."

I wasn't about to be pinned with the guilt of doing in every cowboy. "I don't buy that, Harley. Things change everywhere."

Harley seemed to be more sad than angry. But only for a moment; then the old flame flickered back up.

"There's gonna be a war, Porter. It's being played out right here in the West. And it ain't got nothing to do with the public. It's the government that's building up for an attack, what with their 'copters flying around every night. The war is against us ranchers." A stream of tobacco flew out of his mouth. "What it all comes down to is lock up and lock out."

This thing about nightly government choppers was beginning to drive me crazy. It seemed as if everyone in southern Nevada had seen them except for me.

"The 'copters have to be from Nellis Air Force Base.

They're just out on practice maneuvers,'' I said. Close to Yucca Mountain, Nellis had always considered Clark County its own private shooting range.

But Harley shook his head in disagreement. "Whatever's going on, it ain't no practice session. These are big mother Black Hawks. They're never around during the day. Only at night. And they're always headed in the same direction."

"Where's that?"

Harley turned in his saddle and pointed due south in the direction of the Golden Shaft mine. That made no sense. Either there was one more riddle to unravel or too much desert sun had caused paranoia to run rampant among the local conspiracy loonies.

We reached the top of a butte, where we stopped the horses to look out over hundreds of acres below. Dotted with creosote and the occasional cactus, there couldn't have been any more desolate land.

"Ain't it beautiful?" Harley asked, reveling in the harshness of the desert spread out before us. "This is what life is supposed to be. That's the problem with you easterners and those gobbledygook bureaucrats back in D.C. You think you're roughing it if you can't walk out your front door and see a Circle K or a 7-Eleven. But this is enough for me."

He was right about one thing. What we saw before us was well on its way to becoming a bloody battlefield where everyone—miners, ranchers, and realtors—was scrambling to stake their own claim without regard for the land or its critters.

Harley chewed on his tobacco in silence before turning to me. "Things got out of hand the other day."

I felt that was putting it mildly.

"You don't really believe that environmentalists are dumping tortoises on your land, do you?" I prodded, hoping Harley would admit to the absurdity of the notion.

"Damn right I do," he responded. "Not that I blame you personally. Hell, Fish and Wildlife has been paying those wackos to dump the critters ever since they were placed on that damn pinko endangered list to begin with.''

It was nice to know there was something Harley didn't blame me for. But this was the first time I'd heard that this had been going on for years.

"What makes you think this has happened before?" I asked.

Harley looked at me as though I'd just dropped in from the moon. "This ain't the first time that damn Center's been broken into, you know. How else do you think we got these damned four-legged cabooses all over the place?"

I felt sure he'd been fed this line by someone with an interest at stake. "Who's been telling you all this?"

A smug look spread across Harley's face as he realized the information was news to me. "Ed Garrett. And that's at the risk of losing his job, you know. Garrett says Fish and Wildlife has been salting our land with lots of endangered things.

"That's why we've finally drawn the line in this old desert sand. The Foundation told Garrett that something has to be done, and he agrees. He stands by us ranchers and by God, we're gonna stand by him. We're gonna make sure the county commission is the highest law in this land."

I looked around, realizing that I had yet to see one tortoise so far on our ride across the range.

"So when do you usually spot all these tortoises?" I asked Harley.

"What are you talking about? They're around here all the time," Harley replied indignantly, boosting himself higher in his saddle.

"Then why haven't I seen one the entire time we've been out here?"

Harley's eyes narrowed and his lips compressed into a thin, straight line as he stared at me, his mind working overtime to come up with an answer.

"It's because they're smart," he finally sputtered.

"You mean they know I'm here and they're hiding?" I questioned.

"Could be," Harley spat back, not looking in my direction. His face was a mass of red blotches as he worked hard to control his anger.

I leaned over to give Terminator a pat on the neck and nearly fell out of the saddle. I quickly pulled myself back up, hoping that Harley hadn't noticed. "Maybe they're afraid I've come to take them back to the Center. Do you think that could be it?"

Harley whirled his horse around to face me, one hand twitching above the .45 holstered on his hip.

"Goddammit, Porter," he exploded. "You damn well know that they're being dumped here so that you can swish your fanny onto my land and tell me I gotta stop grazing my cattle. But I got news for you, lady: we went and got ourselves a smart lawyer who's gonna sue the pants off your goddamn agency. If I were you, I'd start looking for another job real fast."

Harley didn't wait for my retort as he nudged his horse and began to move down off the butte. But it wasn't the same way we'd come up; as I watched in horror, Harley disappeared straight down over the vertical side.

"You've got to be kidding," I muttered, my heartbeat pounding into overdrive.

I could opt for the slow and easy way down, but I had the feeling that Harley wasn't in the mood to wait for me— which meant that Pilot and I would be left to aimlessly wander the range. I held tightly onto the saddle horn, the reins clenched in my fists, took a deep breath, and followed Harley over the edge.

Pilot leapt ahead of me, nearly tumbling down the hill before regaining his balance. Mustering his dignity, he looked back at me and then bounded off to catch up with Harley. I now understood how Kim Novak must have felt in *Vertigo*. I shut my eyes tight and clutched Terminator's neck for dear life, hoping he didn't get fed up enough to toss me off. By the time we reached bottom, my clothes were soaked, more out of fear than the heat. When I opened my eyes, I found Harley waiting with Pilot, a maddening grin plastered across his face.

"Have a nice ride?"

I didn't bother to answer. Harley would never have to resort to violence to keep his ranch. All he had to do was drag the big boys in Washington down off their thrones and onto a horse for the ride of their lives. They'd end up giving him whatever he wanted.

We rode together for a while, the quiet of the desert repairing my ragged nerves.

Harley finally broke the silence. "This visit was a one-time deal, Porter. My word still stands as far as federal agents coming onto my land," he warned.

I studied him, wondering if a showdown was in my future.

"Would you really shoot a federal agent?" I quietly asked.

"Like LuAnn said, whatever it comes down to. Whatever it takes. The only way I'll be taken off this land is in a pine box."

I watched Pilot jump back from a whiptail lizard that was standing its ground.

Harley looked me in the eye. "I'm warning you, Porter. Try to seize our cattle or land, and there'll be ranchers here with guns to blow you away. You don't stand a chance. Give it up and head on home."

I had no intention of packing and running. Not on someone else's terms. Not to please Harley or Garrett or Monty Harris or Holmes. What I did have was a final question for Harley. I let go of the horn and finally began to relax in the saddle.

"By the way, Harley, who's footing the legal bills for this lawyer of yours? He must be costing a bundle." It had to be more money than Harley and the other ranchers could afford.

Harley was silent for a long moment. He chewed on his stash while watching the sun begin its descent for the day. "I don't think that's any of your business, Porter."

Maybe not. But I had a gut feeling that whoever was shelling out the bucks had a big interest at stake.

"I don't see why you can't tell me, unless something underhanded is going on," I prodded. "Could it be the reason I haven't seen any tortoises on our ride out here is because you've been rounding them up to sell in Pahrump?"

Harley snorted at me in contempt.

"It would certainly be one way to pay off your legal bills," I added.

I watched as Harley's face turned a deep red.

"You're crazy, Porter."

"That might be," I agreed. "But I could always start an investigation in order to find out what you're up to. Of course, that would mean federal agents coming onto your land. You'd get to have your showdown, Harley—ready or not."

Harley shrugged his shoulders, knocking off a fly that had attached itself to a drop of perspiration on his neck. "Lots of folks are helping us out. Mostly members of the Foundation."

It made sense that the local county supremacy movement would be kicking in money. But I wanted specifics.

"Sorry, Harley. Not good enough," I told him.

Harley stared at me as if pondering whether to kill me now or wait till later. "Alpha Development Corporation. Heard of them? They've been helping us out. Ain't anything illegal about that, is there?"

Nothing illegal, but definitely intriguing. It was also becoming obvious that Garrett was cleverly pulling Harley's strings. As a director on Alpha Development's board, Garrett could only be interested in one thing—kicking the feds out in order to build on public land. If Harley wasn't careful, he might have a 7-Eleven outside his door sooner than he could have ever imagined.

Eleven

By the time I left Harley's, my stomach was rumbling and my stash of junk food was dangerously low. Pilot and I stopped at the Mosey On Inn, where Ruby took pity and fed us both meatloaf for dinner.

"Make any headway on those runaway tortoises yet?" Ruby inquired as she wiped off the counter with a brown, scummy rag.

"Not a bit," I admitted. I had no desire to explain that so far, my major discovery was a can of neon-green spray paint.

"Word has it that a big shipment of those critters landed in Pahrump," Ruby revealed. "But don't get all riled up to hop on over there. Those four-legged Volkswagens have already been scooped up."

"How do you know that?" I wondered if Ruby had somehow been involved in the deal.

"Heard there was some big-ass Chinaman's festival over around Fresno a ways. A wedding or something. Those torts were on special order. At least, that's what I heard. The evidence has probably all been eaten by now." Ruby threw a dollop of thin, gray gravy over a hard lump of instant mashed potatoes on my plate. "By the way, I could use a can of hairspray the next time you're around."

I knew exactly what she liked: the kind of lacquer that would keep the Empire State Building from falling down.

When I finally headed back out, it looked as if someone had thrown an assortment of tempera colors into the sky, fingerpainting the sunset that appeared before my eyes. I pulled out a map, along with Lizzie's piece of paper, and took off to track Dee Salvano down.

Night had closed in quickly by the time I found the wooden sign for Feather Lane Drive. I swung onto the dirt road and turned on my brights, dodging rocks and sneaky ruts along the way. Every once in a while a pair of eyes would flash in front of me, burning into the night with the intensity of meteors ablaze. Surprised by the intrusion, their owner would quickly scamper away. After a few minutes I spotted a glimmer off in the distance, smack dab in the middle of nowhere.

I approached to find the light emanated from a squat concrete structure with a battered red pickup out front. I pulled up next to it and studied the house. An array of colored bottles, all sizes and shapes, was perched on the windowsills. A wooden signpost pointed the way to Hong Kong, London, and Paris—the kind of places most people usually dream about going. A movement caught my eye as one of the window curtains, pulled slightly aside, quickly fell back into place.

I left Pilot in the Blazer and navigated the rocky path up to the house. I was just about to knock when the door was yanked open. Dee stood with a shotgun in hand, bathed in a pool of light. She took a quick glance around and then reached out to grab me. Pulling me inside, she shut the door.

Her mound of brown hair was askew, as if a rabid coon had been trying to claw its way out, and her eyes verged on bloodshot. There was the unmistakable scent of beer on her breath.

"You got a hell of a lot of nerve coming here, Porter," she glared at me. "Maybe you don't give a shit about your own ass, but now you're putting my life on the line."

I hadn't expected this kind of outburst. After all, Dee had been the one who had tipped me off about the mine to begin with.

"It's kind of hard to get you on the phone for an in-depth conversation. I felt face to face in private would be best,'' I responded.

"You take an awful lot for granted, then,'' she snapped back.

"What do you think? That there's someone outside spying on you?'' I joked.

"Wouldn't surprise me a bit. Don't you know who you're playing against, Porter? Nobody screws around with the mining industry in this state. Especially not Golden Shaft. Hell, they just gave NDOW five hundred thousand dollars for being good boys and keeping their nose out of the way,'' Dee groused.

I imagined that with five hundred thousand dollars you could buy an awful lot of fax machines—and a good deal of cooperation.

"Hell, if they're out there, they've seen you by now. So you might as well sit down and have a beer.'' Dee turned and walked over to the fridge.

The place was a lot homier than its outside would have led me to believe. Every spot was filled with knickknacks, as if a carnival had just passed through town, unloading its wares. Small stuffed animals dominated most of the space. I picked up a toy tortoise as Dee flipped me a Coors.

"My husband bought me those,'' she commented, popping open a can.

"Does he work for the mine, too?'' I asked.

"Used to.'' Dee held the cold can of beer to her face. "He died three years ago. His first job was to pick up dead wildlife on the grounds and throw their carcasses into shafts in order to get rid of the evidence. Felt so bad about the whole deal that he'd go out and buy me a stuffed animal each time. I ended up with a hell of a lot of them.''

Dee plucked a toy dog from the pile and hugged it to her breast. "You got that dog of yours out there in that truck?''

I nodded.

"Well, bring him the hell in. No sense in him sitting out there, either,'' she said, putting the toy back in the pile.

I went outside to get Pilot, looking to see if I could spot anyone. But the desert was quiet and dark. Pilot trotted into the house, where Dee gave him a bowl of water and a dog biscuit.

"Have you got a dog, too?" I asked, surprised not to have heard any barking.

Dee gave Pilot a pat on the head and then straightened up. "He was shot. Got onto the mine grounds, where one of the guards killed him."

I started to say I was sorry, but Dee cut me off.

"Hell, Golden Shaft got my husband, as well," Dee sighed. "He fell into a mine shaft one day. Usually you can survive that sort of thing, but he broke his neck on the way down."

I opened the Coors and took a sip. "I'm surprised you still work there."

Dee stared at me a moment. "Like I told you before, there ain't much choice out here. I'm too old be a stripper and the 7-Eleven don't pay near as well. What the hell else am I supposed to do? You gonna give me a job?"

Silence descended, broken only by Pilot lapping the water.

"Tell me, why is wildlife even kept in the freezer if no autopsies are done?" I finally asked.

A sly smile stole across Dee's face. "Nice touch, ain't it? That's so a few can be handed over to NDOW every now and then. They do some kind of slapdash look-see. And sure enough, it always turns out that the critters died of natural causes. Funny about that, huh? Never seen so many things just keeling over dead in one place."

Dee wiped her mouth with the back of her arm. Putting down her beer, she took a plate of stew out of the oven.

"A few autopsies a year by NDOW seems to keep you feds from snooping around, and business goes on as usual." Dee sat down at the table, kicking out a chair for me with her foot. "You had supper yet?"

I looked at the plate of grisly meat and bones, and thought about the dead critters piled up in mine shafts.

"I'm fine, thanks. Is the mine giving money to anyone else that you know of?"

Dee thought for a moment as she chewed on a piece of mystery meat. "There's the county commission. They get a nice chunk of change. The mine calls it community relations. I call it more like greasing the monkey, if you know what I mean."

"I met Ed Garrett the other day. He certainly didn't seem too concerned about winning my vote," I informed her.

Dee wiped up some greasy stew with a slice of bread and stuffed it into her mouth. "Garrett's twenty-five percent jerk, seventy-five percent slime and a hundred percent asshole. But he sure as hell has been stopping by the mine a lot these days."

"Any idea why?" I asked.

"Sometimes the management calls a meeting of all the employees, hoping to get us riled up about federal restrictions. It's all because of Garrett's agenda for county supremacy. But I can tell you that Garrett's got a lot of backing from workers at the mine. Mining is Nevada's gravy train and anything that gets in the way is bound to get run over."

Dee wiped a trickle of gravy from her mouth and put her plate down on the floor, where Pilot promptly lapped up the leftover bits of meat and gravy.

Dee grinned at me. "Betcha didn't know that Golden Shaft has filed a patent to purchase all the land they have claims on."

She was right: it was news to me. Brian certainly hadn't mentioned it. What I did have some knowledge of was the Mining Law of 1872, also known as the Eleventh Commandment. It allows mining companies to purchase public land they have claims on for just five dollars an acre—making it private property on which they can do as they please. One company had recently purchased twenty-seven hundred acres, containing 15.8 billion dollars' worth of minerals, for a paltry sum. Some in Congress called it highway robbery and were working hard to change the law. I mentioned as much to Dee.

"That's why Golden Shaft is pushing to get this patent through as fast as possible," she explained. "They don't want Congress screwing things up."

My guess was that Golden Shaft's next best hope lay with Ed Garrett and his resolution to force the release of all public land in Clark County.

"Do you know if Golden Shaft purchased any of Annie McCarthy's claims?" I probed.

She shook her head. "Nope. Haven't seen a thing on it. But it shouldn't be too hard to sniff around and find out."

I pulled out Annie's quit claim deed that had been signed by Anderson, and showed it to Dee.

"Is that Brian Anderson's signature?" I asked, holding my breath.

"Well, it says Brian Anderson, don't it?" Dee stated, pouring two cups of coffee.

"But does it look like the real thing?" I persisted.

Dee studied it closely. "Sure does to me." She shrugged her shoulders. "Can't blame old Annie. Most small miners dream big-time of selling to a company like Golden Shaft. Otherwise their claims ain't worth dogshit. God knows, prospectors don't have the money to mine for themselves. But if a mining company buys them out, prospectors are usually cut in on a share of whatever minerals are found on that land."

I wondered if selling to Golden Shaft had really been Annie's dream. There were mining companies that played fast and loose, snatching up claims and patenting land without any plans to ever mine it. The land was bought for close to nothing, then immediately sold to a developer for a small fortune.

"By the way, do you know anything about helicopters flying around the Golden Shaft at night?" I inquired.

Dee clearly wasn't counting calories as she dumped three teaspoons of sugar in her coffee along with a dollop of cream. "Oh, yeah. I hear they've been dropping off some equipment at the mine."

"At night?" I asked. "Why would they do that?"

"How the hell should I know?" Dee pulled out an apple pie from the cupboard.

"Are they government helicopters?" I pressed.

"Listen, I usually leave the mine at six-thirty and come straight home, before any of that goes on. What do you want to know for?" she asked, slicing off two big hunks.

I took a bite of the pie. Fortunately it was better than Ruby's. "A lot of ranchers think government helicopters are flying around, planning some sort of invasion."

Dee guffawed. "Yeah. That's their black ops conspiracy theory. Those jackasses are a bunch of loony tunes any way you slice 'em or dice 'em."

She noticed I had cleaned my plate and loaded on another piece of pie before I could refuse.

"So how did you like sleeping with the enemy the other night?" she asked. "Or ain't he the enemy no more?"

"I didn't sleep with him," I replied, guilty about the erotic fantasy that even now spun through my mind.

She gave me a sarcastic look. "All dolled up in that dress? I find that hard to believe."

"Believe what you want," I answered abruptly.

Dee shrugged. "Whatever you say—but it might have been better if you had. Seems our foreman found a bunch of tortoises missing from the freezer and is on a rampage. A word to the wise? Keep out of the way till things blow over." She sipped her coffee. "Of course, if you were to hear of any autopsies verifying that haul paks ran them over, I'd sure like to know."

"You'll be the first," I promised.

Harley had exacted his revenge. By the time I got home that night, every muscle in the lower portion of my body was moaning and groaning. I walked up to my front door with all the grace of a broken-down, eighty-year-old wrestler who'd taken on Hulk Hogan, and been whupped.

Santou was coming in tomorrow. I knew I should spend what was left of the evening cleaning up the debris that littered my house. Instead, I dug out a dirty pot and threw in some oil to pop up a hefty bowl of popcorn.

Pilot grabbed a rawhide chew toy, joining me in the living room, where I turned on the TV and plunked down on the couch, popcorn bowl firmly in hand. After today's Dale Evans adventure, I figured I'd earned a few hours of unqualified rest.

An insistent drumming in the background verified that Lizzie was home and on automatic pilot, her tap shoes pounding to the strains of *42nd Street*. I made headway on the popcorn as an old James Bond movie reeled me in, forcing me to deal with the quandary of deciding who I'd rather be: Bond taking on the bad guys or an eternally young blonde who looked good in both a bikini and an evening gown while lolling on the French Riviera.

I was edging toward the good life as a blonde when Pilot suddenly started to growl, a low, primal rumble that began in his belly and worked its way up to a snarl, threatening to spill into all-out war. I watched in awe as the hair on the back of his neck rose like an unfurling flag. His eyes blazed with a deep reddish glow, reflecting the scarlet gown of the Bond babe, and my arms began to goosebump as I followed Pilot's eyes to the door.

I picked up his chew toy and tried to renew his interest, a blatant attempt to calm my own nerves. But Pilot's eyes remained fixed on the door as his growling escalated, growing more and more intense. Suddenly he broke into an ear-shattering bark, and I jumped, heaving the bowl of popcorn into the air.

A set of car headlights blasted through my front window, framing me in their glare like a deer being jacklighted for the kill. At the same moment, the shrill ring of the phone tore through the room. My heart pounding, I searched for the phone in the blinding light, cursing as I tripped over the popcorn bowl. I picked up the receiver and covered my other ear tightly with my hand.

"Hello?" I screamed over Pilot's frenzied barking.

The same distorted voice I'd heard earlier sliced through the cacophony like a finely honed stiletto. "You're toast, Porter."

The hum of an empty line blended with Pilot's roar as he began to fling himself against the door.

And then the pieces fell into place. My heart clenched as if it were pressed between two heavy steel plates, and a cold wave of shock raced through me, throwing every one of my nerves into fast forward.

Grabbing Pilot by the scruff of the neck, I pulled him away from the door with more force than I ever knew I had, dragging him into the kitchen and out the back, until we were flattened against the chain link fence like two prize specimens about to be mounted. I threw my arms around his neck and pulled him close, burying my face in the warmth of his back. We formed a tight ball of skin and fur as an explosion shook the air, roaring in search of us through the house, burrowing its way under the ground, tracking us to where we were huddled, defenseless, like two sitting ducks with nowhere to fly.

My ears throbbed from the shock wave of sound. After an endless moment, the roar scaled down to a numbing ringing. A shrill shriek penetrated the hum, and I opened my eyes to see where the sound was coming from.

Lizzie stood on the other side of the low fence, her face a mask of fear, her mouth wide open to allow for the scream that shook her body. She held a flashlight clenched in her fist as she stared at the bungalow which was emitting smoke like a chimney.

I wrapped my fingers around the chain link and slowly pulled myself out from under the debris, then staggered toward Lizzie, who burst into tears.

"I thought you were dead!" she wailed, throwing her arms around me.

Funny about that. So had I.

"What the hell happened?" she asked, hysteria tinging her voice. "Did your oven explode?"

Black eyeliner and mascara ran down her face, giving her the appearance of a porcelain clown.

"I think it was something a little more dangerous than the oven, Lizzie," I replied, looking toward the house.

Lizzie's eyes grew wider.

Grabbing her flashlight, I willed my legs to move, feeling like a marionette cut loose from its strings. I warily approached the bungalow with Pilot close at my heels. Automatically pulling my SIG-Sauer from the back of my pants, I held it tight. It gave me the reassurance I needed to approach the dark doorway that loomed ahead.

I walked into what had been my kitchen and stopped dead. I no longer had to worry about cleaning up for Santou. What I needed was a new house. Dishes lay broken on the floor, and shards of shattered glass contributed to the obstacle course. But that was nothing compared to what awaited me in the living room. Dirt and debris were now the main decor, having turned my formerly pink carpet to a morose shade of gray. My living room windows no longer existed. All that was left were remnants of the sills.

I had thought my couch couldn't be any more ragged. I was wrong. Large mounds of shreds were decorated with sharp pieces of metal where my head had been only minutes before. Clumps of foam rubber stuffing were everywhere, looking like runaway globules of chicken fat. But the *pièce de résistance* was the TV. It could have passed as a dead ringer for the ones that Elvis had taken his frustrations out on. Exploded glass lay everywhere. It was at times like this that I was glad I'd never spent money on properly furnishing a place. On the other hand, the Salvation Army was about to have a field day with me now.

I picked my way through the wreckage. Amazingly, the bedroom had escaped most of the damage, remaining relatively intact. It was nice to know I still had a place to stay.

I headed out to the front yard to examine the damage from another angle. Stepping over the remains of my front door, I was confronted with what looked like ragged snow-flakes lying on the ground—except these flakes had deadly sharp, serrated edges glittering under the open expanse of sky. I took a closer look. The pieces had come from my mailbox. I glanced over to where it had once stood and saw that I wouldn't be receiving mail anytime soon. The Postal Service was definitely not going to be happy.

The clash of discordant sirens filled the air, and I watched as a fire engine and police car battled it out to reach the scene first. The Metro car swerved into my drive-way and slammed on the brakes in a show of triumph. Unfortunately it was Brady who pulled his carcass out of the car.

He swaggered over to me, both thumbs stuck in his waistband. A toothpick was lodged in his teeth. Flicking it with his tongue, he took a gander at the house and then eyeballed me.

"What the hell happened here?" he asked, digging out a sliver of food from between his teeth. He removed the toothpick and examined his new-found treasure before swallowing the evidence.

"It seems someone took a dislike to my house," I answered.

I looked at his receding hairline and wondered how long it would be before Brady rushed off to the nearest Hair Club.

He stared at me suspiciously. "Who the hell have you been pissing off lately, Porter?"

"You mean, besides you?" I asked, watching as he dug around for more tidbits from dinner.

Lizzie appeared on the scene, picking her way through the rubble. For the first time, I noticed that she was dressed in a teensy turquoise satin outfit with a flared skirt. The net petticoat just barely covered her rear end. Her black patent leather tap shoes caught the moon, reflecting two pools of light. She must have been rehearsing a number for the one-woman show she swore she was putting together. Either that, or she was even stranger than I had imagined.

But the outfit worked wonders on Brady. He stared at her with the rapture of a man totally bedazzled. In return, Lizzie gave him all the attention she might lavish on a squashed bug.

I allowed a decent interval of time to pass before I dragged his attention back to the matter at hand.

"Brady—my house? Remember? There's been an explosion?"

He wrenched his eyes away from Lizzie and finally noticed the silver fragments scattered about my lawn.

"What's this?" he asked, picking up a piece.

"It used to be my mailbox. Maybe we should consider that the bomb was planted there," I suggested.

"What bomb is that, Porter?" Brady snarled, annoyed that I had disturbed his mating dance.

"You know. The one that just blew up the front of my house." I was at least equally annoyed.

"Don't jump to any hasty conclusions. I'm the officer on the scene. I'll check this out and decide what took place here," Brady intoned with all the authority he could muster. He bestowed a manly smile on Lizzie, who continued to ignore him.

"Then you might not want to contaminate the evidence by picking it up with your bare hands, Brady," I suggested. Flirtation be damned—someone had just tried to kill me. "I think Lanahan should be called in on this. Don't you want him to check for gunpowder residue on some of these pieces?" I asked.

Brady glared at me. "I already thought of that."

"So you've already called him?" I persisted.

"No, but I'm about to! Jesus, let me handle this, will you? Or are you a cop now as well?" Brady shoved past me. "Has anyone ever told you you're a real ball-buster, Porter?"

"Never heard that one before," I retorted as he stomped back to his car.

Firemen were parading in and out of my house in search of a fire when I heard a loud crash. I whirled around to see my neighbor Roy Jenkins stumbling down his front steps, an AK-47 swinging in his hands. He lurched over to where Lizzie and I stood, and stared in silent tribute at the blown-out windows of my bungalow.

"Shit, Porter. You have a party and forget to invite me?" A gooey red liquid that could have been either blood or tomato sauce ran in thick streaks down his beard and onto a dingy white tee shirt. "I told you I'd do bodyguard duty, babe. You should have taken me up on it."

Lizzie and I drew back as his breath slithered over, wrapping around us in a death grip of pizza and booze.

"What a choice," Lizzie commented. "Terrorists or Roy."

She was right; it was a real toss up.

He suddenly began to weave back and forth, as if being pushed and pulled by unseen hands. "I don't feel so good," he muttered.

As we watched, Roy slowly crumpled to the ground and curled up, his AK-47 cradled in his arms.

"Would you believe he started out studying for his Ph.D. in engineering when he first moved here?" Lizzie shook her head sadly. "A living example of one man's evolution from a nerd to a turd."

Roy let out a belch as he rolled onto his back.

Lanahan must have been close by. He made it to my house in under three minutes.

"Lovely place you have here, Porter," Lanahan said with a grin. Stepping over Roy's inert form, he tiptoed around the wreckage. After pulling on a pair of latex gloves, he began to bag and tag the evidence. "I see you're managing to stay as popular as ever. Any idea who did this?"

"That was my question, Lanahan." Brady walked up beside us. "I'm still waiting to hear the answer."

"My list keeps growing," I informed them.

Brady snorted. "Why don't I find that difficult to believe? Look around, Porter. You've made someone seriously angry. If I were you, I'd work hard on narrowing that list down mighty fast. After all, you don't want to put your neighbors, like this pretty little lady, in jeopardy, now, do you?''

Lizzie rolled her eyes as Brady puffed out his chest, pretending to survey the scene. He finally noticed Roy on the ground, snoring away in ignorant bliss.

"Friend of yours, Porter?" he smirked.

I was tempted to pick up Jenkins's AK-47, but held myself back. There had been more than enough excitement for one night.

Brady sauntered over to Lanahan, stepping on evidence along the way. "What have you got so far, big guy?"

He bent down as Lanahan stood up, nearly knocking them both over.

"Man, I hate these late nights," Lanahan yawned. "Vigilantes can be so inconsiderate."

"Did you find anything?" Lizzie asked anxiously, wrapping her arms around her bare shoulders.

Brady noticed she had begun to shiver and diligently ran to his patrol car to fetch his jacket.

Lanahan stretched, glanced over at Lizzie, took in her outfit, and smiled. "Busby Berkeley's *Gold Diggers*. Am I correct?"

Lizzie looked at him in amazement. "Hey! I'm impressed."

"Yeah. People are always bowled over that a guy who spends his time with dead bodies would know about anything else," Lanahan joked.

Enough was enough, already. I felt as if I was going to have to wriggle into one of Lizzie's outfits just to get this investigation off the ground.

"Has any evidence turned up in the rubble so far?" I asked.

Lanahan smoothly clicked into his crime scene mode. "Plenty of it."

He held up a baggie containing metal pieces that glimmered under the near-perfect moon. "Seems someone planted a pipe bomb in your mailbox, lit the fuse, and whammo! You're left with one hell of a mess.''

Brady's car radio crackled off in the distance as the fire engine pulled away, having decided there was little risk of my bungalow spontaneously combusting.

Lanahan was right about the mess. My front yard resembled a battlefield. There *was* a war going on—one that had begun to focus on me.

I felt a heavy weight along my leg. Pilot leaned against me, wondering why we were up so late past his bedtime. I wondered where we were going to bunk down for the night.

Fortunately Lizzie came to the rescue. "Why don't you grab whatever clothes you can and bring them over to my place? You're moving in with me.'' She put her arm around me, and my body relaxed, the adrenaline draining away as if a plug had been pulled. I was tired, though I fought hard not to admit it. Somebody had me dead-on as a target, and I couldn't afford to let my guard down.

"Hey, Porter—you're quite a gal. Seems you landed a doubleheader tonight,'' Brady announced as he pulled the AK-47 out of Roy's arms. Then he gently laid his jacket across Lizzie's shoulders.

"What are you talking about?'' I asked. Fatigue had now settled in like an occupying army. My eyelids felt as if they had ten-pound sandbags weighing them down.

"A call just came over the radio. Apparently your office got hit as well.'' Brady's hand lingered on Lizzie's shoulder. She moved away so his fingers rested on nothing but air.

My first thought was of Sam. He would probably kill me before another bomb could do me in. He had warned me that the last thing he wanted was any kind of trouble, with his retirement inching closer by the day. I had the sneaking suspicion that this would surpass even his worst expectations.

I worked my way through the rubble and back into my house. Quickly packing a suitcase, I also grabbed the duffel bag containing Annie's letters, along with the quit claim deed. Then I headed over to Lizzie's.

A convertible couch was already unfolded and dressed with cool, fresh sheets when I got there. They beckoned seductively and I gladly gave in. I tried my best to convince myself that sleep was just a nod away, but my fears overwhelmed my fatigue. I squeezed my eyes tight, hoping to block out the explosion that had begun a strobe flash in my brain, and breathed deeply as my fingers slowly curled up, hibernating in the palm of my hands. But my nails dug too deep, leaving crescent trails of terror. Hard as I tried, there was no escaping it. My demons had come to taunt me again.

Twelve

The sun was already sautéing Las Vegas by the time I woke Lizzie the next morning. We walked outside, where slivers of metal made a path from the road to my house as if paving the way to Oz. Roy was nowhere in sight. I figured he'd been picked up by a UFO, abducted by a band of roaming gnomes, or had made his way home. What was new was the yellow ribbon of police tape plastered to the front of my house. Ignoring it, we dragged over a roll of heavy plastic and tacked it up where the windows and door had once been, even though it stood about as much chance of keeping intruders away as I had of throwing a sit-down dinner party and serving the meal on fine china.

With that done, I headed over to the office to check out the damage. There had been plenty. The furniture was a total write-off, and wiring and plastic from our only computer were scattered across the floor like day-old party favors. Coffee stains added to the ambiance, splattered against the wall from the pot I'd forgotten to empty. The only upside was that I no longer had to worry about the paper work I'd never caught up with.

I entered Sam's office where paintings of his beloved cows now decorated the floor. Picking up the phone, I discovered that it miraculously still worked—which meant there was no getting around it. I dialed the number to Sam's ranch. Sitting amidst the debris, I was glad there was a state between us.

"Jesus Christ, Rachel! If this is what happens during

your first three months on the job, what's gonna happen after I leave?'' Sam demanded, though his voice was filled with concern.

Fortunately I didn't have to answer.

"And I might as well tell you now," he continued, "it seems the shit has hit the fan."

My heart thumped in my chest as I waited to hear that I had been fired.

"The regional director called yesterday demanding to know what the hell you've been up to. Seems you got Monty Harris's skivvies all tied in a knot. The man is running around screaming about how you've been stepping on NDOW's toes."

Evidently Monty had found out about the tortoises disappearing from Golden Shaft's freezer.

"I told the director that the problem, as Monty sees it, is that you're doing your job." Sam's chuckle took me by surprise. "So congratulations, partner. With all the ruckus that's been stirred up, you've just inherited the title of newest SOB in town."

I let out a sigh of relief. If I had Sam backing me up, everything was alright. At least as far as my employment status was concerned.

"Sorry about all this, Sam," I said, sounding a bit too cheerful.

"Sorry's fine, Rachel. But it ain't gonna keep you alive. Whatever it is you're into, you better back off," he advised.

"That's the problem: it seems I've struck a nerve, but I'll be damned if I know what it is," I told him.

Sam clicked his tongue in disapproval. "You making any headway on those missing tortoises yet?"

"Sam, why didn't you tell me that these break-ins at the Center have been going on for years?"

A long pause crackled over the line before Sam spoke again. "That's because it's news to me. There's never been a report of any goings-on there before. Could be that you've stumbled onto something. In fact, I wouldn't be surprised to find out that Gorfine and Georgia have been staging the break-ins—you know, stirring the pot to brew up some trouble.''

He warmed to the topic. ''Hell, for all we know, they could have set off the bombs! The man's a damn physicist, spending his time frying his brain in the sun, for chrissake. Who knows what he's up to?''

Noah might have been a lot of things, but I doubted that a mad bomber was one of them.

''The way I see it, the bombings could just as easily have been the work of ranchers blowing off steam,'' I responded.

But Sam was determined to place the blame on Noah. ''Don't be crazy, Rachel. These ranchers are solid family men. They aren't gonna kill some female agent and her dog for no good reason.''

Obviously we weren't eye to eye on this one.

''Just don't go running off and doing something stupid,'' he warned. ''I don't need to start over with another replacement just yet.''

Sam paused, and I knew I was in for more pearls of wisdom.

''You gotta be smart and have patience, Rachel. Just like those old wily coyotes. They always get what they want. I've seen 'em take a whole week to kill a calf, just biting a little snippet off the critter's tail each day. You gotta do the same if you want to make any headway on this job. This is the West you're dealing with.''

So everyone kept telling me. I wasn't likely to forget.

''And don't worry. I'll help you fix up the office as soon as I get back,'' Sam promised, before signing off.

I hoped he planned on bringing a construction crew with him, as well.

I was still at the office, picking through bits and pieces of rubble, when the phone rang. Its buzz jangled my nerves, and I picked up the receiver warily, afraid someone was checking to see if I was alone.

''Rachel, are you alright?'' Brian sounded sincerely concerned. ''I heard you had some trouble last night.''

"I'm fine," I answered, the phrase echoing like a skipped record in my mind.

"I was worried," he reprimanded me. "I warned you to be careful, that you were playing with fire. Remember I told you not to dig too deep? Now you can see I was right."

I felt like a truant schoolgirl who'd been called in for a scolding. "Do you know something I don't, Brian? Because I'm having a hard time unraveling what this is about."

Brian's voice scaled back a notch. "All I'm saying is, let things cool off. Take it easy for a while. Deal with routine business only."

"Would you care to define that for me?" I snapped.

"Come on, Rachel; you know what I mean. Do the things every other government employee does: answer phone calls. Write a few letters. Catch up on some old reports," he suggested. "I know that your office got hit, but there must be somewhere you can sit and do that kind of work."

I was as likely to sit around and do nothing as I was to get up on a Las Vegas stage and shimmy. He had pricked a nerve. Once again I was being told to be a good girl and keep my nose out of trouble.

"Is that what you do, Brian? Just enough to get by on the job?" I prodded.

My question was met by a long moment of silence.

"I care about you, Rachel. I just don't want anything to happen," Brian finally responded.

I felt myself begin to soften in spite of my anger.

"How about I pick you up this evening and we go somewhere quiet? Someplace without rattlesnakes in jars or bombs going boom in the night. Just you and me and a nice desert sunset?" Brian asked.

It was tempting. I came close to accepting, when I remembered that Santou was coming to town.

"Sorry, Brian. But I'm going to be tied up for the next few days," I told him.

His voice was tinged with disappointment. "Do you at least have a place to bunk down?"

"Yes, thanks. I'm staying with a friend for a while." I didn't offer to give him the number.

"Then just promise me that you'll watch your back," he said.

I promised, feeling slightly guilty, as if I were cheating on the man by seeing Santou. It wasn't until I hung up that I wondered how he had managed to learn of the bombing so quickly. And how he knew just where I could be found.

With a few hours still to kill before Santou's plane landed, I decided to pay lab boy a visit. My plan was to confront Holmes with the fact that this wasn't the first tortoise theft at the Center; it was just the only one he'd ever bothered to report.

Fortunately he had decided to show up for work today. I walked past the display of dead wildlife and down the hall, where he was conferring with a girl whom I recognized as a pretty, part-time staffer. His hand brushed against her leg as she giggled, making me wonder if I had possibly overlooked a wry sense of humor on his part. I decided not. More likely, the girl was bucking for a full-time position.

Holmes caught sight of me out of the corner of his eye. Leaning in toward the babe, he whispered something in her ear as his palm lightly grazed her fanny. She turned to stare at me before walking away.

"So did you find my tortoises yet, Porter? Or are you too busy dodging bombs these days?" Holmes asked, pushing his tortoiseshell glasses up the bridge of his nose.

It appeared that news traveled fast.

"I wasn't aware that those tortoises were your private property, Bill," I replied. The fact that he thought of them as such made it all the more interesting. "By the way, how did you hear about the bombing?"

Holmes snorted, shoving his hands deep into the pockets of his lab coat. "Are you kidding? You're the talk of the town. Not only are you unable to find three hundred and fifty missing tortoises but you somehow manage to get your office blown up in the process. I'd say that's right up there in the ranks of royal screwups.''

I didn't care whose nephew he was. The kid was going down.

"Well, Bill, that's one of the reasons I came by to see you today,'' I informed him.

"Sorry, but I'm not available to help solve the case,'' Holmes snickered. "I can only do one job at a time. So I'm afraid you're on your own with this one, Porter.''

The overhead fluorescent light cast a shadow on the acne scars that were lodged in his face, giving him a sinister air.

"Speaking of royal screwups, I had an interesting talk with Harley Rehrer the other day. You've got quite a history at this Center. It seems these tortoises are just part of a long line of reptiles that have turned up missing. Why is it that the others were never reported before, Bill?' I asked.

The real question, why he had decided to report the theft this time, hung silently in the air.

Holmes's eyes nervously swept the room before he answered. "Those other tortoises you're referring to were picked off by ravens.''

I knew what ravens were capable of. Sam and I had come across the carcass of a newborn calf one day when we were out in the field.

"You see that? It was pecked and poked and ripped until the poor little fella just laid down and bled to death,'' Sam had observed. "Hell of a way to go, but that's ravens for you.''

While it was common knowledge that the birds considered baby desert torts as irresistible as I do a chocolate sundae, one thing didn't make sense.

"You mean they were snatched up like a platter of hors d'oeuvres from inside their cages right here at the Center?'' I questioned.

Holmes bared a set of incisors that would have been the envy of any rat. "I used to place them outside during the day.''

"Still, there must have been tops on the pens. No one could have been naive enough to put them outdoors unprotected." That would have been like telegraphing a free-for-all at the local Denny's.

"No, Porter," Holmes growled. "Something dug its way inside the enclosures to feed on them."

A faint sheen of perspiration dotted his brow.

"Hmm. So ravens dug their way under the fences. Pretty unusual, don't you think, Bill?"

"I don't know—we're still working on it." William spat out the words.

Like old wily coyote, I kept snipping away at his tail. "But Harley was told the incidents were all thefts. Uncle Ed said the same thing."

"I can't control what my uncle says, Porter. He's his own man. It doesn't necessarily mean that it's true."

"In other words, he has a tendency to lie?" I waited for an answer.

Finally Holmes said, "I didn't say that. What I'm telling you is that I'm not responsible for what those ranchers think."

"I suppose your uncle could have said the tortoises were stolen and dumped in order to rile up the ranchers. It's certainly one way to rouse the natives. If nothing else, I bet that would ensure their vote for your uncle's resolutions. Make sense to you, Bill?" I asked.

Holmes continued to stare without saying a word.

I decided to try a different approach. "By the way, you weren't at work the other day, so I stopped by your house to try and catch you. Those are pretty fancy digs you manage to juggle on a government salary. Wish I could afford something like that."

Holmes ran his tongue along a lip heavily coated with chapstick. When he spoke, his voice was thick and low.

"Maybe something can be worked out to accommodate you, Porter." He waited for me to answer, the skin beneath his eyes beginning to twitch. "Would you like that?"

What I'd like was to catch Holmes red-handed. "If I

didn't know better, I'd say that comes close to sounding like a bribe—which might lead me to suspect you've been stealing and selling the tortoises yourself. A cash business like that would make for a tidy profit."

Though a drop of perspiration rolled down Holmes's temple, he didn't make a move to wipe it away.

"It would be easy enough to blame a group of crazy environmentalists. After all, what rancher around here wouldn't love to believe that eco-nuts are in cahoots with the government?"

William's fingers jerked nervously, as if they had been hooked up to electrodes and were receiving a series of tiny shocks. "Interesting theory, Columbo. But that would be pretty hard to prove," he said.

I decided to call Holmes's bluff. "Not necessarily. There's that wildlife dealer in Pahrump. What's his name? Wes Turley? He's passed on word that he might be persuaded to talk for the right price."

His face turned pale and his body visibly sagged as he leaned against the wall.

I turned up the pressure. "But what I'm still trying to figure out is your tie-in to Annie McCarthy. Other than the tortoise imprint found on her bathroom wall, of course."

"I don't like your accusations, Porter. I had nothing to do with the murder of that woman. I never even heard of her until now." Holmes's twitch traveled up into his hands as he brushed a lock of hair from his brow. "You'd make better use of your time by questioning those eco-nuts I told you about. I'd bet that tortoise symbol is their calling card." He forced a tight smile.

I studied his features, wondering how he had gotten away with the scam for so long. And what it would take to catch him.

"If you didn't know until now who Annie McCarthy was, how did you know she was killed?" I asked.

Holmes pushed away from the wall swiftly, bringing his face to within inches of mine. "Fuck you, Porter. You'd do better to concentrate on your own situation. That bomb didn't get you this time, but it could the next. Or maybe it won't be a bomb at all.''

His eyes danced wildly. ''What is it that frightens you, Porter? Think about it real hard. And then imagine that someone out there knows what scares you as well.''

My fingers strayed to my throat, where I could still feel the blade that had seared through my skin only months ago, back in the bayou.

Holmes gaze followed as he laughed soft and low. ''You've got proof of nothing, Porter. I'd advise you to leave me alone and worry about your own skin.''

I no longer had any doubt as to who had stolen the tortoises or where they had ended up. It was with thoughts of knives and bombs and Holmes's laughter ringing in the air that I headed out to the airport to pick up Santou.

HORICON PUBLIC LIBRARY

Thirteen

I watched from inside the terminal as a long line of passengers made their way off the plane and down the set of portable stairs. One by one, their feet hit the tarmac of McCarran Airport. And then he appeared. At first indistinct, like a far-off mirage in the middle of the desert—but I knew it was Santou from the way my body began to vibrate, like a tuning fork reverberating in perfect pitch.

Santou walked toward me, his black, tousled curls shimmering under a white-hot silver-dollar sun, his gaze locked on mine like a heat-seeking missile. But it was the unexpected lopsided grin that did me in. How could I have ever left the man?

I didn't have time to contemplate that thought as his arms wrapped tightly around me. I shivered and took a deep whiff, breathing him in, drowning in his scent, not wanting to let go. After a moment, he kissed my forehead lightly and broke our embrace.

"It's been so long, I almost forgot what you look like, *chère.*" Santou laughed softly, but there was an unmistakable edge to his voice.

Those weren't the first words I had hoped to hear. I glanced down at his carry-on luggage and didn't need to ask how long he'd be staying. It was obvious the visit would be a short one.

As we walked through the terminal, his fingertips lingered on my back and then just as quickly jumped off, sending every nerve ending in my body on high alert. It was apparent that Santou was as nervous as I was.

It had been three months since I'd seen him, and our phone calls had been few and far between. I glanced at him and wondered if I had only imagined the bond between us. But the heat was still there. I could feel the sexual tension as strong as a magnet, causing my skin to sizzle at the thought of his touch.

Pilot was waiting in the Blazer as we approached, his huge head following our every move. But it was Santou he focused on as he barked, gruffly sounding a warning.

Santou scanned Las Vegas's hodge-podge skyline off in the distance, with its post-modern confection of pyramids and castles. It was only as I went to the driver's side door that he suddenly realized that the giant dog with bared fangs, looking directly at him, was mine.

He silently studied Pilot before turning toward me. "Tell me that's not your vehicle, Rachel. Even better, tell me that *loupe-garou* passing as a dog has nothing to do with you."

I relaxed as Santou's Cajun swept over me, taking me out of the desert and drenching me in the patois of the bayou.

"Sorry, Santou. But they're both mine." I grinned, reveling in the game. "Pilot's part wolf, but he's definitely no ghoul." I opened the door and the dog proceeded to lick the back of my hand, never taking his eyes off the man next to me. "Besides Lizzie, he's the best friend I've got in this town."

I didn't yet fill Santou in on the fact that if it hadn't been for Pilot, I might be splattered across my yard at this very moment along with my mailbox.

Santou cautiously opened the passenger door as Pilot continued to growl, refusing to budge an inch from the front seat.

"Would you mind telling your best friend to back off and give me some room?" Santou asked, a touch of impatience creeping into his voice.

Instead, I handed Jake a dog biscuit and watched as he slowly made the peace offering. Pilot grabbed the cookie in one fell swoop, nearly lopping off Santou's fingertips in the process.

Santou gave me a sidelong glance. "Nice manners. That's one hell of a job you've done training him, Porter. What does he do for his next trick? Bite off my head and play ball?"

I scratched Pilot behind the ears and then ordered him into the back seat. "What can I say? He's very protective."

"And here all this time I thought you didn't need protecting," Santou retorted.

A few more lines had furrowed his brow since the last time I had seen him, and more strands of silver had crept into his hair. Santou had been born brooding. But now something else was there as well.

Digging inside his shirt pocket, he produced a pair of sunglasses and stuck them on. I'd never known Santou to wear shades before, either on the jazz-soaked streets of New Orleans, dripping with steam and *café au lait,* or the humid country bayous with only their ghostly fringe of Spanish moss for shade. I wasn't sure why, but I found it unnerving.

I pulled out of the airport lot, past the imported palm trees, and headed for home. The rosary beads hanging on my rearview mirror swayed in their own rendition of a hula. Santou gently fingered the onyx and garnet strand he had given me.

"Then you didn't forget me, *chère?*" His voice was quiet and low, but a rasp crept into it that scraped at my heart.

"I could never forget you, Jake," I replied, and I meant it. I'd opened my soul to the man, something I considered more frightening than any pipe bomb.

Santou was silent as we drove down the broad streets. We passed one bungalow after another with their picture-perfect patches of lawn as green as newly minted astroturf, denying that this was really the desert.

I pulled into Lizzie's drive and turned off the engine.

"So this is where you live?" Santou asked as he surveyed the place.

"No. Actually, that's where I live." I pointed to the disaster next door, with its littered front lawn and decor of bright-yellow police tape. "This is just where I'm staying since a pipe bomb went off in my mailbox last night."

After a long pause, Santou quietly asked, "Why does that make sense to me?"

He got out of the Blazer and walked over to my ramshackle bungalow to take a closer look. He kicked among the debris before letting loose a low whistle. "I know you like excitement, *chère*. But I think this is taking it a little too far."

As I told Jake about Pilot's frantic barking last night, followed by the phone call, the lines in his face tightened. He took off his sunglasses, and I saw that the crow's-feet around his eyes were deeper than before. Some hidden demon was voraciously eating away at him.

"I think you just used up your second life, Porter. Maybe it's time to rethink things." Santou walked back toward me and for a brief moment a flicker of anger flashed over his face. "This is more than a dart game you're playing here, *chère*."

"You mean that's all I was doing back in New Orleans, Santou?" I snapped without thinking.

Jake studied my face, bringing his fingers up to lightly graze my cheekbones before sliding down to rest on my lips. I knew something was wrong, even as a shot of heat raced through my body.

"Just don't use up the rest of your seven lives too fast, Porter. You'll screw up my plans." Santou stretched and then grinned. "Well, it doesn't look as if we're staying here tonight. What say we find us a big, brassy place in Vegas and get a room? I'm in the mood for a drink and some dinner."

I took a deep breath and let go of the tension that had begun to coil in me. "That's a good idea. Let me just take Pilot inside and write Lizzie a note."

I fixed Pilot a bowl of dry dog chow mixed with beef stew, then tacked a piece of paper onto Lizzie's fridge, explaining that I'd see her in the morning. Pilot quickly ate and then licked my face, settling down on one of my old shirts to indulge in his favorite activity of chewing on a shoe. Satisfied that everything was in order, I headed out the door. Santou was still digging through the clutter in front of my house.

"You might as well come inside. There are a few things I need to get," I said.

I limboed under the police tape to untack the plastic sheet that had become my front door. Santou followed me in.

"Too bad you didn't see the place before this happened. It looked great," I lied through my teeth.

I walked into the bedroom and went straight for my closet, where Lizzie's black dress beckoned like a siren luring me onto the rocks. I pulled it out, along with a few other items as I planned my Vegas weekend. Santou spent the time taking in the damage, then made his way into the bathroom, where he dug through my medicine cabinet.

"What's this? You getting ulcers these days, Porter?"

I turned to find Santou standing in the doorway, holding the bottle of Mylanta. My face flushed, and I busied myself with packing. But his eyes burned into my back. I turned around once more, and this time Santou pulled me close, his breath hot on my hair before moving past my ear to linger on my neck as his lips touched my flesh, sending my pulse rate soaring. His hands slid up my back, where they burrowed under my tee shirt whipping it off in a flash. And then I was pressed against him, caught up in a vortex of emotions. I moaned as his body molded itself to my contours. Even though I'd dreamt of it most mornings and every night, I'd forgotten what Jake's touch was like. His fingers lightly played along the tips of my breasts. I shivered. And then I gave in—not that I really had the willpower to resist him.

We made love with an urgency that took me by surprise, then lay on my bed and let time slow down again. I wanted to ask him if this was the first he'd slept with someone since we were last together. But I held myself back, afraid of the answer. Or even worse, fearing he might tell me a lie.

After showering, I was tempted to put on my tee shirt and jeans again, but decided to be brave and opt for the dress.

Santou gave a low whistle as he walked out of the shower. "Your taste in clothes has improved, *chère*. You look great."

In keeping with Vegas tradition, I let Santou hold onto the illusion.

The sun was just beginning to slide below the horizon like a huge, golden slot-machine slug as we made our way into town. I pulled into the Treasure Island Hotel, where a valet dressed to resemble Blackbeard demanded my keys, holding the Blazer for ransom. We quickly checked in and then headed outside.

"Let's walk around for a while before dinner," Santou suggested, as a horde of senior citizens stampeded by. "I want to get a feel for this town."

We rounded the corner, onto the Strip, where a British frigate and a pirate ship were exchanging cannon volleys in the hotel lagoon. Farther down the road, a fifty-four-foot, man-made volcano was spewing flaming fireworks high into the sky, geysers of ruby-red water running down its smooth slopes. A hurried blur of plaids and polyesters, shorts and mini-skirts, crowded the streets, single-mindedly intent on spinning the wheel and rolling the dice, already mentally making their bets and spending their money.

We hadn't gone far when we spotted a man dragging a huge crucifix strapped to his back. Garbed in a full-length burlap robe and sandals, he sported a long, white ponytail that hung down past his shoulders. A trail of splinters followed behind him.

"A little late for Good Friday, isn't it, fella?" Santou queried as we crossed paths with the Vegas prophet.

"Pray for your salvation," the old man replied tersely.

He nailed Santou with a look, biblical fervor burning in his eyes.

"I think he has a point," Santou muttered as we passed him by.

The infernal clang of slot machines, Vegas crickets, filled the night air, and miles of neon outshone the stars. We came to a Crayola-colored replica of New York City, complete with the Empire State Building, the Statue of Liberty, Grand Central Station, and the Brooklyn Bridge.

Santou ran a hand through his thick, tangled hair, his fingers snarling in the disarray of curls. His shirt clung to his chest as tiny beads of sweat soaked through the thin fabric. He folded his arms tightly against his body and took a long look around, then peered at me over his beak of a nose, like a raptor intent on skewering its prey.

"Looks like you hit the jackpot, Porter." An edgy note crept into his voice. "This is some kind of town. Home away from home, complete with pimps and hookers, crackpots and pipe bombs. Hell, you've even got the skyline of New York to keep you company."

Santou seemed to be spoiling for a fight, and I wasn't about to disappoint him.

"Except for the skyline, do you want to explain to me just how all this differs from Bourbon Street in New Orleans?" I inquired.

"Less silicone there," Santou dryly replied.

A babe dressed head to toe in spandex sauntered by, making me glad I had worn Lizzie's dress. The competition was tough in this town.

"I think what I need is a drink. Lets go someplace typically Vegas. I want to make sure I get the full exposure," Santou remarked, his eyes following the hip-swinging spandex.

The man's attitude was beginning to grate on my nerves. But if that's what Santou wanted, I'd make sure he got a megadose of glitz.

It was a toss-up between the MGM Grand, with its Flying Monkey Bar, laser thunderstorm, and neon rainbow, and the Luxor Pyramid, complete with belly dancers and chariot races, along with an overabundance of whips and chains. I opted for the Luxor. If we were going to duke it out, it might as well be somewhere with weapons on hand.

We arrived at the Antechamber Bar, where a woman swathed in ivory chiffon and a cheap Cleopatra wig held a harp between a pair of monumental breasts that could have been chipped out of marble. A few glassy-eyed drunks stared off into space as she plucked the strings and sang that all-time-favorite lounge tune, "Send in the Clowns."

Santou was rarely relaxed, but tonight he looked even less so. A wound-up intensity radiated from him, and his fingers drummed a hard, uneven tune. It was obvious that the man hated Vegas. I just couldn't figure out why.

"Hey, Santou—lighten up. Just think of this trip as a weekend in a schizophrenic theme park," I suggested. "You know, kind of like Mickey Mouse meets Barbarella."

Santou stopped drumming his fingers as he took in the scene. "You got a point there, Porter. If New Orleans is one big Mardi Gras, this town is the Devil's own version of Disneyland. I keep expecting to find Minnie dancing in a G-string and Mickey standing on the corner selling crack." He pulled a pack of Camels from out of his pocket and lit one up, inhaling deeply.

"Since when did you start smoking?" I asked in surprise.

Jake took another drag and smiled, a nervous twitch tugging at the corner of his mouth. "Bad habit, *chère*. I'd dropped it for a while. But it seems I've started up again."

"Any other bad habits pop up that I should know about?" I asked lightly.

Jake gazed at me from under heavy lids, but his eyes weren't giving away any secrets. I knew Santou was filled with a bevy of them. He'd divvied out a few in the past as frugally as if they were cultured pearls. One had been his former addiction to cocaine.

"What kind of bad habits would you be talking about

now, sugar?'' His voiced wrapped around me in a sinuous embrace.

"What choices have I got?" I teased.

Santou winked as he finished his scotch and quickly ordered another. "You got plenty. But don't worry about me, darlin'. I've got everything under control. What I want to hear about right now is you."

I obliged by filling him in on my interconnected cases along with their growing casts of characters. Jake silently swirled his scotch, meditating on the deep golden liquid, as I ended with the pipe bomb.

Santou took a deep drag on his Camel, emitting a cloud of smoke as billowy and white as a small atom bomb. He watched it slowly evaporate before he spoke. "You know how this stuff works, Rachel. We trip across things all the time during investigations. The problem is you don't even know that it's there until all of a sudden it snaps up at you. And the kicker is that what you've stumbled upon usually doesn't have anything to do with what you were investigating in the first place."

Santou downed his second scotch in no time and motioned to a scantily clad waitress for another.

"It's always something that nobody ever wanted you to trip across. And that's when you get a bomb hand-delivered to your door." He leaned forward, locking his gaze onto mine. "You know what that tells me, *chère?*"

I shook my head, as I watched him take a large slug from the glass that had promptly appeared before him.

"It tells me that you should back off. I got a bad feeling about this one. And this time I'm not here to protect you," he said.

Santou had pushed the wrong button, knowingly or not.

"I wasn't aware that that's what you'd done in New Orleans, Jake. I thought I'd pretty much handled that case on my own," I reminded him angrily.

Santou slowly stubbed out his cigarette, grinding it into the ashtray until only a few shreds of tobacco clung precariously to his fingertips.

"Is that what you thought, Porter? Well, then, let me fill you in." His eyes sliced through me and his voice was low and cold. "Nobody does nothing all on their own. That's how you get yourself killed. You don't want a man backing you up? Fine. Then go find another hotshot woman like yourself to cover your ass. 'Cause there's no way you can do it solo and live long enough to brag about it."

Santou's words hit me harder than I wanted to admit. I prided myself on working alone, on not showing fear, on not depending on a man. If I was with Santou, it was because I chose to be. Not because I needed to be. The same attitude extended itself to my work.

Santou leaned back in his chair, and for the first time I noticed a slight tremor in his hand as he lit up another Camel. A dark curl had fallen onto his forehead, where it hung loosely against his damp brow, giving him the air of a dissolute rogue.

"Look, Porter. All I'm saying is back off of this one. My gut instinct tells me that something's not adding up. There's more to this case than angry ranchers or miners or a few pissed-off animal dealers." A cloud of smoke trailed out of his mouth.

"It must be that Cajun sixth sense of yours, Jake. The question is, would you back off if it were your case?" I quietly asked.

Santou rubbed the stubble on his chin, his eyes dancing over the black dress as he took in every curve. A low chuckle escaped his lips. "No. I can't say that I would."

"Then don't ask me to," I said, trying to keep the lid on my temper.

All the noise and flashing lights seemed to have become louder and brighter than just a moment ago, making me dizzy. It was as if the wine was going to my head, though I had yet to finish my first glass.

Santou reached across the table, slowly entwining his fingers in mine. "It's just that I've got enough on my platter back home. I don't want to have to worry about you out here as well, *chère*."

"That's easy," I responded with a casualness I didn't feel. "Then don't."

Santou said nothing as we paid the tab and headed out to find a restaurant. We ended up instead at the Hard Rock Casino bar, with its head-splitting *ching, ching, ching* of slot machines as hypnotized, dead-eyed johns automatically fed their habit one coin at a time.

I watched as Santou ordered yet another scotch. I was tired of playing the game. "What's going on, Santou? There's something you're not telling me."

"What makes you say that?" he asked, not looking in my direction.

"The way you're drinking yourself into oblivion," I shot back.

Santou turned his laser-sharp gaze on me, reeling me in and not letting me go. "I've already tried that, Porter. It doesn't work."

I glanced around at the autographed Bob Dylan guitar hanging above the window where a few lucky winners cashed in their chips, at the row of slot machines announcing their dedication to help save the rain forest, and wondered what the hell we were doing here.

"Just what is it that you like about Vegas anyway, Porter?" he asked gruffly.

Santou's voice wound itself deeper and deeper through me until it tugged at my heart. At the moment I wanted to be anywhere *but* Vegas, with its nonstop noise and miles of neon, its windowless, time-warp casinos pumping in oxygen to keep you awake, its token-toting grannies and plastic-perfect women who only made me feel anxious about growing older and more out of shape. But I was damned if I would admit it.

"You want to know what I like about Vegas, Santou?" I replied in a voice that dared him to stop me. "What I like is walking into a restaurant at four in the morning and deciding if I want breakfast, lunch, or dinner. I like the fact that I can drive like a speed demon all through this town. I find it comforting that there's a constantly changing world of transients I can get lost in. And I can relax knowing that this place has no past with bayou ghosts dragging me down.''

The scar on my neck had started to throb, bringing back memories of my close call in the swamp. At the same time, I remembered Holmes's mocking laughter from earlier today, and a shiver rippled through me as the roar of last night's pipe bomb echoed in my ears. In my heart, I knew that whatever I was onto was still out there, and more likely than not would strike again.

Santou carefully gauged my mood. "This is also a place with no future, Porter. Or haven't you noticed?"

I dug into a bowl of pretzels that appeared before us, not knowing what to say. Santou was good at letting me rampage on before jumping in to catch me off guard.

"Take a good look around, Rachel. There ain't nothing here. It's all window dressing with empty space inside." He leaned forward with such intensity that I found myself holding my breath. "Stay here, *chère,* and you'll lose your soul."

It was then that I realized that Santou was afraid. I finished my mouthful of pretzels, anxious to ask the million dollar question.

"What frightens you so much about all this, Jake?"

Santou stared at me until I began to wonder if he'd heard my question at all.

"You. You scare me, Rachel."

I felt my mouth drop to the floor. It was the last thing I'd ever expected him to say. "Why?"

Santou downed his scotch, looking as if he were about to take a flying leap off a cliff. "Because I need you in my life and I've never needed anyone."

It was what I'd been waiting to hear for the past three months, ever since I'd left New Orleans and Santou behind. Now that I had, it scared me to death.

"Marry me, Rachel."

My breath caught in my throat, and my pulse took off on a marathon race, charging through every vein in my body. Santou was watching me closely, and I knew I should answer but couldn't think of the right words to say.

"And then what?" I finally managed to blurt out.

Santou shrugged. "I don't know. What do married people usually do, *chère?* Buy a house and go into debt. Raise a couple of kids. Grow old together."

I tried to catch my breath, but my heart was pounding faster and faster until I could barely hear Santou's words over the roar that was filling my ears.

"I want you to come home with me, Rachel. I'm tired. I've been through the wars and more relationships than I want to remember. I'm ready to settle down. What do you say?"

I watched Santou's lips and tried to focus, even as my mind ran at full throttle. Somehow being tired didn't seem like a good enough reason for a lifelong commitment. As for kids, I'd always appreciated the fact that they belonged to somebody else. And I intended to fight old age kicking and screaming every step of the way, no matter the number of nips and tucks or how much liposuction it might entail.

I had finally come face to face with that invisible line of commitment I'd always been afraid of, and it loomed as wide and as deep before me as a bottomless pit.

I said the first thing that popped into my head. "You're drunk, Santou."

I tried to look as calm as I could, given the fact that I'd broken into a cold sweat.

"And you're scared, Porter," he responded, as objectively as a surgeon making the first cut. "What are you afraid of? Settling down and having to deal with another person? Or finally facing yourself?"

It was a question I didn't want to think about it, let alone answer.

"Say yes, Rachel. Jesus, I may be a little worn around the edges, but I ain't exactly dog food yet." He grinned at me as he reached for my hand. "What is it that you New Yorkers say? So what am I—chopped liver?"

I couldn't help but laugh. It was true that Santou was

moody and dangerous. That's partly what attracted me to him. It was also what made him pure trouble. I knew my friend Terri would have been kicking me by now, calling me a fool for not lunging at the offer. And he was probably right. What the hell was I waiting for?

"Come on, Rachel. Let's do it. Right now," he coaxed.

I couldn't tell if Santou was speaking or if it was my inner voice urging me to take the leap. But I felt myself nod as if in a trance, no longer responsible for my own actions.

I immediately found myself walking out the door, following Santou's lead. The night air was thick as Georgia molasses and my limbs felt heavy as dough. I watched Santou hail a cab, and before I knew it, we were standing in front of the Marriage License Bureau. Thirty-five dollars and five minutes later, we were back out on the street.

"You got a preference of chapels, *chère?*" I heard Santou ask.

I shook my head, unable to speak. Hopping back into a cab, we passed the Little White Chapel, famous for its drive-up wedding window along with the fact that such celebs as Joan Collins and Michael Jordan had been married there.

"How about this one, sugar?" Santou's question wafted by me.

I again managed to shake my head, all the while maintaining a plastered-on smile. We whizzed by the Little Chapel of the West, the Wee Kirk o' the Heather, and the Hitching Post before coming to a screeching halt in front of the Graceland Wedding Chapel.

I felt sure I was dream-walking as we entered the chapel door. Inside stood the live embodiment of Elvis, complete with oversized paunch, sideburns, and sunglasses as dark as a lunar eclipse. Looking as placid as an old southern hound dog, Elvis waited to officiate, decked out in a plunging V-neck burgundy velvet jacket studded with rhinestones that fought to stay closed over his girth. Wide lapels framed an array of gaudy gold chains nestled in an overgrown forest of chest hair.

Fortunately another couple was ahead of us, ready to roll the dice, call out 21, and play those fifty-fifty odds by taking the plunge. The bride was a down-home version of Courtney Love, attired in a stained, baby-blue nightgown and a fur headband. The groom stood nearby, shifting nervously from one leg to the other, obviously uncomfortable in his rented black tux.

My legs gave way and I sank into a pew as I heard the ceremony begin. Elvis solemnly recited the vows, which the bride chirped eagerly after him:

"I, Ginny Lee, take you, Tommy Joe, as my hunka hunka burning love. And promise always to love you tender. And never return you to sender. Or step on your blue suede shoes. I'll never treat you like a hound dog. For you'll always be my lovin' teddy bear."

The room started to spin, and I got up and staggered outside. Leaning over, I took in deep gulps of air, hoping that if a UFO was ever going to abduct me, to please let it be now. Then I felt Santou's hand on my back, searing straight through my dress and into my skin, as I struggled to straighten up with some semblance of dignity.

"You're right, *chère.* That's a little too much. How about we just go on back to the Little White Chapel?"

Santou's voice sounded a million miles away.

As much as I loved him, I was terrified out of my wits. "I can't do this, Santou. I can't go through with it. Not now. It's all just too fast."

The truth was that I didn't know if I could ever go through with it. I was petrified that marriage could be the ultimate mistake. To top it off, I wasn't ready to call it quits and head back to New Orleans, placing myself back under Charlie Hickok's imperious thumb.

If Santou had been drunk before, he was dead sober now. He wrapped his arm around me, pulling me tightly to him. Lifting my mane of curls, he nuzzled my neck. His other hand explored the contours of my dress until I felt my self-control begin to waver.

"If this is too fast for you, *chère,* come back with me to New Orleans and we'll do it there," he whispered in my ear.

I pushed away gasping, breathless as a fish out of water. In my mind, marriage meant losing my independence along with losing control. I'd worked too long and too hard to throw that away. To mention nothing of the fact that I wasn't the type to walk in after a hard day, slap on an apron, and whip up a home-cooked meal, let alone keep a house spotless.

Back in New York, I'd failed as an actress. I had no intention of returning to New Orleans to fail as a wife. I had compromised my sense of self too many times for too many men to do it again.

"I need more time, Santou," was all I could say.

Santou looked as if I had slugged him with all of my might. He turned without another word and took off down the street and out of sight.

I stood there as the happy young couple came out, blissfully unaware that anyone else existed. Then I felt a heavy arm drape itself across my shoulders.

"That man of yours gone and got cold feet, darlin'?"

I turned my head to find the pompadoured replica of Elvis at my side.

"I'm afraid it was the other way around, Elvis."

"Darlin', nothing comes easy in the course of true love. Just remember what wise men say: Only fools rush in."

The gold frame on Elvis's sunglasses was alive with the reflection of neon lights, capturing the soul of the Vegas Strip in his wraparound band.

"Isn't that from one of your songs?" I ventured a guess.

"Yes, it is, darlin'," he said. "And don't you forget it. I just want you to know that there isn't a couple or ever will be a couple that won't experience hard times. But there's one thing that always prevails, especially when two people do indeed love each other from the heart. And that's love.''

Great. A dose of Graceland wisdom from an Elvis impersonator. Even worse, I was standing here listening to it. I'd managed to hit a new low.

"You just wait till you're good and ready, darlin'." Elvis gave my shoulder a squeeze.

I caught a whiff of his aftershave and wondered if the real Elvis had also been an Aqua Velva man.

"And if that man really loves you, he'll stick around. Then you come on back to old Graceland to say the I do's with Elvis. Ya hear?" Elvis said, giving me one last squeeze.

I headed back toward the Treasure Island Hotel with a medley of oldie but goodie Elvis tunes stuck in my head. I had a feeling Santou hadn't gone back to the room. My guess was that he was probably sitting at a bar somewhere, cursing me out between shots of scotch and chasers of Mylanta. I couldn't say that I blamed him.

Faced with the choice of going to a bar myself or sitting and waiting for Santou to return, I did what any other sane woman would do. I retrieved my Blazer and raced down the Strip to Lizzie's house. I snuck inside, where Pilot was only too happy to join me for a midnight ride.

Putting the pedal to the metal and our back to the lights, we roared down an empty highway, leaving Vegas and Elvis far behind. Darkness hugged the road as night galloped along keeping pace with my tires, while Bonnie wailed the blues, Pilot sniffed the air, and I tried to clear my head. Santou would have called it running away. I called it running for my life.

Turning off the highway, I swung onto the desert floor and drove for a while before shutting off the engine. A thick blanket of silence enveloped me. Getting out of the Blazer, I stared up at the night sky more full of life than all the neon in Vegas. I knew I'd have to go back and face Santou sometime. But I couldn't just yet. I scrambled up onto the Blazer's roof with Pilot by my side, as the stars gyrated wildly above, pulling me up into them.

Caught up in my own despair, for once I didn't worry about snakes and tarantulas or other bugaboos of the night. Sensing my mood, Pilot lay down beside me and placed his head in my lap.

That was all it took—I started to cry. Just a few tears at first, but they slowly turned into a torrent that threatened never to stop. Santou was right. I *was* afraid. I was afraid of the night and of the dark, afraid of failing at yet another career, and afraid of losing my heart.

Tears ran down my cheeks, crash landing in Pilot's fur. Burying my face in his neck, I hugged him close, eternally grateful to have him. I knew I could love him and never be hurt.

The silence was broken as a coyote howled off in the distance, sending goose bumps up my spine. Pilot quickly sat up, his golden eyes burning holes in the night. Pricking his ears, he listened as the cry was picked up and returned and then picked up again. Throwing back his head, he joined in the chorus with a mournful wail, expressing for me what my heart couldn't say. The cry raced up to the moon and circled the stars before hurtling back down to earth to fill the still valley.

Closing my eyes, I let the sound fill me as well. And for the first time since moving to Nevada, I understood the pull of the desert.

By the time I dropped Pilot off at Lizzie's and tiptoed into the hotel room, the night was half gone and Santou was in bed, fast asleep. Easing in beside him, I barely breathed, not daring to wake him.

But he knew I was there. He raised himself on one elbow as I looked up at the profile I would have known anywhere.

"You don't trust me, do you, Porter?" he quietly asked.

I didn't answer, knowing he would see through me, whatever I said.

"You never have. But you will," he whispered.

Then, leaning over, he kissed me hard. I responded with

a heat I hadn't expected, enveloped by Santou's red-hot anger and white-hot lust. And for once, I was glad there was no light as I let go of all inhibitions.

When I woke the next morning, Santou was already dressed and packed. Sitting up in bed, I clasped the sheet tightly around me.

"Where are you going?" I asked, my heart beating so hard I was scarcely able to catch my breath. He hadn't bothered to shave. The rough edge gave him an undeniable melancholy mystique that came close to breaking my heart.

"I'm catching a cab to the airport, *chère*. There's no reason for me to stay," he said simply.

I stared at him, not wanting to believe that he would leave this way. And then I started to cry again. I'd never been more confused. All I knew was that I didn't want Santou to go.

Jake walked over and sat down on the bed. Taking my face in his hands, he gently kissed the tears away. "I love you, Rachel. You're hard-headed and can be foolish as hell. And lord knows, you make me crazy. But I want you in my life. It's your call, *chère*."

Santou stood up and grabbed his bag. "Get in touch with me when you've made up your mind one way or the other. There'll be no more games between us."

And then he was gone. Just as if it had all been a dream.

Fourteen

My cell phone rang while I was still crying and cursing Santou for turning me into a watering pot. Lunging for my duffel bag, I frantically dug beneath the clothes in search of the muffled ring. Out flew the lacy camisole I'd ordered, the bras I'd never worn, the panties I'd been saving for that special occasion. It seemed they were destined to be buried inside a drawer forever, never to be worn. My hand brushed against the receiver. Pulling it out, I hoped against hope that the caller was Santou.

"Hey, gal! Tell me I didn't disturb anything good."

My heart sank as I heard Lizzie's voice. "You didn't disturb anything at all," I said between sniffles.

"Uh-oh. You guys fighting already? Or can't you talk now?" she asked in a theatrical whisper.

Lizzie loved gossip. Her choice of reading material verified the fact. She devoured everything from *People* magazine to *Soap Opera Digest*. Unfortunately these days, my life was qualifying as filler.

"I can talk. We fought. He's already gone." I figured I might as well tell her. She'd find out anyway.

"Pond scum! That's what they all are!" Lizzie fumed, a true-blue friend loyal to the end. "What did he do?"

"He asked me to marry him," I wailed.

"And?" Lizzie asked, her voice rising an octave. "What did you say?"

"I said no!"

Her shriek sent shock waves through the phone directly

into my inner ear. "What are you? Crazy? This is the guy you're nuts about, right?" she ranted.

"Right," I responded, feeling more miserable than ever.

"Then what's the matter with you? Go and stop him!" Lizzie screamed.

"He's gone already, Lizzie," I reminded her. "He left about forty minutes ago."

"That's nothing! It wouldn't stop Barbra," she said emphatically. "You remember *Funny Girl?* When she jumps on that tugboat to go after Omar Sharif, who's off to gamble his way across the ocean to Europe?"

I couldn't take anymore. "Lizzie! Please stop. I'm not going after him. Is this what you called about?"

There was a long moment of silence and I could tell she was miffed. "No. I called because I came into the office this morning to get some work done and decided to do some snooping around while I was here."

I waited for her to continue. Finally I gave her a prod. "What did you find?"

"First tell me why you said no," she insisted.

I sighed as I thought about it. "Because I'm afraid of being hurt and of losing myself. I know it may not make sense, but there's something I have to prove, and it has to be without Santou's help."

"You're right. You're not making any sense at all," Lizzie agreed, affirming my insanity. "That's why it's lucky you have me around. Don't worry; we'll figure something out. There are a million old movie plots where the lovers fight and then get back together. We just have to decide which one fits your situation best."

Lizzie made a regular habit of turning to Hollywood to solve her problems. "I like to think of it as a lending library of ideas," she once explained. "Screenwriters get paid good money to figure out how to deal with life's problems. Why not take advantage of it?"

"Now will you tell me what you found?" I pleaded.

"Okay. You're gonna love this. You know that quit claim application you found on Annie McCarthy's land?

Well, I don't know when the old broad kicked the bucket, but that deed was filed six weeks ago, signed by both Mc-Carthy and Anderson. And believe me, it wasn't easy finding it, either," Lizzie complained.

"What do you mean? Wasn't it listed with the county recorder's Office?" I asked.

"Sure," Lizzie replied, "if you don't mind digging through every obscure file they have. It would seem as if somebody wanted this deal hidden away real bad."

I didn't have to work overtime to guess at who that might be. I just wanted to know why Brian had lied to me.

"There's more," Lizzie continued. "Believe it or not, Golden Shaft was just granted a patent by the Bureau of Land Management. They're now the proud owners of previously held federal land. Don't ask me how they did it, but somehow they even got McCarthy's claims included in the deal."

"Is that unusual?" I asked, my thoughts still on Santou.

"You bet it is! It usually takes forever to get through the red tape and paperwork that allows mining companies to buy the public land they're working on," she explained. "All I can say is this company must have powerful friends in high places. Golden Shaft barely had any waiting period at all. That's unheard of."

I processed the information while I collected my thoughts and drove home. There was no doubt in my mind that Annie's death was linked to the quit claim deed. The question was, what made her claims so valuable? If they really held a mother lode of gold, it only made sense that other mining companies would have known about it, as well. But I'd been told over and over right from the start that Annie McCarthy's claims were worthless.

As I rounded the corner to my house, I was jolted out of my thoughts by the blare of Jerry Garcia and the Grateful Dead saturating the neighborhood. Sitting in my driveway was a beat-up, turquoise-blue Suburban, its dented license plate hanging on by a screw, emblazoned with the words "Nuke M." I knew it had to be Noah.

I parked my Blazer on the street and walked up to find Noah stretched out inside, with eyes closed and a silver reflector tucked under his chin. A killer ray of sunlight was aimed directly onto his face, while his bare chest heaved up and down, remnants of suntan lotion clinging onto the human blanket of fur. Jenkins's dogs futilely hurled themselves against the chain link fence, foaming at the mouth in a frenzy.

Noah opened an eye and grinned as he sat up. "Hey there, Red. I heard you had quite the fireworks here the other night. Glad to see you're still in one piece."

I was beginning to wonder if the bombing had made front page news without my knowing about it.

"How did you find out?" I asked.

"Word gets around." Noah winked as he turned down the sound. "Had breakfast yet?"

I shook my head, realizing I'd skipped dinner last night, as well.

"Since it doesn't look like your place is fit for company these days, why don't you hop on in and we'll see what we can find?" he suggested.

I casually snuck a peek, just to make sure Noah wasn't driving around nude. "You might have trouble getting in anywhere without a shirt," I offered, not commenting on his cutoff denims and boots.

Noah elevated himself off the seat an inch and whipped a crumpled Hawaiian shirt out from under his rear end with a flourish. He put it on and pulled a pair of Ray Bans from his visor.

"*Voilà!* Who says you can't take me anywhere?" he grinned.

I shook my head and laughed at the thought of what Santou would have had to say about Noah.

"Hey, gimme a break, Red. With this disguise, I'm your Everyman. Your one-hundred-percent, grade-A, all-beef, all-American tourist," Noah defended himself. "What do you think? That you might be knocked off some society list if you're seen with me?"

I had no illusions about that. Besides, I figured breakfast wouldn't make or break the Cindy Crawford figure I'd been yearning for. I slipped in next to Noah.

Once out of town, we saw an IHOP, which beckoned to Noah from the other side of the road. He cut off two cars as he careened across the highway. Brakes squealed and horns blared, but Noah paid no attention. The Suburban was comfortably ensconced directly in front of the restaurant in record time.

I tried to control the trembling of my fingers as I struggled with the seat belt, having come within inches of being creamed.

"Do you always drive like a maniac?" I asked.

Noah pulled a bottle of Jack Daniel's from under his seat and took a good slug. "No. Sometimes I drive faster. It all depends on how hungry I am."

Obviously he had worked up quite an appetite this morning. I watched as he downed an order of scrambled eggs and blueberry pancakes along with two sides of bacon and sausage.

"You done with that?" he asked, as he reached for my plate of French toast.

"You looking to OD on cholesterol?" I asked.

"You got it," Noah nodded.

He stuffed the remains of the French toast into his mouth as he motioned to the waitress for a fourth cup of coffee. While he leaned back to digest, I filled Noah in on Golden Shaft's patent.

"Hmm. Interesting tidbit, Red. Especially since I've been hearing helicopters buzzing over that way at night lately. Sounds like a damn battalion going in and out of the place," Noah replied.

Again with the helicopters! To protect Dee, I couldn't reveal her information, but I was curious to hear his speculations. "Harley chalks it up to black ops. What do you think is going on?" I asked. I watched Noah add five packets of sugar to his coffee.

"Beats the hell out of me. I've been asking myself, what

does a damn mine need helicopters for anyway?'' He belched loudly.

The woman sitting in front of me turned around with a glare of disapproval as I sunk low in my seat.

"And have you come up with an answer yet?"

"Nah. It's going on the list of 'what is it about this hellhole called southern Nevada that attracts military bases, nuclear tests sites, McDonald's franchises, crazy Vietnam vets, whacked-out drug dealers, and eccentric millionaires anyway?' '' Noah grinned and wiped up the few remaining drops of maple syrup with his finger. "But what the heck— it's home sweet home. Here, Red. You pay the bill."

I covered the damage and joined Noah outside, where he was taking deep breaths of hot Vegas air.

"I think it's time we took another look-see at old Golden Shaft. What do you say, Porter? Are you up for a game of hide and seek?" he asked with a wink.

Considering how my morning had begun, I figured it would be the highlight of my day. But first I insisted on stopping by Lizzie's to pick up Pilot.

"Don't you ever go anywhere without that damn wolf?" Noah groused.

"Not if I can help it." I grinned. "Besides, he helps keep me out of trouble."

"Yeah, he's done a helluva bang-up job for you so far," Noah dryly noted as we drove past the bombed-out front of my house.

Noah waited in the Suburban while I went inside to get Pilot. I glanced in each room, but the dog was nowhere in sight. Checking out the kitchen window, I finally found him in the backyard, busy plowing his way under Lizzie's cyclone fence. I opened the back door and whistled, but that wasn't enough to get his attention.

"Hey, Pilot! Want to go for a ride?" I called out.

Those must have been the magic words. Pilot stopped and pulled his nose out of a hole that was beginning to resemble a tunnel to China. Bounding over, he jumped up and licked my face.

"It looks like it's just you and me again, Pilot," I whispered, scratching behind his ears as I thought of Santou.

Pilot jumped in the back of the van and leaned over the front seat. His paws rested on the crumpled Hawaiian shirt as he sniffed Noah's face.

"Jesus, Porter! This mutt's paws are filthy! And I just cleaned my van. To say nothing of my own personal appearance." Noah huffed.

I looked at the strewn coffee cups and empty beer bottles, the Cheez Doodle crumbs that were ground into the van's decrepit gold shag carpet, and let go of my normal guilt.

"You call this clean?"

"For me, this is immaculate." Noah shoved the Suburban into gear.

The sun poured through the windows, baking my skin like a piece of white toast, as Noah tore down the highway. I sat back and enjoyed riding shotgun for once. I willed my mind to go blank, letting the desert work its magic on me.

We drove out of Vegas, through Henderson, and turned south toward Searchlight, as a delicious sense of freedom crept up through my toes, past my legs, and into my arms and fingers, until my whole body tingled. I gazed out the window, and the barrenness of the desert made a surprise attack. Though the air was ringing with silence, I knew that the land was as alive as Las Vegas would ever be.

The sound of gunshots broke through my reverie. I jerked sharply forward and then fell back with a thud, nearly giving myself whiplash. Looking out the window, I saw we were still on the highway and realized I'd fallen asleep. We passed a junker of a car that backfired loudly, repeating what I had heard in my dream.

Noah turned to me and grinned. "Someone walking on your grave, Porter?"

"I'm still a little jumpy after the other night, is all," I explained, annoyed at my case of nerves.

Noah removed the bottle of Jack Daniel's from between his legs. "Here. Take a slug of this."

My good sense told me it was too early in the day to

start drinking, but the part of me I liked best gave the go-ahead.

"Drink. It'll help. Believe me." Noah shoved the bottle into my hands.

I raised it to my lips and took a sip.

"Oh, come on, Porter. You can do better than that. Or are you afraid you might get so drunk that you'll try to take advantage of me?" he snickered.

"Yeah, Noah. That's what I've been thinking." I took a bigger gulp this time, the golden liquid burning straight down through my toes.

"Well, you can relax, Red," he blithely replied. "I guard my virtue like a fortress. It's one of the things Georgia and Suzie Q like best about me. I may bark and growl, but when you come right down to it, I'm just your average neutered, housebroken pet."

The Suburban swerved off the highway and bounced onto a washboard dirt road, leaving civilization behind. Noah grabbed the bottle for another swig. All he needed was a bandana and a tie-dyed shirt to pass as a time-traveler from the sixties.

"Why do you live out in the middle of the desert, Noah?" I asked, curious to know what made him tick.

"You mean why do I prefer it to living like a sardine with all the rest of you in the middle of some goddamn development that's gobbling up the land and sopping up what little water is left?" Noah reached behind him for a beer from his portable cooler.

"Okay. I guess that answers it," I responded as he threw me a Bud.

Noah popped open the tab with his teeth and drank half the can as a whiptail lizard ran for his life, barely evading our wheels.

"Look around you, Porter. This place is absolutely pure. It's the last spot of open freedom left in a country that's overgrown and overrun," Noah quietly explained. Then he winked. "Besides, I can't seem to get along with anyone anyplace else."

"That's interesting. I can't seem to get along with anybody here," I commented.

"Still trying to figure out who set those pipe bombs off the other night?" Noah asked.

"Yeah," I grumbled in irritation. "I've got a list that's growing by the day, while I'm running out of time."

I pulled two Mars bars out of my bag and threw Noah one. I figured worrying would have to burn up at least the candy bar's calories.

"Face it, Porter. You should be scared," Noah said. He released the steering wheel and ripped open the wrapper.

"Thanks a lot. That's very consoling," I replied, drowning my sorrows in a large bite of chocolate.

"I'm serious. You need to be paranoid, Porter. And you need to be careful. I have a gut feeling that we're stepping on some very big toes here. Don't let your imagination limit you on that. Remember, just because you're paranoid don't mean they ain't after you." He downed his bar in two bites.

It seemed I had heard the same warning from Santou only last night. The Mars bar did somersaults in my stomach.

"By the way, what's all this 'we' about? When did we become a team? As far as I can tell, it's only *my* rear end that's been marked as a target."

Noah chuckled. "Hey, Porter—when you got it, flaunt it. And yeah, it's we. In case you haven't already noticed, I'm in on this one. And if I were you, I'd be glad for the help."

"And just what *is* this one, if I may ask?" I was annoyed that Noah claimed to have a handle on what was going on, while I still was kicking at tumbleweeds in the dark.

"I'm not quite sure yet. But as soon as I'm one hundred percent clued in, you'll be the first to know."

"I'd appreciate that," I retorted.

He released the steering wheel again to gather his long oily strands of hair back into a ponytail. Then he pulled a dirty handkerchief from his pocket and doused it with the remaining beer from his can, soaking himself and the car seat in the process. Raising the handkerchief high above his head, he wrung it out, sighing as the beer ran down his face and neck and onto his shirt.

"Ahh. The pause that refreshes. You ought to give this a try, Porter."

Pilot leaned forward, sniffing at Noah. He quickly pulled back with a whine.

"No, thanks. I think Pilot said it all," I remarked. I knew of bums in Central Park who smelled better than Noah did at the moment.

"So tell me, Red, who was that guy at your house yesterday anyway?" Noah asked, catching falling drops of beer with the tip of his tongue.

I turned and stared at the lunatic sitting next to me, wondering if he was more dangerous than I had imagined.

Noah must have read my thoughts. "Whoa! I'm not some frigging wacko. You don't have to worry."

I was beginning to wonder about that. Besides hormonally challenged football players, I didn't know of any men who chose to douse themselves with beer and then bake in the hot desert sun. And to top it off, he'd been stalking me.

"Porter, say something. You're beginning to freak me out." Noah wrung out the end of his ponytail. "I was going to stop by the day after the bombing. But then I saw you and Rambo walking out of the ruins looking mighty happy and satisfied."

"What do you mean by Rambo?" I asked suspiciously.

"Aw, come on. The guy is obviously a cop," Noah retorted.

"And what makes you think that?" If Noah wanted paranoia, I was more than happy to give him a dose first-hand.

Noah snorted. "The way he zeroed in on me and my transport. Rambo gave me the evil eye, so I skedaddled. Since you didn't seem to be fighting him off, I decided to leave the scene and check in with you later."

The fact that I'd been too besotted to even realize Noah had come made me more uneasy than ever. No wonder Santou worried that I needed him around.

"So are you going to tell me? Who was the guy?" Noah persisted.

"Can you give me one good reason why I should?" I countered, angry at myself.

" 'Cause I'm your partner in crime, *compadre*. And it seems like you know a hell of a lot more about me than I do about you," Noah contended.

As much as I hated to admit it, the man had a point.

"He's a detective with the New Orleans Police Department." I felt the heat rise to my face.

Noah pulled a stale powdered donut out of a paper bag from under his seat. "Are you telling me that you've got people after you in Louisiana as well as Nevada these days?"

"I'm dating the man. Okay?" I hoped that would put an end to his curiosity. Unfortunately, it didn't.

"So did he try to talk you into moving back to the land of coonasses and 'gators?" Noah asked with a chortle.

I looked at Noah and wondered if my life was that transparent. "What are you? Psychic?"

"Nah. Just experienced." A shower of powdered sugar fell from the donut onto Noah's beer-stained shirt.

Before I could stop, I found myself confessing all to the man. I told him about my relationship with Santou, his proposal, and my knee-jerk reaction.

Noah was silent as we drove along the dirt road. We passed through an endless series of bumps and ruts, over rocks and around giant boulders, wending our way up the mountain, as the Suburban swayed from side to side. Finally he took a swig of Jack and passed the bottle to me.

"Listen, Porter. There's not much happiness to be had in this world, and what there is of it is fleeting. So grab it while you can. Go, be fruitful, and multiply. The brass ring only comes around once, as far as I can tell. Don't be a fool and think about it for so long that it passes you by. 'Cause if you do, you'll regret it for the rest of your days. And life ain't worth living without it."

I didn't answer, worried that I might have already blown

it. The sharply honed lines of the mountains blurred into soft focus before me. Either I was in danger of becoming perpetually misty-eyed, or Vegas pollution was on the move south. Neither scenario made me feel any better. Only Pilot seemed to sense my mood. I felt his breath on my hair, the wetness of his nose sniffing my neck as his tongue lapped at my ear. Reaching back, I scratched him under the chin, his head resting in the palm of my hand.

By the time we reached the summit, clouds had started to move in, threatening to douse us with rain. But Noah paid no attention to the sky. Shutting off the engine, he grabbed a pair of binoculars and jumped outside, where he stood perched on the mountain's edge, overlooking Golden Shaft mine. I opened my door, and Pilot quickly bounded out, anxious to roam after the long ride.

"Shit. I don't like the look of this at all. Something strange is going on down there," Noah muttered, the binoculars glued to his eyes.

I walked over and joined him, curious as to what could be wrong.

"Here. Take a gander through these." Noah passed me the glasses.

I scanned the scene below, noticing that security had been beefed up. The front gate was now patrolled by three guards instead of just one, all armed with M-16 rifles. And then I saw what Noah was talking about. There was a frenzy of activity, but none of it was directed to hauling ore out of the mine. Instead, it looked as though workers were packing up equipment to leave.

"That's strange. They just bought the land. Why would they be moving out now?" I asked. From this height, the mine resembled a bustling colony of ants.

"That's a good question, Porter. Could be this mine never held all the gold that they originally thought. Or then again, it could be something else," Noah responded.

A flash of silver caught my eye and I zoomed in with the glasses. It was Brian, standing amidst a buzz of activity.

Hovering close by loomed the unmistakable figure of Commissioner Ed Garrett.

"Here's something interesting: It looks like Garrett's involved with whatever is going on down there," I commented. Brian and Garrett disappeared behind the flow of trucks going in and out of the mine.

"Bingo! That's it!" Noah snatched the binoculars from my hands. "You just put the missing pieces together, Red. I'll bet you Frank Sinatra's fur coat this whole thing's been nothing but a scam from the start. Golden Shaft must be in cahoots with Alpha Development," he crowed.

As far as I was concerned, Frank could keep his coat—as long as it was some place far from me. "What would Alpha and Golden Shaft be doing together?" I asked, knowing there had to be more to the punch line.

"Listen, Porter. What's at a premium, making it more valuable than almost anything else in this county?" Noah waited for an answer.

"Land?" I ventured, guessing it had to be either that or water.

"That's right," Noah beamed, pleased with his only pupil. "It's valuable because the government owns almost all of it. Add onto that the fact that this area is going great guns, with more and more people moving in every day. And what does that mean?" He looked at me expectantly.

"A housing shortage," I instantly responded.

"You got it! And what's the easiest and cheapest way to get property out of the government's hands?" Noah tossed me the question as if it were a ball.

"Have something like a mining company patent the land?" I tossed it back.

"That's right. Go to the head of the class." Noah gave me a high five. "Shit, a mine like the Shaft can buy miles of it from the government for close to nothing! All they have to cough up is a measly five dollars an acre. And once they've got that patent, a mining company can legally turn around and sell that same property for up to thirty thousand dollars an acre right here in the Vegas area. That's when scum like Alpha moves in and chops it up into tiny little lots. Before you know it, they're slapping structures down on top of each other and getting up to a half a million bucks a pop for a house.''

Noah beat out a rhythm on his stomach, playing his skin like a bongo. ''The mining company turns a profit, the developers are happy as pigs in slop, and Clark County continues rolling in the dough. Everyone's reaped a huge profit. Except for the government, of course, which has been royally ripped off. Meaning you and me, *compadre.*''

What Noah said made sense.

''That may very well be true. But while it would be sleazy on Golden Shaft's part, none of it is illegal.''

''You're one hundred percent correct, Porter. Just unethical. Still, I'd love to see the bastards thrown behind bars to rot in jail,'' Noah grimly replied.

''The management at Golden Shaft probably just consider themselves to be smart entrepreneurs,'' I observed. I wondered if Annie's claims had also been thrown into the mix.

''Entrepreneurs, entremanures,'' Noah muttered, handing the glasses back to me.

I took another long look at Brian. ''He knows who you are, you know.''

''Who's that?'' Noah asked distractedly.

Brian looked good even from a distance. ''Brian Anderson. He mentioned you once and advised me to stay away.''

''Oh, yeah? And why is that? 'Cause I'm better looking than him?'' Noah joked.

I watched as Garrett and Brian huddled together. ''I'm not sure why. But he seemed to know about your run-in at Los Alamos.''

''Let me see those binoculars again.'' Noah pointed them in Anderson's direction. ''I know I'm a popular boy. But I didn't realize my background had been that well advertised.''

I turned away from the mine to see what Pilot was up to. He was nowhere in sight. I walked back to the Suburban and checked if he was resting inside, but the van was empty. I wanted to call out his name but stopped myself, afraid that the sound would carry. I was beginning to worry—it was as if he had vanished into thin air. I grabbed my own pair of binoculars and scanned the horizon.

Then I spotted him. He had made his way down off the mountain top and was scurrying after a jackrabbit, which escaped his relentless pursuit by popping through the fence surrounding the mine. I watched as Pilot ferociously began to dig, his front paws burrowing a hole alongside the fence as fast as they could.

"What the hell?"

The sharpness in Noah's voice caught my attention. I turned back toward him, raising my binoculars in the direction in which he pointed. Brian was walking beside an enormous flatbed truck that carried a large steel canister.

"Jesus, that guy gives me the willies," Noah remarked, never lowering his glasses.

"Why is that?" Maybe Noah had some male insight into Brian that I was lacking.

Noah slowly shook his head. "That's what gets me. I can't put my finger on it."

We studied the scene for a few more minutes. Then I swung the binoculars back toward Pilot, determined to get his attention. But the dog was no longer there. A fresh gully of dirt snaked its way under the fence just deep enough for Pilot to squeeze through.

I quickly scanned the area, my stomach clenching tightly into a knot. Pilot must have managed to dig his way onto Golden Shaft's grounds, where he was now hidden among the hubbub.

"I'm going down to the mine," I abruptly announced.

Noah turned and looked at me in surprise. "What are you talking about? You've got a sudden yen to play storm trooper and breach the fort?"

I silently cursed myself for not having kept the dog in my sight. "It's Pilot. He dug a hole under the mine fence and got in. I have to get him out."

"What are you, crazy? You can't just burst in there look-ing for your dog!"

A surge of frustration shot through me. "Like hell I can't! Just try and stop me."

I headed for the van, jumped into the driver's seat and turned on the engine as Noah scrambled in beside me.

"Shit, Porter. What are you trying to do? Get us shot?" Noah wailed.

"Hey, you wanted a game of hide and seek. Now you've got one. First we hid. Now I'm seeking," I answered with determination.

The van screamed as I threw the gear into forward mo-tion, its tires grasping for traction in the storm of pebbles that flew into the air. I wheeled the Suburban back onto the dirt path and headed down toward the mine.

"What the hell are you going to say? That you were out here sightseeing?" Noah hugged his arms around his chest as his heels dug into the floorboard.

"Brian knows about the pipe-bombing at my place. I'll say I came by so that he wouldn't worry. What are you so nervous about, anyway?" I asked, gunning the engine.

"There's something about this mine that's sending warn-ing flares up my spine. And when that happens, I've learned to listen. I don't like this, Porter. I don't like it at all," Noah fumed.

I wasn't particularly thrilled about it myself. But if Pilot was on the mine grounds, I wanted him off. I felt sick as I remembered Dee's story about her dog. There was already the possibility that I'd lost Santou from my life. I didn't plan on losing Pilot as well.

Three guards and their guns swiftly surrounded the Sub-urban as we drove up to the gate. I recognized one of the men as the security guard I'd encountered before, and di-rected my attention to him.

"Hi. Remember me?" I gave my best sixty-watt smile. "I'm here to see Brian Anderson. Mind letting me in?"

But there was no nonchalant wave through, as there had been on my last go-around.

"What's your business?" he asked, his expression as blank and unreadable as the other two hulks who stood watching us closely.

I decided to go for what little weight I had. "I'm an agent with the U.S. Fish and Wildlife Service. It's important that I speak with Mr. Anderson."

But the guard didn't budge. "He's busy today. His orders are that no one is to be allowed in."

"He'll see me," I insisted. "Just tell him I'm here." Yeah, me and Cindy, and Sharon Stone might do the trick.

"I'm afraid that's not possible," he calmly intoned. "You'll have to turn around and leave, please."

He shifted the M-16 in his arms, his finger resting lightly on the trigger. The two other guards followed suit.

My fist came down hard on the van's horn, the blast of noise causing Noah to jump in his seat. The three M-16s immediately swung into action, ready to blow us away. I slowly raised my fist off the horn, and a deadly silence engulfed us.

"Good going, Porter," Noah whispered, his voice tightly constricted in his throat.

Brian turned and looked our way from off in the distance. He stood still for a moment and then, waving his hand, motioned us in. The guards immediately backed away with smart military precision.

"I told you I'd get in," I remarked, silently giving thanks to the gods of Sharon and Cindy.

"Yeah. You just forgot to add the part about dead or alive," Noah hissed.

Brian's eyes were dark and hard, his gaze plastered on Noah. He walked over to the van and leaned down toward me with a smile that contained all the warmth of an iceberg about to greet the *Titanic*.

"What are you doing here, Rachel? I thought you were tied up for a couple of days," he said, his voice tight and edgy.

I wondered what had become of the man who'd been so anxious to see me. "My schedule loosened up. Besides, you sounded so worried the other day that I decided to stop by."

Noah chimed in before Brian could respond. "Yeah, any little worry tends to put a crimp in her day. But what's going on here? Has the Golden Shaft finished shafting Nevada so soon?"

I could have throttled him. Instead, I gave a small shrug. "Brian, meet Noah Gorfine."

Brian's picture-perfect features turned their attention onto the shambles of the man sitting next to me. "So you're one of the people who lives in that ark."

"Yep, that's me." Noah nodded enthusiastically. "As I was saying, it looks like you're clearing out of here. What gives?"

It was obvious that whatever was going on, Brian was frazzled. The tension that sprang off the man nearly crackled in the air. Then, almost imperceptibly, Brian took a breath and consciously relaxed as he smiled. "We're just moving operations down to another area. We've got plenty to do here yet."

"Well, you guys sure make one hell of a racket," Noah chattered on amiably. "Would you mind keeping the noise down? In fact, maybe you can have those 'copters of yours make their runs during the day. Those damn things keep me up all night. Gotta get my beauty sleep, you know."

Brian's fingers tightened their grip on the door frame, turning the crescents of his nails pearly white.

"You must be seeing UFOs, my friend. We have no need for helicopters here at the mine," Brian briskly informed him.

Then he turned his attention back to me, markedly cutting off Noah. "Sorry, Rachel. But I'm really very busy right now, though I do need to talk to you." The tips of his fingers brushed lightly along the crook of my elbow. "And believe me, I am relieved you're alright. How about I give you a call in a few days, and we'll get together then?"

He sounded so harried that I wondered if there really

might be a good explanation for what was going on.

I had little time to ruminate, as a ten-gallon Stetson pushed its way into my view. I'd nearly forgotten that Ed Garrett was on the grounds. His light tan suit was sprinkled with a fine layer of dust, as were his lizardskin boots. A bolo tie was held in place by a chunk of turquoise the size of a meatball.

"Hey there, Porter. What are you up to? Out here to rile up the miners?" Garrett's toothy smile jarred with the darkly severe face that stared at me.

"No way—I can't compete with you, Ed. I understand you're down here like clockwork flogging that county supremacy proposal of yours," I sweetly replied.

Garrett gave a belly laugh before slapping a hand down hard on Brian's shoulder. "Sounds like there's an informer in your ranks, Anderson. Guess we'll just have to line 'em all up and start shooting till someone breaks down and talks."

His eyes came to rest on Noah, who was twisted around in his seat grabbing a beer. I felt it only fitting that Garrett should meet the man he'd branded the primary culprit behind the tortoise thefts.

"You know Noah Gorfine, don't you Commissioner?" I sat back and waited for the reaction.

Noah threw him a beer. "Here ya go, Ed. Have one on me. You too, Anderson."

Brian's beer went flying past his head, landing on the desert floor.

Noah took a sip of his Bud and smacked his lips. "Hey, Commissioner. I've got a complaint to make: I hear someone's been taking my name in vain. They've got some angry yahoo ranchers believing I've been dumping stolen tortoises on their leased land. Got any idea who that could be? I plan to sue."

Noah grinned and raised his can of Bud in salute, his middle finger standing straight up at attention.

The smile vanished off Garrett's face. Without a word, he turned on his heels and stiffly walked away.

Brian studiously ignored Noah, his face somber and drawn, as he leaned in quickly toward me. "I've got to run, Rachel. But I'll give you a call soon."

My hand shot up, gripping his wrist with more force than I had intended. "Wait a minute, Brian. Pilot got out of the van on our way here. The last I saw he was digging a hole under the mine fence. Do you think I could make a quick search for him?"

Brian distractedly patted my hand. "Sorry to hear that, Rachel. But there's been no report of a runaway dog in here. He's probably outside somewhere."

Annoyed at the brush-off, I pointedly chose to ignore it as I continued to press my case.

"This just happened. No one would have had time to report it yet. I'm just asking for a few minutes to explore the area," I badgered him.

Brian glanced away, following Garrett's retreating form. "This is a bad day, Rachel. You can see how crazy it is around here. Listen, I'll keep my eyes open for him. If anyone finds him, I promise to give you a call."

I loosened my grip but kept hold of his arm. "Not good enough, Brian. I want to get him now. He could get hurt in all this commotion. What's the harm in letting me scout around?"

A wariness crept into Brian's eyes that hadn't been there before.

"Sorry, but I can't let you do that. It's against policy rules for visitors to roam unaccompanied, with all the heavy equipment around. And right now there's no one to spare." He looked pointedly at me. "There was a recent theft in the freezer room, and management's come down hard. That means no exceptions—even for you. Pilot will turn up eventually. Besides, if he's in here, he's safe."

I shook my head in disagreement. "That's just it. He's not safe at all." I was damned if I'd play the good girl and meekly go home. "There was a dog that was shot while wandering around Golden Shaft's grounds. I'm not going to let that happen to Pilot."

Brian zoomed in on me with the precision of a top gun jet pilot. "Who told you that?" he brusquely demanded.

I was startled by his reaction until I realized what I had just let slip. As far as I knew, the only dog that had been shot on Golden Shaft grounds belonged to Dee.

As my mind raced to cover my tracks, Noah nonchalantly replied, "She got that mixed up with something I told her. It was my dog that was shot, when I worked at Los Alamos."

Brian momentarily lasered in on Noah as if I weren't even there, then finally swung his attention back to me.

"Stop worrying, Rachel. I swear that no one will harm Pilot." Brian smiled reassuringly, his old self once again. "Hey, they'd have to answer to me. I'll even keep him safe in my office as soon as he's found."

Anderson slipped out of my grip, giving my hand one last indifferent pat, before walking off to join Ed Garrett.

"I believe that's called the classic kiss and dodge technique," Noah pronounced, donning his Ray Bans. "Too dangerous, my ass. Speaking of which, you can thank me for saving yours, by telling me what all that was about."

"Let's just say I might have blown the cover on a source," I distractedly replied.

My attention was on a series of dragmarks, each approximately six inches wide. The marks could have easily been made by rocks pulled along the ground, except for the tiny foot impressions running laterally alongside. They were desert tortoise tracks. Leading off into the distance, the tracks angled around to the side of the mine. My best guess was that the tortoises had found a source of water. I wondered if they had made it to their destination or if their carcasses were now stacked inside the mine's freezer, replacing those I'd previously stolen.

We drove past the gate, leaving Pilot behind. Sick to my stomach, I cut the engine and climbed onto the Suburban's roof, refusing to give up my search. Finally Noah joined me with his cooler of beers as I called Pilot's name over and over until it was branded in the desert air and seared into my heart.

Fifteen

It wasn't until midafternoon, when my voice was as raspy as Roy Jenkins's dogs', that Noah managed to drag me back inside the Suburban. The unrelenting sun had turned my skin hypertender by the time I was finally deposited home. I gave a moment's fleeting thought to straightening up some of the bungalow's mess, but the walls began to close in on me without Pilot around. I decided to head for the office to bury myself in work.

Once there, I discovered I had as much ambition to tackle that debacle as the one I'd just left at home. Fortunately the blinking red light on the office answering machine temporarily solved the problem for me. I hoped it would be Brian, calling to say he'd found Pilot. But it was Henry Lanahan's voice that boomed out loud and clear.

"Hey, Porter. I've got some information that I think you'll find intriguing. God knows, it's proven to be enthralling for all of us here at the lab. You might want to get in touch with me ASAP. Better yet, haul your butt on over as fast as you can. And I ain't talking sometime soon. I mean NOW!"

I stepped over the ragtag piles of wire, plaster, broken glass, and papers that were strewn about, and locked the door to what remained of the office. Jumping inside the Blazer, I hightailed it over to Lanahan's lab. If he'd found that the tortoises had indeed been run over by the mine's haul paks, it would give me a legitimate reason to head back to Golden Shaft and search the grounds to my heart's content!

I sped through Vegas and down the Strip, cutting off senior citizens who poked slowly along in rental cars. I waved in silent apology as they slammed on their brakes, surprised to find such discourteous behavior west of the Rockies. Siegfried and Roy fumed down at me in mute disapproval from atop their marquee as I beat a red light, scaring an unsuspecting tourist who'd stepped off the curb. Quarters and dimes flew out of his plastic bucket, glittering brighter than stars as they were embedded in steaming black asphalt by the trail of cars behind me. I spotted my ponytailed prophet with his crucifix still strapped to his back. He spotted me as well, stopping long enough to release one hand from his cross and flip me the finger, damning me to hell for eternity.

My head told me to slow down, but my adrenaline kept my foot pressed to the pedal until the Forensics lab came into view, beckoning me like a beacon to a ship lost at sea. I rushed into the building and hurried down the hall, passing lab employees as quiet as the corpses they attended. I rounded the corner, the pounding of my heart echoing the beat of my shoes on the white-tiled floor. By the time I reached Lanahan's office my pulse was tap-tap-tapping as fast as Lizzie's feet. I poked my head into Lanahan's office to find him hunched over his desk, working on a report.

"I made it," I croaked. My throat was still raspy and sore as I stepped into his lair.

Lanahan glanced up and grimaced at the sight of my swollen, sunburned skin and frazzled mass of red hair.

"My favorite woman. What the hell did you do to yourself? Stand in front of an atomic blast? Haven't you ever heard of skin cancer, Porter? For chrissake, use a self-tanning lotion if you're so concerned with being fashionable," he lectured.

"Thanks for the advice, doc. Next time I'll be sure and take a beach umbrella along. So what did you discover?"

Lanahan leaned back in his chair and laced his hands

behind his neck. He gave me the once-over before shaking his head.

"If nothing else Rachel, you certainly liven things up. There's always some sort of surprise whenever I see you," he replied.

"Are you telling me the tread marks weren't made by haul paks?" I asked. My heart dropped like a molten lump of lead, heavy with disappointment.

"Let me fill you in on something, Porter. Right now, if I were to tell my employees who was sitting in my office, you'd probably be strung up like a plucked chicken and heaved above a large pot of boiling water.

"What the hell did I do?" I asked, completely flummoxed by having added an angry mob of scientists to the list of people out to nail my rear end.

"Sit down and I'll walk you through it, Porter," he ordered.

Lanahan got up from his chair and poured two cups of java from the coffee machine. I watched, making sure he didn't slip anything tasteless, scentless, and deadly into my brew before handing it to me. I waited until he took a sip of his coffee before tasting my own.

"We examined those tortoises you foisted on me. It appears they weren't killed by tires," Lanahan began.

"Jesus!" I exploded in disgust. "So you're saying that they just dropped dead while they were crawling around in the desert and then were run over?" That was the lame explanation Brian would have handed me.

"Hey! Do I have to call in my employees, or are you going to shut up and behave?" Lanahan threatened.

I squirmed in my seat, trying to find a patch of skin that didn't hurt, as I impatiently waited for him to continue.

"I handed your stack of reptilian buffalo chips over to our rookie pathologist for analysis. It seemed a pretty cut-and-dried case. I figured all you were looking for was some official paperwork to nail the bad guys with."

He was right, which was why this momentary holdup was driving me crazy. I bit the tip of my tongue as he took the time to slowly stretch. If Lanahan was out to torture me, he was doing a good job. I decided to take my chances with his troops.

"Those torts looked pretty well crushed to me. Maybe your rookie made a mistake. How can he be so sure it wasn't a truck that killed them anyway?" I demanded.

Lanahan glared at me a moment. "Because there was no bleeding in the capillary areas. That's why."

I looked at him blankly.

Lanahan took a sip of his coffee and rubbed his eyes. "If a truck had caused their death, there would have been internal bleeding. There was none. Their hearts had already stopped pumping by the time those tire tracks were made," he explained.

"Maybe it was cyanide ingestion," I suggested. "Did you check for that?"

"Yes, Madame Curie," Lanahan retorted. "The tortoises were handed over to our toxicologist, who examined tissue samples for a multitude of poisons. They came up spanking clean. Ted even checked to see if they might have died from lack of water. But the critters were relatively well nourished."

I made one last valiant stab at remaining outwardly calm. That lasted all of two seconds before I erupted in a firestorm of frustration.

"Alright! I'm impressed. You're thorough. You checked everything out. That's great. But dammit, something killed those tortoises and I refuse to believe it was nothing but old age!"

"Very perceptive, Porter," Lanahan shot back. "You're so smart, you want to tell me what it was that did these critters in?"

I opened my mouth and shut it just as quickly.

"That's what I thought."

I pounded my head against my own mental brick wall, having little choice but to sip my coffee and wait until Lanahan was good and ready to pick up where he'd left off.

"X-ray machines are potential sources of radioactivity. You're aware of that, right?" he asked.

I nodded my head. At this point, I would have agreed to almost anything in order to move him along.

"Since our toxicologist and chemists work around X-ray machines, they're required to wear special badges that can tell whether or not the radiation inside our equipment is contained. The patches are then turned in every thirty days to a company where they're analyzed." Lanahan paused dramatically. "Well, all our badges were sent in a few days ago."

He hauled himself up and headed back over to the coffeepot, where he refilled his cup.

"This morning I got a call informing me that our lab has a potentially huge problem on its hands. In fact, huge is a mild way of putting it. Through the roof would be more exact." Lanahan's eyes pinned me down as if I were a mouse about to be dissected. "It seems that badge number 27325 was turned in showing a massive exposure to radiation. That just happens to have been Ted's badge. It's the type of news that gives everyone in here a heart attack, Porter. Especially me."

I held my breath, trying to figure out what he was getting at and how the hell I was involved. Lanahan slowly stirred sugar into his coffee, the clanging of the metal spoon loud as a warning bell.

"The first thing I suspected was that something had gone wrong with the shielding on one of our X-ray machines," he continued. "So we went into every room where Ted had been working and methodically swept it with a Geiger counter. When we hit the toxicology lab, the Geiger spun right off its scale."

Lanahan's body shook as if something had crawled on him that had to be knocked off. "We got our asses out of that room as fast as we could. Our entire staff was also rushed outside, where they kept themselves busy plotting what hotshot lawyer in Vegas to call in case of contamination."

"What happened next?" I was, afraid to think of where all this was leading.

"You mean before or after my coronary, Porter?" Lanahan asked, running his fingers through his hair. A few strands came out and he held them toward me accusingly. "Look at this! Not only am I losing my hair, but it's also turning white!"

"It was already white, Henry!" I cried out in exasperation. "I'm begging you, get to the point and tell me what this is about!"

Lanahan rested his elbows on his desk and leaned in close to me, his eyes riveted on mine. "What this is about are those damn tortoises, Rachel. They're radioactive enough to glow in the dark."

I tried to speak, but nothing came out, my mind having momentarily melted into a giant pile of toxic slush. I'd heard what Henry had said, but none of it made any sense.

Lanahan's voice cut through my haze. "I need to know where you got those tortoises."

His eyes remained focused on mine like twin barrels of a shotgun cocked and ready to fire.

My moral compass was gyrating as wildly as Lanahan's Geiger counter must have been when it hit those torts. Though I felt no loyalty to Golden Shaft, I needed to know what exactly was going on. From past experience, I knew that once the information leaked out, another agency would quickly step in and take over the case. I had no doubt that I'd be kept out of the loop.

I put on my best poker face. "What will you do with whatever I tell you?" I asked.

"I'll turn it over to the local FBI," Henry stated.

"Have you told them about this yet?" I pondered what my old boss Charlie Hickok would do.

"No. I wanted to speak to you first," Henry responded, watching me closely.

"Then you still have the carcasses?" I asked, wondering what the hell I was thinking.

Henry stared at me a moment before answering. "Some

men in special-protection suits came in early today and hauled the stuff off for further testing. They need to confirm that my Geiger counter isn't screwy and that I'm not some paranoid nut whose bolt has been loosened once too often," he replied. "Other than that, the room has been sealed. As for Ted, I gave him the rest of the week off. I hate to think what he would have done if I hadn't."

"Then my name hasn't been mentioned to anyone?" I persisted. A surge of adrenaline began to work its way through me.

Henry sat back in his chair, his fingers drumming on his desk as if it were a tom-tom.

"Are you involved in this somehow, Porter?" His eyes narrowed in on me. "Or are you just crazy enough to try and take on whatever this is by yourself?"

"I know this is going to sound crazy, Henry. But give me a week before you hand my name over to the FBI or whoever the hell was here," I pleaded, barely able to believe my own audacity.

"Where did you get those tortoises?" Lanahan growled.

"Okay. Five days tops, and I'll tell you all I know," I countered.

"Listen to me, Porter. Once the testing on those reptilian frisbees and their tissue samples is finished, the FBI will be on me like white on rice," Henry protested.

"Can't you just slide over the fact that I gave you the torts? Maybe say they were anonymously dropped off at the lab's door?" I implored. I couldn't believe what I was asking. Even worse, I didn't care. "Give me four days' head start. That's all."

"Are you crazy, Rachel? How do you know this doesn't involve terrorists?" Lanahan demanded. "My guess is that the tortoises went in search of water and ended up drinking from a radioactive source. Which means who the hell knows what some bunch of loonies is up to."

I had no idea. For all I knew, it was the work of a local militia group or even well-connected ranchers burning with a cause. In fact, the more I thought about it, the more I realized that the tortoises could have stopped to drink just about anywhere. It might have been nothing more than a matter of timing that had caused their deaths to occur at the mine.

"Give me three days, Henry. I swear to you that I'm not involved. But you're right: I do want the chance to look into it, and once the FBI gets my name, I'll be locked out of the case for good." I hoped that he would understand.

Henry ran his hand over his head. He pulled out a few more loose hairs and placed them on his desk like a phalanx of toy soldiers.

"Forty-eight hours, Porter," Lanahan rumbled. He stared forlornly at the visible sign of age creeping up on him. "I'll try to stall until then, but I can't make any promises. After that I want every detail you've got."

"I promise, Henry." I held my hand up in an oath and crossed my heart as I edged my way toward the door.

"And by the way, Porter—try to not get yourself killed. We don't need any extra bodies on our slabs," Lanahan added.

"Then you like me. You really like me," I joked.

"Nah. Its just that we're already overworked. Besides, there's a need even for people like you around." Lanahan gave a tired smile.

"What's that mean—crazy?" I queried.

He turned his attention back to the work on his desk. "Be careful, Porter. You've got a lot of fire, but that doesn't mean you won't get burned out."

I just hope it didn't burn me up.

The sun was already beginning to set by the time I walked outside. I had forty-eight hours. I took it on faith that Lanahan's clock was starting as of first thing in the morning.

The idea of heading home without Pilot held all the allure of spending an intimate evening with Frank Sinatra— the furry one. I pointed my Blazer back towards the Strip, intent on drowning my sorrows.

All I needed to do was find out what had happened to

three hundred and fifty desert tortoises, discover the source of some radioactive water, reclaim my lost dog, and resolve a conflicted heart. At the moment, it was easier just to order a drink.

There is no such thing as a quiet bar in Vegas. I headed inside the MGM Grand and followed the neon rainbow past the Emerald City Casino to the Flying Monkey Bar, where I sat beneath a laser thunderstorm and listened to a witch maniacally demand, "Surrender, Dorothy!" over and over as I downed a vodka martini.

Although Vegas is a city without a past for people who want to forget theirs, tonight it wasn't working. At least not for me. Having few other options, I waved good night to the Wicked Witch and headed back outside.

When I arrived home, I was pleasantly surprised to find that my landlord had been busy at work. Along with my front door, the living room window was now miraculously repaired. Though Lizzie's lights burned bright, I decided to stay in my own place tonight.

I wended my way past the bits and pieces of rubble that I was beginning to view as a new form of interior design. Padding into the kitchen, I fixed myself a makeshift martini and then headed for the bedroom. I hoped to find the red light blinking on my answering machine, but all was quiet on the electronic front. Which meant that Brian had yet to find Pilot. Or that a trigger-happy guard had gotten to him first.

I didn't want to think about that as I turned on the tap in the tub, stripped off my clothes, and stepped in. I didn't want to think about much of anything as the water worked its way up my toes, past my thighs, encompassing my waist and engulfing my breasts like a slow and tender lover. I laid my head back against the cold white porcelain rim, feeling depressed. For the first time, I was beginning to realize that too much of what I'd been taught as a child was a lie. Things don't get any easier as you get older. They just get tougher. The darkness at the end of the tunnel gets darker, and it gets harder and harder to find your way home.

The night air chilled my skin as I stepped out of the tub. I dried off thinking of Annie McCarthy. Annie had had the courage to follow her heart and her man to Nevada. Could I be equally brave and admit that right now I needed to speak with Santou?

I gathered my nerve and went into the bedroom, where I picked up the phone and dialed his number before I could change my mind. Each ring of the phone danced through my veins. My heart hammered as the receiver on the other end was lifted, and I waited to hear Santou's warm drawl.

"Hello?"

The voice was feminine, as cool and light as a mint julep on a hot southern day. My own voice caught in my throat, the heat vanishing from my veins as an Arctic chill quickly set in.

"Who is this, please?" she asked.

Oddly enough, I had the same question. Only I didn't bother to ask. I slowly set the receiver down. And then I remembered: Annie had followed her fiancé to the Nevada desert, and look where it had gotten her. I wasn't about to make the same mistake.

I didn't bother to check and see if I had dialed the wrong number. I crawled into bed and sipped the remains of my martini, hoping to keep my nightly demons at bay. A trail of coarse hairs clung to the sheets and worked their way up to my pillow. I didn't brush them off but took what comfort I could at the sight of them. Right now, they were all I had left of Pilot.

I'd been able to turn out the lights when Pilot had been around. That wasn't about to happen tonight. Even so, I fell into a restless sleep where no amount of light could keep the night's darkness from creeping in, until I was confronted by demons from the outside world as well as within. Strangely, they were beginning to look the same.

Sixteen

I woke up feeling as if I'd never slept, my mind groggy and my body begging to stay in bed. I decided to make my first call of the day with the sheets pulled up to my chin.

"Golden Shaft Mine." Dee's voice clipped the words like a machine gun rattling off rounds of ammo.

"It's Rachel," I replied. "I have to speak with Brian. I don't know if you heard, but my dog dug his way onto the mine's grounds." My stomach tightened into a knot.

"There's no way Anderson's going to speak with you," Dee tersely replied. "He's tied up in top-level meetings all day. But I can tell you this much—as far as I know, your dog hasn't been found."

It was what I had expected to hear. Still, the news stung like an ember being burned into my heart. I tried to take my mind off Pilot by focusing on business.

"Is the meeting with Garrett?" I felt sure that Alpha Development was somehow involved. "I saw him at the mine when I stopped by yesterday."

"No. He's not here," Dee answered abruptly.

Something was wrong. It wasn't like Dee to be so remote.

"Listen, Dee. I know that Golden Shaft's patent went through. But when I came by yesterday, it looked as if the mine was shutting down. Yet security around the grounds was tighter than ever." I paused and waited, but there was no response.

"Then when I bumped into Garrett, I began to wonder

239

if Golden Shaft might have worked out some sort of deal. You know, maybe sell Alpha some land and pocket the profits. Am I on the right track? Is the mine closing?" I pressed.

Dee finally answered, "You're partially correct. Alpha did receive some land."

"Really? Do you know how much?" I asked, trying to sound casual. It seemed that Noah had been right after all.

"Fifteen thousand acres." Dee's voice was low, but the information tore through me with the impact of a major quake.

That would give Alpha enough land to create a multi-billion-dollar development empire. I sat up in bed and threw off the sheets.

"That's a lot of land. Golden Shaft must have done well on the deal." I prayed that Dee wouldn't let me down now.

"The transaction went through for the price of one dollar," came her whispered response.

"What!" I exclaimed. I could scarcely believe what I'd heard. For the first time, I began to distrust Dee's information. "But how is that possible?

"Believe me, it is. I have to go now." The tension in Dee's voice snapped at me through the wire.

"Wait a minute—I got back a preliminary autopsy report on what those tortoises died from. Does radiation poisoning make any sense to you at all?"

I could hear Roy Jenkins yelling at his dogs next door as I waited for Dee's reply. A heavy deadness was the only response except for the faintest of clicks.

"Dee, are you still there?" I asked, wondering if we'd been cut off.

"Listen, Porter. There's something I have to tell you. But not over the phone. It's too dangerous," Dee whispered softly. So softly that I had to strain in order to hear. "Come by my house this evening and I'll talk to you then."

Dee hung up before I could question her further.

Anticipation of what she might know had me jumping out of bed and into the shower. The stream of cold water washed all my remaining drowsiness away, and I remembered that the clock was now ticking. The pressure was on to make good the time between now and my meeting with Dee. I decided to pay another visit to Bill Holmes at the conservation center, and this time confront him about the neon-green spray paint in his garage.

I was already in the Blazer and heading out when my stomach began to rumble, and I remembered that I hadn't eaten since losing Pilot. Yesterday morning seemed like ages ago. Apparently my stomach felt the same. Still, the thought of sitting down to solid food made me feel queasy. I stopped at the nearest 7-Eleven, where I opted for a Hickok special—a jumbo Coke and a buttered roll to go. That would carry me at least until noon.

The expanse of the desert seemed larger and more desolate than ever as I rode alone, its silence settling down on me as heavy as a buzzard picking at my bones. I pulled onto the unmarked dirt road heading to the conservation center and willed my mind to go blank. If nothing else, maybe I'd be able to meditate my way to some answers. A swift movement off to the left caught my eye. An antelope squirrel was running for its life with a coyote not far behind. I found myself rooting for the squirrel's escape with more intensity than usual. These days, I was feeling pretty low on the food chain myself.

A cyclone fence sprang up, cutting the result of the chase from my sight. But I had little time to ponder the outcome, as the locked gate of the Center came into view. I didn't bother wasting my time beeping my horn, I just pulled out my Leatherman, flicked the lock on the gate, and drove on through.

I walked into the entrance hall, this time feeling as if the stuffed wildlife was watching my every move. I heard a rustle and glanced over at the exhibit. It wouldn't have surprised me to find each critter awake and fully intent on laying waste to the building and everyone in it.

Hurrying past, I made my way to Holmes's office, but he was nowhere in sight. I checked the lab room with its empty tortoise cages. While the neon-green imprint was still boldly etched on the door, that room was deserted as well. I searched for the assistant whose fanny Holmes had caressed, and bumped into the portly biologist I'd encountered on my last visit. Formerly dressed in baggy jeans with ragged cuffs, he was now decked out in a white lab coat complete with pocket protector, and a pair of neatly pressed khaki slacks.

"May I help you?" he asked, seemingly unaware of our prior meeting.

"Remember me?" I reminded him. "I was here not long ago looking for Bill Holmes. Well, I'm here again. Same mission."

My biologist straightened the pens in his pocket protector before clearing his throat. "I'm afraid William Holmes is on an extended leave of absence. I'm taking his place for now," he informed me in a lofty tone of self-importance.

"When did this happen?" I silently kicked myself in the butt. I should have known to expect some sort of move on Holmes's part after our last meeting.

"Fairly recently," my biologist said, standing perfectly straight. His hands were nestled inside the lab coat pocket, so that only his thumbs were in view.

I glanced at the name tag on his lapel. "Just how extended is this leave of his, Charles?"

"It's indefinite." Charles gave a smug, satisfied smile as if pleased that he knew something I didn't.

"Then I take it there haven't been any more thefts since the last batch of tortoises were reported missing?" I figured I might as well pump him for whatever information I could.

Charles gave me a funny look. "What theft are you talking about?"

"You know—the three hundred and fifty juvenile tortoises that were stolen," I prompted him.

"I was told that was due to predation," he slowly replied.

"Who told you that?" I asked, beginning to wonder which one of us had lost our mind.

"William Holmes did," Charles answered uneasily.

"That's interesting. Did you ever happen to catch the critter that was snacking on all those torts?" For all I knew, Charles was also in on the scam.

"Well, no," Charles stammered, before making a quick recovery. "For goodness' sakes, it's not as if the perpetrator signs in and out, even though I know you'd like a full confession."

"Out of curiosity, when was it that Bill Holmes began working here?" I asked.

Charles stopped and thought for a moment. "I'd have to say two years ago."

"And when was it that the staff first began to notice batches of tortoises were suddenly missing?" I inquired. I knew watching Court TV would pay off one of these days.

Charles jammed his thumbs inside his pockets, his ever-inquiring mind humming almost audibly. "Now that I think back, it had to have been somewhere around the same time."

Biologists. You had to love them. I let Charles out of the witness box and headed to Holmes's residence, eager to see what was cooking.

My Blazer nosed its way through one subdivision after another, passing modest ranch houses on toothpick plots of land, before turning into the upscale development where Holmes resided. Rounding the corner, I slammed on the brakes. For the first time, I noticed a sign partially obscured by transplanted palms. If you were daydreaming, it was easy to pass it by. I got out of the car and parted the fronds to make sure my eyes weren't playing a trick. But the bold lettering left no doubt, proudly announcing, "You Are Entering An Alpha Development." Uncle Ed must have offered Holmes a deal he couldn't refuse.

I pulled up to the house, where all was quiet as before. I didn't bother to ring the bell this time; instead, I headed straight for the front window, as eager as a voyeur on his way to a peep show. The purple bean bag chair and big-screen TV were gone, along with my personal favorite, the black velvet portrait of Elvis.

I didn't need to jimmy the lock on the garage. It opened with an easy tug. Not surprisingly, the sporty red Miata was no longer sitting idle in its place. However, the can of neon-green paint had been left nestled in the coils of the garden hose, as if mocking my thwarted efforts to solve the case.

I was about to pull the garage door closed when something warm and furry brushed against my leg. Imagining a giant, mutant tarantula, I let out a screech followed by a high jump as I twisted around to view the demon behind me. Holmes's tabby cat calmly stared at me, daintily licking its paw, then washing its face. When Holmes had hightailed it out of town, he'd left the tabby to fend for itself. It was obvious that the cat was hungry; there was no hissing this time. Instead, Tabby rubbed against my leg as if I were a walking can of tuna.

"Alright, already!"

Scooping up the cat, I closed the garage door and headed for the Blazer, where I placed the feline on the backseat. Tabby immediately went to work digging its claws into the vinyl upholstery. Suddenly the cat got a whiff of Pilot. Arching its back, it hissed.

"Get used to it. He's coming back, " I responded.

I backed the Blazer out of the driveway and headed for the nearest convenience store.

7-Eleven is about as gourmet as it gets along the side roads of Nevada. I stopped at the same store my high-energy breakfast had come from. This time I picked up two prepackaged tuna sandwiches, three cans of cat food, a pack of Ring Dings, a can opener, and a couple of Diet Cokes. The cashier looked at me and sneered, remembering my morning purchase.

"You must be on a health kick," he noted, his pimply face a monument to his own highly disciplined diet.

I turned around, leaned down, and picked out a packet

of Yodels, allowing him a view of the gun handle sticking out of the back of my pants.

"Let's add this to the list." I slapped the Yodels down alongside the Ring Dings, daring him to make my day. I figured if being a wildlife agent didn't work out, I could always play Bonnie. I just needed a Clyde.

Being that it was lunchtime, I headed for the Clark County administrative building, where I pulled out my cell phone and gave Lizzie a call.

"Have you eaten yet?" I asked, knowing she wasn't one to ever turn down food.

"Yeah. But I'm still starved anyway," she informed me.

I would have killed for her metabolism. "Meet me down in the parking lot. I've brought lunch," I told her.

"Why can't you come up?" Lizzie asked petulantly.

"I've got Ring Dings and Yodels." I knew the temptation would be too great.

"Alright. I'm coming down," Lizzie sighed.

Soon I saw the top of her dark curls bouncing and heard her feet tapping as Lizzie maneuvered her way between the rows of parked cars.

"What was so important that I had to come all the way down here?" Lizzie asked, holding her hand out for the pack of Ring Dings.

I pointed to where Tabby sat on the backseat, chowing down a can of cat food I had just opened.

"What are you becoming—a home for wayward strays?" Lizzie asked. She tore apart the cellophane packet of goodies with her teeth.

"Tabby belonged to Holmes. It appears he flew the coop and left the cat behind," I told her, between bites of my dry tuna sandwich.

"What a guy. What a guy," Lizzie mumbled. Polishing off the Ring Dings, she started on the Yodels. "But how's Pilot going to feel about the new addition? A feline, no less."

The dry bread caught in my throat. I took a swig of Diet

Coke, silently convincing myself that Pilot's disappearance was just a temporary situation.

"I was scouting outside Golden Shaft yesterday and let Pilot out of the car. He never came back."

Lizzie stopped eating. "What do you mean, he never came back? How did he get lost?"

"He dug his way under the mine's fence. He must have gotten onto their grounds," I explained, working hard to maintain a calm exterior.

Lizzie breathed a sigh of relief. "Then it's okay. Brian will find him for you."

I looked at my friend and held back the urge to scream. "It seems that Brian is pretty busy at the moment."

I filled Lizzie in on the arrangement between Alpha Development and Golden Shaft.

"What kind of deal is that?" she retorted. "It sounds like that scum Garrett is making out like a bandit, without Golden Shaft getting much in return."

"I know, and it doesn't make sense," I agreed. "Do you think you can check if any record of sale has been officially logged in?"

"Sure," she nodded. "We can do that right now."

I left Tabby to another round of face-washing and followed Lizzie inside.

She quickly went to work punching in commands on her computer, where she scanned one record after another before finally giving up.

"There's nothing here. It's as if the exchange never took place." She looked completely mystified. "What do you think's going on?"

I had no idea. But I knew there had to be a catch for Golden Shaft to have given so much of their newly acquired land away.

I shook my head, feeling as puzzled as Lizzie. "I don't know. But I'm stopping by Dee Salvano's tonight and I'm willing to bet she's got some of the answers. Can I leave the cat with you for the evening?"

Lizzie nodded, having moved on to her tuna sandwich.

"Sure. In fact, the cat can stay with me permanently. That way, Pilot won't feel he's been replaced when you get him back home."

Lizzie spoke so matter-of-factly that I felt she had to be right. I gave her a hug and told her I'd call later on in the evening.

"You'd better," she warned. "If you find anything we can bury that bastard Garrett with, I want in."

I drove home and let Tabby play among the ruins while I made a half-hearted attempt to clean before heading out to Dee's. No calls had come in on my answering machine. I checked the office, hoping for some sort of diversion, but all was quiet there as well.

I took Tabby over to Lizzie's bungalow at six o'clock and let myself in. The cat acquainted himself with his new surroundings as I opened a can of mackerel and placed it in a dish on the floor. It didn't take him long to discover the jeweled turbans that lined the bedroom bureau. But what really caught the cat's eye was the colorful array of feathered boas nesting in the limbs of the coatrack. By the time I got to Tabby, he was poised to pluck the boas as bare as a flock of Perdue chickens.

I swooped down and picked up the cat as he let out a howl. Obviously Lizzie was going to have to rearrange her furnishings. I placed the cat in front of his bowl of food and locked the bungalow up behind me.

It was still too early to go to Dee's, so I headed for the Mosey On Inn. The drive seemed endless tonight. Purple mountains popped out against a deep-tangerine sky, urging me to press forward as I chased the light of the desert. Finally Paul Bunyon loomed up ahead. Usually a comforting sight, there was something sinister about the statue this evening as he glared off into the distance. I tried to shake the mantle of gloom that had begun to descend, but I knew that my time was quickly slipping away.

I walked in to find Ruby at her usual spot behind the counter. But tonight her kewpie-doll face held an air of the grotesque, her ruby red lips more Bette Davis as Baby Jane than Bernadette Peters.

"Mosey on in here, sugar. You haven't been around for a while," she said with a smile.

Streaks of red lipstick were smudged on her teeth, giving her the appearance of a vampire that had just fed. A shiver ran through me as I sat down.

"What's the matter? A ghost walk on your grave?" a voice croaked out from behind.

I had heard almost those same words from Noah only yesterday. Turning around, I found Cammo Dude ogling me, his one good eye jumping strangely back and forth inside its battered nest of scar tissue.

"Buy me a beer!" Cammo commanded.

I nodded to Ruby, who pulled out a Bud. Cammo aimed for what there was of his mouth, but the liquid squirted down the lower half of his face and onto his shirt.

"Shit. Give me a damn straw," he ordered.

My appetite was gone, but I ordered Ruby's special of the day, a bowl of chili. I immediately regretted it. The small chunks of ground beef were as hard as kernels of unpopped corn, and the beans tasted like metal. I felt Cammo Dude's breath over my shoulder and thought about giving him my food.

"Your tortoises are all dead," he cawed, like a crow announcing his presence. "But they sure do make damn good soup."

A pink tongue waggled out of his mouth as he futilely attempted to lick his lips. I put down my spoon, the chili turning sour in my stomach.

"How do you know what happened to the tortoises?" I asked.

" 'Cause I spoke to the fella who bought them over in Pahrump." Cammo's eye flickered with a hint of glee. "I know who he buys them from, too."

"And who would that be?" I inquired. I tried to keep the edge of excitement out of my voice.

"I want that chili!" Cammo demanded.

I was more than happy to oblige.

"And crackers, too!" he barked, a dribble of saliva working its way into the crook of his chin.

Ruby pulled out a packet of Saltines and slid them down the counter. I watched Cammo slurp at the chili. More landed on his clothes than went into his mouth.

"Who did he buy the tortoises from, Cammo?" I asked again. I wondered if the old goat was pulling a fast one or if he really had something to sell.

Cammo Dude cackled. "You think you're such a smart girl, doncha? But the whole time it's been right there under your nose!"

He laughed again, this time choking on a kidney bean. His hand lashed out as he desperately searched for his beer. I picked up the bottle and handed it to him. His lips latched onto the straw. Cammo finally disengaged himself from the bottle and sighed in relief. I waited until I was sure he had caught his breath.

"So who sold the tortoises to Turley?" I asked, my voice taking on a harsh edge of impatience.

"How do you know about Wes Turley?" the Dude suspiciously countered.

"I'm psychic," I shot back. "Now spill the beans." I looked at the bowl of chili and hoped he didn't take it literally.

"You never did get rid of those damn helicopters like you promised. How about that? Huh? That was part of the deal."

By now I was ready to grab the Dude by his camouflage gear and shake the answer out of him if I had to.

"I'm working on it!" I spat between clenched teeth. Standing up from the stool, I stared him straight in what was left of his face. "Now, give me the answer, Cammo. Or I swear I'll turn you in for squatting on public land."

I wasn't sure if I would have actually done so, but the threat worked like magic. Cammo backed away, the beer bottle quivering in his hand. His mouth gaped open and closed, like a fish in a life-and-death struggle to free itself from a hook. I felt so bad that I was just about to relent when Cammo beat me to the punch.

"Alright. But you gotta swear you won't turn me in," Cammo blubbered.

I only wished I had this much power over all the men in my life. "I swear, Cammo. Now tell me who was responsible."

The Dude slyly smiled. "What's got a roof and four walls and is something you live in?"

A riddle. Even worse, it was a bad one.

"A home," I automatically replied, and then realized what he was getting at. It was who I had suspected all along. "Bill Holmes?"

The Dude nodded his head. His lips sucked on the straw, drawing up nothing but air from the empty bottle.

"Give him another beer, Ruby," I said.

The Dude eagerly plucked the straw out of the old bottle and plunged it into a new Bud, his face grimacing into what I chose to interpret as a smile.

"What better set-up, eh?" Cammo sniggered.

He was right. Ten to one, Uncle Ed had gotten Bill the job based on that very understanding. Holmes would reel in the bucks while helping his uncle fuel rancher paranoia. So far, it had proven to be excessively easy.

"You still haven't found the poison though, have you?" Cammo quizzed, an impish tone to his voice.

"What poison are you talking about?" I asked.

The Dude simply stared at me, not bothering to answer.

"Was Holmes using poison for something?" I persisted.

"Tick-tock goes the clock. Find a way or there'll be hell to pay," Cammo recited in a singsong voice.

I turned to Ruby, who drew tiny circles in the air near the side of her head. I had little patience with Cammo's new-found fondness for rhymes. If he wanted to play the prankster, so be it. I didn't have the time to hang around for his games.

I paid Ruby and headed outside. The sun had set, leaving a tinge of vermilion painting the sky. The desert usually cooled down in the evening, but tonight was different. The air still hung heavy with the heat of the day. I shifted the Blazer into gear and took off, following the last of the light.

A bevy of cars raced by, manned by drivers eager to get to Vegas. The glare of their high beams was blinding, forcing me to slow down as my eyes searched for the wooden sign that marked the turnoff for Feather Lane Drive.

When I swerved onto the dirt road, a pervasive eeriness instantly enveloped the vehicle, and I shivered under the cloudy, starless sky. I fall asleep with the TV blaring, fire engines wailing, even turning on a fan just to break up the quiet of night. Noise helped to fend off the darkness that threatened to grab me up whole and eat me alive. But there was no release from the overwhelming silence of the Mojave.

I decided to shatter the stillness. Leaning my head out the window, I called Pilot's name. It came echoing back, vibrating off mountains cloaked in a dark ether. I called out again, and this time, the echo was followed by the blast of a shotgun piercing the desert solitude. I jumped at the sound, and told myself it was varmint-hunters.

I knew that the desert was filled with nightstalkers: nocturnal people who preyed on coyotes and mountain lions, even wild horses, shooting at anything that moved. I grasped the steering wheel tighter, determined to ignore the shaking of my hands.

One of the Blazer's tires bounced in and out of a rut, and I focused my mind back on the road. I told myself it wouldn't be much longer before Dee's abode came into view. I was so absorbed in my thoughts that it took a moment for me to notice the red glow that stained the night sky. The color quickly grew, intensifying as it ate up more and more of the darkness, until it seemed that night had turned into a molten version of day.

My foot pressed down hard on the gas pedal, the Blazer's shock absorbers howling in protest as the vehicle flew over rocks and ruts. The scent of the air changed and I picked up a whiff of smoke. Pinpricks of cold sweat broke out on my body. I ordered my mind to be still, not wanting to conjure up the worst. But it was no use. Visions of sugar-plum flames danced in my head, scorching the desert floor into burnt butterscotch ribbons. I drove as fast as I could, the Blazer creating its own gust of wind. And then I was outside the vehicle, staring at what should have been a fe-verish dream. Dee's house was ablaze, with licks of fire curling inside and out like a den of snakes hissing a warn-ing. Nearby, her red pickup had become a mass of charred metal contorted into odd shapes.

I called out to Dee in the hope that she had escaped and was hiding even now behind a nearby Joshua tree. A heart-wrenching cry tore through the air. I quickly scanned the area. The anguished shriek came once again, and I ran to-ward a nearby yucca, where the sound had come from. But Dee was nowhere in sight. Instead, I watched in stunned fascination as the yucca burst into flames, its screech more human than I could have ever imagined.

A sledgehammer pounded where my heart should have been, as smoke rushed deep into my lungs. My body tingled and my face was as hot as a piece of burnt beef, while the taste of ash coated my tongue. By now the house was a roaring inferno. I knew there was no hope left for Dee, if she was still inside. The only thing to ever be found would be her scorched bones.

The sledgehammer moved from my heart to my head as I made my way back to the Blazer and pulled out the cell phone. I placed a call to the local police. Then I dialed a second number.

"Ursula Unger's residence."

"Lizzie, it's Rachel."

My throat felt as though a bough of thorns had been raked across it, scraping it raw.

"What do you think, Rach? Tamara Twayne just wasn't working, so I moved on to names beginning with U. Should it be Uma or Ursula? What's your gut reaction?"

"Listen to me, Lizzie. I'm out at Dee's. There's been a fire."

An explosion of throbs produced an extravaganza of fireworks in my head.

"Oh, my God!" Lizzie gasped. "Are you alright?"

"I'm okay. But Dee may not be. There's some information I need to check, and I'm hoping you might remember." I spoke slowly, believing it might help the pain go away.

"Shoot. What do you need?" Lizzie asked.

I heard a crash in her bungalow, and for a moment my heart stopped.

"Get out of there, Tabby!" Lizzie firmly commanded. "Sorry about that, Rachel. Go ahead."

"Do you remember how many acres were in Annie McCarthy's quit claim deed that was signed over to Golden Shaft?" I asked.

I closed my eyes, but the fire still twirled in front my sight, performing perfect pirouettes.

"Oh, sure. That's easy. There were fifteen thousand. I remember that because fifteen is my lucky number."

I heard her voice chatter on, but I stopped listening as one more piece of the puzzle clicked in my brain. Fifteen thousand acres was exactly the amount of land that Golden Shaft had sold to Alpha Development for one crisp dollar bill.

I got off the phone as quickly as I could. More than likely, Dee had discovered the reason behind the sale. I didn't have to wait for a team to sift through the smoking debris to confirm that she had been murdered. I knew it as surely as if I had been witness to the act myself.

Except for the burning funeral pyre, night loomed stealthy as a panther around me. I turned on the Blazer's engine and pulled away, the blackness swallowing me, until the fire was no larger than the dot at the end of a sentence. And I could very well have been the one who lit the match that began the flame.

It's too dangerous, Dee had said. *Not over the phone.*

Whatever she had decided to reveal must have been important. It had cost her her life.

Lanahan's clock was still ticking. I knew that by this time tomorrow, the FBI would have moved in. I was also aware that a female wildlife agent carried about as much weight as a thimbleful of soot. I would be thrown off the case. Not knowing what else to do, I headed for the only place I had left to go.

I threaded my way between rocks and cactus, hugging close to the base of the mountains. I knew it would have been smarter to get back on the main road. This way, it was too easy to get lost. One wrong turn, and I would wind up driving all night. If I drove all night, I could run out of gas. And if I ran out of gas, I was good as dead.

I didn't let any of that sway me from my course. It was a streak of stubbornness that had nearly gotten me killed once before, but it was important to me to prove that I could do whatever a male agent could. It was the reason I would never admit to being tired or cold or hungry. I would never give up, never give in.

I heard a coyote yip in the distance. The call was picked up and answered by a second critter, and then a third and a fourth, until a chorus of yips merged into one long, mournful coyote song. The melody slowly melted back into the desert, where it was replaced by the dim echo of a scream in my head. I knew it was Dee's scream, and that it would always be there.

Seventeen

My headlights sliced through the dark, searching for the trail that led to Noah's. Pairs of eyes floated in and out of the night like fluorescent marbles, startled by the huge metal creature invading their turf. I heard a low, throaty cough—a sure sign that a mountain lion was lurking nearby, probably licking his chops at the sight of the potential meal on wheels.

The vehicle's brights picked up a dirt road that headed into the mountains. I quickly swerved onto it, hoping I'd made the right choice. The Blazer began its slow ascent toward the sky. I stayed as far away from the path's uneven edge as I could, following the precarious trail higher and higher. One wrong move, and I'd find myself plunging down the steep mountainside and crashing to earth, just one more casualty of the Mojave to be tripped across some day.

I kept going, my eyes focused on the road, while I strained to catch a glimpse of a light. The likelihood of becoming lion chow was beginning to haunt me when I finally caught sight of a flicker in the distance. The mountain leveled off, and I followed the tiny beam, latching onto it as my guiding star.

There was no moonlight to reflect off the life-size ark, but the faint yapping of Georgia Peach's matted menagerie was all the hard-core proof I needed that I had managed to find my way. I drove the remaining distance almost giddy with relief. The ark had never looked so good, its weathered wooden boards a welcome sight as I pulled up beside

Noah's battered Suburban. Georgia met me at the door with a drink in her hand.

"What are you, out for a stroll, Porter? Or did they fire you already?" She stepped aside to let me in. "Either way, you're just in time. I'm whipping up a batch of Fuzzy Navels."

Georgia's rear end hung out of the bottom of her short shorts, the dimpled skin more in need of exercise than of alcohol. I pushed my way past the motley mob nipping at my feet as Georgia turned around and caught sight of my face.

"What the hell happened to you? Have a bad experience at a tanning salon?" she asked, unable to take her eyes off me.

I knew what she was talking about. My face felt as though a blowtorch had been held up against it. I took a deep breath in an effort to hold myself together before I could speak.

"Something's going on. I need to talk to Noah." My voice quivered as my knees began to shake. Now that I was here and safe, the fire at Dee's was beginning to hit me with the force of a clenched fist driven into my chest.

The sound of a snore barreled through the ark. Noah lay spread-eagled across a mound of foam pillows on the floor behind me, his bare belly rising and falling to the rhythm of his snores. Clutched in one hand was an empty can of Bud. The other held a small bottle of nail polish, the cap barely hanging on. I looked down at Georgia's feet, where balls of cotton carefully separated each toe, half of which were painted flaming-red.

Georgia padded over to Noah and nudged him gently with her unpainted foot. It produced no response. She tried again, this time lifting her foot and giving him a swift kick in the ribs.

"What? What's the matter? What's going on?" Noah sputtered, struggling to sit up. Then he spotted me through half-closed eyes. "What the hell are you doing here?"

Georgia wended her way into the shambles of their

kitchen. "I'm gonna make coffee," she called out over her shoulder.

The next thing I knew, she shoved a shot of whisky into my hands. "Here, drink this."

I stared numbly at the glass, seeing flames dancing within the amber liquid. "I thought you were making coffee."

"Not for you. For him," Georgia replied, heading back to the kitchen. "You need some booze."

I gulped the liquid down. Its fire spread through me almost as quickly as the blaze that had engulfed Dee's house.

Georgia returned with a cup in one hand and a bottle of whisky in the other. The coffee inside the cup splashed back and forth with each step, spreading a trail of liquid onto the floor. It was quickly lapped up by the band of hair balls behind her. Noah gratefully accepted the cup and slowly sipped what was left as Georgia refilled my glass.

"Now what happened?" he asked, finally fully awake.

"Remember yesterday, when I told you that I might have blown the cover on a source?" I heard Dee's scream ring again in my ears.

"I remember," Noah said quietly.

"Well, I think I really did it this morning." Taking a deep breath, I tasted the fumes of the fire. "I called Dee Salvano, my source at the mine, earlier today. She told me that Golden Shaft just handed fifteen thousand acres of their newly patented land over to Alpha Development for the sum of one dollar."

"I knew it!" Noah exulted.

"It gets better," I told him. "Remember the claims that Golden Shaft obtained from Annie McCarthy right before she died?"

"Let me guess. The claims totaled fifteen thousand acres," Georgia said softly, sinking down onto one of the pillows.

"Yeah, okay. Still, what's the big deal?" Noah reasoned. "That information is public knowledge; it's not going to compromise your source. Besides, I'd bet my life you won't find anything tying those fifteen thousand acres into what happened to old Annie.''

"You don't understand.'' I paused and took a large drink of whisky, hoping to dull the throb in my head. "Last week I stole five dead tortoises from the storage freezer at the mine.''

"You *stole* them?'' Georgia gave a deep chuckle.

"Let's just say I didn't bother to tell anyone that they happened to fall inside my bag,'' I said. "Anyway, I had them autopsied. I felt pretty certain they had died as a result of being crushed by haul paks.''

"And what did you find out?'' Noah asked.

"Lanahan at Forensics thinks it might be radiation poisoning. His Geiger counter went wild when he put it next to the tortoises,'' I revealed.

Noah suddenly straightened up, leaning forward so intensely I was afraid he might topple over, his eyes burning as bright as two laser beams.

"When I told Dee about it this morning, she said she had something important to tell me but refused to talk over the phone. That's where I was, just before coming here. I went to Dee's house.''

"Get to the point, Porter. What did she say?'' Noah demanded.

A chill ran through me. "Nothing. Absolutely nothing at all.'' I began to choke up. "Her house had been set on fire. I have every reason to believe that Dee was inside.''

There was a long moment of silence as Noah absorbed what he'd just been told.

"That's it!'' Noah whispered. "Goddammit! That's where I know the guy from.''

I looked at Noah questioningly—and I realized that the man had come alive.

"Your friend Anderson? That bastard's with the Department of Energy!'' Noah slapped a hand down hard on the pillows, startling Georgia's sleeping dogs. Leaping up en masse, they yapped at an imagined intruder.

"I saw him at Los Alamos a couple of times. He was

attending high-level meetings that even I wasn't privy to.''

I watched his mind run at one hundred miles a minute, the hum almost audible. Then his eyes widened, witnessing something from his past.

''Holy shit! If this is what I think it is, they've fucked us and gotten away with it!'' he fumed.

The man was beginning to scare me. At the moment, I'd rather have had the old Noah that I knew and trusted.

''What are you talking about?'' I asked warily.

''Come on, Porter—think about it. You ever peel an onion? You peel one layer and there's another and then another and another. There's a game being played that I'm just beginning to understand.'' Noah shook his head in frustration. ''Look, those tortoises you snatched from Golden Shaft died from radiation poisoning, right? Well, don't you get it? Shit, we've got to get to the mine.''

He lumbered up, pushing away the pillows.

''Now?'' I asked in disbelief.

''Now!'' he roared.

''I'm coming, too,'' Georgia volunteered, pulling the cotton balls from between her toes.

''No. Someone's got to stay here,'' Noah quickly said. ''Just in case.''

''Just in case of what?'' she asked suspiciously.

''Just in case! That's all. We don't want to attract any attention. Two people are already more than enough. Three are way too many,'' he gruffly explained.

I had the distinct feeling Noah was trying to protect her.

''Great,'' Georgia pouted. ''So I'm the one who gets to stay home. What am I? The happy housewife?''

She poured the remaining vodka into the blender and flipped on the switch, drowning out the possibility of any further conversation.

We walked out the door, the whirring of the blender following us like an angry hornet. Noah quickly made a beeline for his Suburban before I could say a word.

''Why don't we take my Blazer for a change?'' I suggested. I was getting tired of playing sidekick in his wreck of a vehicle.

Noah stopped abruptly. "Listen, Porter. I don't like the idea of you coming along either. So don't push it."

I turned and stared him down. "Noah, you couldn't stop me if you ran me over with your damn truck."

"I know that," he growled. "Why the hell do you think you're coming?"

Noah jerked open the door of his Suburban and jumped in as I made a dash for the passenger side, afraid he might leave me behind. Reaching under his seat, he produced the same rumpled Hawaiian shirt he had worn yesterday, complete with the sour aroma of day-old Bud.

"Yeah. That's a good cover. Pretend you're a drunk going to a luau. That shouldn't attract too much attention," I commented snidely.

He pulled on the shirt, not bothering to retort. Turning on the engine, he headed out into the night.

Noah knew the way better than I ever would have. He navigated past each rock and perilous slope in the dark as if he had done it countless times before. I snuck a glance and was taken aback by the focused look of determination on his face. The overwhelming silence gnawed at me. Noah had provided more questions to think about than answers.

"Are you certain it was Brian Anderson that you saw at Los Alamos?" I asked. "After all, it was a few years ago. Maybe you have him confused with someone else."

With all the booze Noah must have consumed between then and now, I wasn't sure how much his memory could be trusted.

"Of course I'm certain," Noah snarled. "I've got the mind of a souped-up computer. I never forget a thing. I knew I'd seen that silver-haired freak somewhere before."

I didn't remind him that it had taken until now for his souped-up mind to click in.

"If you're right and Anderson really does work for DOE, why would he pose as the manager of a mine?" I countered.

"Good question, Red. That's exactly what we're going to find out," Noah replied.

The clouds were beginning to break, allowing the moon to slip in and out of its cover like a child playing a game of hide and seek. Just enough light shone for Noah to drive with only his dims. We had barely reached the summit overlooking Golden Shaft when a noise ripped through the blanket of night, slapping the air in an unexpected assault, and quickly escalating into a whirring roar. Noah immediately cut the engine and doused the lights before jumping out of the Suburban to get a better view. I joined him, hunkering down close as I approached the ledge.

The lights were on at the mine, where a group of people were busy milling about. But it was what had caused the noise that caught our attention. A large, unmarked black chopper hovered just above the ground, a canvas sling attached like a kangaroo's pouch below its belly. Sticking out of the top was what appeared to be part of a boring machine. We watched as the chopper slowly pulled up and away. Silhouetted against the moon, the cargo was anchored by a large metal hook held firmly in place with a thick coil of cable.

"It looks like they're moving out. But why at night? It doesn't make any sense," I whispered.

Noah didn't respond. I turned around, my stomach lurching, to find he was no longer there. A wave of panic rippled through me. I quietly backtracked to the Suburban, where I found Noah banging his head on the steering wheel over and over again.

"Stupid! Stupid! Stupid!" he exclaimed.

I slid into my seat and took a deep breath, relieved that he hadn't mysteriously disappeared, as I watched his head bob up and down.

"Exactly what is it that you're referring to in this particular instance?" I asked.

Noah stopped and raised his head. A curved red line looked as if it had been permanently carved into his brow.

"Those tortoises of yours were the tip-off. But the 'copters are how they did it!'' Noah exclaimed and then laughed at the thought. ''It really was just that simple! How the hell could I have been so blind?'' He slapped himself on the forehead.

''Clue me in here, Noah—because there's obviously something you know that I don't.''

Noah leaned toward me and whispered in my ear. ''Spent nuclear rods, Porter. They've been bringing them in here on government Black Hawks at night, all along.''

I looked at him and froze, the implication more than I was willing to imagine.

''You're saying the mine is a front? That this is really a nuclear waste facility?''

''Welcome to the wacky world of DOE, Red Riding Hood.'' Noah gave me a wicked grin. ''I'll bet Granny's house that what they're doing is testing the stuff here.''

''What do you mean, testing it?'' I asked apprehensively.

''Look around you, Porter. The rock structure here is exactly the same as the rock structure at Yucca Mountain,'' Noah explained, an edge of excitement creeping into his voice. ''Because of all the ruckus by anti-nuke activists, DOE has never been able to fully test their system for storing spent nuclear rods there. And they need to see just how well it will work. Think about it,'' he continued. ''What better place to test how effective your set-up is than out here in the middle of nowhere? A place that everyone thinks is a gold mine? And to top it off, one that's about to be closed to keep unwanted visitors away! Shit, I couldn't have planned it better myself.''

I was tempted to accuse him of having watched one too many episodes of *X-Files*. I really wanted to believe that Noah was just one more nut case feeding off conspiracy theories.

''We're being shafted alright, Porter. DOE set up this mine as a shell company in order to secretly lease the land and then buy it. And while I've been keeping my eye on Yucca, they've probably been conducting all their testing on nuclear waste right here.''

I continued to look for loopholes in his theory, though everything Noah said was beginning to make scary sense.

"But how can they legally get away with it?" I asked.

"That's the beauty of it, Red. Everything changed when Golden Shaft's patent went through. The fact that DOE doesn't own all of the land at Yucca was part of their problem. Other agencies were involved, which meant that their work had to be out in the open. But here DOE has total control. They don't have to squabble with other government agencies about what they can or can't do. Hell, nobody even knows that they're here. For chrissake, they just overcame the last legal impediment that stood in their way!" Noah urgently explained.

It suddenly all began to make sense.

"That would explain why those fifteen thousand acres were given to Alpha. The land must have been offered as a kickback to Garrett to help buy the county commission's silence," I reasoned aloud.

Noah nodded in agreement, his unkempt hair illuminated by a ray of moonlight that glimmered in through the windshield. "You got it, babe. Funny what an offer of free land in Clark County can accomplish. Especially when it's to be used for a multi-billion-dollar development deal."

Clearly it had been enough to buy DOE what it most wanted: anonymity, with its guarantee of no public hearings, no public protests, no public knowledge.

"Garrett and his cronies get rich off their real estate holdings; meanwhile, the county is kept fat and happy as Las Vegas Valley continues to grow," I surmised.

Noah beamed. "Red, if you weren't already in love, I'd marry you myself."

I felt my face flush and was glad for the cover of night.

"Let's see what's going on now," Noah suggested.

He shimmied out the van door and crept back to the ledge. I followed close behind, glad to have Noah with me. We watched in fascination as a crew of men scurried about, diligently loading equipment and boxes onto a waiting convoy of trucks. The lead lorry's engine rumbled to life, its low roar filling the valley below. Almost immediately the second truck joined in, and then the third and the fourth until the valley floor reverberated with their growls. I could almost feel the gear shifted out of first and thrust into second as the head truck heaved and then slowly pulled forward. The lorries lumbered past the guarded gate and headed down the road. We watched the slow procession go.

"If this is a nuclear waste facility, why is everyone leaving?" I asked, mystified by what was going on.

Noah pulled at a lone blade of grass and began to nibble on it, deep in thought. "They're probably just leaving a skeleton crew. In fact, they may not need any staff at all. With the proper computer equipment, this baby can be monitored from anywhere in the U.S."

He studied the scene below as he continued to munch on the blade. "Still, I can't see them locking it up and just walking away. Someone will have to be down there."

Noah began to walk back toward the van. "Come on, Red. It's time to head out."

The Suburban's ancient engine whined and complained before finally kicking in, the sound muffled by the din of the departing cavalcade. Noah carefully guided the vehicle along the top of the ridge until the far side of the mine came into view. Ahead of us lay a faint dirt path that appeared to plunge straight to the valley below. I found myself praying that Noah wouldn't be crazy enough to take it. But before I could wrap up my prayers, Noah had swung the Suburban's nose onto the path and we headed over the ledge.

My stomach leapt up to my throat as our roller coaster plunged down to meet the earth. Once I was sure we had landed, a rush of words came pouring out in one long, continuous flow.

"Listen, Noah, now that we know about this facility, we can stop it from operating. We can go back and tell—"

Noah cut me off at the pass. "Tell *who* Rachel? Just *who* is going to listen to us?"

I stopped and thought about it for a moment before Noah

continued. "We need proof, Porter. Without it, we're just two nuts picking our noses out in the desert in the middle of the night."

He was right. I would never have believed it myself until now.

Noah studied me and then pulled something out of his pants pocket. He reached for my hand, turned it over, and placed his palm on top of mine. When he took it away, a gold medal of St. Christopher dangling on a chain glistened in the palm of my hand.

"That's to protect you wherever you go," Noah said, looking at me intently.

"But you're Jewish," I blurted out, taken by surprise and not sure what else to say.

"Yeah? So?" Noah groused. "What does that mean? That a saint can't help me out every now and then?"

"Why are you giving this to me?" I asked.

Noah chewed on his bottom lip, focusing his attention back on the mine. "At least two people have already been killed over this. And those are only the ones that we know of. DOE's playing for keeps, Rachel. I want you to stay here and keep watch while I go in and find out what's going on."

My hand shot out and grabbed his wrist as his other hand reached for the door.

"If I'm not going in, then neither are you," I informed him. "What are you trying to do? Get yourself killed?"

Noah grinned at me. "Didn't I say something like that to you just the other day? When you barged up to those guards like a bat out of hell?"

I didn't answer.

Noah sighed and patted my hand. "Don't you get it yet, Porter? I don't care. I died two years ago along with my family in that flood. This is all I've been hanging around for."

He released my hand as he reached behind the seat, grabbed a large backpack, and headed out the door. I followed close on his heels until he stopped and turned around.

"You're not going in without me," I told him defiantly.

Before I knew what was happening, Noah planted a kiss that smelled of Jack Daniel's and Bud on my lips. I stared at the overweight man in his loud Hawaiian shirt, hairy legs, and cowboy boots, trying to imagine what he must have been like when he was cleaned up and working five years ago.

"Hey, those kisses used to be great," he smirked, breaking the awkward silence.

"I'm not going to scream sexual harassment and run, if that's what you're thinking. Don't try to scare me off, Noah. I'm coming in with you," I said, standing my ground.

Noah gave me a wink. "That's what I like about you, Porter. You're as crazy as I am."

Turning back toward the mine, we examined the fence, searching for a way in. Noah had begun to pull out an unwieldy pair of metal snips when I stumbled upon a gully under the wire that was just large enough for us to squeeze through. I realized it must have been the hole Pilot had dug only yesterday. The knot that had formed in my stomach tightened as I motioned to Noah.

Noah looked at the hole skeptically. "Sure. It's fine for you. For me, crawling under there is gonna be like trying to squeeze through an iron lung."

I wanted to attract as little attention as possible if we were going to do this. I was worried that the sound of metal snips cutting away at the fence would echo throughout the valley. In addition, it was possible that an alarm could be triggered.

"Listen, if we slide under, no one at the mine will ever know that we've been here," I reasoned. "I promise I'll help you get through."

Noah rolled his eyes, dropped his backpack, and hit the dirt. He maneuvered his body between the fence and the ground until he resembled a hot dog stuck in a bun.

"Okay, Porter. Brilliant idea. Now what?" he grumbled.

I sat down next to him, drawing my knees close into my chest, and braced my hands behind my back.

"Now I push," I said as my feet shot out, propelling his butt under the wire.

"Hey! That hurts, Porter!" he hissed in surprise.

"Just once more for the shoulders," I promised, setting myself in position again.

"Oh, shit! You're scraping my tan right off me," Noah complained. I pushed while he wriggled his shoulders, clearing the fence.

Noah brushed off his back and scrambled to his feet. "If you think I'm going out the same way, think again," he groused as I slid his backpack under the wire. "I expect a night on silk sheets after this, just to soothe my ravaged skin." He pulled me through to join him.

Though no guards were in sight, a heavy stillness bore down upon us, as though we'd just breached forbidden ground.

"Now what?" I whispered, afraid of disturbing the silence. "You're not planning an assault on the main office, are you?"

Noah snorted. "What do you take me for? Rambo? My motto is, If you've got a brain, use it. And the first thing it tells me is to stay away from the coffee machine. That's usually where everyone congregates late at night."

Noah hesitated, and I wondered if he'd begun to change his mind.

"You sure you want to go through with this?" I asked.

"You chickening out on me, Porter?" Noah taunted.

I'd sooner face Harley and his friends on a bad day. "Lead the way."

Noah turned and headed off across a large open space as I kept pace behind him. We made it to the base unobserved and then quickly scrambled up the far side of the mine, intersecting with a dirt road built into the mountain. The path led to an overhang, in which an electric meter box and a telephone were mounted. Closing off entry to the interior was a large steel door.

"Here's your first tip-off, Red," Noah noted. "You've gotta ask yourself what the hell an electric meter and a phone are doing outside a mine shaft."

"How did you know this was here?" I asked, not quite ready to believe Noah had the instincts of a bloodhound.

Noah grinned, adjusting the pack on his back. "You think you're the only detective in town? I started to get suspicious after our visit yesterday. So I set myself up on the ridge early this morning with a pair of high-powered binoculars and a couple of cans of beer, kicked back, and watched the show."

"Sort of your proverbial fly on the ledge?" I chuckled.

"You got it, Red," Noah agreed, pleased with the recognition.

I pulled out a pen and jotted the phone number listed on the meter onto the back of my hand. Noah looked at me, raising an eyebrow.

"Hey, you never know," I said in my own defense, not quite sure why I had done it.

Noah twisted the knob on the door, pressing against the steel with his shoulder. It gave way with a low creak that reverberated loudly in my ears. We walked ten feet inside and found a locked steel grate blocking our way. A second door stood behind it, slightly ajar. I half expected an armed guard to appear and blow us away, but the only thing I could hear was my heart pounding like a battering ram.

We stood still, barely daring to breathe, for what seemed an eternity. If a guard was on duty, he'd apparently taken a break. I pulled out my Leatherman and jimmied the lock. The grate swung silently open.

Noah shook his head in disbelief. "Pathetic, isn't it? Don't you think they'd take the time to put a decent latch on the place?"

He closed the outer door behind us as I peeked into a room ablaze with light. It was as if we had been magically transported into a technological wonderland, far away from the barren desert outside. Millions of dollars' worth of electronic equipment and gear filled the room, each instrument alive with an assortment of lights that glittered and gleamed and blinked on and off. I stood in the looming silence and gaped in astonishment. If I'd been Dorothy in the land of Oz, the Wizard's voice would have nailed me by now. I'd stepped into a secret world far beyond any I'd ever known, and I knew it would do no good to click my heels. There was no going home now.

I became aware of a low hum that pervaded the area, seeping into my bones so that my body joined in the vibration. A massive mainframe computer stood protectively in the corner of the room like a glowering samurai warrior. Blinking angrily at us, its screen spat out a flurry of red numbers in dizzying succession, protesting our brazen intrusion. A multitude of umbilical cords sprang from the electronic brain's back, connecting it to every gadget in the place, which contentedly fed off their host. Additional wires from each instrument ran into conduit attached to the wall, leading back into a tunnel like the beckoning tail of a dragon.

"Eureka! We've just hit the mother lode," Noah murmured, following me inside.

Noah's fingers wandered lovingly over every piece of equipment as though they were long-lost friends, cooing to them softly. When he saw the conduit, his body suddenly jerked and he quickly turned and followed the cables into the tunnel, disappearing from my sight.

My own attention had been lured to a chalkboard that held an array of phone numbers, each followed by a person's first name. I hurriedly began to scribble down as much of the information as I could, before Noah's voice brought my writing to a halt.

"Porter, get back here! There's something I want you to see."

My breath came in short, rapid bursts as I headed off, afraid that his voice would carry through the tunnel, past the mine, and up to the front office, where the gang was probably even now gathered about the coffee machine. The tunnel wound further and further back until the outer room was no longer in sight, the only source of light a row of tiny bulbs that illuminated the way. My eyes were drawn to irregular clusters of white fungus that haphazardly dotted the walls and ceiling like a secret government mushroom farm.

I spotted Noah at the end of the tunnel, standing next to an enormous block of cement. Looking like a massive, squat peg, it rose two feet above the floor. Studded into the slab were the hundreds of cables and wires that had snaked their way back through the tunnel, connecting the mainframe directly with the giant block. It was the ultimate computer nerd's dream, strewn with a wide assortment of gauges and screens. Endless streams of numbers flashed from some, while other screens danced as if possessed, kinetic green lines high-kicking and swaying like a chorus line of alien worms.

"What the hell is this?" I asked in astonishment, wondering if we'd just blundered upon a cousin to the monolith in the film *2001*.

"My best guess?" Noah rubbed the stubble on his chin against the back of his hand. "I'd have to say that this is where some of the rods are buried."

I felt the hair bristle on the back of my neck. "Inside this slab?"

"No. Underneath it. They would have buried them and then poured this cement block on top," Noah explained. "Either that, or they've got hot waste encased down there."

"Hot waste?" I asked, astounded at the thought of what lay beneath our feet.

"Sure. Heavy water—the waste water from nuclear storage, Porter. That stuff will keep generating heat and radiation long after it's been removed from a power plant. All these gauges and instruments are probably measuring temperature, compression, expansion—that sort of thing," Noah elaborated.

I must have looked like I was about to be left back in science class.

Noah sighed and tried it again. "In other words, scientists are studying to see how any rainwater that might trickle through cracks in the tunnel would behave and if the rock chemistry then changes. The theory is that heating this block will keep the waste and rods dry for thousands of years to come. So that if water does seep through, this block here will act like a big old percolator, turning it into steam," he clarified.

"Theoretically, what would happen if the waste managed to get wet?" I queried, paddling as fast as I could to try to keep up.

"Then you make tracks the hell out of Nevada on the first plane you can catch. If this stuff cools down, water will condense, seep through the rock and into the containers that hold those nuclear rods and fuel. When that happens, waste will begin to leach out and your groundwater becomes contaminated. That's the time to start buying stock in Evian water. Consider it a hot tip, Porter."

I stepped away from the huge block as Noah pulled a Geiger counter out of his backpack.

"Here we go," he said, holding it out in front of him.

"What are you doing with that?"

"This little beauty is going to let us know if there's any kind of radiation leak in here," he grinned.

I watched as Noah's smile abruptly disappeared, his face turning grim.

"What's up?" I asked, not sure I really wanted to know.

Noah silently turned the Geiger counter in my direction so I could see the dial. The needle had swung clean off the scale.

Noah stuck the counter in his pack. "Time to haul ass, Red. We probably started to glow in the dark about two minutes ago." He quickly headed out the tunnel.

I ran to keep up with him, surprising us both as I slammed into the back of his pack in the main room. Noah had stopped dead in his tracks.

"Shit, Porter! Will you watch where you're going? At this rate, I won't have to worry about radiation when I've got you to scare me to death!"

He pointed toward the chalkboard he'd been studying before our collision. "I know these people and I can damn well read their equations," he said angrily. "What they're doing is more than just a little testing. It looks like they've decided to permanently leave in the rods that they've buried here."

I felt sure Noah had to be wrong. "But Alpha's planning a housing development that will probably come right up alongside the mine."

"Yeah. Real thoughtful of Garrett and the gang. Not only do you get a house, but enough radioactivity to light it for free. Let's go check out what our friends at DOE have planted in the tunnel below this one."

"There's another?" I asked in alarm.

"Well, there's a second steel door the next level directly down from here, and I have a feeling it's not the entrance to the employee cafeteria," Noah retorted.

Noah ran outdoors and then barreled down the side of the mountain like a runaway train, his weight propelling him past the lower level. Unable to stop, he finally fell on his butt, flinging his arms out as he grabbed onto handfuls of gravel. After watching his performance, I chose to sit on my rear end to begin with. I slowly slid my way down, digging my heels in and braking to a gentle halt.

"That's impressive, Porter," Noah sarcastically observed as I stood up and brushed off my pants.

"I'm bowled over by your fancy footwork, too," I retorted.

Noah dumped his backpack on the ground and pulled out a flashlight as we examined yet another steel door. A thick chain was stretched across the metal, secured by a heavy padlock. I got down on one knee and immediately lost my balance, sliding into a deep depression that had formed beneath the doorway.

Noah flashed his light on the gully and shrugged. "Probably rattlesnakes living inside. Or maybe a coyote.''

I jumped up and backed away until I heard Noah begin to snicker. Cursing him under my breath, I straddled the hole, focusing on picking the lock. But the catch wouldn't budge.

''Fuck that,'' Noah snarled, stuffing the end of the flashlight into his mouth.

He pulled out his metal snips and cut the chain as easily as a knife slicing through butter. Then, stepping around his backpack, he pushed open the door. The flashlight prowled the subterranean walls like the eyes of a nocturnal cat, pouncing upon the power switch that came into view. Noah flicked it on, and a row of bare bulbs sprang to life, dimly illuminating the tunnel before us. We walked a short distance, the rough-hewn, craggy walls our only guide, until we came to a corridor that branched off to the right. Noah aimed his flashlight down the unlit passage and turned into it as I followed behind. I tried to peer around his massive frame, but my eyes remained glued to the bright Hawaiian flowers on his shirt, which undulated in psychedelic lunacy, their fluorescent gleam appearing to mutate in the dark.

We had only gone about twenty feet in when Noah came to an abrupt halt. The small tunnel had ended, cut off by an airshaft that revealed the night sky. Glancing up, I saw a peek-a-boo moon wink as it escaped from behind a cloud, a silent co-conspirator to our break-in. My eyes followed a ray of moonlight back down and came to rest on the ghostly skeletons of a pair of raptors. Spotting them at the same time, Noah knelt beside the remains of the birds, their bare bones shimmering as though illuminated from inside.

''They must have flown in here and then evidently became too sick to fly back out,'' Noah softly said.

''Too sick from what?'' I queried, the words forming like heavy lumps of clay in the back of my throat.

Either Noah didn't hear or he was too engrossed to answer. Scouring the area, his searchlight focused in on yet another open burial site. The small frame of what had been a coyote lay quietly on its side, its perfectly intact skeleton settled in for the night, not expecting to be caught by un-invited guests. A shiver formed at the base of my spine, snaking up through my body until my teeth began to chatter.

Noah retraced his steps without a word as we connected once again with the main tunnel. By now, the shaft exuded the closeness of a tomb. My arms pressed protectively against my sides as my clothes clung to my body in a moist layer of fear. I had always sworn I'd be cremated, fearing the suffocating confinement of a coffin and the impenetrable darkness of night. Now I wondered if this was what it felt like to be buried alive.

My senses heightened, I glanced around, noticing large patches of the same white fungus I'd seen in the passageway above. But this time the formations appeared to erupt from glistening crystals that grew out of the walls of stone. Eerily fascinated by their shimmering gleam, I reached out, wanting to caress their crystalline surface, as if that would somehow reassure me that I was still alive.

But Noah grabbed onto my wrist in midair. "Don't touch that, Rachel. Don't touch anything inside this tunnel," he sternly warned. "I've never seen formations like these before. But I can sure as hell tell you they aren't your normal everyday crystals. The less physical contact we have with anything in here, the better off we'll be."

I found myself wondering what the consequences were of just being in the place, but didn't dare ask. Having come this far, neither of us planned on turning back now. We continued on our trek, pushing further into the shaft.

"We should be right below that concrete slab about now," Noah informed me.

But I barely listened, suddenly aware of the sharp smell of ammonia that had begun to fill my lungs. My stomach performed a series of skydiving somersaults as the odor continued to grow. I brought my hand up to cover my mouth, then remembered where I had smelled that same scent before: at Annie's house.

Noah noticed the odor as well. "That's the smell of

death, Porter. Something's decomposing in here.''

Noah focused the flashlight into a corner, where the decaying carcass of a coyote lay, an odd puddle of liquid on its side shining in the light. A short distance from the carcass lay a couple of large shells from which leg, neck, and head bones protruded: the skeletons of two desert tortoises.

Noah slowly raised his flashlight from the disintegrating corpse, up along the tunnel wall, one maddening inch at a time. The focused rays picked up tiny fractures that sparkled in the stone, their surfaces slick and shiny, the crystals growing out of them gleaming with dew. Noah's flashlight continued its upward journey, the beam traveling still higher, until the source of the moisture was finally found. A small stream of water dripped with a silent, steady beat from the uneven ceiling, the drops obscenely muted by the cadaver below.

"Shit. The damn place is leaking! That's why they're moving out," Noah whispered in a hoarse rasp. He looked like a living corpse, his usual sunburned complexion transformed into a pallid mask of gray.

"But what about that heated block?" I said frantically. "I thought that was supposed to keep water from reaching any of the waste."

More than anything, I wanted to shake Noah as hard as I could, forcing him to say he was wrong, that this was all some ludicrous mistake.

"It had to be that earthquake," he muttered, half to himself.

"What are you talking about?" I asked, even as I remembered the tremor that had rocked my kitchen, breaking my few pitiful secondhand dishes, only a week ago. "What would an earthquake have to do with any of this?"

And then the final piece of the puzzle fell into place. "The radiation poisoning those tortoises died from! Their water source must have been here, inside the mine. They were just the ones that got out alive."

But Noah didn't answer, his mind already moving ahead at warp speed.

"I left my pack outside the tunnel. I need to take a reading on this place. I'm going to get it and you're coming with me. I want you out of here now, Porter."

Noah swiftly turned around to leave, then he came to an abrupt halt and stiffened. I drew alongside him and looked down, furiously exploring the dark without any clue as to what I was searching for. Until I heard the whisper of a sound, and my eyes latched onto three tiny pack rats huddled together, their bodies pressed tightly against the rough tunnel wall. Fearing our attention, the rodents drew closer still, pathetically whimpering as they tried their best to hide from our sight.

Noah carefully knelt down and flashed his light on their quivering bodies, and I heard a sharp cry. The sound echoed in my ears, and I realized that the cry was my own. A steady trickle of blood wept from their eyes, their noses, and their mouths, transforming them into a perverse science fiction version of the three blind mice.

"Take a good look, Rachel," Noah whispered, his voice sounding a thousand miles away. "What you're seeing is radiation poisoning. Let's get the fuck out of here now."

Noah quickly retraced his steps toward the exit. I immediately began to follow when another sound, coming from further back, reached my ears. Halting, I watched Noah's retreating form pass under each bare bulb, the brilliant colors of his shirt fading like the last rays of sun on a hot summer night. My mind told me to run as fast as I could, to think of nothing but getting out of the tunnel. But my feet had a mind of their own. Knowing I had little choice, I found myself turning away from Noah and heading deeper into the shaft.

The bulbs became fewer, the light more dim, and my head pounded with each step, the air pungent with death and decay. I heard the cry again, though I tried not to listen. I told myself it was nothing more than my demons toying with me, mocking my fear. But by now my body was on automatic pilot. Noah's voice called to me from off in the distance, but I didn't bother to answer, knowing I had to face whatever it was on my own.

Wrapped up in my thoughts, I was caught off guard by the rock that jutted in front of me. I tripped, and a sharp jolt of pain shot up my leg as my ankle twisted and I went down. I called out in dismay, angry at my foolhardy pride. But Noah was no longer there. I pulled myself up and hobbled a few steps, deciding I'd had enough. It was time to head back. Then a loud whimper stopped me dead in my tracks, turning my blood ice-cold.

I continued on, limping slowly toward the sound, my eyes focused on the form that was beginning to take shape under the shaft's shadowy light. Trembling, I moved in closer. My breath caught in my throat, and a wave of nausea surged through me.

Pilot lay on his side, a rivulet of blood streaming from his mouth. He tried raising his tail, only to have it thump weakly down to the ground. Then he looked up at me and let out a cry, as if to tell me he was hurt, trusting I would make it all better. My knees buckled beneath me and a sob racked my body, my cry blending in with his. I wrapped my arms around his neck and buried my face in his fur. Then, grabbing a tissue from my pocket, I tried as best I could to wipe away the blood, my vision blinded by tears. But the flow wouldn't stop, staining his muzzle a deep crimson red.

"Oh, no, Pilot, not you," I whispered, knowing I couldn't leave him.

My prayers were answered when I heard Noah call my name, followed by a gunshot that rang out in the distance. In my desperate relief to hear from the man who was fast becoming my guardian angel the sound didn't register.

"I'm back here! I've found Pilot. We need to get him out!"

Noah didn't answer. But his footsteps echoed down the long hall, raising my spirits as they drew closer. It was only as my rescuer came into view that I knew all of my hopes had been dashed.

Brian Anderson stood before me, a .357 Magnum held in his hand. I stared at him through my tears, continuing to stroke Pilot's fur, as the dog let loose a low growl.

I didn't ask about Noah. I already knew what had happened.

Brian shook his head in dismay, his eyes looking first at Pilot and then back at me. "I'm so sorry, Rachel."

I truly believed him, and for the briefest moment, I felt as if we still might be saved.

"I didn't want things to end like this. I tried to warn you," he said gravely.

It was then that I finally knew where Brian's allegiance lay.

"But why?" I asked, barely able to form the words over the sob that was lodged in my throat.

"It's simple." Brian shrugged. "We're dealing with a public that wants cheap energy, but no one wants nuclear waste buried in their own backyard. As it stands now, DOE already has to ante up damages for coming in behind schedule."

Brian looked tired, as if dealing with the issue had taken its toll.

"Yucca Mountain would have solved the problem. But your friend Noah put the brakes on that when he brought in the press. So we set up the Golden Shaft mine. The idea was to prove our case here—that Yucca Mountain could be made safe," he explained. "Unfortunately the earthquake last week was centered in this area. The waste canisters came loose, and some leakage occurred."

I gently laid Pilot's head down on the ground with a final kiss, then pushed my way up along the wall.

"Did DOE buy the county commission's cooperation by promising land for development if they remained silent?" I asked.

Brian smiled sadly. "Life is a series of murky compromises, Rachel. It's amazing the power that developers have in this county."

I felt faint at the sight of Pilot's blood on my pants but

forced my mind to stay focused. I had to keep Brian talking. "What about the houses that are going to be built? The people that will be living here?"

"Developers are a greedy, unconscionable lot, aren't they? Makes you stop and wonder about human nature," Brian smiled grimly.

"Is that why Dee was murdered?" I asked, playing for time.

Brian's finger rested on the Magnum's trigger. There was no way I'd ever outdraw the man.

"You know why, Rachel. You were partially responsible. She knew too much and was beginning to talk." Brian restlessly shifted his weight.

My fingers latched onto the chain that hung from my back pocket. "And Annie McCarthy? Did she know too much as well?"

Brian sighed. "I'm sorry about that. Alpha Development wanted her land and she wouldn't sell."

He began to raise the gun as I wrapped the chain tight in the palm of my hand.

"What I still can't figure out are the tortoise symbols that were found," I said desperately.

Brian stared at me blankly, the gun frozen in place. Then he smiled as he realized what I was talking about.

"Oh, that was Garrett's nephew. The idea was to send Metro on a wild-goose chase after animal activists." Brian shook his head. "Kids and their crazy ideas."

I brought my hands out from behind my back, the pounding in my head making it hard for me to think. I racked my brain, at a loss on how to distract Brian.

But Anderson had reached his limit. "I'm sorry, Rachel. Time's up. No more questions. That's been your problem right from the start. You should have talked less and listened to me more." Predatory eyes flickered coldly, his voice turning flat and hard. "You don't know how much I hate this part of the job."

My lungs had begun to burn with the fury of a stoked furnace, while my heart was beating like a locomotive out of control. I could feel the weight of Pilot's head against my legs as I took a deep breath and said a silent prayer. Then, opening my eyes wide, I focused my attention behind Brian.

"Noah! Watch out!" I screamed loud enough to bring every dead soul in the cave back to life.

Brian glanced over his shoulder, and I quickly threw the St. Christopher medal down the tunnel hall as far as I could. Brian went for the bait. Turning around, he took off toward the sound as I dodged past Pilot and pushed deeper into the mine. I spotted a passageway that veered off to the right and hobbled inside.

But any hope of evasion was mere illusion. Brian's voice curled with serpentine menace down the floor of the hall, smoothly rounding each corner until it nailed me.

"Good try, Rachel. But I can't leave you here, and you can't get away. Don't make this any harder than it already is."

I stumbled blindly, crying out as I stubbed a toe hard against a rock. At the same moment, I discovered that my escape had been cut off, dead-ended by yet another wall. Bracing myself against it, I tore the SIG-Sauer pistol from the back of my pants and held it in both hands, trying my best to be cool and steady.

I aimed at the entrance and calculated where Brian's chest would be, my finger pressed lightly against the trigger. I held my breath until I felt I would burst—then Brian's silver hair finally came into view. I silently cursed every demon in my life, every poacher that had gotten away, the forces that had caused Pilot to be poisoned, and any man that would take me for a fool. I focused Anderson's chest in my sights, and firmly squeezed the trigger. But instead of the inevitable roar, a deadly silence became my earthly shroud. My gun had jammed, just as it had on the day I'd met Noah. I stood with my back to the wall, now the perfect target.

A fine layer of sweat defined each flawless angle in Brian's handsome face as I sensed the tension in his body relax. He serenely raised his revolver and pointed it in my direction.

"Oh, Rachel. You almost had me. That makes this so much easier now."

My life didn't flash before me and I wondered if it was because I didn't have one as I heard a roar and waited to die. It took a splitsecond before I realized that the sound hadn't come from a gun but from Pilot, who had managed to follow us in. The dog leapt against Brian's back, the full force of his weight catching the man off guard and sending my adrenaline soaring.

Anderson's revolver clattered to the ground. I flung my own useless pistol at his head and dove forward, determined to claim his .357. My fingers wrapped around the Magnum's handle, then Brian's hand clamped onto mine, bearing down with the strength of a vice.

I hung on tight as Anderson rose to his feet, pulling me up along with him, all the while fighting to pry the gun from my grip. Gritting my teeth, I refused to let go. I kept one hand on the Magnum and the other on Brian's wrist, fighting to ignore the pain that tore through me. Finally, unable to hold him off any longer, my arms quivered and began to give way as Anderson steadily pushed the gun in toward me. The cold steel of the revolver lodged itself tightly beneath my chin like a brace, thrusting my head back until it could go no further.

My throat rested heavily on the mouth of the barrel, imprinted with each tiny ridge. My last thought was that you could only be betrayed by the people you trust. I was still holding tight onto Brian's wrist when Pilot lunged once again, his fangs sinking into Anderson's arm. Brian screamed at the dog and struggled to shake him off, but Pilot's grip only grew stronger. My heart hammered against my ribs as I called up every last bit of strength I could muster to propel the gun away from my neck, slanting it in Brian's direction. His eyes caught mine in a riveting stare, and his voice gave one last command.

"It's over, Rachel."

I'll never know if the pronouncement was meant for my own death or his. I concentrated on squeezing my fingers as hard as I could against Anderson's, which covered the trigger. Then the sound of gunfire roared through my limbs and my body flew backward, the revolver clutched tight to my chest. I looked up and saw Brian still standing, even as the sickeningly sweet scent of blood filled the air. My mind frozen in terror, I held the gun out before me and shot twice more. When I stopped, his body lay crumpled, as lifeless as everything else in the tunnel.

I wanted to laugh and cry in relief—until I saw Pilot. He was lying on his side, blood running from his nose, each breath racking his body with pain. I knew he was dying and that I was losing my closest friend.

I also knew there was only one thing left I could do, breaking the only vow I'd made when I'd taken this job. Cradling his head in my lap, I brushed my lips against his fur and thanked him for saving my life. Then, standing, I held the magnum steady in both hands and taking careful aim, shot Pilot between the eyes.

My mind was numb as I limped back through the tunnel, my hands pressing blindly along the wall to guide the way. It seemed forever before I began to smell the desert air, sweeter than any perfume. For the first time, I knew that my demons had never been monsters or things that go bump in the night. They were tangible, made of real flesh and of bone. Even worse, they now had a face, bringing the terror closer to home.

Already light-headed, I felt almost giddy as the entrance came into view, and I picked up my pace. But something was blocking my way. Losing my balance, I tumbled to the ground, where Noah stared blankly, a bullet hole smack through his head. A wave of panic crested, threatening to burst, as death closed in around me. I scrambled up, fear propelling my body out of the tunnel and past the steel door, until I was standing under the night sky with a ceiling of stars burning blissfully in their orbs. I wanted to cry until there were no tears left. Instead, I threw back my head and howled in rage, my screams covered by the roar of haul paks as they continued to make their way down the road.

Eighteen

I don't remember how I made it back to the ark. All I knew was that when I opened my eyes, Georgia was hovering over me, a spoon in her hand and the smell of chicken soup filling the air.

"Thank God," Georgia said, her eyes uncharacteristically brimming with tears. "You scared the hell out of us, Porter."

"Us?" My tongue felt heavy and dry, making it an effort to speak.

Suzie Q poked her head out from behind the tie-dyed curtain. "Yeah. Georgia, Frankie S., and me," she said, though the tarantula was nowhere in sight. Her eyes were swollen and red as if she had been crying.

"I have to tell you what happened." I struggled to sit up, my stomach grumbling loudly.

"What you have to do is eat," Georgia ordered, shoving a spoonful of soup in my mouth. "You've been going back and forth between a high fever and chills for the past two days. As for food, I'm on my last pot of soup. Let's hope you can keep this one down."

"But I have to tell you about Noah," I insisted, not knowing when I had ever been so hungry.

The spoon came to a halt in midair as Georgia's face froze into a mask of grief.

"You already did, Porter," she informed me softly. Then she cleared her throat. "We know what happened. Don't you remember?"

I shook my head as I inhaled the soup. Looking up, I saw Georgia and Suzie Q silently watching, their cheeks wet with tears. Then the flood of events came rushing back to me.

"We have to get to the mine! Noah's body is still there. So is Pilot's." My voice cracked as the two women continued to stare, neither saying a word. "We need to prove what DOE has been doing!"

Georgia shook her head slowly, as if dealing with an unruly child. "It's over, Porter," she said, echoing Anderson's very last words.

Icy fingers ran their way up my spine, the soup turning cold in my stomach.

"Do you really think you can prove anything?" Georgia continued, a hard edge to her voice. "Trust me. You'll never be able to beat DOE."

But by this time, my feet were already on the floor and I was shakily heading for the door.

"I'm damn well going to try. I'll need help in getting both Noah and Pilot out, and there's no time to call anyone and explain." I looked at both expressionless faces, wondering if they had even heard what I'd said. "Who's going to come with me?"

Suzie Q slipped wordlessly behind the curtain. I didn't bother to wait for Georgia Peach's answer, certain of what she would say.

I walked outside and blinked, surprised to find daylight. Noah's beat-up Suburban was parked in its usual place, his backpack lying beside it. Grabbing the pack, I headed over to the Blazer, where I found Georgia leaning against its side.

"Jesus Christ, you're stubborn as hell," she sniffled, and then blew her nose. "Wasn't the other night enough for you? Do you want to die as well?"

That was the last thing I wanted. But even more, I wanted to prove what DOE had done. Otherwise nothing in my life would ever make sense.

"Don't you care about what happened to Noah?" I quietly asked, hoping to goad her to action.

Georgia's eyes hardened and then bore straight through me. "Hell, Porter. We may not do the usual pissing and moaning and groaning, like I suppose you're used to. But Noah was part of our family. So what say you cut the moral crap and let's get under way."

We headed out in the Blazer without another word, silence stretching between us until we reached the former Golden Shaft mine.

The front gate was locked and the place deserted, without a soul in sight. I didn't bother to beep the horn or wait for guards. It was obvious no one was there. Breaking and entering was fast becoming my second profession. I picked the lock and slowly drove through the gate, inspecting the site that had become part of my fate.

Every haul pak was gone, the absence of their roar more deafening than the thunder of their engines had been. I searched for the spot where Noah and I had begun our assault. Daylight bathed the area in quiet indifference. A golden eagle circled lazily overhead, the desert caught up in a midday yawn. I parked the vehicle and handed a flashlight to Georgia, glancing up at the cloudless sky. I was fully prepared for a Black Hawk to swoop down upon us, its cacophonous din invading my soul. But the only sound was the overpowering silence of the deadly still land.

I led the way, scrambling up the hillside to the top level, not yet ready to witness the remains of Noah and Pilot. A skull and crossbones had been newly painted on the door and a padlock put back in place. A sign warned, "Abandoned Mine. Danger. Keep Out." The electric meter box and phone were nowhere in sight.

I pulled out the metal snips and cut my way past the front door, no longer giving a damn about DOE property. Though the inner steel grate was now gone, the second door stood open, almost as if someone knew we'd be there. My heart picked up its pace as I flicked on my flashlight and expectantly shone its golden beam around the room. Just as quickly, my heart came to a stop. Everything I had seen only two days ago was no longer there.

My body broke into a drenching sweat, my eyes refusing to believe what they saw. The mainframe samurai warrior had vanished, as had every single piece of equipment. It was as if the very tunnel had swallowed up the miles of conduit, along with hundreds of electrical cords, snuffing out their circulatory powers. My brain buzzed, clouding my thoughts, as I tried to figure out where I had gone wrong. I was certain we were on the right level. But the room that once blazed bright as the Rockefeller Center Christmas tree was now as barren as snowfall under the hot Mojave sun.

"Everything I described to you was here! I swear it!" I exclaimed, trying to reassure myself as well as convince Georgia, who looked blankly at me without saying a word.

I was rushing back through the corridor, afraid I was either dreaming or had truly gone mad, when the block of cement finally appeared, as solid and reassuring as an ancient artifact from a faraway land. But even this was stripped of the gauges and instruments that had adorned it.

"What did you expect?" Georgia sarcastically asked, perching herself on top of the block. "That there would be a neon sign up announcing, 'Nuclear test facility. Come right this way'?"

I ran out of the empty room and slid down to the lower level, where a spanking new lock had been attached to that door as well and the gully beneath it filled. Cursing silently, I wielded the metal snips like an executioner's sword, quickly severing the chain.

In my mind's eye, Noah lay on the tunnel floor, the bullet wound in his forehead puckered and red. But his body was nowhere in sight. I made a mad dash for the air shaft, my heart beating so hard I felt faint, only to find that each skeleton had been removed. I hurried on, the whimper of pack rats filling my ears, yet no trace of them could be found. Finally I entered the room where I'd fought for my life, my pulse pounding in a combination of anger and fear. Nothing of Pilot was left. It was as though all the bodies had vaporized into thin air, their very existence expunged, my memory mocked and denied.

I wanted to tear down the walls, blast open the cave, find Brian's corpse, and strangle it with my bare hands. Instead, I was left to swallow my rage.

"You're right, Georgia. They've won," I finally conceded, my anger building inside.

Laughter nipped at my heels with razor sharp teeth, ghostly taunts whispering that I'd failed. Frustration devoured me as I scoured the room again, but any telltale signs had been forever obliterated.

Wordlessly I began to head back, my mind racking up losses, when a glitter of gold caught my eye. My feet froze in place. There, nestled between two small rocks, lay the St. Christopher medal, which had protected me just as Noah had promised. I picked up the necklace with its memories branded inside and after a moment turned and offered it to Georgia. It was the only proof there would ever be of what we both knew had taken place.

Georgia Peach held it in her hands as carefully as if it were the last of its kind, then slipped the chain over my head.

"It's yours, Porter," she said. "You earned it. If I were you, I'd hold onto it tight for a very long time."

We drove back to the ark as silently as we came, the gold medal burning against my skin. The stillness was finally broken by the crazed barking of the whirlwind of Lhasas. Georgia got out of the passenger door and leaned in on the open window as Suzie Q slinked to her side.

"What are you planning to do now?" Georgia asked, brushing a strand of hair from her face.

I thought about it for a moment, unsure of what the next step would be. I knew I had better odds trying to break the bank at a casino in Vegas than I did going up against DOE.

"Yeah. Sure, you could go back to Disneyland. But why the hell would you go there when you've always got the ark?" Suzie Q chimed in.

I smiled, appreciative of the invitation. But I could already feel the ark's ghosts settling in.

"What bothers me is that Garrett and Holmes are still out there. They've gotten away scot-free."

"Don't bother worrying about Holmes." Suzie Q giggled mysteriously. "He's being taken care of even as we speak."

I noticed that her shoulder was again empty of one very large and intimidating tarantula.

"Listen, not that I'm looking to befriend him or anything, but where's Frank Sinatra these days?" I asked.

Suzie Q gave a sinister grin. "Frank's pretty busy right now. It seems he got hold of something that he'll be feasting on for a long time to come."

Georgia Peach chirped in before I dared question Suzie Q any further. "I wouldn't worry too much about Garrett either. He shouldn't be hard to deal with."

The Blazer's engine kicked in and I started to pull away, not really wanting to think about either Frank Sinatra or his meal at the moment. But Georgia stopped me, coming over to my window.

"I was wrong about you, Porter," she simply said.

"You mean you've changed your mind? My body isn't completely shot to hell?" I asked with a slight grin. Okay, I admit it—her initial critique still bugged me.

Georgia gave a weary smile. "You're not ready for the body shop yet. But don't let that go to your head. You'll be there soon enough."

She leaned in further, her face more serious now. "What I meant is, don't ever let them run you out of your job. Those bastards in Washington may not know it, but they need someone like you in the field, kicking butt."

At the moment, I wasn't so sure I agreed with her. "Fish and Wildlife could always use a good biologist," I ventured.

But Georgia Peach shook her head. "I served my time, Porter. Remember? I'm the disgruntled government employee. You're the one with that damn burning fever to help. I hope that it lasts forever.''

Pushing away, she waved her hand in farewell.

Everything felt slightly off-kilter as I drove out of the desert and onto the razzle-dazzle terrain of the Strip. I knew I'd have to check in with Sam at some point, although I didn't have the slightest idea of what I would say.

I pulled into my driveway to find a mailbox had been erected, as bright and shiny as a brand-new bullet. Opening the lid, I extracted an armload of mail, most of it intimately addressed to Resident.

My bungalow looked better than I had remembered, though the silence was louder without Pilot around. Tears sprung up at the thought, and I knew they'd be there for a long time to come.

I threw the mail on my bed and hit the Playback button on my answering machine, which was flashing faster than a broken traffic light. Lizzie had left five separate messages, each one more anxious than the last.

"That's it, Rachel. Either you ring me back or I'm going to be forced to call the police. Isn't there some sort of charge for ignoring your best friend? By the way, Tabby here has destroyed my entire boa collection. I think it's time we discussed joint custody.''

I picked up the mail and sorted through unpaid bills as Lanahan's voice boomed out next.

"Hey, Porter. All is forgiven. It seems my Geiger counter was wacky, after all. Damn those labs and their RAD counters! But I've been getting some very strange phone calls. What say you and I talk? By the way, you owe me at least coffee and a doughnut for the mailbox.''

I let my mind go blank, not wanting to think right now about DOE and the length of their reach. Later on I would decide just what Lanahan really believed and how much he really knew.

I wasn't surprised to hear Duff Gaines of the *Las Vegas Sun* pop up on my line, still chipping away at the tortoise story. But it was the next call that caught my attention. Santou's voice gently wound around my heart.

"Listen, *chère*. Maybe I pushed too hard last weekend when I was out there. What say we blame it on the voltage sparking off those Vegas chapel signs? I'm thinking we should spend some quality time together and try to sort things out. How about we meet somewhere on neutral ground?" There was a moment's pause. Then Santou cleared his throat, his voice turning soft and low. "What will never change is that I love you, Rachel. Give me a call as soon as you can."

His message left me feeling not quite so alone. Maybe Noah had been right after all. I'd waited almost too long to grab hold of the brass ring, afraid of taking a chance, fearful of losing it all. If Santou was willing to give it another try, I promised myself not to blow it this time.

I threw the remaining mail off my lap, anxious to pick up the phone, when a large manila envelope caught my eye. It's funny how some things can grab you without your knowing why. The envelope nearly jumped into my hands as I pulled it out of the pile and quickly ripped it open. Goose bumps worked their way up my spine, past my neck, gathering for a powwow at the top of my head.

The letter had been sent by Dee. My heart pounded at the possibility that she might still be alive until I examined the envelope more closely. It had been postmarked the day of the fire.

I pulled out the contents, trying to steady my hands as I focused my mind. But all thoughts of remaining cool, calm, and collected were trashed as my eyes settled on the papers inside. Neatly clipped together was a bombshell big enough to blow both DOE and Alpha Development clear out of Nevada.

Topping the pile was a deed from Golden Shaft granting fifteen thousand acres of prime real estate to Alpha Development for the bargain basement price of one dollar. But Dee's revenge went further than that. Official papers spelled out the exact extent of DOE's cover-up, along with a blueprint revealing how Golden Shaft was set up to be used for the storage of high-level nuclear waste. Best of all was the document that reported that leakage had now taken place.

Dee had chosen her material wisely, handing me everything I could possibly need. The only decision to be made was whom to give the information to first.

My spirits soared. Along with the realization that DOE hadn't won after all came an end to the whispering taunts that had trailed me ever since I had left the mine.

I was still rejoicing in my new-found victory when the ringing of the phone took me by surprise. I quickly picked it up, hoping it would be Santou—but the robotic voice that greeted me was like a shot of freon injected straight into my veins.

"This is being said just once, Porter," the voice warned. "If you're smart, you'll forget everything you saw the other night. Otherwise someday you won't come home. Your boss will wonder what happened for a while. Your little neighbor? She'll think you packed up and moved. As for your boyfriend, he'll just pickle his brain in booze. You won't ever be heard from again."

The mechanical voice gave a malicious chuckle. "It's a big desert out there, princess. Piss us off enough, and you'll end up a lab rat at Area 51."

The phone clicked dead in my ear as a bolt of recognition tore through me.

I now knew who had been responsible for the threats and the pipe bombs all along. It hadn't been Harley and his two pals or even Garrett and his nephew. Only someone involved with the government would have been able to know my every move. And only one person had ever referred to me as princess. My mind screamed in rage at the undeniable truth: Brian Anderson was alive.

I sat stunned. I knew that DOE could track me down wherever I went, haunting my every move. And then I remembered a basic tenet I'd learned from old Charlie Hickok.

"Sheet, Bronx. Every criminal and case has its weak spot. Ya just gotta figure out what that is. Then after you've done that? You just drive a goddamn stake right through the sonofabitch."

I chuckled to myself, knowing Charlie would be pleased, even though he'd never admit it. If DOE had one weak spot, it was their fear of the public's right to know. And what the hell—while they might be supremely angry with me for a while, my best protection lay in placing what I knew right out in the open.

I pulled out my cell phone, certain that a tap on my residence line was already firmly in place. There was the call to be made to Santou and plane tickets to be purchased. But I had one task that had to be dealt with first. My fingers quickly punched in the numbers, my exhilaration revving back up as my adrenaline kicked into gear. My call was answered on the second ring by a voice eager to be given the bait.

"Duff Gaines, *Las Vegas Sun.*"

"Hi, Duff. This is Rachel Porter, with the U.S. Fish and Wildlife Service. Have I got a story for you."

Explore Uncharted Terrains of Mystery
with *Anna Pigeon, Parks Ranger* by

NEVADA BARR

LIBERTY FALLING 0-380-72827-3/$6.99 US/$9.99 Can

While visiting New York City to be with her sister, Anna invesigates when a teenager falls—or is pushed—to her death from the Statue of Liberty.

TRACK OF THE CAT
0-380-72164-3/$6.99 US/$9.99 Can

A SUPERIOR DEATH
0-380-72362-X/$6.99 US/$9.99 Can

ILL WIND 0-380-72363-8/$6.99 US/$9.99 Can

FIRESTORM 0-380-72528-7/$6.99 US/$9.99 Can

ENDANGERED SPECIES
0-380-72583-5/$6.99 US/$8.99 Can

BLIND DESCENT 0-380-72826-5/$6.99 US/$8.99 Can

Available wherever books are sold or please call 1-800-331-3761
to order.
BAR 0900

The Joanna Brady Mysteries by National Bestselling Author

An assassin's bullet shattered Joanna Brady's world, leaving her policeman husband to die in the Arizona desert. But the young widow fought back the only way she knew how: by bringing the killers to justice . . . and winning herself a job as Cochise County Sheriff.

DESERT HEAT
0-380-76545-4/$6.99 US/$9.99 Can

TOMBSTONE COURAGE
0-380-76546-2/$6.99 US/$9.99 Can

SHOOT/DON'T SHOOT
0-380-76548-9/$6.50 US/$8.50 Can

DEAD TO RIGHTS
0-380-72432-4/$6.99 US/$8.99 Can

SKELETON CANYON
0-380-72433-2/$6.99 US/$8.99 Can

RATTLESNAKE CROSSING
0-380-79247-8/$6.99 US/$8.99 Can

OUTLAW MOUNTAIN
0-380-79248-6/$6.99 US/$9.99 Can

And in Hardcover

DEVIL'S CLAW
0-380-97501-7/$24.00 US/$36.50 Can

Available wherever books are sold or please call 1-800-331-3761 to order.   JB 1000